BRIGHID'S QUEST

P.C. CAST

LUNA™
www.LUNA-Books.com

LUNA™

First edition December 2005

BRIGHID'S QUEST

ISBN 0-373-80242-0

www.LUNA-Books.com

Printed in U.S.A.

To my stepmom, Patricia Ann Cast,
with much love and appreciation.
Thank you for knowing how to heal a shattered soul.

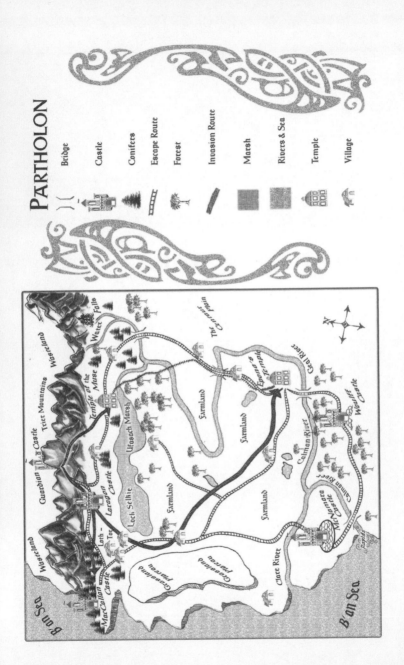

PARTHOLON

Bridge

Castle

Conifers

Escape Route

Forest

Invasion Route

Marsh

Rivers & Sea

Temple

Village

PRELUDE

"Through the blood of a dying Goddess your people will be saved."

More than one hundred years ago, women began disappearing from a green, prosperous land called Partholon. At first the disappearances were sporadic, seemingly random. It wasn't until an invading horde attacked MacCallan Castle, slaughtered the Clan's brave warriors and enslaved their women that the awful truth became known. The Fomorians, a race of winged demons, were using human women to breed a new race of monsters. It meant nothing to the vampiric creatures that birthing the mutant fetuses caused the death of the unwilling mothers. The human women were incubators—their deaths were no more than an evil means to a ghastly end.

The Goddess Epona's rage was terrible, and through her Chosen One, the Goddess Incarnate Rhiannon, and her centaur lifemate ClanFintan, the peoples of Partholon united to defeat the Fomorians. The demon race was destroyed, but the people of Partholon did not realize that the war's legacy was more than death and evil. In the Wastelands, far away from the heart of Partholon, winged children were born to human mothers who miraculously survived. Part demon, part human the small group of hybrid beings struggled to carve a life for themselves out of the Wastelands. They held firm to their humanity, even when refusing the call of their fathers' dark blood caused them pain…pain that slowly eroded their will until madness became their only respite.

"Through the blood of a dying Goddess your people will be saved."

But Epona had not forgotten the women who never lost hope and stayed faithful to their Goddess, though they could not return to Partholon with their winged children. The great Goddess whispered The Prophecy to her deposed children, and the promise of salvation breathed hope into the race of half-demons.

A century turned slowly and the winged people waited for the answer to their prayers. Partholon recovered and prospered again, and the Fomorian War became a memory, entombed in history.

And then a child was born, part human and part centaur. Touched by Epona's powerful hand the babe was given the name Elphame. Through dreams she called to Lochlan, the leader of the winged half-demons who waited in the Wastelands. The child grew to adulthood, and Lochlan followed the threads of his dreams to MacCallan Castle where Elphame awakened more than the stones of the ancient ruin.

"Through the blood of a dying Goddess your people will be saved."

Out of love for Lochlan and trust in her Goddess, Elphame fulfilled The Prophecy, sacrificing a piece of her own humanity as well as her brother's heart to save the race of hybrid Fomorians. Now this new breed of beings was finally coming home. But their struggle had just begun. Remember, the Path of the Goddess was not an easy one to tread…

Chapter
One

Elphame was exactly where the Huntress had thought she would be—not that it took a centaur Huntress's skill to track the Clan Chieftain. The MacCallan's habit of visiting this particular set of cliffside boulders had become well-known. From the vantage point of the highest of the large, weatherworn rocks, Elphame could sit and look northward toward the Trier Mountains, which were just a jagged purple line of peaks jutting into the horizon. She would stare at that distant line, trying to see past it into the Wastelands beyond.

Brighid approached Elphame quietly, reluctant to disturb her. Even after living and working closely with Elphame for more than two complete cycles of the moon, Brighid could still be moved by the sight of the unique being who had become her friend as well as her Clan Chieftain. Born eldest daughter of Partholon's Goddess Incarnate and the centaur Shaman who was her lifemate, Elphame was human only to her waist; her two legs had been fashioned more equine than human. They were powerfully muscled and covered with a fine coat of glossy fur, ending in two ebony hooves.

But her physical differences were not all that set Elphame apart. She carried within her the powers given to her by Epona. She communed with the Realm of Spirits through an affinity for Earth Magic. Elphame could hear the spirits in the stones of MacCallan Castle. She also had a special connection with Epona, and Brighid often sensed the presence of the patron Goddess of Partholon when Elphame invoked the morning blessing, or thanked the Goddess at the close of a particularly productive day. And, of course, they had all witnessed Epona's favor when Elphame had called upon the strength and love of a Goddess to defeat the madness of the Fomorians…

Brighid shuddered, not wanting to remember that ghastly day. It was enough to know that her Clan Chieftain was a miraculous mixture of centaur and human, goddess and mortal.

"Was the morning hunt successful?" Elphame said without turning to look at the Huntress.

"Very." Brighid wasn't surprised her Chieftain had sensed her presence. Elphame's preternatural powers were sharp and accurate. "The forests surrounding MacCallan Castle haven't been properly hunted in more than one hundred years. The game practically leap before my arrows, begging to be culled."

Elphame's full lips turned up in the hint of a smile. "Suicidal venison? That sounds like a truly unique dish."

Brighid snorted. "Don't tell Wynne. That cook will demand I choose the beast's temperament more carefully so her stews will have a more perfect flavor."

The MacCallan pulled her gaze from the distant mountains and smiled. "Your secret is safe with me."

Looking into Elphame's eyes, Brighid was struck by the sadness there. Only her lips smiled. The MacCallan didn't show this haunted face to the general public—it was a rare privilege to be allowed such an intimacy. For a moment, Brighid feared the Fomorian madness lurking deep within her friend's blood had awakened, but she quickly discounted the thought. Brighid didn't see hatred or rage within Elphame's eyes, she saw only deep sadness. She had little doubt as to its source. Elphame was happily mated to Lochlan. The rebuilding of MacCallan Castle was well underway. The Clan was healthy and thriving. Its Chieftain should be content. And Brighid knew Elphame would be, except for one detail.

"You're worried about him." Brighid studied Elphame's strong profile as her gaze shifted back to the horizon.

"Of course I'm worried about him!" She pressed her lips together in a sharp line. When she spoke again her voice was sad and resigned. "I'm sorry. I don't mean to take it out on you, but I've been worried about him since Brenna's death. He loved her so much."

"We all loved the little Healer," Brighid said.

Elphame sighed. "It's because she was special. Her heart was so incredibly big."

"You're worried that Cuchulainn won't recover from her loss."

Elphame stared at the distant mountains. "It wouldn't be so bad if he was here—if I could talk with him and know how he's doing." She shook her head. "I couldn't stop him from leaving, though. He said everything here reminded him of Brenna, and that he'd never learn to live without her here. When he left he was just a ghost of himself. No—" she reconsidered her comparison "—not a ghost of himself. He was more like a shadow of what he used to be…"

Elphame's voice faded. Brighid stayed by her side while the Chieftain struggled silently with worry for her brother, and Brighid's own thoughts turned in remembrance to the little Healer, Brenna. She had come to MacCallan Castle as had Brighid, looking for a new life and a new beginning, but the scarred Healer had found much more. She had found love within the arms of the Chieftain's warrior brother, who was able to see past her terrible burn scars to the beauty of her heart. Brighid remembered how spectacularly happy her friend had been—up until the moment of her untimely death. That her death had set into motion the events that led to the salvation of a people did little to salve the wound left by her absence. And now Cuchulainn had gone to the Wastelands to lead back into Partholon the very people who had brought about his lover's murder.

"It was at his insistence," Elphame said quietly, as if she could sense the path of Brighid's thoughts. "He did not blame the other Fomorians for Brenna's death. He understood her murderess had been under the control of the madness they all struggled against."

Brighid nodded. "Cuchulainn blamed only himself. Perhaps bringing the hybrid Fomorians home will serve as an act of closure. Lochlan says many of his people are still children. Maybe they will help Cu to heal."

"Healing without the touch of a Healer is a difficult process," Elphame murmured. "I just hate to think about him in pain and without—" She broke off with a dry laugh.

"What?" Brighid prompted.

"I know it sounds silly, Cuchulainn is a warrior renowned for his strength and courage, but I hate to think of him without his family near while he's hurting."

"Especially his big sister?"

Elphame's lips twisted. "Yes, especially his big sister." She sighed again. "He's been gone so long. I really thought he'd be back by now."

"You know the report from Guardian Castle said there was a major spring snowstorm that ravaged the mountains and closed the pass into the Wastelands. Cuchulainn would've had to wait for the next thaw, and then he would be traveling slowly, being careful not to overtax the strength of the children. You must be patient," Brighid said.

"Patience has never been one of your virtues, my heart."

The deep voice came from behind them. The Huntress and her Chieftain turned to watch the winged man finish his silent approach. Brighid wondered if she would ever get used to the fact that such a being existed. Part Fomorian, part human, Lochlan had been born an anomaly. More human than demon, he and others like him had been raised by their human mothers in secrecy in the harsh Wastelands north of the Trier Mountains. He was tall and leanly muscular. His features were chiseled and attractively human, but the luminescence of his skin hinted at his dark heritage. And then there were his wings. Right now they were at rest, tucked snugly against his back, with just the storm-colored topside visible. But Brighid had seen them fully spread in terrible magnificence. It was a sight the Huntress would not easily forget.

"Good morning, Huntress," he said warmly as he joined them. "Wynne tells me you returned this morning with a spectacular kill and that we have venison steaks to look forward to at the evening meal."

Brighid inclined her head in a brief bow, acknowledging his praise as she moved aside so Lochlan could greet his wife.

"I missed you this morning," he said, reaching up to take Elphame's hand and kissing it softly.

"I'm sorry. I couldn't sleep and I didn't want to wake you, so I…" She shrugged.

"You are impatient for your brother's return, and it makes you restless," he said.

"I know he's a warrior, and I know I'm thinking with a sister's heart instead of a Chieftain's mind, but I'm worried about him."

"I am a warrior, but if I lost you I would lose my soul. Being a warrior does not prevent a man from feeling pain. Cuchulainn has been in my thoughts lately, too." Lochlan paused, choosing his words carefully. "Perhaps one of us should go after him."

"I want to. I've even thought of it, but I can't leave." Elphame's frustration spilled over into her voice. "The Clan is too new, and there is still so much work to be done rebuilding the castle."

"I will go." Brighid spoke in a simple matter-of-fact voice.

"You will?" Elphame asked.

The Huntress nodded and shrugged. "The forest is so lush with game that even the human warriors can easily keep the castle fed—at least for a while," she added with a smile. "And it will take the skill of a Huntress to follow the path Cuchulainn took through the mountains." She looked pointedly at Lochlan. "Will it not?"

"It is an obscure trail, and though I know Cuchulainn and the others will have marked it, still it would be difficult to find and follow," he agreed.

"Besides, game is scarce in the Wastelands. At least I can ease their burden of hunger as they ready themselves to travel." Brighid smiled at her Clan Chieftain. "A Huntress is always welcome company, especially when there are hungry young mouths to feed."

"A friend is also always welcome company," Elphame said, her voice catching with emotion. "Thank you. You have relieved my mind greatly."

"Cuchulainn will probably think me a poor substitute for his sister," Brighid said roughly to cover up her own emotions. She had come to care for Elphame as she would a member of her own family. *No,* the Huntress silently amended, *it was from my family I escaped by joining Clan MacCallan. Elphame is far easier to care for.*

"He will think no such thing." Elphame laughed.

"I will sketch a map that will help make your path clear," Lochlan said. Then he rested his hand lightly on the Huntress's shoulder. "Thank you for doing this, Brighid."

She looked into the winged man's eyes and stifled the urge to flinch under his touch. The majority of the Clan was slowly accepting Lochlan as Elphame's lifemate. He was half Fomorian, but he had proven his loyalty to the Chieftain and their Clan. Yet Brighid could not quell the nagging feeling of unease that being in his presence always evoked.

"I will leave first thing in the morning," the Huntress said resolutely.

* * *

Brighid hated snow. It wasn't that it was a physical discomfort. As with all centaurs, her natural body heat effectively insulated her from all but the most drastic weather changes. She hated snow in principle. It shrouded the earth with a blanket of numb dampness. Woodland creatures either burrowed away from it or fled to warmer grounds. She agreed with the animals. It had taken her five days to travel from MacCallan Castle north through the thickening forest to the mouth of the obscure pass Lochlan had sketched in his detailed map. Five days. She snorted in disgust. She might as well have been a human riding a mindless horse in circles. She had expected to have traveled twice the distance in half the time.

"Goddess-accursed snow," she muttered, her voice sounding odd against the walls of the looming mountains. "Surely this must be it." She studied the uniquely fashioned rock formation for some sign that Cuchulainn's small party had passed within. Brighid thought he would have marked it, though it was unlikely there was another grouping of red rocks that looked exactly like the open mouth of a giant, complete with distended tongue and jagged teeth. Her hooves made muffled wet clomps as she approached the gaping tunnel.

Suddenly the air was filled with the wind-battering sound of heavy wings and a black shape swooped past her to light on the tongue-like rock.

Brighid came to an abrupt halt and ground her teeth together. The raven cocked its head and cawed at her. The Huntress frowned.

"Begone wretched bird!" she shouted, waving her arms at it.

Unruffled, the raven fixed her with its cold, black stare. Then slowly, distinctly, it tapped the side of the rock with its beak three times before unfurling its wings and beating the air neatly, skimming low enough over Brighid's head that her hair stirred and she had to force herself not to duck. Scowling, the Huntress approached the rock. The bird's feet had drawn claw-shaped marks in the snow so that the red of the rock was visible in rust-colored lines against winter's canvas. She reached out and brushed at the area, unsurprised when Cuchulainn's trail slash became visible, pointing into the mouth of the tunnel.

Brighid shook her head. "I don't want your help, Mother." Eerily her voice bounced back to her from the tunnel walls. "The price you place on it has always been too costly."

The raven's cawing drifted down on a wind that suddenly, magically, felt warm, bringing with it the scents and sounds of the Centaur Plains. Brighid closed her eyes against a tide of longing. The green of the waving grasslands was more than a color—it held scent and texture as the warm breeze shushed through it. It was spring on the Centaur Plains, and completely unlike this cold, white world of mountains. The grasses would be midhock high and dotted with the proud show of blue, white and violet wildflowers. She drew a deep breath and tasted home.

"Stop it!" She jerked her eyes open. "It's a sham, Mother. Freedom is the one thing the Centaur Plains does not offer me!"

The raven's call faded and died, taking with it the warm home-touched wind. Brighid shivered. She shouldn't have been surprised that her mother had sent a spirit guide. The anticipatory sense she had felt all day had been instigated by more than nearing the entrance to the mountain passageway. Brighid should have sensed her mother's hand. No, Brighid corrected herself, she *had* sensed it—she should have acknowledged it.

I have made my choice. I am Huntress for the Clan MacCallan—an oath-sworn member of the clan. I do not regret my choice.

The Huntress squared her shoulders and entered the tunnel, physically and mentally shaking off the lingering effects of her mother's presence. She was suddenly glad that the pass was snow-covered enough that it would take all of her concentration and much of her vast physical strength to navigate her way through it. She didn't want to think about her mother or the familiar beauty of the homeland she had decided to leave forever.

The day was still young. According to Lochlan, she should be able to clear the most treacherous parts of the trail before dark. If all went well, tomorrow she would find the Fomorian camp and Cuchulainn. She picked up her pace, careful not to misstep and catch a hoof in a snow-hidden crevice. Brighid focused on the trail. She did not think of her mother or the life from which Brighid had turned. She ignored the guilt and loneliness that shadowed her every decision. She had made the right choice. She was sure of it. But just because she had chosen wisely didn't mean she had taken the easiest path.

As she scrambled around a slick, narrow corner in the treacherous trail, she smiled in grim irony. The physical path she had chosen to travel was quickly proving to be almost as difficult as the life path she had chosen.

Distracted by her inner turmoil and her outer challenges, the Huntress's keen senses only registered the watching eyes deep in her subconscious as a brief feeling of unease. A feeling cast aside as vestiges of irritation at her mother's interfering spirit emissary.

Unhindered within the darkness, the eyes glowed the color of old blood as they continued to watch and to wait.

CHAPTER TWO

The damned wind was never-ending. Cuchulainn thought it was the thing he disliked most about the Wastelands. The cold he could bear, at least in limited doses. He could even find the open land and the oddly low-growing plants unusual and interesting. But the Goddess-cursed wind was a constant irritant. It howled incessantly and chafed exposed skin to raw roughness. The warrior shivered and pulled the cowl of his fur-lined cloak over his head. He probably should return to camp. Evening was quickly approaching, and though he had only been in the Wastelands for less than two full cycles of the moon, he had already learned to respect how dangerous it was to get caught in the open after sunset, even for a short time.

Cuchulainn paused and squatted to study the sharp hoof indentations in the snow. The tracks were fresh. The whipping wind hadn't had time to obscure them. The wild bighorn sheep couldn't be far ahead.

The young wolf made a muffled whine as she pressed her cold snout into his side. Absently Cuchulainn stroked the wolf's ruff.

"Cold and hungry, too, are you, Fand?"

The wolf whined softly again and nuzzled her wet nose under his chin. Abruptly he stood and tightened the lacings of his cloak. "All the more reason to finish tracking the sheep. Come on, it's not far ahead of us. Let's get this business done."

The wolf's whining stopped as she moved forward at his side. Though not even half grown she was totally devoted to her surrogate parent. Where he went, she would follow.

Cuchulainn stepped up his pace, imagining the happy cries of the children when he brought game back to camp. For the briefest of instants, the warrior's thoughts softened. The children had certainly been unexpected. Not that he hadn't known they existed. They had been the impetus for his mission. It had been his task to travel to the Wastelands and guide the children of the hybrid Fomorians, or New Fomorians as they liked to call themselves, to Partholon, the homeland of their long dead human mothers. But the thinking of a thing and the actual doing of it was often as dissimilar as the stark Wastelands and the green prosperity of Partholon.

The New Fomorians, quite simply, had been one surprise after another.

When Cuchulainn had thought ahead to the actual meeting with the hybrid Fomorians his warrior's mind had imagined them as barbarians who were quite likely dangerous. That Lochlan was civilized made no difference. As unlikely as it had seemed at first, Epona had fashioned him to be Cuchulainn's sister's lifemate. Of course Lochlan would be different, but Cuchulainn knew only too well that the hybrid Fomorians were capable of great savagery.

They had survived in the harshness of the Wastelands for more than a century. And even with the madness recently excised from their blood, they were still the spawn of demons. His sister had insisted they return to Partholon, as the land was part of their heritage. She was his Clan Chieftain and he would obey her, but he was also an experienced warrior. Cuchulainn would not lead enemies into Partholon. So he would be wary and wise. It was one of the reasons he had insisted on traveling with no other human warriors. By himself he could discover the truth, and by himself he could return to warn Partholon if need be.

As he and the hybrid Fomorian twins, Curran and Nevin, traveled from MacCallan Castle through the northern forest and into the hidden pass in the Trier Mountains, Cuchulainn had waited, watched the twins, and nursed the raw wound that was his grief. That he woke every morning able to force himself to move through the motions of another day was a small miracle. Looking back, the trip to the Wastelands had been one long, painful blur. Curran and Nevin had been silent traveling companions. They had appeared to show no predilection for violence. They did not complain about the pace he set, nor did they react to his gruff, withdrawn manner. Cuchulainn told himself their benign demeanor meant nothing. When he got to their camp he'd planned to gauge the reaction of the other Fomorians to his news, and then he would do what was best for Partholon.

So Cuchulainn had journeyed into the north, battling grief within and imagining demons without. He'd no physical injuries from which to recover, but the wound Brenna's death had left in his soul was a gaping, invisible hole. The passage of time hadn't begun to whittle away any of the sharpness of his pain. He would not ever truly recover from it. He would only survive it. There was a distinct difference.

His mind skittered away from the pain thinking about Brenna caused. Not that his loss wasn't always with him. She was never far from his thoughts, but he had learned that if he gave in to despair by dwelling on might-have-beens the pain went quickly from smoldering coals to a hot, flaming need. It was a need that would never be slaked. Brenna was gone. That was unalterable fact. It was far better not to think—not to feel—at all.

Just track the sheep. Kill it. Return to camp. He ordered his mind to stop its restless roving.

Cuchulainn turned a corner. He and the young wolf quietly worked their way between the snow-covered rocks that nestled against the northern slope of the Trier Mountains. He was pleased that the snow had markedly lessened. Just days ago he couldn't have followed the sheep to the base of the mountains. If luck held and they didn't have another unexpected bout of snow the pass might be clear enough for travel in another few days. Of course he would have to make sure. The children were tough and willing, but they were, for all their eagerness and precocity, still just children.

They were unusual, though. He would never forget his first glimpse of them—or their reaction to the first completely human man they had ever seen. It had been an overcast, gloomy afternoon. The sky had been heavy with the spring blizzard that would seal the pass and close them into the Wastelands. He and Curran and Nevin had emerged from the mountains and traveled the short distance from the pass to the small valley that sheltered the New Fomorian camp. It had been a young sentry named Gareth who had glimpsed them, and like any good guard he had rushed to alert his camp. But instead of meeting the small party with drawn weapons and wariness, the New Fomorians had rushed from their encampment with open hands and welcoming smiles. Children! By the Goddess, he hadn't expected so many children. Laughing and singing a beautiful melody Cuchulainn was shocked to recognize as an ancient Partholonian song of praise to Epona, the hybrids had embraced the twins. Then their attention had quickly turned to him—the lone human rider in their midst.

"This is Cuchulainn," Nevin had said.

"He is brother to the Goddess Elphame who has saved us," Curran finished for him.

The joyful singing had instantly been silenced. The cluster of winged people had gazed at him. Cuchulainn remembered thinking they looked like a flock of bright, beautiful birds. Then the crowd parted to let a slender figure emerge. The first thing he noticed was that her skin had the odd luminous paleness of the other hybrid Fomorians, but her hair, wings and eyes were much darker. And then he saw the tears that washed her cheeks. Her dark, almond-shaped eyes were bright with them. Her gaze locked with his and Cuchulainn saw compassion and a terrible sadness. He wanted to look away. He didn't want her emotions to touch him. His own pain ran too deep, was too fresh. But as he turned his head to break their locked gaze, the winged woman dropped gracefully to her knees. And then, like she was a pebble thrown into a waiting pool, the crowd of winged people, adults and children alike, followed her example and rippled to their knees.

"Forgive us. We are responsible for your sister's death." The winged woman's sweet voice was filled with the sadness he'd read within her eyes.

"My sister is not dead." Cuchulainn's voice was flat and so devoid of emotion that it sounded alien to his own ears.

The woman reacted with obvious shock. "But the curse has been lifted. We all feel the absence of the demons in our blood."

"You misinterpreted the prophecy," Cuchulainn said in his gruff, empty voice. "It did not call for the physical death of my sister. Instead of her life, the prophecy led her to sacrifice a piece of her humanity. She lives. And it is only through the grace of Epona that she is not mad."

Still on her knees, the woman looked from Cuchulainn to Curran and Nevin.

"What he says is true," Curran said. "Elphame drank of Lochlan's blood, and with it she accepted the madness of our people. Through the power of Epona she has defeated our fathers' darkness, but it lives within her blood."

"Lochlan? Did he survive?" she asked.

"Yes. He is mated to Elphame," Nevin said.

"Keir and Fallon?"

"They have chosen another path," Nevin said quickly.

Cuchulainn felt ice slice through him. Fallon had chosen the path of madness and in doing so she had murdered Brenna. But before she could be executed for her crime she'd revealed that she was pregnant. Elphame had imprisoned Fallon at Guardian Castle to await the birth of her child. Keir was her mate, and he had chosen to stay with her.

Ciara watched the human warrior's face carefully. She recognized the numb, hopeless look that was the shadow left behind by tremendous loss. He had not lost his sister, but he had borne terrible sadness. Much had happened that they all needed to know, but not now—not at this moment. Later, she told herself. Later she would discover what could be done to relieve the warrior's pain, as well as hear the tale of Fallon and Keir. Right now all that was important was that this man was the brother of their savior. For that alone they owed him a debt of gratitude.

She smiled, filling her words with the joy that was part of her soul. "Then we will give thanks to Epona that your sister lives, Cuchulainn."

"Do what you feel you must," he said in his dead voice. "My sister asks that I lead you back to Partholon and to our Clan's castle. Will your people come with me?"

Her hands flew to cover her mouth. All around her she heard gasps of happiness and surprise. She couldn't speak. Breath-stopping exultation swelled within her. This was it! This was the fulfillment of the dream their mothers and grandmothers had nurtured and kept alive within each of them. Then, bursting through the circle of kneeling adults came a tide of laughter and excitement as a horde of children, no longer able to contain their exuberance, crowded into the empty space that surrounded the warrior and his horse. The adults hurried to their feet and rushed forward, clucking at their young charges and trying in vain to restore some semblance of order and dignity to the warrior's welcome.

The children clambered around Cuchulainn, their eyes large and round. With wings extended they jostled against one another like an overcrowded nest of baby cuckoos. He felt suddenly like a lone, overwhelmed sparrow.

"Partholon! We go to Partholon!"

"We are to meet the Goddess!"

"Is the land really warm and green?"

"Do you really not have wings?"

"May I touch your horse?"

Cuchulainn's big gelding snorted and took two skittering steps backward, away from a tiny, winged girl who was trying on tiptoe to stroke his muzzle.

"Children, enough!" The winged woman's voice was stern, but her eyes sparkled and she smiled as she spoke. "Cuchulainn will believe that the lessons of courtesy your great-grandmothers taught have been forgotten."

Instantly the young winged beings dropped their heads and muttered soft apologies. The little girl who had been trying to touch his horse bowed her head, too, but Cuchulainn could see that she was sidling forward, one hand half raised, still trying for a covert caress. The gelding snorted again and took another step back. The girl followed. *Just like Elphame when she was young,* Cuchulainn thought fondly. *Always reaching for things she shouldn't.* And for the first time since Brenna's death, Cuchulainn almost laughed.

"Yes, child," he said to the top of her blond head. "You may touch him. Only go slowly, he is not accustomed to children."

The small head tilted up and the child gifted Cuchulainn with a tremendous smile of gratitude. Sharp canine teeth glittered in odd contrast to her innocent appearance.

"Her name is Kyna."

The winged woman moved to the child's side. She gave Kyna a nod of encouragement and Cuchulainn tightened his grip on the gelding, holding him firmly in place so the girl could carefully pat his slick chest. The rest of the children watched and whispered to each other.

"And I am Ciara, granddaughter of the Incarnate Muse Terp-sichore. You are most welcome here, Cuchulainn." She, too, smiled brilliantly up at the warrior with a sharp-toothed grin. "I believe the children have answered your question for all of us. We have waited for more than one hundred years for this day. Yes, it will be our great pleasure to follow you to Partholon."

Pandemonium greeted her proclamation. The adults cheered and the children danced around as if they had springs as well as wings. Afraid someone would get trampled, Cu had been forced to dismount, which brought on another tirade of questions from the children who wanted to touch his back to make sure he wasn't hiding wings under his cloak. Ciara and the other adults had quite a job calming the jumping, dancing, laughing group of excited youngsters.

Trying to keep his veneer of detached observer in place, Cuchulainn had silently watched the cacophony of jubilation. The winged people obviously looked to Ciara for leadership. She had laughingly apologized for the overenthusiastic welcome while she called for one of the lodges to be made ready and introduced him to several smiling adults. But when he asked her if she had been made leader during Lochlan's absence, she had only laughed and said she was the same now as she had been when Lochlan was with them—just an ordinary Shaman to her people.

Her words had been completely unexpected. Shaman? Where were the barbaric hybrid demons he had expected to watch warily and judge harshly? Cuchulainn remembered how stunned he had felt standing there that first day. Then little Kyna had shrieked. He had lunged, pulling his claymore free from its pommel. Crouched and ready for battle he had followed the child's pointing finger to discover that Fand had finally crept from a clump of concealing brush and was slinking toward him. Cu had hastily sheathed his sword and knelt down to reassure the nervous wolf cub, while he fielded rapidly fired questions from Kyna. He felt Ciara's gaze and looked up to find her dark eyes studying him knowingly.

"You have no enemies here, Cuchulainn, except those that war within you," she had said quietly.

Before he could respond the sky had opened and huge, wet flakes of snow had begun falling.

Fand and the big gelding temporarily forgotten, Kyna had tugged on Cuchulainn's cloak for his attention. "Watch me catch the snow with my tongue!"

Still crouched beside his wolf cub, Cuchulainn had watched the little girl throw her arms wide and spread her dove-colored wings. With the innate innocence of childhood she stuck out her tongue, twirled and jumped, trying to catch the elusive flakes. Soon she was joined by dozens of other children and he was surrounded by the timeless laughter and joy of youth. For an unexpected instant he'd felt the suffocating pain of losing Brenna shift and ease and become almost bearable.

Cuchulainn thought he would remember that moment for the rest of his life. Though he didn't realize it, thinking about the children relaxed the tight sadness that had claimed his handsome face since Brenna's death. He almost looked like himself again, the Cuchulainn who had been quick to smile and laugh and had been filled with life and hope and the promise of a full and happy future.

Now, with a soft woof, Fand slunk low to the earth, pulling Cu's thoughts back to the present and shifting the focus of his attention to the trail ahead. Silently Cuchulainn moved forward. Readying an arrow, he peered around the next boulder to see the wild, white sheep pawing through the snow at a patch of yellow lichen. Taking a long, slow breath he notched the arrow, but before he could draw and aim, he heard the distinctive twang of a loosed bow and the sheep dropped, a quivering arrow neatly embedded at the base of its neck.

Fand's growl changed to a yip of welcome when the centaur Huntress stepped from behind a concealing ledge.

CHAPTER
THREE

"Y̶ou took my shot, Huntress." Cuchulainn's words were gruff, but he smiled and grasped the centaur's forearm in greeting. He was surprised at the pleasure he felt at the sight of Brighid. With her came a vision of MacCallan Castle. Until that moment he hadn't realized how much he had begun to long for home. And then on the heels of his remembrance came a wave of fresh pain. Brenna would not be there. All that remained of her was a monument carved in her image and a cold grave.

"Took your shot?" The Huntress's unusual violet eyes sparkled. "If I remember correctly the last time we hunted together you hit nothing and chose to bring your prey back alive." She returned Cuchulainn's smile, even though his had faded into an odd grimace. She clasped his forearm warmly before frowning down at the young wolf that was leaping around her hocks. "I can see the creature is still alive."

"Fand is an excellent companion." He motioned for the jubilant cub to leave the Huntress alone. Fand ignored him.

"She hasn't learned any manners." Brighid kicked a hoof absently at the squirming cub, who decided it was a game and began biting at her hock.

Cuchulainn growled low in his throat, sounding remarkably wolflike, and, looking dejected, Fand stopped her mock attack and flopped down on her belly to stare with soulful eyes at the warrior.

Brighid lifted a brow. "Seems I have come just in time. You obviously need some civilized company."

"Meaning you?"

The Huntress nodded. "There is nothing more civilized than a centaur."

She waited for Cu's return gibe, which did not come. Instead the warrior tucked his arrow back in its quill and began striding toward the sheep.

"My sister sent you, didn't she?"

"I volunteered. I don't like to see her worried. And—"

Cuchulainn whirled around and cut her off. "Elphame is well?"

Brighid heard the thinly veiled panic in the warrior's voice and was quick to reassure him. "She's quite well. Renovation of the castle moves ahead. The Clan is happy and healthy. The first new MacCallan clan member has been born within the castle's walls. And, as I was about to explain, the game in the forest is so thick that even humans can easily hunt it. So I thought I would kill two birds with a single arrow." She grinned, raising her empty bow. "I'd alleviate my Chieftain's worry for her errant brother, as well as hunt something more challenging than deer that are practically domesticated."

As she spoke she studied Cuchulainn's face. The panic had dissipated, leaving him looking tired and relieved, and then, as she watched, even those small emotions fell from his face, until it seemed he was wearing an expressionless mask. He had lost weight. His eyes were shadowed by darkness and new lines feathered from their corners. Was that gray in his sand-colored hair? He bent to pull her arrow from the sheep's body and she looked down at him. Yes, it was, indeed, gray that glinted around his brow. The man before her looked easily a decade older than he had two moon cycles earlier.

"Here," Brighid said, swiveling at the waist to pull two long leather cords from one of the travel packs slung across her back. "Tie this around its legs. I'll drag it."

Cuchulainn returned the arrow to her after wiping it clean in the snow.

"My gelding isn't far from here."

Brighid snorted. "I hope your camp isn't far from here. I've seen little of the Wastelands, but I already do not savor the thought of spending the night in the open. Not in this Goddess-be-damned wind."

For an instant she thought she saw amusement flash in his eyes, but all he said as he took the cords was, "The camp is not far, either. But we should hurry. The nights are cold."

Methodically he squatted by the sheep's rear haunches and began tying its legs.

Elphame had been wise to worry. It was obvious that the Cuchulainn his sister knew and loved was disappearing under the weight of grief and guilt. Brighid could only imagine how much the sight would wound her Chieftain. Brighid hated seeing what Brenna's death had done to him, and he was just her friend.

She smiled sadly at the warrior's back. Theirs had been an unlikely friendship. Cuchulainn had known too well the segregationist beliefs of her family concerning humans and centaurs and he had been leery to trust Brighid. And, quite frankly, the Huntress had thought Cuchulainn an arrogant womanizer. At first they had snapped at and circled one another like restless beasts protecting territory. But as the Huntress had watched the rakish young warrior fall in love with the Clan's newly appointed Healer, she had seen the real

Cuchulainn—the compassionate, loyal man who lived within the skin of the dashing warrior. And she had won his trust in turn. First, by helping him track Elphame after she had taken a nasty fall, and finally, regrettably, by fighting at his side when they captured the hybrid Fomorian Fallon after she murdered Brenna.

"Brenna's death is a heavy burden to bear," Brighid said solemnly.

Cuchulainn's head was bowed in concentration as he finished securing the cords, and she could see his back stiffen. He stood slowly and met the Huntress's sharp gaze.

"Yes." He bit out the word.

Brighid didn't flinch from the anger in his voice. She knew from her own experience that anger was part of grief's healing process.

"Your sister planted those blue wildflowers Brenna liked so much all around her grave. The Clan talks about how beautiful the tomb is, and how much Brenna is missed."

"Stop," Cuchulainn said between clenched teeth.

"As long as we remember her, she is not completely gone, Cu."

"Not completely gone!" Cuchulainn laughed humorlessly. He threw the cords he had been holding to the ground and spread his arms, palms up, looking around them. "Then show her to me. I don't see her. I don't hear her. I can't touch her. To me, Huntress, she is completely gone."

"Brenna would hate to see you like this, Cuchulainn."

"Brenna is not here!"

"Cu—" the Huntress began, but the warrior's gruff voice cut her off.

"Leave it be, Brighid."

She met his gaze squarely. "I will leave it be for now, but you cannot continue like this. Not forever."

"You are right about that. Nothing continues forever, Huntress." Abruptly he bent and retrieved the leather cords. Handing one to her he wrapped the other over his shoulder. "This way." He pointed his chin back the way he had come. "We need to hurry. Night will fall soon."

Mimicking Cuchulainn's motions, Brighid placed the cord over her shoulder and together they dragged the sheep's body. As the Huntress glanced at Cu's haggard profile she thought grief had already caused night to fall within Cuchulainn's wounded soul. Could anything, even his Goddess-touched sister's love, ever bring the light of happiness to his life again?

They spoke little as they traveled steadily in the direction of the waning sun. Together they had quickly dressed the sheep and folded it into the leather carrier Cuchulainn strapped over the big gelding's hindquarters. There were several questions Brighid wanted to ask, but the warrior's manner was so withdrawn, his few words so brusque, that she had learned little more than that he'd easily found the hybrid Fomorian settlement, that there were almost one hundred of them, and that they were eager to return to Partholon. When she asked him what they were like he'd said only, "They're just people," and withdrawn again into silence. Brighid had decided that conversing with him was like cuddling a porcupine. Not worth the trouble. She was a Huntress. She would observe the hybrids for herself as she would any other creature of the Wastelands and then form her own opinion.

And she would always keep in mind that they had been fathered by a race of demons.

"Do you like children?"

Brighid raised her brows at the strange question, not sure she had heard Cuchulainn correctly. "Children?"

He grunted and nodded.

"I don't know. I don't particularly like or dislike them. They don't usually figure into the life of a Huntress, unless you count that I have to consider them as extra mouths to feed. Why do you ask?"

"We are almost to the settlement. There are—" he paused and glanced sideways at her "—children there."

"I expect children. Lochlan told all of us about them back at the castle. You know that. You were there."

"Lochlan didn't exactly tell us everything," Cuchulainn said cryptically.

"That's no surprise to me." Brighid snorted.

The warrior gave her a lidded look. "You don't sound like you trust Lochlan."

"Do you?"

"He saved my sister's life," Cuchulainn said simply.

Brighid nodded slowly. "Yes, he did. But it was Lochlan's coming to Partholon that placed her life in jeopardy in the first place."

Cuchulainn said nothing. He'd already thought over and over again about how Lochlan's presence had changed all of their lives. But he found it hard to blame his sister's lifemate, which did not mean he was willing to fully embrace the winged man. It only meant that Cuchulainn was most willing to blame himself for the events that had culminated in his sister's sacrifice and Brenna's death. He should have known. He *would* have known had he listened to the warnings from the spirit realm. But Cuchulainn had always turned from the use of spirits and magic and the mysterious power of the Goddess, even though it was obvious from an early age that he had inherited his Shaman father's spirit gifts. Cu was a warrior. It was all he'd ever wanted to be. His affinity with the sword was the only gift he desired.

His stubbornness had sealed his lover's doom.

"I thought you said we were almost at the camp. I see nothing ahead except more of this empty, dismal land."

Cuchulainn dragged his dark thoughts back to the silver-coated centaur who trotted by his side.

"Look more closely, Huntress," he said.

Brighid glowered at him. Friends they may have become, but the warrior still had a knack for getting under her skin.

Cuchulainn almost smiled. "Don't feel bad. I didn't see it

at first, either. If I hadn't been with Curran and Nevin I would have probably toppled blindly over the edge."

"I don't…" At first the landscape appeared to be a snow-patched, treeless plain. Red shale, the same color as the great boulders that flanked the Trier Mountains, littered the ground. But then her vision caught an almost imperceptible change. "It's a gorge. By the Goddess! The land is so bleak and similar that one side matches the other almost perfectly."

"It's an optical illusion, one the human mothers of the New Fomorians thought to use to their advantage more than one hundred years ago when they were desperate to find a safe place to build their settlement."

"New Fomorians?"

"That's what they call themselves," Cuchulainn said.

Brighid snorted.

"The path winds down from there."

He pointed at Fand's disappearing hind end and clucked his gelding into a gentle canter, pulling him up just before the land dropped away beneath them. Brighid moved to stand beside him and drew in breath sharply at the sight below. The gorge opened as if a giant had taken an ax and hewed an enormous wedge from the cold, rocky earth. The wall on which they stood was taller than the opposite side of the canyon. The sheer drop must have been at least two hundred feet. A small river ran through the middle of the valley. And nestled against the gentler northern wall of the canyon was a cluster of round buildings. Brighid could make out distant figures, and she strained to see wings as the self-proclaimed New Fomorians moved between circular-shaped houses and corrals and low, squat structures she thought might be animal shelters.

She could feel Cuchulainn watching her.

"The human women chose wisely. There's shelter in the walls of the canyon and a ready water supply. I can even see a few things that might be masquerading as trees," she said. "If I had been with them, this would have been the site I would have recommended." In actuality if Brighid had been with them, she would have recommended they slit their monstrous infants' throats and return to Partholon where the women belonged. But that was a thought the Huntress decided was best kept to herself.

"It's an unforgiving land. I have been surprised at how well they have survived. I expected…" Cuchulainn's words trailed off as if he was sorry he'd said so much.

Brighid was looking at him with open curiosity.

Cu cleared his throat and pointed the gelding's head down the steep trail. "Watch where you step. The shale is slick."

Brighid followed Cuchulainn, wondering at the changes in him. Were they all because of Brenna's death, or had something happened here in the Wastelands? Even had he not been her friend, the Huntress owed it to her Chieftain to find out.

CHAPTER
FOUR

The first hybrid Brighid saw was doing something totally unexpected. He was laughing. The Huntress heard him before she saw him. His laughter rolled up the trail to meet them, punctuated by mock growls and youthful snarls.

"They like Fand," Cuchulainn muttered in explanation.

The warrior and the Huntress finally stepped onto level ground and walked around a rough outcropping of rock to see a winged man sprawled on his back in the middle of the trail. Tongue lolling and mouth open as if she were smiling, the young wolf cub's paws were planted squarely on his chest.

"Fand rolled me, Cuchulainn. She's growing so fast that in no time she'll be a proper wolf," he said, chuckling and scratching the cub's scruff. When he glanced up and saw the centaur by Cu's side, his eyes rounded in shock.

"Fand, here!" Cuchulainn ordered. This time the wolf

chose to obey, hopping off the hybrid's chest and loping back to her master.

The winged man stood quickly, brushing dirt and snow from his tunic, all the while keeping his large eyes fixed on Brighid.

"Gareth, this is—"

Gareth's excited voice cut him off. "The Huntress, Brighid! It is, isn't it?"

"Yes, Gareth. This is MacCallan's Huntress, Brighid Dhianna."

Gareth executed a quick, awkward bow, and Brighid realized that he was really just a tall, gangly youth who stared at her with open, awestruck delight.

"Well met, Brighid!" Gareth gushed, his voice cracking on her name.

Brighid could hear Cuchulainn's sigh and she stifled a smile.

"Well met, Gareth," she returned the greeting.

"Wait till I tell the others! They won't believe it. You're even more beautiful than Curran and Nevin described."

Gareth started to rush away, then stopped, turned back and bowed sheepishly to Brighid again. The Huntress could have sworn that the youth's cheeks were reddened with an embarrassed blush.

"Pardon me, Huntress. I'll go tell the others that we have a visitor. Another one!" Then he turned and, with wings spread, all but flew down the path.

"Foolish boy," Cuchulainn muttered.

Brighid raised a brow at the warrior. "I'm even more beautiful than Curran and Nevin described?"

Cuchulainn lifted his hands in a gesture of quiet frustration. "The twins tell stories in the evenings. You are a favorite subject."

"Me? How can that be? Curran and Nevin hardly know me."

"Apparently they put the short time they spent at MacCallan Castle to excellent use. They listened and observed. A lot. You know how the Clan likes to talk, and the more they talk, the more deeds grow. You didn't just track Elphame in the night through the forest to find where she had fallen—you did it all in a lashing storm, too," he said.

"I did nothing of the sort. The storm began on our way home. And it wasn't full dark until after we found Elphame." Brighid tried to sound annoyed, but she couldn't help the smile that played at the corner of her lips.

"And then there's the story of Fand," Cuchulainn said, shifting in the saddle as if he was suddenly uncomfortable.

Brighid's brows went up. "And who told them about that, Cu?"

Cuchulainn shrugged and kneed the gelding to follow Gareth's path. "They asked. And they can be very persistent when they want to know something."

"They being Curran and Nevin?" Brighid asked his broad back.

"No. They being the children."

And then a noise drifted to the Huntress's acute hearing. She thought it sounded like the chattering of many birds.

Cuchulainn's horse's ears pricked forward. "Remember that I forewarned you about the children," he called over his shoulder.

Brighid frowned severely at the warrior's back. Forewarned her? He hadn't forewarned her about anything—he'd just asked if she liked children. What in the darkest realm of the Underworld was going on here?

They took another turn in the path and the trail opened up. Brighid moved quickly so that she was beside Cuchulainn. The road widened and led straight into the heart of the neat little settlement, which was currently filled with small winged bodies chattering excitedly. When they caught sight of her, the children's talking was instantly replaced by a collective gasp that reminded Brighid of the coo of doves.

"Oh, great merciful Goddess," the Huntress murmured. "There are so many of them."

"I tried to tell you," Cuchulainn said under his breath. "Prepare yourself. They are as energetic as they are small."

"But how can there be so many?" Her eyes were roving the group as she tried to get an accurate count...ten... twenty...forty. There were at least forty young bodies. "I thought you said there were less than one hundred hybrids in total. Do they have multiple births?"

"No. Not usually. Most of these children no longer have parents," the warrior said grimly.

"But—"

"Later," Cuchulainn said. "I'll explain it all later. They won't stay still much longer."

"What are they going to do?" Brighid asked warily.

The warrior gave her the briefest of smiles. "Nothing you can defend yourself against, believe me."

The waiting group rippled and Cuchulainn caught sight of Ciara's dark head.

"Come on. It's best to face them head-on."

Side by side Cu and Brighid came to a halt before the waiting group just as a lovely winged woman stepped out to greet them.

Cuchulainn made hasty introductions. "Ciara, this is Mac-Callan's Huntress, Brighid Dhianna. Brighid, Ciara is Shaman for the New Fomorians." He gestured at the two winged men who had followed Ciara through the children. "And, you will remember Curran and Nevin."

The twins nodded their heads, smiling widely at her. She was instantly struck by how well they looked. The last time she'd seen them their wings had been dreadfully torn. Now they looked whole and healthy, with only pale pink lines scarring the delicate membranes. One of the twins spoke, but Brighid had no idea whether it was Curran or Nevin.

"It is good to see you again, Huntress."

"We are all so pleased that you have come, Brighid Dhianna, famed Huntress of the MacCallans," Ciara said.

Brighid tried not to be distracted by the horde of watching children, even though her eyes were drawn to their small faces. All different sizes and shapes, they were beaming sharp-toothed smiles at her as their wings quivered with barely suppressed excitement. Puppies, she thought. They looked like a wriggling mass of healthy, happy, winged puppies.

Pulling her gaze from the children she nodded politely first to Ciara and then the twins. "The MacCallan thought you might need a Huntress to ease the burden of feeding your people during your journey. I was glad to be of service to her," Brighid said.

"And now I understand why I have dreamed of a silver hawk with gold-tipped wings these past several nights," Ciara said, looking from the Huntress's silver-white hair to the golden gleam of her equine coat.

Brighid kept her face carefully neutral, but the mention of the Shaman's dream was like a fist to her gut. Even here, in the far off Wastelands, she could not escape her childhood.

"Oooh, you are even more beautiful than I imagined!"

The Huntress's eyes sought and found the miniature speaker—a small girl child standing near Ciara. Her hair and wings were an unusual silver-gray, like the breast of a dove. Her large eyes were bright with intelligence.

"Thank you," Brighid said.

"That is Kyna," Cuchulainn said.

At the mention of her name the child bobbed excitedly on her tiptoes.

"Cuchulainn, can I come closer? Please! Pllllease!"

Cu looked questioningly at the Huntress. Not knowing what else to do, Brighid shrugged.

"Come on then," Cu said. As the child sprinted forward with several of the other children close behind, Cuchulainn lifted his hand and said sternly, "Remember your manners!"

Kyna's headlong rush instantly slowed and the children jostling behind her almost knocked her over. Brighid had to be careful not to laugh when the girl elbowed one of her friends and ordered, "Remember your manners!" sounding unerringly like Cuchulainn. She folded her little wings and walked much more sedately to stand in front of Brighid.

"You're the famous Huntress Cuchulainn's told us stories about, aren't you?" The little girl's face was bright with more than just the Fomorian's distinctive luminous skin. She was a beautiful, fey-looking little thing, sparkling with intelligence and curiosity.

"Well, I am the Huntress Brighid. I don't know how famous I am, though," Brighid said, throwing Cuchulainn a look of mild annoyance.

"Oh, we do! We've heard all about you!"

"Really? You'll have to share those stories with me," Brighid said.

"Not now," Cuchulainn said brusquely. "Now there is dinner to prepare." He dismounted and began unlacing the ties that held the fresh meat behind his saddle.

"Did you get another deer, Cuchulainn?" Kyna asked, bouncing up and down.

"A wild, white sheep this time, Ky. And you can thank the Huntress for it. She is the one who brought the beast down," he said, neatly turning the child's attention back to Brighid.

Dozens of sets of round little eyes refocused on the Huntress. Brighid shrugged. "I just beat him to the shot."

"No, you're special. We already know," Kyna said. "May... may I touch you?"

Brighid looked helplessly at Cu, who was suddenly oh-so-busy handing the wrapped meat to Curran and Nevin.

"Please?" the child asked. "I've always wanted to meet a centaur."

"Yes, I suppose that would be fine," the Huntress said helplessly.

Kyna walked closer to Brighid and then reverently stretched out her hand and touched the Huntress's gleaming golden coat. "You're soft like water. And your hair is so pretty, just like Cuchulainn said. I think he's right. It's good that you keep it long even though most Huntresses cut theirs short."

"I—I've never felt the need to cut it," Brighid stuttered, completely take aback by the child's comment. Cuchulainn talked about her hair?

"Good. You shouldn't."

"I want to be a Huntress when I grow up!" shouted a voice from the throng.

Kyna rolled her eyes and shook her head. "You can't be a Huntress, Liam. You're not a centaur and you're not a female."

Brighid watched one of the taller children's faces fall and she felt a panicky knot within her when his eyes filled with tears.

"You could still be a hunter, Liam," Brighid said. "Some centaurs agree to train humans in the ways of a Huntress." As soon as she said it she realized her ridiculous error. The little winged male was definitely not human. He'd probably really cry now. What if he started the rest of them crying? But Liam didn't notice anything wrong with what she'd said. His fanged smile was radiant.

"Do you really mean it? Would you teach me?" The boy rushed up to her and soon his small, warm hand was patting her sleek side.

Teach him? She had no intention of teaching him or any-one—especially anyone whose head didn't reach her shoulder. Brighid's panic expanded. She had just been trying to keep the child from crying.

"If she's going to teach Liam I want her to teach me, too!" Another child disengaged from the group and skipped up to Brighid, hero-worship shining in his big blue eyes.

"Me, too!" said a little girl with hair the color of daisies.

Brighid had no idea how it had happened, but she was sur-rounded by small, winged beings who were chattering away about their lives as Huntresses. Warm little hands patted her legs and flanks while Kyna asked never-ending questions about how Brighid kept her hair out of her eyes while she hunted, and what she rinsed it with to make it shine so, and did she use the same rinse on the horse part of her, and…

Brighid would've rather been thrust into a pack of angry wolves, at least she could kick her way clear and escape.

"Perhaps we should give the Huntress time to unload her packs and fill her stomach before we ask more of her," Ciara's firm voice cut through the high-pitched, childish jabbering.

Little hands reluctantly dropped from the centaur's body.

Undaunted, Kyna still chirped with excitement. "Can Brighid stay at our lodge?"

To Brighid's intense relief, Cuchulainn spoke up. "I think it would be best if the Huntress lodged with me. She's part of my Clan, remember?"

"Yes, I remember," Kyna said softly, kicking at a dirt clod with bare feet that Brighid noticed ended in remarkably sharp-looking talons.

They are such anomalies, the Huntress thought. *Not really human and yet obviously not Fomorian. How will they ever find their place in Partholon?*

"Cuchulainn, why don't you show Brighid to your lodge. I'll send for you when it is time for the evening meal."

Cu surprised Brighid by tossing the reins of his gelding to little Kyna.

"Take care of him for me."

"Of course I will, Cu! You know I'm his favorite." The child giggled. "Bye, Brighid. I'll see you again at the evening meal," she said before clucking and tugging fussily at the big gelding's reins. The horse blew through his nose into the child's hair and then plodded docilely after her.

"Go on now, the rest of you! You have chores to finish before we eat," Ciara told the children.

In clusters of two and three, they rushed off like darting fish, calling goodbyes to Brighid and Cuchulainn.

"I think they were better this time," Ciara said to the warrior.

"Well, at least there was a lot less jumping and dancing," Cu said.

"Better than what?" Brighid asked.

Ciara smiled. "Better than when they first met Cuchulainn."

Brighid snorted.

"You laugh, but we're serious," Cu said.

"I didn't laugh. I scoffed disbelievingly. There is a distinct difference," the Huntress said, wiping at a smudgy handprint that had been left on her golden coat.

"You'll get used to them," Ciara said. And at the look on the centaur's face she laughed.

Brighid thought she had never heard such a lovely, musical sound.

Cuchulainn harrumphed. "Now it's my turn to scoff."

"Oh, Cuchulainn, you're getting along with the children just fine. They adore you!" Ciara said.

"I'm not interested in their adoration. I just want to be sure they arrive safely at MacCallan Castle," Cuchulainn said sharply, his face hardening into a blank, emotionless mask.

"Of course," Ciara said, her smile never wavering.

It was interesting, Brighid thought, to watch how familiarly the beautiful winged woman spoke to Cu. And how she ignored the way he had turned cold and withdrawn.

"I'll leave you with Cuchulainn. He knows his way around. If there is anything you need, he will know if we can provide it. We do not have much here, Brighid, but what we have we willingly share."

"Thank you," Brighid said, automatically responding to Ciara's openness and warmth.

"Cuchulainn, the evening meal will be in the longhouse, as usual, after the dusk blessing ceremony. Please bring Brighid. And it would be nice if this time you chose to stay and share the meal with us." Ciara nodded politely to Brighid before she turned and gracefully walked away.

CHAPTER
FIVE

Cuchulainn motioned for Brighid to enter the small building ahead of him. She ducked through the thick animal skin
that served as a doorway and was pleasantly surprised to feel
warm, still air instead of constant cold wind. The lodge was
circular, and the walls were made of the red shale that was so
plentiful in the Wastelands. It was patched snugly together
with a mixture of mud and sand. There was a hearth that
wrapped around almost half of the curving room. Two small
windows were covered, so there was little light, but it was
bright enough for Brighid to see that the roof was unusual. It
appeared to be mesh, woven of reeds or thin branches. Placed
over the matting was a substance Brighid couldn't identify. It
had been firmly pressed into the weave, but now it appeared
to be hard and dry.

"It's moss," Cuchulainn said. "They cut it from the ground
and while it's still pliant they press it into the web of woven

tubers. When it dies it hardens until it's like rock, only lighter. Nothing can get through it."

"What's this on the floor?" Brighid bent and picked up a handful of short, fragrant grass.

"They call it dwarf heather. It only grows to about hock-high, but there's a lot of it, especially in canyon areas like this. It makes for good insulation. The ground here is damnably cold and hard." Cuchulainn motioned to the other side of the room, opposite the stretched animal skin hammock that served as a bed. "You can put your packs there. Ciara will have pelts brought in for you to sleep on. You should be comfortable and warm enough—and anyway we'll be traveling in just a few days."

"Cuchulainn, what's going on here?"

"I'm preparing to lead the hybrids back to Partholon, of course. The snow has almost thawed enough for the pass to be open again—as you know better than I," he finished curtly.

Brighid shook her head. "That's not what I mean. I counted at least forty children. I saw only three adults. What is going on here?" she repeated slowly.

Cuchulainn pulled off his cloak and ran a hand through his hair, which Brighid noticed was uncharacteristically long and unkempt.

"I'm not exactly sure," he said.

"Not sure?"

Cuchulainn scowled at her. "That's right. They're not what you think. The only thing I know for sure is that the New Fomorians are different."

"Well of course they're different!" Brighid wanted to shake Cu. "They're a mixture of human and Fomorian. There has never been a race like them."

Cuchulainn walked over to the hearth. Stirring the glowing embers to life he fed them blocks of dried peat from the stack nearby and the coals flamed into a lively, crackling fire. Then he turned and gave Brighid a weary, resigned look.

"Take off your packs. Relax. It isn't much, but I'll tell you what I know."

As Cuchulainn helped her unload she watched him carefully. Grief and guilt had aged and hardened him, but there was something else about him, something that tickled the edge of her mind but which she couldn't quite understand.

Had the hybrids cast some kind of spell over him? Cuchulainn shunned the spirit realm, and he would have little protection against a magical attack. Though Brighid did not have the training and experience of her mother, she was not a stranger to the powers of the spirit world. Nor was she a stranger to the ways in which powers granted by the Goddess could be twisted and misused. Silently she promised herself that later, when she was free to concentrate, she would see if she could detect any malevolent energy hovering around the settlement. Until then all she could do was what she was best at—finding a trail and following it.

"Here," she said, tossing the warrior a fat skin from her last pack. "Your sister sent you this."

Cuchulainn uncapped the skin, sniffed the liquid within, grunted in pleasure and took a long drink. He wiped his mouth with the back of his hand and settled onto his cot. "It's been too long since I've tasted wine from Epona's Temple. My mother would say there is no excuse for living like a barbarian."

"That's exactly what your sister said."

Cu's smile looked almost normal for an instant. "I miss her."

"She misses you, too."

He nodded and took another drink of the rich red wine.

"Cu, why are there so few adult hybrids?" Brighid asked softly.

He met her eyes. "Here's what I know. I have counted twenty-two full-grown, adult hybrids—twelve females, one of whom has just announced that she is pregnant, and ten males. And there are seventy children ranging in age from infants to young adults. Ciara and the others say that everyone else is dead."

"How?" Brighid's head reeled at the disparity in numbers.

"It was the madness. Ciara says it was more difficult to withstand the older they became. Of the original hybrids born of human mothers only Lochlan, Nevin, Curran, Keir and Fallon remain." Cuchulainn paused, clenching his jaw. "Of them Fallon is mad."

Brighid nodded. "Her jailors at Guardian Castle say she remains mad. Elphame's sacrifice didn't touch her."

"It was too late. She had already accepted the darkness of her father when El drank Lochlan's blood and took on their madness. Apparently there is no reversing it once it has taken hold." His stomach tightened as he remembered the horrific scene when Elphame had slit her own wrists, forcing Lochlan to share his blood to save her life. With the hybrid's blood she had taken within her the madness of a race of demons. "It should have driven El mad, too. It was only through Epona's power that she remains sane even though the madness lies dormant within her blood."

"But accepting the madness didn't kill your sister, and it didn't kill Fallon. How did it kill the other adults?"

"Suicide. Ciara says that when a hybrid was no longer able to bear the pain of withstanding the evil within him, he chose suicide rather than a life of violence and hatred."

The Huntress tilted her head and sent him an incredulous look. "So what she's saying is that someone who has pretty much decided to accept hatred and evil has the capacity to make the ultimate sacrifice of taking his or her own life?"

"Yes. As a last act of humanity."

"And you're believing all of this?"

Instead of the anger with which Brighid expected him to respond Cuchulainn's expression turned introspective. He took another drink from the wineskin.

"At first I didn't believe any of it. For days I walked around armed, expecting winged demons to jump out at me from behind every rock." His brows tilted up and some of his old sparkle lit his eyes. "Demons failed to appear. But can you guess what did jump out at me?"

Brighid snorted a quick laugh. "If you'd left me to lodge with them I think I would have called them demons. Very small demons, but none the less frightening."

"The children are everywhere. There are so many of them and so few adults that it's a constant struggle to care for them and keep them fed. Not that they're helpless—or at least not as helpless as human, or even centaur, children would be at their age. They're hardy and intelligent. Despite their rather exuberant show when welcoming strangers, they're incredibly well-behaved." Cuchulainn met and held Brighid's sharp gaze. "And they are the happiest beings I've ever known."

"There's nothing new about the young being happy, Cu. Even your silly wolf cub runs and frolics. It is the way of youth before the responsibilities of the world encroach upon their unrealistic dreams for the future."

Cuchulainn heard the bitter undertone in the Huntress's voice and wondered what had happened in her youth to put it there.

"But before Elphame's sacrifice, the New Fomorian children had no carefree period of innocence. From the day they were born, not only did they have to struggle to survive, but they had to wage a constant war against the dark whisperings within their own blood as they watched their parents succumb to the evil and die around them."

"If that is actually what happened."

"I'm tired, Brighid." Cuchulainn ran a hand across his brow. "I didn't come here as a hero who would lead them back to their ancestral homeland. I came here filled with hatred."

Brighid nodded her head slowly. "I know."

"Elphame didn't. At least I hope she didn't. I wouldn't

want her to think that I would betray her trust." He shook his head and held up his hand to stop her when she tried to speak. "No, I don't mean that I came here with the intention of slaughtering the hybrids. But I was looking to cast blame and to find a battlefield on which to avenge Brenna."

"That wouldn't bring Brenna back, Cu."

"No, it wouldn't. And instead of a battlefield or a race of demons I found a people who are imbued with happiness." He rubbed his brow again. "Happiness is all around me. I'm surrounded by it. But I can feel none of it."

Brighid felt a rush of sympathy for him. Living within a face that was too old for his years, he looked lost and alone.

"You need to go home, Cu."

"I need—"

Cuchulainn's words were cut off by a tapping sound against the door flap followed closely by Kyna's shining head.

"Ciara said I should come for you." She grinned at Cuchulainn. Then her bright eyes and smile flashed at Brighid. "And you, too, Huntress. The evening blessing is about to begin. You don't want to miss it, do you?"

"We'll be right there, Ky," Cuchulainn said.

The child's head disappeared.

"Evening blessing?" Brighid asked.

"They honor Epona every day, both at sunrise and sunset. It's a little like being back at my mother's temple."

"Except for the cold, dreary land, the absence of the riches of Partholon, and the presence of hordes of winged children," Brighid said.

Cuchulainn tossed the wineskin back to the Huntress and grabbed his cloak.

"Exactly like that." He paused in front of her on his way out of door. "I am glad you're here, Brighid."

"So am I, Cu. So am I."

The long, low, rectangular building Brighid had mistaken as a shelter for animals when she'd looked down at the settlement from above was really the general meeting place and, Cu explained, it served as a Great Hall for the hybrids. It was there that Kyna, skipping and dancing, led them, and then, with a parting grin and the promise to sit near them during the meal, she scampered to one of the clusters of waiting children.

Although Cuchulainn had prepared Brighid for the number of children, the centaur found herself gaping like an inexperienced foal. There were just so many of them! Winged children were everywhere. It looked as if the entire settlement had gathered in front of the longhouse in a large, loose circle. The children clustered in groups, each surrounding an adult who attentively talked to and kept watch over his or her charges. The sun had almost fallen below the distant western horizon, and the incessant wind had turned even colder and more biting, but not one child cried or complained. They didn't run around in the undisciplined gamboling typical of youth. They simply stood and waited patiently, even the smallest ones with their tiny wings and wide, bright eyes. Of course they did stare openly at Brighid. But when she met a young one's gaze, the child returned her look with a wide, sharp-toothed smile. Several of them waved at her. She noticed the boy child, Liam, right away because he made a point to catch her attention by executing a very grown-up bow and sending her a look of total adoration. As if she really was his mentor, she thought with a silent groan.

What in the world would she do with a small winged shadow?

The door to the longhouse opened and Ciara stepped out. She walked quickly to the center of the circle. The winged woman's gaze skimmed over the group until it came to rest on Brighid. Her smile turned radiant.

"It is a blessed day that is closing!" she proclaimed.

The children made small happy sounds while their heads bobbed up and down in vigorous agreement. All eyes turned to the Huntress.

"Until today we knew of the noble race of centaurs only

from memories of our mothers and our mothers' mothers, and from the stories we have told. But today we are honored by the presence of the famous MacCallan Huntress, Brighid Dhianna. Let us give thanks to our Goddess for yet another day and the new blessing with which she has gifted us."

Feeling the weight of all of those young eyes, Brighid wanted to fidget or, better yet, escape. Thankfully, when Ciara raised her arms and turned to face the west all the children and adults turned with her, focusing their eyes on the horizon. But as Ciara's clear voice rang out strong and sweet, evoking the timeless ritual of Epona's evening blessing, Brighid found curiosity and surprise pulling her eyes from the west to the delicate form of the winged woman.

O Epona, Goddess of beauty and of magnificence
Goddess of laughter and joyous strength.
At this setting day we begin our thanksgiving looking to the west,
the way of water,
and we are washed in the blessings of another day.
Today we thank You for guiding the Huntress to us,
she who is born of a noble race.
Bound in honor.
Rich in tradition.

Ciara was standing with her arms raised and her head thrown back. Her dark wings unfurled and lifted around her, rippling smoothly against the cold evening wind. Brighid drew in a surprised breath. The winged woman's body was outlined by a glittering haze that during the past two moons had become very familiar to Brighid. It was the same shimmering power she had seen countless times when Elphame called upon Epona's name.

"You didn't expect that, did you?" Cuchulainn whispered.

Brighid could only shake her head and continue to stare at the Goddess-touched hybrid.

O Goddess of our hearts
protectress of things wild and free
we thank You for Your bright presence here
and for Your power that works through water...

Arms still raised, Ciara turned to her right, and the group followed her movements.

Through earth...

She turned again to the right.

Through air...

Again, the group followed her in the sacred circle by turning to face the south.

And through fire.

Then Ciara and the group closed the circle by turning again to the west. At the moment the sun sank into the earth, she lifted her voice joyously, threw wide her arms, and called,

Strike, Goddess lights!

Brighid gasped as two torches staked just outside the longhouse door flamed into bright, burning light.

This is a day of bounty and of joy,
worthy to be celebrated,
as in times far ancient

our mothers taught us
to honor You, O Goddess.
Your light will ever guide
those who have been lost in the dark.
All hail Epona!

"All hail Epona!" the group shouted and the circle broke as smiling children made their way amidst lots of giggling talk into the longhouse.

Brighid felt like her hooves had been rooted to the cold ground.

"By the hot holy breath of the Goddess, she has fire magic!" Her words exploded at Cuchulainn. "Why didn't you tell me?"

"Over the past two moons I have learned that some things must be seen to be fully appreciated. Come on, Huntress." Much like he would have his sister, Cu wrapped his arm through Brighid's and guided the stunned centaur toward the longhouse. "I told you understanding them is not as easy as you might think."

CHAPTER
SIX

"Y ou couldn't have told me about this, either?" Brighid muttered to Cu as she stepped inside the longhouse.

"There really wasn't time," he said under his breath. "And I don't think the simple telling of it would have been adequate."

It was a beautiful building. More rectangular than circular the two longest walls supported huge hearths in which fires crackled merrily around enormous, bubbling pots that, from the wonderful smells drifting throughout the room, must be filled with well-spiced stew. Long rows of trestle tables were formed by smoothed wooden planks resting snugly atop stone pillars that had been carved to look like blooming flowers. But what drew Brighid's eye were the walls of the great building. From the outside they looked like the walls of Cu's small lodge, but on the inside they had been meticulously smoothed and covered with painted scenes so lovely they rivaled any of the treasured pieces of art gracing the marble walls and hallowed halls of Epona's Temple.

The centermost scene was breathtaking. A silver mare, silhouetted in the golden light of a rising sun, arched her proud neck and presided regally over the room. The mare's eyes were wise—her gaze benevolent. All around her vignettes of Partholon had been brought to life with a master's hand. There was the Temple of Epona, glistening with pearlized walls and stately carved columns. The Temple of the Muse's elegant grounds were filled with silk-clad women, frozen in time, clustered around each of the nine Incarnate Goddesses, listening in rapt attention to their daily lessons. There was even a scene wherein two centaurs raced through wither-deep grass that Brighid easily recognized as the Centaur Plains. Framing each one of the scenes were intricate knots that hid birds and flowers and animals indigenous to a land much more hospitable than the Wastelands.

"It's truly amazing," Brighid said.

"I'm pleased you like it," Ciara said. With an elegant unfolding of her hand she motioned to a section of one of the tables that had been arranged away from the others. The benchlike sitting area on one side of it had been removed to accommodate Brighid's equine body. The other side remained fashioned for more diminutive human hindquarters. "I hope this will be comfortable for you. I thought Cuchulainn and I could join you, here apart from the others, so that you would not be deluged with the constant questioning of the young." Ciara led them to their seats as Liam and Kyna hurried over with trays of steaming food. "Well, with two possible exceptions," Ciara whispered to the Huntress.

Brighid eyed the eagerly waiting children with suspicion. Their inquisitive looks made her more uncomfortable than a pack of starving coyotes. The moment she sat beside the table, Liam rushed forward and ladled for her a generous portion of thick stew filled with chunks of potato, meat and barley, and a side dish of warm greens that smelled a lot like spinach.

"The wildgreens are special for you, Brighid." Liam's nervous excitement brimmed over and spilled around them. "They're a real treat so early in the spring. I, um, I mean we hope you like them."

"I'm sure I will. Everything smells wonderful." Brighid smiled tentatively at the boy. He practically wriggled out of his skin with pleasure.

"Can Fand eat at our table, Cu?" Kyna asked the warrior as he helped himself to the wildgreens she offered.

"Of course, but be sure she stays under the table. Not on it," Cu said.

"Leave the trays and go eat now," Ciara prompted when the two children looked as though they would be content to stand all night and watch every move Brighid made as she attempted to eat under their intense scrutiny. They obeyed, but reluctantly, still throwing curious looks over their shoulders at the beautiful centaur.

"The children are enamored with you, Huntress," Ciara said with a smile.

Cuchulainn glanced up at Brighid from under his brows. "It's a relief to have them obsessed with someone else," he said around bites of stew.

Ciara laughed. "Oh, do not think they have forgotten you, Warrior."

Cu scowled and turned his attention back to his bowl.

Brighid ate silently, letting her eyes dwell on the incredible scenes that filled the walls.

"I sense that you are surprised by our artwork," Ciara said.

Brighid's gaze shifted to her. "Yes," she said frankly. "I am."

Ciara's warm smile didn't waver. "You wouldn't be if you knew the story of our birth."

"I know some of it—that your people come from a group of women stolen from Partholon by the Fomorians during the war more than one hundred years ago. When the Fomorians realized they were losing the war, they escaped into the Trier Mountains with as many human women as they could capture. They planned to hide there and grow strong again, replenishing themselves with a new generation of demons born of human women. Eventually they would return to attack Partholon again."

"Yes, that much is true. What else do you know?"

Brighid lifted one shoulder. "Only what Lochlan told us. That the Fomorians escaped the Partholonian warriors, but they couldn't escape the plague brought to them by Epona's outrage at the violation of her women. The demons grew sick and weakened. Then a group of pregnant women, led by Lochlan's mother, attacked their captors, killed them, and searched through the mountains, helping the other groups of women rise against their captors, too."

Ciara nodded and took up the thread of the story. "Their plan was to return to Partholon. They knew their pregnancies meant death sentences for them. No human woman had ever survived the birth of a child fathered by a demon. It was their desire to return to their homes where they would die surrounded by their loved ones."

Ciara's beautiful face glowed with the telling of the tale and Brighid listened, entranced by the Shaman's singsong voice.

"But then the impossible happened. As they began the journey back to Partholon, Morrigan MacCallan went into labor and survived the birth. She brought forth a boy child who had wings as well as the spark of humanity. She looked upon her son with the fierce love of a mother, and named him Lochlan. And then another woman survived the birth of her infant. And another. And another." Ciara paused, holding Brighid's eyes with her own. "What were the women to do? Some would say they should have killed or abandoned their children and returned to the lives that waited for them in their beloved Partholon. The infants were, after all, the spawn of demons. But their mothers did not see them as such. They saw their humanity instead. So Epona led the young mothers here, to our canyon, where they built new lives from the dreams of their old world. And here we have stayed for more than one hundred years, waiting to fulfill those mothers' dreams by returning to the world they loved with a depth of spirit second only to their love for their children."

"And Epona gave Lochlan's mother the Prophecy, which he fulfilled after dreaming of Elphame and following that dream to Partholon," Brighid said quickly without looking at Cuchulainn. She didn't want to speak of the events that had led Fallon to follow Lochlan to MacCallan Castle. She had despaired of Lochlan fulfilling the Prophecy because she knew he had fallen in love with Elphame. So Fallon killed Brenna to lure Elphame away from the safety of her clan. "That I know, but it doesn't explain all of this." The centaur pointed at the lovely paintings.

"Oh, but it does. You see, the largest group of pregnant women were captured during the great battle at the Temple of the Muse."

Brighid's eyes widened in understanding. "So many of you are descended from either Incarnate Goddesses of the Muse, or their acolytes."

"That's right. You already know that I am granddaughter of the Incarnate Goddess Terpsichore, Muse of the Dance. This room is filled with descendants of all nine of the Goddesses. Our mothers and grandmothers knew the magic of the Muses, and they passed that knowledge along to us. It was their greatest wish that the wonder of Partholon not die in the Wastelands. Does the beauty surrounding you now make sense?"

"It does indeed," Brighid said softly. Throughout Partholon the Temple of the Muse was known for its various schools of learning and the exceptional women who lived and trained there. Epona's own Chosen was always educated by the Incarnate Goddesses of the Muse. The Huntress considered Ciara's words. There were many more layers to this situation than she had anticipated. And layers meant things were rarely as they at first seemed. "Your mother was daughter to Terpsichore's Incarnate Goddess of the Dance, and your father?"

Sadness crossed the winged woman's expressive face. "He was the son of an acolyte devoted to Calliope who was captured by the Fomorians, raped and impregnated when she was thirteen years old. Really just a child herself..." Ciara's voice trailed off.

"Where are your parents now?" Brighid forced herself to ask.

Before she answered, Ciara looked at Cuchulainn. The warrior returned her gaze steadily, with eyes that had once more gone flat and expressionless. She turned slowly back to Brighid. When she spoke her voice was shadowed with grief.

"More than two decades ago my parents committed suicide. They chose to die in each other's arms before they succumbed to the evil that was choking the humanity from them. As they wished, I scattered their ashes into the south." Ciara's eyes pierced Brighid almost as fully as did her next words. "I am my people's Shaman. Trained by my mother, who followed the ways of her mother, the Beloved of Terpsichore. I would not lie to you, Huntress. I sense you have knowledge of the Shaman Way. Can you not discern the truth in my words?"

Brighid felt more than saw Cuchulainn straighten in his seat. She hadn't told anyone—not Cu, not even his sister. How did Ciara know?

"Shamans can lie," Brighid said. "I know that from my own experiences."

"Yes, they can." Ciara's open, honest face was tinged with sadness. "But I do not."

"They all committed suicide," Brighid said.

"Not all. Most did. The others..." Ciara looked away. She laced the fingers of her hands together. Her knuckles whitened under the pressure with which she held herself together. "The madness claimed the others and shortly afterward they died, too."

"It pains you to speak of it," Brighid said.

"Yes, very much." Ciara forced her hands apart and pressed her palms into the smooth wood of the table. "You have to understand what happened to us when Elphame fulfilled the Prophecy and took the madness from our blood. All these long years we fought against the evil within us, even though it caused us pain and each battle cost us a piece of our humanity. And then suddenly that great, sucking evil was gone." Ciara's breath caught and her eyes glistened as she relived the moment. "What is left within each of us now is what we fought so hard to keep. Our goodness. Our humanity. We want to move forward—to become the people our human mothers believed us to be so long ago. When I remember the horrors of the past and those of us who were defeated before salvation came, it feels like I am deconstructing the fortress of goodness within my mind. Grief and sadness drift into darkened corners. Disillusion moves in until breathing in remembrance does nothing but barricade the doors and seal in pain." She didn't turn to look at Cuchulainn, but Brighid felt that Ciara was speaking more to him than to her. "Dwelling on tragedy makes grief become like a dripping icicle that begins as a small, harmless sliver of coldness. But slowly, as the winter of mourning progresses, layer after dripping layer hardens into an unbreakable dagger of pain." Ciara straightened her back and turned her hands, so that they rested palm up in a gesture of openness and supplication. "Test me, Huntress. I know you have the ability to discern any falseness in my words. I welcome your scrutiny."

Brighid ignored Cuchulainn, who had stopped eating and was staring at her with a mixed expression of surprise and revulsion. She drew in a long breath and focused her keen powers of observation—powers that were, just as Ciara had sensed, enhanced by the rich Shaman heritage that was her birthright—upon the winged woman. As when she searched out prey for her Clan, the Huntress scented more than the air. She breathed in the spiritual essence of that which she sought. And what she sought there in the longhouse was the dark spoor left by evil and lies.

Ciara sat still and serene, waiting patiently for the Huntress to search her spirit and see what lived there.

"You're not hiding anything from us," Brighid finally said.

Ciara's smile was radiant again. "No, Huntress. I am not hiding anything from you. But if it would rest your mind, I invite you to travel with me on a true spirit journey to the Upperworld, and I will pledge before Epona Herself that my words are truth."

Brighid felt a cold fist close around her heart. Using her innate powers to feed her Clan or to know the truth about Ciara and therefore keep the MacCallans safe, was one thing. To her it was no different than piercing the heart of a noble stag with an arrow. It was not pleasant, but it was something she must do in order to fulfill the path she had chosen for her life. But she would not travel on a spirit journey. She knew only too well who she would meet.

"No," she said a little too quickly. "That won't be necessary, Ciara."

"You have the power within you, but you do not take the Sacred Journey?"

"No. I am a Huntress, not a Shaman."

Ciara opened her mouth, and then changed her mind and simply nodded slowly. "We each must find our own path."

Cuchulainn stood so abruptly that he almost knocked aside the bench. "It is time I retire for the night."

Ciara made no attempt to hide her disappointment. "But the storytelling will begin shortly. The children will be asking for you."

"Not tonight," he said curtly.

"I, too, must ask your indulgence that you allow me to retire early. My journey here has been a long and tiring one," Brighid said, rising gracefully and walking around the table to stand beside Cuchulainn.

Ciara's disappointment turned quickly to a gentle look of understanding. "Of course. Rest well tonight, Brighid."

Before they turned to leave, Cuchulainn said in his terse

voice, "Tomorrow I want to explore the pass. I think it might be clear enough that we can begin our journey soon."

"That's an excellent idea. I'll make plans to join you," Ciara said.

Cuchulainn grunted. Without waiting for the Huntress, he strode briskly out the door, leaving Brighid to smile and wave apologetic goodbyes to the disappointed children.

Torches were lit all over the settlement and it didn't take long for Brighid's sharp eyes to pick out his hunched back as he walked briskly between lodges. She caught up with him easily.

"You have Shaman powers," he said without looking at her.

"Yes. Though I choose not to, I do have the ability to travel the Sacred Journey and to commune with the spirit realm. It's in my blood—" she paused and glanced at his stony profile "—from my mother. She is Mairearad Dhianna."

Her words brought him up short. "You are the daughter of the High Shaman of the Dhianna herd?"

"I am."

"Which daughter?"

Brighid set her face in carefully neutral lines. "The eldest."

He shook his head in disbelief. "But your herd's tradition is that you follow your mother as High Shaman."

"I have broken with tradition."

"Yet you carry that power within you," he said.

"Yes! You sound like I just announced that I carry within me a rare plague. Your father is a High Shaman, too. Don't you know a little of what it's like to have the power and to choose not to walk the exact path it wishes to lead you down?"

Cuchulainn's jaw clenched and unclenched. "You already know the answer to that, Brighid. I want no traffic with the spirit realm."

The Huntress threw up her hands in frustration. "There are other ways to deal with the powers that touch our lives than to totally reject them."

"Not for me." He ground out the words between his teeth.

"Your sister is the eldest daughter of Epona's Chosen. Tradition holds that she should follow her mother as The Beloved of Epona, yet all who know her understand that it is her destiny to be The MacCallan. She has not turned from the powers inherent in her blood. She used her affinity for earth magic to bring MacCallan Castle alive. Like her, I have chosen not to follow tradition, but I do not completely reject the gifts of my heritage."

He was silent, staring at her like she was a pariah. Brighid sighed, keeping her growing anger in check by reminding herself it wasn't her he battled against—it was himself.

"My affinity is for the spirits of animals."

His eyes narrowed. "That's why your abilities as a Huntress are so vast."

Brighid snorted. "I like to think that I use my affinity to enhance rather than to create my abilities."

"I don't see any difference in the two."

"Be very careful, Cuchulainn. Remember that you speak to your Clan's Huntress. I will not tolerate your slander." Brighid's voice was tightly controlled, but her eyes were bright with anger.

Cuchulainn hesitated for only an instant before he nodded slowly. "You are quite right to remind me, Huntress. Please accept my apology."

"Accepted," she said shortly.

"Would you rather lodge elsewhere?" he asked.

She snorted again, letting some of the tension relax out of her shoulders. "Is sending me into a lodge filled with children how you plan to torture me for my transgression into the spirit realm?"

"No," he said quickly. "I just thought that you might not—"

"Let's just get some sleep."

"Agreed," he said.

They walked on in silence. Brighid could sense the turmoil within the grim warrior who stalked beside her. He was a notched arrow waiting to explode. When he spoke suddenly, his voice sounded like it came from a tomb.

"You would have used your powers to save her, wouldn't you?"

She looked quickly over at him, but he did not meet her eyes.

"Of course I would have, but my gift isn't one of preordination. I already told you I simply have an affinity for..." But her voice faded as she realized what he was really saying. He had been forewarned of Brenna's death by a premonition of danger. A warning he had rejected just as he had always rejected anything from the spirit realm. She stopped and placed a hand on his shoulder, turning him so that he had to look at her. "No matter how much you punish yourself or me or your sister, Brenna will remain dead."

"I'm not punishing you or Elphame."

She raised one eyebrow.

"I—I can't seem to get away from it!"

"It?" she asked.

"The pain of her loss."

She felt the tightness of his shoulder muscles under her hand. What could she say to him? She wasn't good at dealing with raw emotions. It was one reason she had chosen to become a Huntress. She'd wanted to leave the emotional turmoil of her old life behind. Animals were simple. They didn't agonize or manipulate or lie. Cuchulainn needed to talk to a Shaman, not a Huntress. But the warrior wouldn't turn to a Shaman. By process of elimination she was all he had.

"I don't know what to tell you, Cu," she said honestly. "But it seems to me that you can't run away from that kind of pain. You have to face it. And then you decide if you're going to heal and go on, or if you're going to live life as one of the walking wounded. I do know which Brenna would choose for you."

He looked at her with old, tired eyes and tunneled a finger down the center of his forehead. "I know, too. I keep thinking that if I make her angry enough at me she will at least come to my dreams to berate me." His dry, humorless laugh sounded more like a sob. "She doesn't come. She won't. I've rejected the spirit realm and that's where she is."

Helplessly Brighid watched his agony. "You need to rest, Cu."

He nodded and, like a man sleepwalking, he moved forward again along the path to their lodge. He reminded Brighid of a wounded animal. He needed a miracle to heal him, or someone needed to put him out of his misery.

CHAPTER
SEVEN

The hearth fire had burned down to glowing coals, but Brighid's sharp eyes needed very little light. She thought he was finally asleep. From her side of the lodge, she had watched the warrior struggle into sleep. It was as if his body fought against relaxation as another way to punish himself. No wonder he looked so haggard. What he needed was a cup of one of Brenna's notorious tea concoctions to make him rest. The Huntress let out a long, slow breath. No, what Cuchulainn needed was Brenna.

She was tired, too. What she had told Ciara about needing to retire early had been true. She rearranged her folded equine limbs and curled more comfortably on her side, breathing in the light, pleasing fragrance of the dwarf heather that covered the floor of the lodge. Her eyelids felt heavy, but she resisted the urge to sleep. Not yet. She had something she needed to see to first. And now that Cuchulainn was asleep she could begin.

Staring into the glowing rust-colored coals she relaxed her body while she deepened and slowed her breathing. She would not take herself into the trance state that led to a Sacred Journey, but she did need the focused concentration of meditation, which was only the first step to the spirit world.

Brighid wouldn't travel farther, though. She wouldn't allow that. She never allowed that.

Against the backdrop of the glowing coals, the Huntress pictured herself as she had been earlier that day when she had stood at the edge of the canyon precipice and first glimpsed the hybrid settlement below. She saw the neatly arranged camp and the well-constructed buildings. Then she looked again, but this time she saw with the senses beyond her eyes. The scene rippled, like breath blowing over water, and the colors changed. The dull gray and rust of the Wastelands shifted and was suddenly washed in a bright halo of green—a color that radiated life and health and the promise of spring. Brighid allowed herself to fall deeper into the trance and she expanded her senses. The halo of green intensified and her spirit sight became clearer. The light was actually coming from dozens of shining orbs that flickered brilliantly against the dreary colors of the Wastelands.

Before she could focus her concentration more, she Felt something else, but she sensed it wasn't coming from the settlement. In her vision there came a sudden tingling awareness from behind her. She imagined turning, and the mountains wavered and became red, as if they were bathed in blood. Startled, Brighid's concentration broke and she was once more staring into the remains of the hearth fire.

What did it all mean? She wished she had her mother's knowledge. *Think!* she ordered herself. The hybrid camp had been painted in ethereal green. There were no negative connotations with that color. In the spirit realm it represented what it did in the physical world—growth and prosperity and life beginning anew. Had she seen any dark tinges within the verdant halo? No…Brighid sifted through the memory of her meditation. Ciara had been telling the truth. She was hiding no evil—at least no evil that Brighid could discover.

Then her thoughts turned to the brief glimpse she'd had of the mountains. Their aura had definitely been scarlet. And the Feeling radiating from them had been different, more complex, tinged in darkness. Her brow furrowed and she restlessly shifted her bent legs. The mountain range had been named Trier, which was the word in the Old Language for the color red, for the red rocks and the small red-leafed plant that carpeted the lower slopes during the warmer months. Was that what her vision had reflected? That the mountains were aptly named and even in spirit they were red. Or did it go deeper than that? In the spirit realm the color red carried complex, conflicting symbolism. It stood for passion, but it also represented hatred. It foretold birth as well as death.

She simply wasn't certain—she glanced at the restlessly sleeping form of Cuchulainn—she wasn't certain of anything here, except that she would remain alert and guard against anything that threatened her clan. Brighid closed her eyes, but sleep didn't come easily. She kept hearing the phantom sound of wings and seeing the horizon drenched in the scarlet color of blood.

The morning was still young. The day had dawned bright and breezy, with an almost imperceptible shifting of the ever-present wind from the relentless frigid north to a slightly gentler northwesterly current that brought with it the distinct and enticing scent of the sea. Cu and Brighid had joined Ciara in the morning blessing ceremony, and after breaking their fast the three of them retraced the path Brighid and Cu had taken the day before, all the way to the mouth of the hidden mountain pass.

But something wasn't right. Ciara Felt it deep within her spirit. The closer they got to the mountains the more intensely she Felt the wrongness. It was more than just her lifelong dislike of the rocky barrier that divided them from

Partholon and all that was good and green and growing. Today she Felt the warning crawl across her skin and lodge inside of her like the bite of a venomous spider. She wanted to believe it was just her imagination, just the fact that the Trier Mountains symbolized so many negatives. But she wasn't an ordinary maiden. Ciara was her people's Shaman; she didn't need to be on a Sacred Journey to recognize a message from the spirit realm.

She needed to get away from the mountains and the unease they seemed to be evoking. Then she could retreat to her lodge and open herself to the Sacred Journey. There Ciara could call upon her spirit guides to help her sort through the warning that had shaken her all the way to her soul. She realized she had been ready to bolt from the shadow of the mountains when Cu's voice broke through her inner tumult and anchored her back in the physical world.

"It's melted quite a bit. If the weather holds, and all the signs say that it will, the trail should be passable in the next couple days," Cuchulainn said thoughtfully, nodding his head while he squinted into the still snow-speckled path that led between two sheer edges of red rock and directly into the mountains.

"You really think so?" Ciara forced her voice not to betray the fear that his words had sent spiraling through her.

"I can't see why not. It will, of course, be a difficult journey. But you said yourself that winter has broken." He nodded his head at the narrow path. "At least there won't be any more snow to block the way."

The Huntress watched Ciara and Cuchulainn as they peered into the dark slash in the ancient walls of rock. She folded her arms across her breast and shook her head at them. "You two must be totally mad."

The warrior frowned, but the winged woman simply shifted her gaze to the Huntress.

"What are you talking about?" Cu asked.

"What am *I* talking about? Better ask yourselves that question."

"Explain yourself, Huntress," Cu growled.

Brighid curled her lip at him. "By the Goddess, it's simple! You cannot take seventy children through that pass. Not in a couple days, nor in a couple turns of the moon."

Cuchulainn opened his mouth to bluster, but Ciara's calm voice interrupted his rant. "What do you mean, Brighid?"

"I mean it's clearly too dangerous. Maybe it was different when Cu came through it two moons ago, but today it would be a difficult journey for a party of adults. For children it is impossible."

"Our children are special," Ciara said softly. "They are not normal children."

"Regardless, they are still children. No matter how strong, their legs are only so long. I've watched them. Some of them are barely gliding, which means adults, or the older children, would have to carry the littlest ones. That would double the danger and difficulty." Brighid spoke matter-of-factly, in the logical emotionless voice of a Huntress discussing the tracking of game.

"You're certain? Even if we took them through in small groups?" Cu asked.

"Small groups would be better, but still dangerous. Travel would be slow, so they would be forced to spend the night in the pass. And that would be a night without fire." Brighid glanced at the Shaman who had so easily wielded the power of flame. "Fire would weaken the snow that is already thawing on the walls of the pass."

"Avalanche," Cu said. The warrior shook his head in self-disgust. He hadn't thought of that, and he should have. "But small groups could work?"

Brighid lifted one shoulder. "I suppose."

The Shaman's dark eyes caught hers. "If they were your children, would you chance taking them through the pass, even in small groups?"

"No."

"If you would not lead your own children through, I will not lead ours," Ciara said.

Cuchulainn raised his brows at the quickness of the winged woman's decision, but they were her people and it was her choice to make. "Then we'll have to wait until late summer to lead the children through, when there is no more snow on the walls of the pass," he said slowly. He could already feel the weight of the children's disappointment when they found out that they would not be traveling to the land of their dreams for several more turns of the moon.

"Not necessarily," Brighid said.

"But you just said—" Cu said gruffly.

"I said this pass was too dangerous for the children. But this is not the only pass into Partholon."

Cuchulainn jerked in surprise. "Guardian Pass!"

"Exactly." The Huntress looked pleased with herself.

"I hadn't even considered it, but you're right. It does make the most sense. It's wider, well-marked and well-maintained. Probably even passable today."

"It's guarded by warriors from Guardian Castle." Ciara's soft voice shook only slightly. "Their sole charge is to keep Fomorians from entering Partholon."

"You aren't our enemies. My sister's sacrifice promises that," Cu said gruffly.

"But that is where *she* was taken to be imprisoned."

Cuchulainn's body jerked as if someone had struck him. The *she* Ciara spoke of was Fallon, the mad hybrid who had murdered Brenna. After Fallon had been captured, Elphame had sentenced her to death as retribution for the taking of Brenna's life, but the hybrid had been pregnant, and not even Cuchulainn had been willing to sacrifice an unborn child to pay the debt its mother owed. So Fallon had been taken to Guardian Castle to be imprisoned until the birth of her child. It was there that she would eventually be executed.

"Yes," Cuchulainn clipped the word. "Fallon is jailed there."

"So won't the people assume we are as she is?" Ciara asked, eyes luminous with feeling. "Won't they already hate us?"

"You aren't responsible for Fallon's actions," Brighid said. "She chose madness and violence. None of the rest of you did."

"The warriors are honorable men and women. They will treat you justly," Cuchulainn said.

Brighid slanted a look at him, considering the irony of the situation. Here was Cu, reassuring Ciara about something that he had struggled with himself. He had been ready to treat the New Fomorians unjustly—he had already admitted that to her. But their goodness had been obvious, even to a grieving warrior. If Cuchulainn could look past their wings and their father's blood, wouldn't the Guardian Warriors be able to do the same, too? Brighid desperately hoped so.

"If they were my children, taking them through Guardian Pass is the only way I would lead them into Partholon," the Huntress said.

Ciara looked from the Huntress to the warrior. "If you believe it is for the best, then it is through Guardian Pass that we will enter Partholon."

Cuchulainn grunted and looked eastward.

"What do you think? Is it about a two-day trip?" Brighid asked, following his gaze.

"With children? I'd say you better double that."

"I thought you knew the children better than that, Cuchulainn."

Before Cu could answer the winged woman Brighid snorted. "You'll have ample opportunity to show us how special your young ones are. How soon can all of you be ready to travel?"

"Whenever you say. We have been ready since the snow began melting. And we have been awaiting this journey for more than one hundred years."

"We leave at first light," Cu said.

"First light it is then," Ciara said firmly. "We should hurry back so I can tell the others."

With those words, Ciara spread her dark wings and moved quickly over the rocky ground in the distinctive gliding run her people had inherited from their fathers. She heard the pounding of hooves as the centaur and Cuchulainn's gelding galloped behind her. She had Felt the tightness within her loosen when they decided not to take the hidden path and instead chose the way through Guardian Pass, but the suffocating sense of wrongness did not dissipate until they were well out of the shadow of the mountains and back on the rough flat terrain of the Wastelands.

The Shaman's mind whirred as her legs pumped rhythmically. Why had she been sent the warning? The obvious answer was that the spirit realm agreed with the Huntress—the hidden path was too dangerous for the children to navigate. But the answer seemed too simplistic for such an intense reaction. The Huntress had easily recognized the danger, and Ciara already believed the centaur's judgment was honest and accurate. She would have listened to her, as did Cuchulainn, without any prompting from the spirit realm. It seemed a waste of time for the spirits to compound the warning needlessly. One thing she understood very well from her experience with the world of the spirits was that they never wasted their powers and their warnings should never be discounted as needless.

She must find time to take the Sacred Journey and discover what the other realm was trying to tell her. It was always wise to heed the warnings of the spirits.

CHAPTER
EIGHT

"I didn't think they could do it," Brighid said under her breath as she and Cuchulainn approached the heart of the settlement where every member of the New Fomorians had gathered. From the smallest winged child to the beautiful Ciara, they were all waiting expectantly for the centaur and the warrior who would lead them into the land they only knew from paintings and stories and the dreams of women who were long dead.

"It is first light, and we are ready," Ciara said. "We were just waiting for the two of you."

Brighid noted the very obvious glint of pride in the winged woman's eyes, but she found it hard to blame her. The children were lined up like little warriors, each with a pack strapped to his or her back. The adults were more heavily burdened, and the Huntress counted five of them who carried leather slings across the front of their bodies in which rested the smallest of the children. The majority of the provisions for the trip were neatly piled onto litters which, Brighid snorted with surprise, were strapped to shaggy-haired goats. They were definitely ready to travel.

Cuchulainn found his voice first. "Well done." He nodded at the grinning children but didn't return their smiles. "Our way lies first to the east before we turn south and enter Partholon." He swung astride his gelding and, clucking, trotted off toward the rising sun.

Brighid moved to his side and jumped only a little when the group behind them started out with a deafening cheer. Then one small voice began an ancient song sung for generations by the children of Partholon as greeting to Epona's sun.

> Greetings to you, sun of Epona
> as you travel the skies on high,
> with your strong steps on the
> wing of the heights
> you are the happy mother of the stars.

Soon another child joined the song and then another and another, until the morning echoed with the happy sound of children's voices raised in praise to their Goddess.

> You sink down in the perilous ocean
> without harm and without hurt.
> You rise up on the quiet wave
> like a young chieftain in flower...

"It's going to be a damned long journey," Brighid said with a sigh.

"That it is," Cuchulainn said. "But it could be worse."

"How?"

"They could be riding you."

Brighid couldn't tell for sure over the blaring noise of seventy singing children, but she thought the warrior might have been chuckling softly.

As midday moved toward afternoon and then evening, Brighid decided that without a doubt the Wastelands was the gloomiest place she'd ever had the misfortune to visit. It had only taken them a few hours to reach the mountains. Once within the shadow of the stark red giants Cuchulainn had turned their group east, and for the remainder of the morning they'd been paralleling the mountain range.

Brighid's gaze slid over the land. *Ugly,* she thought as she took in the jutting shale and the low, spindly plants that masqueraded as foliage. Besides being damned ugly, the place set her nerves on edge. It appeared flat and easy to navigate, but in truth the land held sudden gorges like wounds slashed into the ground. Shale littered the cold, hard landscape. It would be too easy for a hoof to misstep. One mistake, even at this sedate pace, and it would be a simple thing to snap her leg.

The mountains were no better than the land they bordered. Red and intimidating they looked like silent sentinels, which, oddly enough, wasn't a positive connotation. But maybe mountains were supposed to be intimidating and awe-inspiring. Brighid had little experience with such terrain. The only landmark she could use for comparison was the Blue Tors, the soft, rolling hills that separated the northwestern edge of the Centaur Plains from the rest of Partholon. The Tors didn't qualify as actual mountains, even though they appeared impressive when compared to the flatness and open freedom of the Centaur Plains. They definitely weren't anything like the looming red barrier of the Trier range. The Blue Tors were round and so covered with thick, flourishing trees that from a distance they appeared to be a hazy sapphire color. Where the Tors were welcoming and filled with greenery and wildlife, the Trier Mountains were the exact opposite. Brighid eyed the hulking Triers uneasily, once again glad Cu and Ciara had heeded her advice and not tried to take the children through the dangerous hidden pass.

From behind her the shared laughter of two young girls drifted on the endlessly restless wind. The Huntress didn't need to look back to know what she'd see. Little wings unfurled to almost skim the ground, the girls would have their heads together, giggling with delight over...over... Brighid snorted. *Over the Goddess only knew what!* How those children could find such joy and blatant happiness when all that surrounded them—all that they'd ever known—was the dismal Wastelands and a struggle for life that would have been daunting for an adult centaur was beyond Brighid. And they were mere children! It amazed her as much as it confused her.

"You're looking almost as pensive as the warrior," Ciara said.

Brighid glanced over at the winged woman who had matched her gliding pace with the Huntress's steady gait.

"That can't be a compliment." Brighid jerked her head sardonically at the pole-straight back of Cuchulainn. "I can't imagine a gloomier traveling partner."

The warrior had consistently kept ahead of the group so that, even though he led almost one hundred gregarious travelers, he had spent most of the day alone. He spoke as little as possible, and rarely interacted with them. By midday Brighid had given up trying to engage him in conversation and she had decided—reluctantly—that she preferred to travel on the outskirts of the children's jubilation rather than in the dark cloud that shrouded Cuchulainn.

Ciara's smile was as warm as her voice. "It was meant as neither compliment nor insult. It was simply an observation, Huntress."

Brighid acknowledged the winged woman's words with a slight nod. "Actually I wasn't thinking about Cu. I was thinking about the children. They're doing well. Much better than I anticipated," she admitted.

Ciara's smile widened. "I told you they were special."

More happy laughter drifted to them on the wind. Brighid snorted. "They're aberrations!" Ciara's bright look instantly faded and Brighid realized her unintentional slur. "Now it's me who must explain. What I meant was not an insult," she said quickly. "I admit I have not spent much time around children—a Huntress's life rarely includes a mate and offspring. But what little I know of them did not lead me to expect such…" She trailed off, searching for the right word before concluding, "Optimism."

Ciara's face relaxed back into its familiar, open expression. "It would be difficult for them not to be filled with optimism. Their every dream is coming true—*our* every dream is coming true."

As usual, the Huntress spoke her mind. "You cannot believe that returning to Partholon will be an easy thing."

"Easy is relative, don't you think?"

Brighid raised a questioning eyebrow.

"Consider, Huntress, how it would feel if your people had been living for over one hundred years in a barren, dangerous land with demons in your very souls—demons that were slowly, methodically destroying you, as well as those you loved. And then, unbelievably, you survived it. What wouldn't seem easy after such a life?"

"Ciara, Partholon is a beautiful, prosperous land, but you must remember that there are many types of dangers and many ways to destroy a soul."

Ciara met and held her gaze. "With Epona's aid we will survive this transition."

Brighid studied Cuchulainn's rigid back. Sometimes survival could be crueler than a quick, painless end.

Ciara followed the Huntress's gaze, and as if reading her mind she said, "The warrior's soul is shattered."

Brighid's eyes jerked back to the winged woman, but she said nothing.

"May I ask you something, Huntress?"

"You may ask. I cannot promise to answer," Brighid said curtly.

Ciara's lips tilted up. "It is not my intention to pry—or to offend. But as a Shaman it is difficult for me to watch another's suffering without attempting to…" She hesitated, moving her shoulders restlessly.

"He won't accept your help," Brighid said bluntly.

"I realize that. But there are ways a Shaman can be of aid whether or not the subject is particularly willing." At Brighid's narrowed gazed Ciara laughed. "I can assure you that I harbor no ulterior motives, and I would not intrude upon the warrior's privacy." Then her expression sobered. "But he is in such pain I cannot stand by without at least attempting to give him some relief."

Brighid felt the truth of Ciara's words settle deep within her. "Ask your question, Shaman."

"What was Cuchulainn like before the death of his lover?"

The Huntress raised her brows, taken aback by the question. She had expected Ciara to ask about Brenna or about her death, or even about how Cuchulainn had reacted to the murder, but Brighid hadn't expected the winged woman to ask about *before*.

Reacting to Brighid's obvious surprise, Ciara lowered her voice to be certain none of her words carried on the wind. "Sometimes, when fate has been too harsh and the trauma of life's personal tragedies, illnesses, or crises are more than can be borne, a person's soul literally fragments—disintegrates—and pieces of it are lost in the Realm of Spirits, leaving the individual feeling broken… lost…not all there. At first it is a defense mechanism to help us survive that which would otherwise destroy us. But the person is still…" She struggled to put her understanding into words.

"Still damaged?" Brighid supplied.

"Exactly." Ciara smiled appreciatively. "You have the instincts of a Shaman, Brighid."

The centaur's expression flattened and her violet eyes narrowed. "You are mistaken."

Ciara did not falter or flinch under the Huntress's glare. "You will find that I am rarely mistaken. Perhaps it is because of my affinity with fire, which I have always thought of as a purifier not a destroyer, but my instincts do not fail me. Even before I met you, I dreamed of the coming of a silver hawk, one of the most powerful of the spirit guides."

"I do not have a spirit guide. I am not a Shaman." Brighid's voice was steel.

"We shall see, Huntress," Ciara said softly before shifting the subject back to the warrior. "As you said, a shattered soul causes the person damage. And if the pieces of the soul do not rejoin... Imagine an invisible, gaping wound that refuses to close and then begins to fester and putrefy. That is what happens."

"And you can fix that?" Brighid asked sharply, forcing herself to push aside the mixed feelings of irritation and panic Ciara's comments had evoked.

"Not always. Sometimes the soul does not wish to heal."

"What happens then?"

"Often suicide. Sometimes the person continues to cling to life, but is only a shell of what once was," Ciara said sadly.

"Knowing about the kind of man Cuchulainn was before he lost Brenna would help you fix him?" Brighid asked, but her instincts, whether she wanted to acknowledge them or not, were already mirroring Ciara's answer before the winged Shaman spoke.

Ciara sighed. "Perhaps. A shattered soul is difficult enough to heal when the patient openly accepts aid. Without Cuchulainn's cooperation there is little anyone can do except to try to contact that part of him he has lost and to coax his damaged soul into choosing life and healing instead of despair and death."

Brighid nodded, thinking back to her early childhood and the times her mother had been able to salve the sadness of another centaur's life. Her mother had been healing shattered souls, the Huntress realized, ashamed that she had never thought about it before. There had been a time when Brighid had seen her mother as a shining example of all that was good. But that was before Mairearad had become obsessed with the power her position granted her. Brighid had stopped seeing her mother as a spiritual healer long ago, and that thought unexpectedly washed Brighid in sadness. *Cuchulainn,* she reminded herself. *This is about Cu, not about me and not about the Dhianna herd.* She was part of the Clan MacCallan now and Cu was more of a brother to her than her own had been for years.

Swallowing past a sudden thickness in her throat, the Huntress spoke. "Cu was a rogue. Elphame often called him incorrigible, and she was right. He was a terrible flirt. You wouldn't know it now, but a smile looked natural on his face, and he laughed with an openness that I used to think was blatantly boyish and ridiculously endearing—which I will deny ever saying if you repeat that to him."

Ciara's own smile widened. "Go on, I wouldn't think of repeating any of this. What else do you remember? Just speak the first thing that comes to your mind."

"Women loved him, and he loved them," Brighid blurted, and then she snorted, remembering how confused the warrior had been when he had first tried to woo Brenna. "Except Brenna. She openly rejected him when he attempted to court her." Brighid chuckled. "I remember how he blundered about, trying to win the Healer's affection. He was remarkably inept. Actually I once compared him to a bull in rut, marking his territory around her with all the finesse of a roaring beast."

Ciara's burst of laughter caused the warrior's head to turn briefly in their direction. Both women were innocently silent until he resumed his statue-like pose. Even then, Brighid was careful to keep her voice low when she continued.

"He didn't understand how to woo a woman who told him

no and no and no again. Cuchulainn was a man few women refused."

Ciara blinked in surprise. "Brenna rejected him?"

"She didn't trust men. She was only used to being rejected and ostracized."

"Why?"

"Brenna had been terribly scarred from an accident in her youth. I assumed you knew. Haven't Curran and Nevin told stories about her?"

"No, not directly. It is too obviously painful for the warrior to hear or to speak of his lost love. I had no idea she was anything but a beautiful, gifted Healer."

"She was—but she was also much more."

"Apparently there is much more to Cuchulainn, too, if the rogue he used to be had the ability to look beyond the physical and find the love that hid beneath."

Ciara's words sounded like high praise, but her expression had become strained and serious.

"Is that a bad thing, Shaman?"

"It complicates things."

"Explain," Brighid said.

Ciara brushed a long strand of dark hair from her face and took her time in answering. "Love comes in many forms. For instance, the love we feel for our family—even within that dynamic, love differs. Do you have siblings?" she asked suddenly.

Caught off guard by the question Brighid's voice was strained as she ground out a clipped, "I do" between her narrowed lips.

"Then you understand the difference between the love you feel for a brother or a sister, and the love you have for your parents."

The Huntress nodded quickly, hoping Ciara would not follow that line of questioning. She needn't have worried, the Shaman's voice had taken on an almost singsong quality as she settled into explaining the nuances of love.

"As within our family, the love between a man and a woman can take many forms, too. Some love passionately but rashly, and like a fire that burns too hot their love is consumed quickly, often leaving cold ashes in its wake. Others do not feel the intense passion, their love is like embers smoldering year after year, keeping their lives warm and fulfilled. There is love that is almost exclusively of the mind or of the heart or of the body. It is rare, but sometimes all three mix."

"All three mixed with Cuchulainn and Brenna."

"And that is the most difficult from which to recover."

"Will you still try to help him?" Brighid asked.

"Of course, but—"

"But what?" Brighid prompted.

"But I am not what he needs. Cuchulainn has drawn within himself. He needs the aid of a Shaman who cares for him on a much more personal level." She sighed softly. "I respect the warrior, and perhaps in time I would be able to become close enough to reach his innermost emotions, but I'm afraid that Cuchulainn's need is more immediate."

"His father is High Shaman of all Partholon. Couldn't he help Cu?"

Ciara pressed her lips together and shook her head.

"Why not? Midhir is a great Shaman."

"Remember the different types of love?"

Brighid nodded impatiently.

"To heal from the wound of Brenna's loss, Cuchulainn will need intimacy with a Shaman that is different from that of a parent's bond to a child. He will need someone who can reach more of the lover and less of the child," Ciara said.

Brighid frowned. "That makes no damned sense at all. The only Shaman Cu would come close to trusting is his father. There is no one else—except for you."

"Is there not?" Ciara smiled cryptically. "I can feel our Goddess's hand upon the warrior. I do not believe Epona will leave him bereft of aid, but the ways of Epona are often mysterious and difficult for us to fully understand. Until another

Shaman comes forth, I will attempt to ease the warrior's suffering."

Ciara's words made the hair on the nape of Brighid's neck prickle, and when she spoke her voice sounded more clipped than she intended. "Waiting for maybes or what-ifs is ridiculous. Do what you can to help Cu. But I wouldn't say anything to him about it."

Ciara bowed her head in gentle acknowledgment.

CHAPTER
NINE

T hat first night's campsite came to order with amazing efficiency as children worked quickly and skillfully in little groups supervised by the adults and the eldest of the youngsters. The poles from the litters were easily transformed into the skeletons of tents and then covered securely with stretched goatskins. The makeshift shelters grew in a tight circle around a flat, rocky area Ciara had chosen carefully. The front flap of each tent was left open.

"I understand the circle formation," Brighid had murmured to Cuchulainn as he joined her where she was skinning the half dozen hares she had snared while the tents were being erected. "But why leave the front of them open? Seems like it's just inviting this Goddess-damned cold to freeze them while they sleep."

"Watch," Cu grunted, taking a rabbit and unsheathing his knife.

Before the Huntress could tell Cu just how irritating his uncommunicative company had become, Ciara's voice rang clearly through the fading day.

"It is time! Bring the firestarters."

With squeals of joy and more chattering than Brighid thought was good for anyone's nerves, the winged children fluttered to the litters. Filling their arms with what looked like large clumps of hard gray dirt, they swirled around their Shaman, who pointed to an area in the middle of the flat rock. Gleefully the children heaped their armloads into a growing pile. When the mound was almost to Ciara's waist, she motioned for the children to stop, and they fell blissfully silent as they, and the adult New Fomorians, formed a loose circle around their Shaman.

The Huntress sent Cuchulainn a questioning look, but he only repeated his earlier command of "Watch."

Brighid frowned at him, but her eyes were drawn back to Ciara, who smiled at her people before turning to the west. Following her lead, the circle rustled and likewise faced the setting sun. Brighid's hands, which had been efficiently skinning one hare after another, stilled as Ciara spoke.

Gentle Epona, blessed Goddess, You close another day,
changing the warmth of sky to dark of night.
Facing the way of fire, we hearken and pray,
shield us from darkness, cold and fright.

Ciara's wings unfurled and the air around her shimmered with the tangible presence of Epona. She lifted her arms, and her voice was magnified and filled with happiness and confidence and the power of a Goddess's touch.

Blazing force of cleansing fire,
dancing flames of Epona's light;
Hear me, for our need is dire,
aid me in this evening rite.
Gift of flame, O fiery flower,

Ever glowing in my sight;
Fill me with our Goddess's blessed power,
Touch me with Her blazing might.

Ciara flung her open hands forward, toward the mound. Instantly the pile ignited. Flames blazed cheerfully, casting dancing winged shadows against the tents as the adults called for their children and the circle dispersed. The clatter of pans announced they would soon be ready for the Huntress's catch, but Brighid could not take her eyes off the Shaman.

Ciara remained where she had been at the end of the invocation, standing so close to the fire that Brighid thought it likely her clothing would catch. Her head was bowed and her eyes were closed, and Brighid could see that her lips moved silently. For a long moment Ciara stood there, statuelike in her concentration. Then, slowly, she raised her head and opened her eyes, meeting the Huntress's curious gaze with her own clear, guileless one. Brighid was the first to look away.

"You know, you could tell me more than 'watch' or 'you'll see' when I ask you questions about…" Brighid gestured vaguely at the fire and the encampment.

"I think you should get the same experience I had," Cu said.

"Which is?"

"Surprise. No," Cu raised a hand smeared with rabbit blood, cutting off the Huntress's snort of annoyance. "I'm not doing it to be irritating. I want your honest reaction to them—to this." He met her gaze. "I trust your instincts, Huntress, better than I trust my own."

Brighid opened and then closed her mouth. Cuchulainn was damned hard to talk to. One moment he was distant and evasive, the next he was disarmingly honest and almost like the Cu she used to know. It was as if he had become an incomplete picture of himself. His responses were off, and he knew it. *The warrior's soul is shattered.*

"Maybe your instincts are still trustworthy. Maybe you just need to call them back to you, and start believing in yourself again," Brighid said haltingly. She felt out of her element trying to counsel the warrior. She'd rather take him out on a long hunt and have him work himself into exhaustion chasing elusive prey, than try to advise him on matters of his soul. And from his silent response to her words and the lack of expression on his face as he returned to skinning the hare, he'd probably rather she knocked him over the head and be done with it. But she knew that what was wrong with Cu couldn't be fixed through the physical realm as surely as she knew that if he didn't find a way to heal he would continue to fade away. That would hurt Elphame, and Brighid didn't want her Chieftain and friend to know the pain of losing a family member. Brighid knew the pain of that kind of loss all too well.

She glanced at the warrior. His face was set into what was becoming its typical expression of stony withdrawal. Perhaps it was the talk she'd had with Ciara, but the contrast between Cuchulainn now and Cuchulainn just two moons ago suddenly made Brighid heartsick. She remembered clearly how he used to laugh and joke easily, and how his very presence could enliven a gathering. Even when she'd first met him and thought him insufferably arrogant she had envied the dynamic aura he radiated.

"Stop looking at me like that." Cuchulainn's voice was as expressionless as his face.

"Cu, I hate it that you—"

"Ciara says we're ready for the rabbits now!" Like a winged whirlwind, Kyna swirled up to them, Liam close on her trail.

"Next time could I go with you to hunt? I could help. Really I could. Really." Liam's eyes blinked enthusiastically as he hopped from one taloned foot to the other.

Brighid told her face not to frown. This was exactly why Huntress's rarely had offspring. They interrupted when they shouldn't and made entirely too much noise.

"To hunt hare, you must be very quiet, Liam," she said severely.

"Oh, I am! I can be! I will. Just watch and see, I will," he assured her, still dancing from foot to foot.

"You're *never* quiet, Liam," Kyna said with disgust.

"I am so!"

"You are not!"

"I was quiet during the evening blessing," Liam said. His wings rustled as he fisted his hands and raised his chin defiantly.

"*Everyone* was quiet during the evening blessing." Kyna rolled her eyes.

As the two children bickered, Brighid looked helplessly at Cuchulainn. The warrior met her gaze briefly and Brighid thought for a moment a shadow of good humor flickered through his eyes.

"Kyna, I left the gelding tethered with the goats," he said nonchalantly.

Looking a little like a baby bird, the girl instantly swiveled her attention to him. "But he doesn't really like the goats. They're too small and they bother him."

Brighid thought she knew exactly how Cu's gelding felt.

"I should check on him," Kyna said determinedly.

Cuchulainn lifted one shoulder. "As you wish."

"Liam, you take the rabbits to Ciara," Kyna ordered, tossing the basket she had been carrying to the boy before she hurried away. Then she threw over her shoulder, "That's probably as close as you'll get to catching a rabbit!"

Liam scowled after her. "I can be quiet."

"To trap rabbits, you must be fast, too," Cu said. "Isn't that true, Huntress?"

"Definitely," Brighid said.

"Then watch me! Just watch me. I can be fast!"

And as he scooped up the skinned rabbits and glided quickly away from them, basket clutched to his narrow chest, Brighid had to admit that the boy really did move with amazing speed. He'd never be quiet, but he certainly was fast.

"By the hot breath of the Goddess those children are annoying! How have they not driven you crazy?" Brighid asked, staring after the boy.

"You learn to tune them out. After a while, it's like they're not even here."

Brighid's gaze snapped back to Cu. He had crouched down and was wiping his blade clean on a small clump of frost-dampened moss. His voice was again dead and detached. He stood up and sheathed the blade. Then, without another word, he turned and walked back toward the camp.

As Brighid settled herself comfortably near the brightly burning campfire and accepted a bowl of thick stew from an eager young server, she thought that even though Partholon was prosperous and thriving, there were many things Partholonians could learn from the New Fomorians—especially about traveling in comfort. The winged people had little, and their land was stark and harsh, but she had rarely experienced such a cozy, harmonious campsite.

The cold, ever-blowing wind had been neatly blocked by the sturdy design of the goatskin tents, which fitted snugly in a warm circle around Ciara's blazing fire. Every so often someone would feed the fire with another chunk of what one of the winged women had said was a mixture of dried lichen and goat dung. The fodder explained the vague scent that drifted with the smoke, but it was much less offensive than she would have thought—and it accomplished its job. The fire burned hot and steady.

Dinner had been put together as quickly and efficiently as had the tents, and in an amazingly short time everyone was sitting near the fire or within the warmth of the open-fronted tents, sharing a robust stew. Brighid chewed thoughtfully on a piece of rabbit and looked around the unusually quiet camp. The children looked tired, the Huntress realized with a jolt. Not long ago they had flitted about, tending the goats and chattering nonstop while they spread soft goatskin rugs within the tents. Now it was as if someone had turned off their youthful exuberance.

Without being obvious about it, Brighid cut her eyes to her left, where Liam had insisted he had to sit because he was, after all, her apprentice. *When had he quit babbling?* she wondered. *When had they all stopped babbling?* Maybe Cuchulainn wasn't as far gone as she had thought—it seemed she, too, had the ability to tune out their ceaseless talking.

"Here—" Cu tossed a wineskin to her as he joined the circle, sitting cross-legged to her right. "You brought it. You should drink some of it." He nodded his thanks at the boy who handed him a steaming bowl.

"It's weird when they're not constantly talking," Brighid said, lowering her voice so that it didn't carry over the crackle and pop of the campfire.

"They came a long way today, twice as far as I expected. Any other children would have stopped hours ago." Cu's gaze traveled around the silent circle and he almost smiled. "I suspect it has finally caught up with them."

"Thank the Goddess," Brighid mumbled and took a long pull of the excellent red wine.

"I suspect they'll be ready to go again at first light."

"I suspect you're right," Brighid said. The warrior seemed more relaxed than he had been earlier, or perhaps he was just tired, too. Did keeping everyone at a distance take its toll on Cu, especially since he had spent the vast majority of his life drawing people to him?

"Maybe we'll get lucky and they'll skip the storytelling," Cu said between bites of stew.

Brighid raised an eyebrow at him. "You mean the infamous tales of a certain Huntress?"

Cuchulainn grunted and jerked his chin in the direction of Liam, who had finished eating and was yawning sleepily. "You can't say you don't understand how persuasive they can be when they want to know something."

Brighid snorted, but was careful not to look at the boy,

afraid any show of attention would cue him to begin prattling once again about how quiet he could be.

"Well," she said softly. "I might admit to knowing something of what you mean…" she began, but a rustling from the opposite side of the circle drew her attention.

Brighid hadn't had time to speak to many of the adult hybrids. Everyone had been too involved with setting up camp, and the adults were kept especially busy with their flocks of children. Other than a passing word or two, she had spent her time in the company of Cuchulainn and Ciara. And, she added silently, the too-exuberant Liam and Kyna. But she easily recognized the two adults, who were now standing, as the twins, Curran and Nevin.

"I spoke too soon," Cuchulainn said caustically. "When those two stand that means there are going to be stories."

Brighid felt him gather himself to leave, and then, before she could stop herself, she reached out and put her hand on his shoulder.

"Stay," she said, surprised at the unfamiliarly husky sound of her voice. It was as if her impulse to keep Cu there had come from deep within her, and her voice reflected that well of emotion.

Cuchulainn turned his head and met her eyes.

"If you leave one of those children might come and take your place. Then I will be completely surrounded," she whispered, feeling suddenly too exposed and vulnerable.

"Harrumph," he said roughly, but he resettled himself beside her.

"Our journey has finally begun," said Nevin.

"We have waited long for this day." Curran picked up the thread of his twin's words. "Our mothers in the spirit realm rejoice."

"They smile that their hearts' desires are coming to fruition," Nevin said. "Do you feel their presence, children?" The winged man smiled at the small faces turned in his direction and the children nodded sleepily.

"Their love is in the wind," Curran said. "It lifts our wings."

"And our hearts," Nevin completed. "And as long as the wind blows, we will not forget their love, or their sacrifice."

Brighid couldn't help but be intrigued by the twins' performance. They truly were bards. Their voices weren't simply powerful, but had that indescribable note of magic that so clearly separated a bard from the rest of the populace. She thought she could listen to their rich, emotion-filled voices forever, and she was chagrined that the twins had spent all those days at MacCallan Castle without any of the Clan knowing of their gift. She snorted lightly to herself. That would certainly change when they returned. Bards were always a welcome addition to any clan.

"Tonight we must rest well for the coming day," Curran said.

"So our tale will be a short one."

"But well-loved." Curran's smile flashed brilliantly across the campfire at the surprised Huntress. "With your permission, Brighid. We will tell the tale of how you tracked the young Fand and saved her from certain death."

The tired children stirred and Brighid heard delighted murmurs from the youngsters sitting nearest to the wolf cub sprawled by the fire. Beside her Liam came back to life and wriggled happily, staring at the Huntress with wide, adoring eyes.

"Glad I stayed," Cu grunted under his breath to her. "I like this one, too."

Ciara's musical voice interrupted the scowl Brighid was aiming at the warrior.

"Now that we have been blessed with the presence of the Huntress, perhaps Brighid would be so gracious as to tell us her own version of the saving of Fand."

Brighid's scowl turned instantly from Cuchulainn to Ciara. What was she thinking? Brighid was no bard, and she certainly didn't want to tell some ridiculous story about herself to a group of already annoyingly infatuated children. And anyway, she hadn't actually saved the damned cub, she'd just led Cu to the den. It had been Brenna who had made sure that… The Huntress's eyes met the Shaman's and Brighid felt a jolt of gut-deep understanding. Ciara was looking at her steadily with a serene, encouraging expression.

"Will you tell us the real story, Brighid?" the Shaman asked.

"I'm no bard, but if you want the real story, I'll tell it."

She was glad her voice didn't betray the tumult going on within her. Her gut was tight and her heart thumped like she had been running all day after an elusive prey. She could feel Cu's eyes on her and she allowed herself one fast glance at the warrior. His brows had gone up and surprise curled one side of his lips. She looked hastily away. He probably thought she was going to brag about how hard it had been to track the two-day old trail of the dead mother wolf. Brighid drew a deep breath and hoped that she *did* have the instincts of a Shaman. Right now she was following those instincts, and it felt a little like following a cold trail through a darkened wood during a thunderstorm.

"Well, it seems you already know the story of how Cuchulainn discovered the body of the dead mother wolf while we were hunting, and how Cu challenged me to track the wolf's

trail back to her den to see if any of the cubs could be saved."
Brighid paused and her attentive audience nodded enthusiastically, making little sounds of agreement. "But what you don't
know is why Cu wanted to find the cub, or who really saved
Fand." Brighid ignored the warrior at her side, even though
she could feel his slouching body suddenly tense. "It was all
about Cu trying to get a young woman's attention—a woman
who acted like she wasn't interested in him at all." Brighid
grinned and a few of the children giggled.

"Brenna was Clan MacCallan's Healer. She was also my
friend," Brighid added in a voice she carefully kept free of sadness or regret. She would tell the story, but she would not tell
it as a lamentation, mourning Brenna. She would tell it as a
joyful tribute to the Healer.

The Huntress squared her shoulders and tossed back her
hair. "Did I mention that Brenna was smart?"

Little heads bobbed up and down.

"Well, she was smart enough to say no to a certain arrogant warrior who thought he could snap his fingers and have
whatever woman he desired." Brighid jerked her head at
Cuchulainn, careful not to look at him. "So when Cu pulled
Fand from the den—and let me tell you, that wolf was in a
sorry state—he thought the perfect way to get the Healer to
spend time with him would be to bring her a sweet young animal that needed healing." The Huntress snorted and shook
her head in exaggerated disgust. "Not that Fand was very
sweet. You should have seen her then. She was pathetic. Tiny,
dried-out, and covered with wolf dung."

Brighid did not react to the waves of tension radiating from
Cuchulainn. Instead she caught the bright gaze of the children sitting closest to Fand. She rolled her eyes and wrinkled
her nose, causing the children to laugh.

"So instead of making the very smart Brenna swoon with
desire, the appearance of the dirty, half-dead wolf cub only annoyed her, and I think, it also made her question Cuchu-

lainn's commonsense." More laughter drifted with the fog-colored smoke from the campfire. "But Brenna was as kind as she was smart and beautiful, and she took pity on the little wolf. She showed Cu how to feed Fand, and she kept a careful watch on the two of them, coaxing the warrior into being the perfect wolf parent. I remember how she described what the two of them looked like that first morning after Cu had spent all night trying to keep the cub alive. Brenna had laughed and laughed, saying she'd almost had to hold her nose because of the smell." Brighid paused again, letting the children's soft, sleepy laughter fade. "But I supposed Cu's plan worked, because it wasn't long after that Brenna accepted his suit, and they were formally betrothed. And that is the real story of how Fand was saved. It was not me, but Cu's love for Brenna, and the Healer's kindness, that saved the cub."

The children broke into spontaneous applause. Brighid drew a deep breath and turned to face Cuchulainn. The warrior had gone so pale that the dark smudges under his eyes looked like wounds. He was staring at her and it seemed his face had frozen into a harsh, painful grimace.

"That was cruel." He ground out the words from between his teeth. In one fluid movement, he stood and stalked away into the darkness.

"To bed now!" Ciara's voice hushed the applause and the children obediently started disappearing into the warmth of the tents, calling good-nights to each other and to the Huntress.

Brighid jumped in surprise when Liam's little arms wrapped around her and he squeezed her with unexpected strength.

"That was a wonderful story, Brighid! Good night!" He rushed off in a flutter of wings, barely giving the Huntress time to call good-night to his back.

"You did the right thing."

Brighid looked up at the Shaman who seemed to materialize from the fringes of the fire.

"I don't think Cu would agree with you," Brighid said.

Ciara went on as if Brighid hadn't spoken. "Follow him. Don't let him be alone right now."

"But he's—"

The Shaman's eyes flashed with a flame-colored light. "He is not whole. If you care for the warrior's soul, follow him."

Flexing her powerful equine muscles, Brighid rose and left the campfire. Heading in the direction she thought Cu had taken she considered Ciara's words. Of course she cared about Cuchulainn's soul. He had been betrothed to her friend, and he was her Chieftain's brother. She *should* care about him, just as she should want to help his shattered soul to heal. The centaur stopped short with a sudden realization—that had been it! What she had sensed that first night when she and Cu had discussed the New Fomorians—the tickle at the edge of her mind. She'd known then that something beyond Cu's grief was affecting him. It had been his shattered soul, and something within her—that elusive, indefinable something she had inherited from her Shaman mother—had recognized the warrior's loss.

By the Goddess, she didn't want this! She had no experience with it. She had turned from The Way of the Shaman when she'd left the Dhianna herd. But the choices she'd been forced to make weren't Cuchulainn's fault, and if there was something, anything, she could do to help him, her problems shouldn't compromise that help. But beyond all of that, Cuchulainn was in pain, and Brighid had never been able to stand by and watch anything suffer. She wished she hadn't been made that way. It had caused her more than a little trouble. The centaur snorted in self-mockery. That was the ultimate in understatements. Her sympathy had caused her to leave her beloved Centaur Plains and her family and to break with tradition.

It had been the right choice. She was following the right path for her life. Now she would find Cuchulainn, let him know he wasn't alone, and then do the only thing her Huntress training had prepared her to do. She'd tell him she'd take first watch so he could get some much needed sleep. Simple. Clear. Just as she preferred her life to be.

But where was Cu? By the Goddess, it was dark beyond the circle of tents and the campfire's friendly light. Dark and cold. Brighid shivered as the insatiable wind licked against her skin. She would be damned glad to return to Partholon and the warmth of MacCallan Castle.

A muffled sound to her left brought her to an instant halt as she listened with the acute senses of a centaur Huntress. The sound came again, and she angled to her right, almost stumbling over Fand, who growled low in her throat.

"Don't tempt me to kick you," Brighid told the half-grown cub. Fand slunk off, casting a look at the Huntress that was partially contrite and partially a warning.

At least Brighid knew Cuchulainn was near. That cub was never far from him. Of course Fand's semi-aggressive reaction also told her that Cu must be upset enough to have shaken the wolf into growling at a friend.

She almost didn't see him. If the moon hadn't cast its wan light through the veil of high clouds at the same moment Cu lifted his tear-streaked face, she would have walked right past him. But his tears had given him away. Damn it! She hadn't expected him to be crying! She'd expected anger—let him rail at her and get it over with. She understood that. She could handle that. But as he turned toward her something totally unexpected happened. She felt a mirroring of his pain that was caused by more than their shared clan ties or even their friendship. She was reacting with a Shaman's empathy and the knowledge almost undid her. Brighid wanted to walk away, to deny the inherited purpose that flowed through her veins, but she could not. That would be cowardly, and Brighid Dhianna, MacCallan's Huntress, was not a coward.

"Cu," she said softly, reaching to touch his shoulder.

He jerked away as if her touch scalded him. "Does it make you happy to cause me pain?"

"No."

"Then why?" The warrior didn't sound angry. He sounded defeated.

"You have to go on, Cu. You have to find a way to live without her. And you can't do that by avoiding all mention of her."

"How do you know?" Anger was beginning to stir the apathy from his voice. "How would you know anything about it?"

"You're not the only man to have ever lost a loved one. Grief isn't exclusive to you, Cuchulainn!" She quickly considered telling him her own story. But her gut told her not to make this about her. She was decidedly out of her element, so all she could do was follow her gut. "Look around you. How many of the hybrids have lost lovers or parents or children to suicide and madness? How is Brenna's death more tragic than that? For the passing of two moons you have been surrounded by a people who have overcome losses that would have decimated any other race, yet they have done more than survive. They still find joy in life. You've seen it yourself. How has that not reached you? Maybe Brenna was right when she called you self-absorbed."

With the lightning reflexes of a well-trained warrior, Cuchulainn's dagger was unsheathed and pressed against the centaur's neck. But she did not flinch from him. She held his wide, pain-filled gaze with her own.

"This is not you, Cuchulainn. The man I know would never take arms against a member of his clan."

Cuchulainn blinked twice, and then stumbled back. "What am I doing?" With a growl he hurled his dagger to the ground and wiped both hands across his thighs as if he were trying to eradicate a stain. "I've lost who I am," he said in an emotionless voice. "Sometimes I think I died with Brenna."

A chill of warning shivered through the centaur's body. "You aren't dead, Cu. You're shattered."

Cu bent wearily and retrieved his dagger. "Aren't the two really one and the same?"

"No, my friend. One involves the body, the other the spirit. And I'm afraid your trouble rests within the spirit realm."

His bark of laughter was humorless. "That is something I've known for most of my life."

"This is different." Brighid sighed in frustration. "Damn, I'm doing a poor job of this!" She rubbed a hand across her brow, wishing her head wasn't pounding in time with the beat of her heart. "I think you have a shattered soul, Cu. That's why you don't feel like yourself and why you're not able to heal from Brenna's death."

Cuchulainn narrowed his eyes. "Is this more of that Shaman affinity nonsense you say you inherited from your mother?"

"No! Yes…I don't know!" She rubbed her forehead again. "By the Goddess, you make my head hurt, Cu. The truth is I don't know much more about Shamanistic dealings than you do! But I do trust my instincts. As a Huntress they have never failed me. Now they're telling me that Brenna's death damaged your spirit, so it is your spirit that must be healed if you are to recover."

"What if I don't want to recover?" he said slowly. "Maybe I should have died with her, Brighid."

Everything within the centaur became still. How she answered Cuchulainn might change whether the warrior lived or died. *Epona, help me to say the right thing,* she beseeched silently. And, like a candle flaring to light in an unused room, she suddenly understood what to say.

"Maybe you should be dead—maybe you shouldn't. I don't know, but I do think I know how you can decide for sure." Brighid was careful to sound calm and matter-of-fact, like she was discussing whether they should hunt deer or boar.

"How?" His voice was ragged.

"Well, it's really simple. You're not yourself. So, as you already admitted, you don't trust your own judgment. But if you fix your shattered soul, you'll be able to rely on your own instincts again. Then if you choose death, you'll know your choice is valid."

"You make it sound simple, but I have no idea how to go about fixing something I didn't even realize was broken."

"Neither do I. All I know is what I've observed from my mother, and that was too many years ago to count." She didn't need her Shaman-inherited instinct to know that it was best not to mention that she and Ciara had been discussing the state of his spirit that very day. "But I do remember that she helped those whose souls had been shattered to become whole again."

"I don't want any Shaman meddling with my spirit, shattered or not."

"Then how about me?"

"You?"

Brighid shrugged. "As you said, I do have 'that Shaman affinity nonsense,' which I inherited from my mother. But I'm decidedly not a Shaman. So how much meddling could I actually do?"

A bark of real laughter escaped from him, and for an instant he sounded like the young, rakish warrior she had once known. "Shouldn't the question be how much fixing could you actually do?"

"I think the question should be how much do you trust me?" Brighid retorted.

"You've proven yourself trustworthy many times, Huntress. If I have made you believe otherwise, it is due to my failing, not your own."

"Then will you trust me to try to fix your soul?"

The warrior hesitated. His face was no longer devoid of expression, and Brighid could clearly see the emotions that warred within him. Finally he met her gaze. "Yes."

Brighid didn't think that hearing any one word had ever made her feel quite so much like she wanted to run in the opposite direction. Instead she jerked her head in a quick, acknowledging nod.

"Now what do I do?" Cu asked leerily.

"You give me your oath that you won't do anything to harm yourself until your spirit is whole again."

"What if you can't fix it?"

Brighid drew a tight breath. "If I can't fix it, then your oath would not be binding. You'd be free to do as you will."

"Then you have my oath."

Cuchulainn held out his arm and Brighid grasped his forearm in the warrior's way of binding an oath. His grip was strong and he felt so alive. She hoped desperately that her instincts hadn't just blundered her into a suicide pact with the brother of her best friend.

"Where do we go from here?" Cuchulainn asked.

"Back to camp. I'll take the first watch over the fire. You get some sleep. I'll wake you when the moon is at half point."

"What does that have to do with fixing my shattered soul?"

"Not a damn thing," she muttered. "But it'll give me time to think about the mess I've gotten us into."

As they walked side by side back to the camp, Brighid heard Cu chuckling. She might very well be helping his suicide, but at least she was amusing him.

Her family had been right about one thing. Humans certainly were odd creatures.

CHAPTER
ELEVEN

Brighid fed the fire another compacted log of moss and goat dung, and grunted in wordless approval at the heat that radiated from the flame. The night was cold and the wind was brutal, but within the tight circle of tents there was warmth and light and a more than adequate measure of comfort. The Huntress wondered silently whether the strength of the fire was because of Ciara's affinity for the spirit of flame or the right mixture of goat dung.

"A little of both," Ciara said, joining the Huntress.

"Are you practicing Shaman mind reading on me?"

The winged woman smiled. "No, of course not, but I have always been good at reading expressions. Your face did not hide the question on your mind." She gestured at the neat pile of fuel. "It burns well, and it lasts long. But the truth is that my presence intensifies its natural attributes. Were I not with the camp, it would still be good fuel." Her dark eyes sparkled. "But because I am with the camp it is excellent fuel."

"You'd be good to have along on a cold winter's hunt," Brighid said.

Ciara's laughter made the flames leap and crackle. "Bringing fire is the only way I would be helpful on a hunt. I'm hopelessly inept at tracking, and I cannot bear killing of any kind. I even dislike harvesting grain or pulling wild onions from the earth. You would find me a poor hunting companion."

Brighid snorted. "That's how I feel about attempting to be a Shaman. Inept is an excellent way to describe me. When I spoke to Cuchulainn I felt like a fish attempting to nest in a tree."

Ciara's expression saddened and she sighed heavily. "If he would not listen to you then he is more lost than I believed."

Brighid glanced sharply at the tent Cu had so recently disappeared into. "Walk with me," she said, moving away from the warrior's tent. Still, she lowered her voice. "He listened."

Ciara's eyes widened with her returning smile. Brighid held up a hand.

"Don't go all happy on me. Yes, he agreed to let me help him. But he only agreed to it so that he could be whole again and decide with a clear mind to kill himself."

"When his soul is no longer shattered the warrior will not choose death."

"How can you be so sure?"

"I feel it here." Ciara placed one slender hand over her heart. "When Cuchulainn is whole, he will love again."

Brighid didn't want to destroy the Shaman's optimistic delusion, so she stayed silent. She knew Cu better than Ciara knew him. She could imagine him healed and returning to his life as one of Partholon's most respected warriors, but loving again? She thought about how he had looked at Brenna and the joy that had blazed from him. Cu's soul might heal. His heart was a different matter.

"But one step should be taken at a time. You must not rush the process and get ahead of yourself," Ciara said.

"And just exactly what is our next step?"

"You mean *your* next step."

"No, I mean *our.* I'm totally out of my element here. It's like hunting for you, remember? I'll do it because I have to, but you have to guide me through the steps."

Children called to the centaur and the Shaman as the two traced their way slowly around the circular camp. Soon they found it impossible to converse without constant cheerful interruptions.

"Shouldn't you check on the outer perimeter?" Ciara asked, smiling wryly as yet another child's sleepy voice drifted through the night.

"This time you did read my mind," Brighid said, thinking that the wind and the darkness would be less annoying than the exuberance of seventy children.

The wind slapped cold and hard against Brighid's face the moment they left the tight shelter of the tents. The moon's light was still weak and far away, only illuminating the Wastelands' bleak emptiness.

"By the Goddess, this is a wretched place!" The Huntress shivered and rubbed her arms.

"It is true that it is harsh, but there is some warmth and beauty here." Ciara searched the ground around them until she found a thin, oddly light-colored twig that was barely the length of a centaur's hock. Ciara crouched and gently screwed it into the hard, rocky soil so that it stood on its own, like an anemic sprout. Then she whispered something Brighid couldn't hear and blew on the twig. It responded by bursting into a white-hot flame that flickered crazily in the wind but showed no sign of sputtering or dimming. Ciara sat, spreading her wings so that she blocked the worst of the wind and trapped some of the flame's heat. She motioned for Brighid to sit beside her, and the Huntress folded gracefully to her knees, shaking her head in awe at the purity of the flame that was so white it was almost silver.

"What is that? I've never seen anything burn that color before."

"It's from an oak tree. No," she said before Brighid could finish forming the question in her mind, "it didn't grow in the Wastelands. The wind brings them here from the south, and something about our rather intemperate climate changes them from green to white." She smiled at the burning twig. "I like to pretend that the small dried limbs are a gift from Partholon to us. It was through one of them that the spirit of the flame first spoke to me."

"An oak—the most venerated of trees—known for divination, healing and protection," Brighid said, echoing knowledge she had learned from her mother when she had still been young enough to believe in following family and tradition.

"Exactly." The Shaman's voice sounded dreamy and very young as she stared into the white light. "A real, living oak is one of the things I most look forward to seeing when we finally enter Partholon."

Ciara's idealism made Brighid's gut clench. What would happen to that joy when she was confronted by the truth of Partholon? Did she not understand that her wings alone would be reason enough for her to be hated and feared?

"But we're not here to talk about trees or about Partholon." Ciara pulled her gaze from the flame. "We're here to talk about Cuchulainn and how you can help him. First, before I give you any details about soul-retrieval, I'd like to know your thoughts. Tell me—if you didn't have me to guide you—what would you do?"

"Not a damned thing!" Brighid snorted. "I wouldn't have even known his soul was shattered had you not told me."

Ciara's brows lifted. "Really? Nothing within you whispered that there was something wrong with the warrior beyond the normal grief of losing his mate?"

Brighid frowned. "I don't know…maybe…I did sense something," she admitted reluctantly.

"And had I not been here, you would've ignored the intuition that told you your friend needed your help?"

"No. Probably not." Brighid moved her hands restlessly. "But I wouldn't have known what to do! Just like I don't know what to do now."

"You take the first step. Stop, center yourself, and listen for that voice within. That voice of instinct and spirit that was breathed to life by Epona when you were born, and still carries the magic of a Goddess's touch." Ciara smiled encouragement. "What does your instinct tell you, Brighid?"

"My Huntress instinct tells me Cu needs to be knocked over the head," Brighid grumbled.

"Then you must not think with your Huntress instinct. Listen more carefully. Find the voice of the Shaman that is carried within your blood."

Brighid looked sharply at Ciara. "Why are you so insistent that I have these instincts?"

"I already told you, Huntress. I sense it, and I am rarely wrong. Actually my guess is that you do use the Shaman within you, and you use her quite often."

"What do you mean?"

"Your gift is an affinity for the spirits of the animals, is it not?" Without waiting for her answer, Ciara continued. "The instincts that help you to be such a successful Huntress are the same that will help you heal Cuchulainn's soul. If it disturbs you to think of the act as one of a Shaman, can you not simply consider the quest as just another hunt?"

The centaur blinked in surprise. "You mean all I need to do is track the pieces of Cu's soul?"

"Perhaps…" She flashed a small, secret smile at Brighid. "Listen carefully within and tell me."

Stifling the urge to shake the winged woman, Brighid took a deep breath and concentrated. Cuchulainn's soul was shattered. How could that be fixed? Instead of throwing up her hands and shouting that she had no damned idea, she took another breath. *Think*, she ordered herself. *Make it a hunt. The prey would be different—instead of a deer or a wild boar, I would be tracking a spirit, which meant I must go where spirits dwell—*

into the Otherworld, the Realm of Spirits. The Huntress shivered again, and this time it had nothing to do with the cold or the wind.

"I have to track Cu's broken soul into the Realm of Spirits," Brighid said with much more confidence than she felt. "And bring it back with me. Somehow."

"Yes," Ciara agreed, "but you need to understand that your goal differs from that of a hunt. You cannot attack or entrap. A Shaman should never coerce, threaten, or force any soul to return. In doing so, you would be interfering with the free will of the individual."

Brighid sighed and squinted into the silver flame. "So it's not just a matter of finding the broken pieces of Cu's spirit?"

"No. Think of yourself as a guide, or more accurately as a mediator between the warrior and his retreated soul. That is why it is important that Cuchulainn agree to the retrieval. Without his approval his soul will never become whole."

"Does it matter that the only reason Cu agreed to this is so that he can have a clear conscience when he kills himself?" Brighid asked sardonically.

Ciara's kind smile didn't waver. "Once his spirit is whole again, the warrior will not kill himself—and part of Cuchulainn already knows that."

"I hope you're right about that, Shaman."

"Trust me," Ciara said.

Brighid met the Shaman's steady gaze. Just days ago she would never have imagined trusting any of the hybrids, but wings or no wings, Ciara exuded honesty and goodness. She was trustworthy. Slowly the Huntress bowed her head respectfully to the winged woman, just as Brighid had seen so many centaurs acknowledge their trust in her mother.

"I choose to trust you, Shaman," Brighid said.

"Thank you," Ciara breathed, visibly moved by the centaur's show of respect.

"So, what is my first step on this spirit hunt?" Brighid asked.

"You've begun the first step. Before soul retrieval can be attempted there must be a bridge of caring and understanding between the warrior and you. You are his friend. Simply strengthen the bond that is already in place between you."

Brighid snorted. "That's damn difficult to do when Cu's as withdrawn and surly as a bobcat."

"Then you must explain to him why he must be open to you. It is your job to do the journeying and to expose yourself to the spiritual rigors of the Otherworld. His part in the process is to allow you access to his spirit—in this world, as well as the other."

"Cu's not going to like that."

"The warrior is an intelligent man. Like it or not, he'll understand the necessity of it."

Brighid wanted to say that she didn't like it either. The idea of trammeling around within another's spirit felt like an invasion of the worst type. And, unexpectedly, she thought how much easier this would be if she could speak with her mother, but it was a desire she tamped down almost as quickly as she thought it.

"So I talk to him. I'm friendly with him. Then what?"

"In order to retrieve his soul, you will need to journey deep within the Realm of Spirits, and that is something you cannot safely do while we travel. It would not do to have your body and your spirit both displaced. I am an experienced Shaman, and even I would be reluctant to journey to the Otherworld before we're settled in Partholon. Instead what you must do now is lay the foundation for your quest." She paused and flashed Brighid a quick smile. "Or, as you would call it, your hunt. When you return to MacCallan Castle, and your body is safe at your home, then you will take the Shaman's Path to the Otherworld."

Relieved she wouldn't be doing any spirit traveling in the near future, Brighid felt the nervous tension in her body relax.

"Between here and MacCallan Castle think of Cuchulainn

each night before you sleep, for it is during our sleeping hours that we are closest to the Otherworld. Send positive thoughts of him into your dreams. Begin to imagine him as he once was—whole and happy."

Brighid nodded. "I can do that."

"You will also need a soul-catching stone. This stone is always a gift from the spirit realm. Sometimes it comes directly from Epona. Sometimes it is brought to the Shaman from her animal ally."

"But I'm not a Shaman, and I certainly don't have an animal ally!"

Ciara shrugged. "Perhaps you won't need the gift of a soul-catcher. All I'm suggesting is that you stay open to the possibility."

"Fine. If a stone drops from the sky onto my head I'll be sure to pick it up and keep it."

Ciara laughed. "Be careful. Too often the spirit realm takes our jests seriously."

More good news, the Huntress thought.

"And while you're watching out for stones, you might also want to keep your eyes open for your animal ally."

"My animal ally?"

"It's just a thought. Even though you are not a Shaman, your affinity for the spirits of animals is strong, so it wouldn't be beyond belief for you to be gifted with an animal guide from the spirit realm."

Thinking of the raven that was so closely allied with her mother, Brighid frowned.

"I hunt animals and then I kill them. That's not exactly being allied to them," Brighid said shortly.

"You do not slaughter animals for the pleasure of it, or as some vainglorious, self-gratifying act of ego. You do what you must to feed your people. Do you not respect each animal you kill, as well as give thanks to Epona for Her bounty after each hunt?"

"Of course," the Huntress said.

"The spirit realm knows this—perhaps even better than you do, Huntress."

Brighid shook her head and rubbed her arms again as another chill worked its way through her body. "Doesn't it ever make you feel...I don't know how to put it...violated?"

"It?"

"It! It!" Brighid gestured at the silent darkness that surrounded them. "The Otherworld—the Realm of Spirits. Isn't it like having someone, or a group of someones, constantly watching your every move?"

The Shaman tilted her head to the side, considering. "It's not a violation because the Realm of Spirits rarely encroaches where it is not welcome."

"It might not encroach, but I know from experience that when warnings from that realm are ignored or denied, there is usually a high price to pay," Brighid said solemnly.

"Isn't that how life is? If you're given a gift, be it an affinity for a part of the spirit realm, or be it a talent to make music or to tool leather, and you ignore it, isn't there always a price to be paid?" Ciara paused and pressed her lips into a tight line before continuing in a sad, heavy voice. "I had a sister. She was the most gifted artist among our people, but as she grew to adulthood, she refused to use her skill. She said there was too much ugliness around and within her—she refused to find beauty anywhere, not even in the stories from the past. From the day she quit painting, I think her soul began to die. Eventually her body followed it."

"I'm sorry for your loss, Ciara," Brighid said quietly.

"Thank you, Huntress. But I did not share my sister's story with you to evoke your pity. I'd simply ask that you learn from it."

"Understood."

They sat together silently, each lost in her own thoughts. The silver light between them fluttered with the wind, casting moving shadows against Ciara's wings. In the light from the flame of her own creation Ciara looked like she belonged

more to the Otherworld than to this one. She should be the
one doing this soul-retrieval stuff, not Brighid. Ciara looked
up from the flame, and Brighid was surprised to see lines of
worry furrowing her brow.

"Would you allow me to ask you something that has nothing to do with the warrior or his soul?" Ciara asked abruptly.

Brighid nodded, hoping that the perceptive winged woman
wouldn't ask any questions about her family.

Ciara's gaze drifted outside their small circle of light toward
the silent mountains.

"You passed through the mountains. What was your impression of them? What did they make you Feel?"

Brighid started to say they didn't make her *Feel* anything
except a bone-deep cold and an eagerness to end her journey.
But then she remembered the visit from the raven, and the
sense she had of being watched.

"I don't know that they made me Feel anything in particular, but I will admit that I was distracted as I traveled the hidden pass. The only thing I can tell you with any certainty is
that I like them no more or no less than I like this desolate
land of yours." But instead of the soft smile of response she
expected, the centaur watched Ciara's look of worry deepen.
"What is it, Shaman?"

"I cannot tell. Perhaps it is nothing except that the mountains have always represented a barrier to all that my people
have been taught is good, and that I despise them for that. But
recently I've begun to wonder if it isn't more… They make
me…" She spoke hesitantly, searching for the right words as
she stared into the darkness. "Wary. The more I'm around
them—the closer I get to them—the more wary and on edge
I Feel."

"What does the spirit realm tell you of this Feeling?"

Ciara shook her head, causing her wings to move restlessly. "Nothing more than I already logically know. That the
Trier Mountains are a cold, harsh place filled with death and
lost dreams."

"Death and lost dreams?"

Ciara's eyes caught the Huntress's gaze again. "Many of my people chose to use the mountains as the place to end their lives."

Brighid grimaced as she remembered navigating steep red ridges and jagged chasms that seemed to open down to another world. The Trier Mountains definitely provided ample opportunities for suicide.

"Restless souls…" Brighid didn't realize she'd spoken the thought aloud until Ciara nodded.

"Perhaps that is all I sense—the restless, unsleeping souls of my people."

"Still, I'll keep a watchful eye turned south. As you have said, your instincts rarely fail you," Brighid said, not liking the prickling sense of warning Ciara's words had evoked within her.

Finally the Shaman's face cleared as she smiled. "It's a good thing you have the sharp eyes of a Huntress—you certainly have a lot to be watchful of…a soul stone, an animal ally, and now a faceless Feeling of unease not even a Shaman can put a name to."

"Well, I do like to keep busy."

"It's a good thing you do." Ciara laughed out loud.

"One might think so," the Huntress muttered, wondering what she had managed to get herself into this time.

CHAPTER
TWELVE

The day dawned thoroughly miserable. The winter chill might have been absent in the wind that blew constantly from the southwest, but the steady drizzle it carried was cold enough to have the children wrapping themselves in thick, water-resistant cloaks that cowled around their small faces. They quickly repacked the tents, ate a fast breakfast, and were ready to follow Cuchulainn again with an enthusiasm that did not appear to be dampened by the weather.

Brighid was just thankful that the hoods muffled their chattering and singing. She was in no mood for gleeful children. She had a headache. She'd awakened with it, and she knew why. It was that damned dream.

After she and Ciara had finished talking, Brighid had patrolled the outer perimeter of the camp twice before she'd returned to the warm circle of tents and the fire. Not wanting to wake even a single child, she was careful to be quiet as she fed the fire and then settled herself to keep watch over the sleeping camp. As a Huntress, she was used to dividing her attention. She could easily follow a deer's trail along a winding stream bank while she planned the next day's hunt. So while she fed the fire and made occasional circles around the campsite, listening carefully for anything out of the ordinary, her mind chased the trail Ciara had set. The Shaman had said that Brighid needed to imagine Cuchulainn as he once was, whole and happy, and Brighid had assured Ciara that she could do that—and she could. Truthfully it was easier than thinking of the warrior as he was now.

The Huntress fed another chunk of fuel into the fire and let her mind wander. The first day she'd met Cuchulainn he'd been working at clearing century-old debris from the heart of MacCallan Castle, and he had instantly bristled when she'd introduced herself as part of the Dhianna Herd. She snorted quietly, remembering the arrogant way he had challenged her motives for joining MacCallan Castle, and how she had met his challenge with her own sarcasm. Elphame had stepped in to mediate on more than one occasion, and still they had snarled at and circled one another like wolves from opposing packs.

She shook her head and laughed softly to herself. It had taken her tracking Elphame the night she had gone missing, and then carrying Cu's wounded sister and the warrior himself on her back during the stormy return to the castle, before he had begun to trust her. Brighid's full lips tilted up. She shouldn't have forgiven him so easily for his distrust, but the warrior was damned hard to dislike when he turned on his charm. He was, as his sister had often called him, an incorrigible flirt.

Women had been drawn to him like bees to fragrant flowers, although comparing the virile man to a flower was laughable. He was tall, with the athletic build of a warrior approaching his prime. The Huntress didn't usually consider humans attractive—they were typically too small to catch her interest, even though her beauty guaranteed her attention from males in general, be they human or centaur…or New Fomorian, she added silently, recalling the appreciative glances she'd received from Curran and Nevin. But she had noticed Cu. How could she not? Like his sister, he had an aura that was larger than life. Though, unlike Elphame, his body was completely human, he carried himself with a confidence and pride that said to the world, *Bring it on! I can handle anything!* And it wasn't an empty boast. Cuchulainn was an incredibly gifted warrior—stronger, faster, more skilled with a claymore than any warrior she'd ever known, and that included centaurs.

But his confidence was tempered by his sense of humor. Cuchulainn knew how to laugh at himself—an attribute that served to keep his arrogance from becoming boorish and unbearable. His laugh… Brighid's smile widened. He used to laugh with such boyish exuberance!

It was the memory of boyish laughter that stayed with Brighid as the night waned—as she awakened the groggy Cuchulainn so he could take his turn watching over the camp— and as she settled herself into the tight confines of the tent she shared with the warrior and quickly drifted to sleep amidst thick bedding that was still warm from Cuchulainn's body and scent.

It began as so many of her dreams did—with her watching the wind roll over the tops of the tall grasses on her beloved Centaur Plains. In her dream it was early spring and the plain was colored with wildflowers in magnificent full bloom. The light green of the prairie was infused with bursts of lavender and aquamarine and saffron. In her sleep she felt the soft breeze caress her face, so different from the obnoxious wind of the frigid Wastelands. On the Centaur Plains the wind soothed, and brought with it the seductive fragrances of verdant grass and wildflowers. She breathed deeply and allowed her dreaming self to soak in the scents and sounds of her homeland.

On the wind she heard laughter. It came from behind her and she instinctively turned toward the sound. She smiled, noting that she was dreaming of one of her favorite places, an area of crosstimbers that was not far from her family's summer settlement. She followed the laughter along the lazy Sand Creek that ran musically through the middle of the shady grove of oak and ash and hackberry trees. Brighid trotted around a gentle curve in the creek and came to an abrupt halt. Sitting on the bank with his bare feet in the clear water, was Cuchulainn. He was laughing.

Brighid must have made some unintentional sound of surprise, because he swiveled at the waist and looked over his shoulder at her.

"Brighid! I wondered if I might see you here." He waved for her to come closer. "Join me. The water's cold, but so clear and sweet that it's worth the chill."

"Cuchulainn, what are you doing here?" The words tumbled from her mouth as she approached him.

He looked up at her and laughed heartily. "I have no idea!" Then he leaped to his feet and flourished a chivalrous bow in her direction, grinning his rakish smile of old. "Will ye come sit beside me, bonny Huntress?" he asked, putting on the thick brogue of western Partholon.

She tried to hide her own smile in a snort. "I will if you quit acting like you've forgotten that I'm half equine."

"Can't a man show simple appreciation for female beauty, even if she is part horse?"

Brighid made herself glare at him in mock severity. "Centaurs are not horses."

"I stand corrected, my beautiful Huntress!"

"Oh, just sit back down. By the Goddess, I'd forgotten how annoying you could be!"

Cu chuckled as he flopped down, reclining back on his elbows and sticking a long piece of sweetgrass in his mouth. Warily Brighid settled herself beside him.

"Relax, I'm not going to bite you." He grinned boyishly at

her. "Probably won't kiss you, either, although I'm considering it."

"Cuchulainn!"

"You sound exactly like Elphame when you say that," he said. "Which is not necessarily a compliment. You know how uptight my sister can be."

She shook her head at him. "Act right. It is my dream."

"We're in your dream, huh? Well, that explains what I'm doing here. You must have been thinking about me before you slept, and, like a Shaman, you've conjured me here. What is it you want with me, Brighid? Are your intentions honorable?" He waggled his eyebrows at her. Her shocked expression had him pulling the grass from his mouth, throwing his head back and laughing heartily again.

And there it was—that endearing, infectious, totally happy laugh that used to boom through MacCallan Castle regularly, causing women's heads to turn as they stopped and listened and smiled with secret thoughts, and causing men to eagerly join Cu in whatever renovation Elphame had set him to, no matter how filthy and difficult. By the Goddess, he looked young and relaxed and so very happy. Then, with a little spark-like shock, his words registered.

She *had* conjured him. Just like a damned Shaman. But what had she conjured? Ciara had said that it was during sleep that they were closest to the Otherworld. Could this dream apparition be more than an image created by her own mind?

"What?" Cuchulainn asked, still chuckling softly. "Since when have you become so serious you can't joke with a comrade?"

"No, it's…it's not that." Brighid fumbled, not knowing what to say. Then she blurted the first thing that came to her mind. "It's just so damned good to see you!"

"Ah, there, you see? My charms are not totally wasted on you," he said, chewing the stalk of sweetgrass again.

Brighid snorted. "You needn't be so cocky. I'm surprised that I have missed you—charm and all."

"Harrumph," he snorted back at her. "Huntress, you are a confusing creature—decidedly beautiful, but confusing."

Brighid raised one eyebrow at him.

"Well, it's you who said you've missed me, but how could that be? We've been working side by side for days clearing out that wreck my sister calls a castle." He winked at her. "Or is this your subtle way of telling me you'd like to spend even more time with me?" He made a great show of sighing. "Go easy with me, Huntress, I am only one man."

Brighid's mild annoyance changed to something that felt almost like fear.

"Brighid?" He reached forward and touched her arm gently. "Have I offended you? I thought you knew I only jested."

"No…I…" She floundered. What was she supposed to say? She stared at the man sitting next to her. He was carefree and kind and charismatic—everything that the Cuchulainn who was at that moment watching over the New Fomorian camp was not. And she knew with a feeling as sure as her knowledge of the habits of the animals he wasn't a figment of her dreaming imagination. He was the part of Cuchulainn that had been shattered at Brenna's death, and this part of Cu seemed to be caught in a time before the tragic event. Brighid searched desperately within herself. What should she say to him?

"Brighid? What is it?"

"Cu, you know we're in my dream?"

The warrior nodded.

"In the waking world we are no longer at MacCallan Castle," she said slowly.

Cuchulainn sat up straight and took the sweetgrass from between his teeth. "But that's not possible. Just this evening we worked together to clean out the Chieftain's quarters as a surprise for El." His smile faltered only a little. "We can't be traveling. We're busy working."

"Who?" she asked quietly. "Who is busy working on El's chamber, Cuchulainn?"

"Have you been overimbibing my sister's stash of red wine, Brighid?" he asked with humor that was obviously forced. "It's mostly been the three of us—you, Brenna and me."

Brighid drew a deep breath. "Cu, what you're remembering…it happened in the past…more than two full cycles of the moon since—"

"No!" With a sharp, jerky movement the warrior stood. "No…" He backed away from her.

"Cu, wait!" Brighid reached toward him, but all she touched was the darkness of her tent as her eyes opened to the fading night.

That was when her headache began. The cold drizzle of the morning had done nothing to dispel it. Brighid had tried to catch Ciara's eye and pull her aside. She needed to talk to the Shaman about her dream. But the Shaman had been kept busy herding the waterlogged goats.

"You're setting a fast pace for such a miserable day."

Cuchulainn's gruff voice jolted through her thoughts. She looked around and felt a little like she was waking from another dream.

"Sorry," she said shortly. "I hadn't realized I'd pulled away from the rest of them."

A grunt was his only reply. She expected him to turn and ride away, but as Brighid slowed her pace Cu's gelding stayed beside her. His hair was damp and too damned long. He looked like one of the semiwild goats Ciara had spent the morning wrestling.

"You need a haircut," she said.

His eyes widened in surprise before they narrowed into the flat, cynical expression that had overtaken his face in the past months. "I do not care about my hair."

Huh, Brighid's mind whirred. *He was visibly shaken by a normal, personal comment.* And something suddenly made sense to her. Everyone had been tiptoeing around Cuchulainn since Brenna's death, treating him like he was a delicate egg that needed to be sheltered. Even the hybrids were careful with him—not expecting him to stay for dinner and most of the storytelling—allowing him to escape to his tent so he could brood alone. No wonder the joyous part of him had retreated. If she had a choice, she wouldn't want to spend time with the black cloud that had become Cuchulainn, either.

"Obviously. Your hair looks awful," she snapped. "You also need a shave and a change of—" she gestured at the stained kilt that was barely visible beneath the goat's pelt he'd thrown over his shoulders "—whatever it is you claim to be wearing."

"The more delicate aspects of a gentleman's toilette have not been foremost on my mind these past cycles of the moon." His voice was thick with sarcasm.

"Perhaps you'd like to reconsider that Goddess-be-damned attitude, *boy*." The Huntress purposefully drew out the word. Granted, she was probably only a year or two older, but she drew her seniority around her like a rich cloak and sent the warrior a haughty look. "By this time tomorrow we'll be entering Guardian Pass. The children, as admittedly annoying as they are, deserve our help greeting Partholon. *Our* help, Cuchulainn. That doesn't mean me playing the Huntress and you playing the Long-Suffering Warrior." She rolled her eyes and shook her head. "Look at you! Your sister would barely recognize you."

"Huntress, I warn you. I am in no mood for your—"

"Spare me!" She interrupted him, tossing her hair back and curling her lip. "Try to remember that what we're doing isn't for me or for you. It's for them." She jerked her thumb over her shoulder at the mass of children following them. "Get yourself together and don't let them down."

"Do you think this is a good spot for the midday meal?" Ciara rushed up to them in a flutter of dark, wet wings. If she sensed the tension between the centaur and the warrior, her happy, open expression showed no sign of it.

"Yes," Cuchulainn said in a clipped tone.

"Fine with me," Brighid said.

"Lovely! I'll tell the children. But we shouldn't stop long.

We're all so excited about the possibility of entering Guardian Pass tomorrow. We don't want to fall behind schedule."

The winged woman rushed off and Brighid could hear her calling the children to order and organizing the brief break. The Huntress slowed to a stop. Squaring her shoulders she turned to the warrior, ready to do battle. But instead of cynicism or anger, Cuchulainn just looked old beyond his years and very, very tired.

"So I look that bad?" he said.

"That bad and then some," Brighid said.

"Is this part of the soul-fixing thing you have to do?"

The Huntress shrugged. "It might be. It might not be. I don't exactly know what I'm doing."

"Well, you're certainly being an irritant."

"And you're not being much better," she said.

He slanted a considering look at her. "Does that make us a team?"

"You mean together we're not as irritating or, in your case, as pathetic?" Brighid said.

"I think your manner with patients needs some work."

"Probably. I usually kill my 'patients.'"

"That could be the problem," Cu said.

"Yeah, but it's only one of them," Brighid said.

CHAPTER
THIRTEEN

The drizzle kept up the entire day until even the children were subdued and comparatively quiet as they made camp that night. When Ciara completed the evening prayer with, "…Fill me with our Goddess's blessed power, Touch me with her blazing might," Brighid didn't think she'd ever been so relieved to hear any words in her life.

The homey warmth of the Shaman-enhanced campfire worked like a magical charm. Soon pots were boiling with stew supplemented with several stringy snow geese Brighid had shot not long before they stopped for the night. The Huntress rested beside the fire and the musty scents of the fuel and the stew mingled to lull her into a relaxed, contented state. By the Goddess, she was tired. Her dream the night before had definitely not provided her with much rest. The Huntress was used to going several days without sleep— sometimes hunts were exhausting, and a centaur's stamina was always greater than a human's. But one night flitting about the Otherworld had worn on her as if she had been hunting nonstop for a week.

"Here, eat this. You look as bad as you claim I do." Cu handed her a bowl of steaming stew and flopped down beside her.

She blinked her eyes sleepily at him. "Is it safe?"

"Like I'd poison you? I'd have to drag your carcass back to Partholon."

Brighid sniffed the stew apprehensively. "You're probably not strong enough to drag me," she muttered.

"Don't underestimate me," he said.

Brighid met his eyes. There was something behind the flatness. It wasn't that he looked like the Cu she'd spoken with the night before—the happy, carefree young warrior whose charisma drew others to him—but she was sure she saw a spark of something, and that spark suddenly eased her exhaustion. He was talking to her. Actually he was bantering with her. It had to be a step in the right direction.

"I like the goose, Brighid!" Like an annoying habit, Liam took his place beside her with an impish grin. "Kyna said she thought goose tasted like grease, but I don't."

"Well, grease is good for you," Brighid answered inanely as she struggled for something adult and wise to say to the boy.

"I knew it!" he said joyously, digging into his bowl of stew.

"Good for you? Grease?" Cuchulainn said under his breath.

"Do you want to trade places with me and sit next to him?" Brighid whispered back.

"Harrumph," Cu said, becoming very busy with his own meal.

"That's what I thought," she murmured, and then concentrated on her own stew while she let the warmth of the tightly circled tents and the gentle sounds of tired children wash over her. When Cu passed her the wineskin, she nodded her thanks and drank deeply from it, feeling the strong, red liquid spread its heat throughout her body.

She was just about to tell Cu to take first watch so she could retreat to their tent before she embarrassed herself by falling asleep sitting up, when Nevin and Curran stood. Anticipatory whispers swelled and then stilled as the twin storytellers waited patiently for the children to settle themselves.

"Our journey to the land of our foremothers continues," Curran said, looking from one upturned face to another.

"Today we feel their ancestral pleasure in the joyful tears they send from the sky," Nevin said.

Brighid snorted softly to herself. If the miserable drizzle was tears of joy then she wished the damned foremothers would contain their happiness. She felt eyes on her, and looked across the fire at Ciara, who caught her gaze with an amused smile that said the Shaman was reading her expression again. The Huntress looked hastily away.

"Bathed in ancestral approval, our tale tonight evokes a time long past," Curran said.

"It begins in a place of legends, celebrated for the beauty, wisdom, and integrity of the women educated there," Nevin continued.

Brighid's curiosity was pricked and she roused herself from her sleepiness. They had to be talking about the Temple of the Muse—there was no single place in Partholon more celebrated for its rich history of higher learning or for the gifted women who studied there.

"Tell us, children," Curran said, "what are the names of the magical nine Incarnate Goddesses who dwell at the Temple of the Muse?"

"Erato!" Liam's voice called eagerly from beside her. "She is the Muse of Love!"

Brighid ignored the besotted look he gave her, as well as the soft laughter that followed from the adult hybrids. Thankfully Kyna was quick to call out the next goddess's name.

"Calliope! The Muse of Epic Poetry."

And then the other seven names and titles followed, shouted by young, eager voices.

"The Muse of History is Cleio."

"Euterpe, Muse of Lyric Poetry."

"Melpomene, the Muse of Tragedy."

"Polyhymnia, Muse of Song, Oration and Mathematics!"

"My grandmother!" A small winged girl said as she jumped up and down, wings fluttering wildly. "Thalia, Muse of Comedy!"

"Urania is my great-aunt, and she's Muse of Astronomy and Astrology!" said the young man Brighid recognized as Gareth.

"And don't forget Ciara's grandmother, Terpsichore, Muse of the Dance," Kyna called.

"We would not forget Terpsichore, child," Curran said.

"She is the subject of our tale tonight," Nevin continued.

His pronouncement was followed by a smattering of claps and delighted sounds from the children. Brighid looked at Ciara. The winged woman was smiling happily along with the rest of the New Fomorians. How much time had passed since Terpsichore's death? Or, for that matter, how long had it been since Ciara's mother, the Incarnate Muse's daughter, had committed suicide? With a start, Brighid realized she had absolutely no idea how old Ciara was. She knew one of the attributes the hybrids had inherited from their demon fathers was an unusually long lifespan. Elphame's hybrid mate, Lochlan, appeared no older than a man in his prime, yet he had lived almost one hundred and twenty-five years. The Shaman looked as if she had lived barely twenty years, but she must be older. She carried herself with the same confidence that Brighid's own Shaman mother exuded.

Curran's words reined in Brighid's wandering mind with the threads of the story.

"Each of the nine goddesses was lovely in her own way, but Terpsichore was a rare beauty even amidst those divine. I remember her well from my childhood. Her beauty was not based simply upon the perfection of her face or figure."

As if they were one being, Nevin picked up the strand of the story neatly. "Terpsichore's beauty lay in the magical grace with which she moved. Even as the fragility of her battered body kept her from dancing prayers to her Goddess, she never lost that singular way of moving that clearly marked her as goddess-blessed."

Battered body? Brighid wondered, already intrigued. It had long been believed by Partholon that after the battle at the Temple of the Muse was lost, the Incarnate Goddesses and their acolytes had been slaughtered by the Fomorian horde. The Huntress thought about the amazing beauty of the paintings and carvings left behind at the New Fomorian settlement. Her eyes slid around the circle of winged people, noting the delicately carved bone jewelry so many of the children wore and the fine tooling of their roughly cured hides. *The historians were definitely going to have some rewriting to do.* The thought made her lips curve up. That was just one more in a long list of surprises for Partholon.

"Ah, but we get ahead of ourselves," Curran said. "Terpsichore was the first of our foremothers to die, but not before she left a legacy of life in the bringing of death."

"Makes no sense at all…"

Cuchulainn's grumble echoed Brighid's thoughts, but she frowned at him and shushed the warrior, not wanting to miss any of the story.

"It was a summer's day like any other at the Temple of the Muse. The trees spread their green coolness throughout the smooth ivory halls of learning. As the women went from temple to temple, studying dance and poetry and the stars, the sweet scent of golden honeysuckle perfumed the walkways. Jewel-colored songbirds darted amidst ceiling frescoes that seemed to be alive."

"Emerald ivy and bright ropes of flowers cascaded curtainlike from the roofs of the temples." Nevin smiled at the children who were listening as attentively as the Huntress. "Even in the rooms dedicated to the learning of medicine and nursing of the sick, there was comfort and joy. The Temple of the Muse is a place of great beauty."

"It is also a place of peace," Curran continued. "Unlike Partholon's patroness, Epona, the Muses are not goddesses of war, and thus their temples were ill-equipped to be used as fortresses for anything more violent than the war against ignorance. Terpsichore had been entertaining the young acolytes who had fallen ill with a debilitating pox. Those of us who knew her, understand that the Incarnate Goddess used her talents to bring others joy and to honor her Goddess, even if in doing so she put herself at risk. So it is not surprising that she, too, became ill."

Nevin's expression darkened as his voice neatly stepped into his brother's pause. "And those of us who knew her understand that on the day of the great battle, when she had an opportunity to escape the invading demons, instead of fleeing and saving herself, she chose to stay with those who were more ill than she."

"Like my great-aunt, Urania!" Gareth called.

"And my grandmother!" another child said.

"And mine!"

Little voices echoed throughout the night. The storytellers waited, patiently nodding and acknowledging each child until Brighid wanted to yell at them all to be quiet so she could hear the rest of the story. But soon they settled into listening silence once more, and Curran spoke again.

"The demons overran the Temple of the Muse. The brave centaurs and Partholonian warriors could not hold back the invading army. Many women were captured, Incarnate Goddesses and their students—women who were the most talented and beautiful of Partholon. The demons ravaged them and used them to sate their own twisted desires."

Brighid's chin jerked and her eyes darted hastily around the circle, disturbed by the blunt honesty of the tale, but no one else appeared shocked or upset, and Nevin hardly paused for the beat of a breath before he continued.

"Terpsichore's incomparable beauty caught the eye of the leader of the enemy, Nuada, and that night he commanded that she dance. He thought she danced for him, but for whom did she really perform?"

"Her Goddess!" came the enthusiastic answer from the crowd.

"It's true, and while she spun the lovely dance that was meant to celebrate a Partholonian mating ceremony, she made her way through the demon camp, touching as many of them as she could, and leaving disease in her wake instead of her Goddess's ceremonial blessing."

"We know this," Nevin said, his voice lifting once again, "because even though she was infected with the horrible pox and impregnated by a demon—she survived."

"She survived long enough to teach her daughter the ways of her Goddess, and, in turn, that daughter survived long enough to pass on that precious learning to her daughters."

Curran paused and he and Nevin turned to face Ciara.

Curran bowed to his Shaman, the granddaughter of the Goddess Incarnate Terpsichore. "The women of Terpsichore are all lovely flames. It is a sad truth that some of them have burned too brightly too fast."

Then it was his twin's turn to bow his respect to Ciara and speak. "Would you honor us tonight, Ciara, with a dance of your ancestress?"

The children let out a collective sigh of pleasure; and as their Shaman stood Brighid heard the scuffling of little feet and the rearranging of winged bodies. *What are they up to?* she wondered.

Ciara tilted her head in acknowledgment to the twin storytellers. Then she shrugged off her thick pelt, stepped lightly out of her leggings and kicked off her thick-soled moccasin-like boots. She approached the campfire in only an undyed cotton tunic that reached almost to midthigh. Brighid's eyes widened. Ciara's feet did not end in talons! Instead she had perfect, smooth limbs and delicately arched human feet.

"Tonight I thank the Goddess Terpsichore for my grandmother's strength, and Epona for our victory over darkness. I dedicate this dance as a celebration, remembering those we have loved, and those who have died and by dying gifted us with a legacy of life."

Brighid could have sworn the Shaman spoke the last directly to Cuchulainn.

From somewhere within the circle came the beat of a drum, which was soon echoed by another and another. Then the clear, high trill of a pipe joined the haunting drumbeat. Obviously all the scampering and rearranging had been the children rushing for instruments.

Like the spreading of a dark, living veil, Ciara's wings unfurled and she began to dance. Before that night, if Brighid had been asked to describe the Shaman, she would have used words like petite and delicate, but as Ciara twirled and leaped, and traced intricate patterns in the air with her graceful hands and arms, the Huntress realized just how wrong she had been. Ciara was long, lean, feminine muscled, honed to an astonishing perfection of grace and suppleness. She was not small or soft, though she appeared nymphlike with her luminous skin and dark hair and wings. But a delicate woman would not be able to order her body to perform the feats of sheer athleticism that Ciara completed so easily.

Amazed and entranced, Brighid couldn't take her eyes from the winged woman's performance. Her dance was graceful and sensual. Brighid recognized many of the movements Ciara performed as steps that every Partholonian child knew—even centaurs adapted many of the country's celebratory dance steps to their equine bodies. But the Huntress had never seen anything like the performance Ciara was giving. She did not simply move to the music—the winged woman *became* the music. She seemed to shine. At first, Brighid thought it was just the sheen of sweat glistening against her skin in the flickering firelight, but soon she realized it was Ciara herself—the longer the winged woman danced, the more she glowed from within. At the climax of the music, when she twirled at a dizzyingly speed, her dark hair crackled and sparked with an unearthly, lustrous light.

"I've never seen anything like that," Brighid whispered to Cu without taking her eyes from Ciara. When he didn't respond with even his typical grunt, she glanced sideways at him. He was staring at the dancing woman, his face a study in dark intensity. Brighid tried to identify the expression. Was it lust? Obsession? It was certainly more animation than she'd seen on his face since…

Riotous claps and cheers broke into her thoughts and her gaze returned to Ciara, who was curtsying and smiling grandly to her appreciative audience. Briefly she caught Brighid's eye and waved at her before returning to her place amidst the clapping children.

"A legacy of life…" Nevin said.

"…from death," Curran completed. "Tomorrow we continue to follow that legacy back to Partholon, and to the future our foremothers dreamed for us."

Curran and Nevin bowed neatly, and the adult hybrids began rounding up the children. This time when Liam hurled himself into her arms, the Huntress was a little more prepared.

"Good night, Huntress!" he said after hugging her tightly.

"Sleep well," she called absently after his departing wings. Her mind wasn't on the child. She turned back to Cuchulainn. The warrior was sitting very still, staring into the campfire. His face was again an expressionless mask, but his eyes hadn't quite made the transition back to blankness. They were narrowed in contemplation, as if he was worrying through a weighty problem.

She should ask him what he was thinking, but by the Goddess, she didn't want to! She didn't want to intrude…she didn't want to pry…and then, with a small, stunned jolt she realized that she also didn't want to know that Cuchulainn desired Ciara.

CHAPTER
FOURTEEN

"The three of us should talk about how best to handle tomorrow," Cuchulainn said.

"The three of us?" Brighid raised an eyebrow at him, which he didn't notice because his gaze remained fixed on the winged Shaman.

"You—me—Ciara," he said.

"I think we should include *all* of the adults," Brighid heard herself say.

Cuchulainn finally turned to look at her, a slight frown tugged down one corner of his mouth. "It's not practical to meet with all the adults. They're busy putting the children to bed. And I have already discussed what it will be like entering Partholon with all of them—many times over during the past two moons."

"But now we're entering through Guardian Pass and Guardian Castle itself. That changes things."

Cuchulainn's frown deepened. "Not enough to warrant disrupting the night."

Brighid snorted. "Disrupting? Aren't you exaggerating?"

"Do *you* want to put them to bed, or deal with seventy children who haven't had enough sleep tomorrow?"

"It wouldn't take very long to talk to the adults as a group," Brighid insisted. "They need to be prepared for the fact that one of their own is being held prisoner there."

Cuchulainn's face darkened. "They know that."

"Yes, but I think we should talk to them about it. Again."

"Why are you being so difficult?" Cu said.

"Why are you being so stubborn?" Brighid shot back.

"Is there a problem?" Ciara smiled sweetly at them.

"No!" Brighid and Cuchulainn barked together.

"Good. I think we should talk about tomorrow," Ciara said.

"I agree," Cu said, slanting a look at the Huntress.

Brighid ignored him and spoke directly to Ciara. "It'll be important that the children and the adults stay together. None should rush ahead or straggle behind."

"That's exactly what I've been saying for the past two moons," Cuchulainn broke in. "And also remind them to contain their—" the warrior paused, and it almost looked like he was fighting a smile "—enthusiasm." Then his expression sobered and the lines in his face deepened. "The people of Partholon know that you exist, and not just because Fallon has been imprisoned at Guardian Castle. As Epona's Chosen my mother will have made sure the news of your discovery and impending arrival have been blazed across the country. Partholon has been prepared for you—in theory. But hearing about winged children and *seeing* the group of them..." He lifted one shoulder.

"Are two entirely different things," Brighid finished for him, thinking once again about the small winged surprises that would soon descend upon Partholon. The humans had no idea what they were in for. She glanced at Cuchulainn. His face had fallen back into its familiar mask of nonexpression. But were his eyes still unnaturally bright and focused too sharply on Ciara?

Something prickled down Brighid's spine, twitching her skin and making her Feel preternaturally aware of the vast Wastelands that surrounded their little camp.

"So that's settled." She rose restlessly. "Tomorrow we stay close together—we all keep our eyes on the children. No straggling—no exploring."

"And we enter Partholon." Ciara breathed the word like a prayer.

"With caution," Brighid said more sharply than she had intended.

"What is it, Huntress?" Ciara asked. "Have you been warned of something to come?"

"No!" Brighid said a little too quickly. She hadn't been warned about anything—she'd just been caught totally off guard by Cuchulainn's reaction to Ciara's dance. And now the Shaman was studying her with those perceptive eyes of hers. Brighid stood and shifted her weight restlessly. "No," she repeated in a more controlled voice. "I'm just tired. And I don't get premonitions anyway—that's Cu's area, not mine."

The warrior's head snapped around and he narrowed his eyes. "I don't have premonitions anymore."

"That might not necessarily be a good thing." Brighid met his eyes squarely.

"You are tired, Huntress," Ciara spoke into the tension-charged silence. "Perhaps you would like to sleep first?"

Brighid nodded tightly.

"I wish you a good-night then. I will speak with the other adults about tomorrow. Cuchulainn will take the first watch."

Brighid nodded again. Without speaking to Cuchulainn she retreated into the tent they shared and settled herself amidst the thick pelts. She closed her eyes and took a deep breath.

What was wrong with her?

She was angry to her core. And she had no reason to be.

Cuchulainn had responded to Ciara. What was wrong with

that? Nothing. It would be wonderful if Cu could love again. Actually it would be miraculous.

When his soul is no longer shattered the warrior will not choose death. When Cuchulainn is whole he will love again.

When Ciara had spoken those words Brighid had thought it impossible that Cuchulainn would ever love again—she hadn't considered that Ciara had been speaking of herself.

Brighid restlessly rearranged her long, equine limbs. Cu was her friend. She had agreed to help him recover the shattered piece of his soul because she cared for him. She wanted him to be whole again. She hadn't taken the soul-retrieval journey yet, but already Cu seemed more animated. He'd bantered with her, and noticed that she was looking tired. She should be pleased he was showing an interest in Ciara, too. The winged woman was beautiful and kind. Elphame would approve.

Brighid was happy for him, she told herself firmly. She had just been taken unawares. That was all. And she was tired. Her dream last night had sapped her energy. It had also obviously worn on her patience. She needed sleep. Then she would be herself again.

Brighid drew another deep breath and focused on relaxing the tension from her body. Exhaustion pulled her under, and sleep came easily. Her last coherent thought was that she would make a conscious effort to accept the relationship that was forming between her friend and Ciara. Cuchulainn deserved to be happy….

Her dream began with a flash of movement.

"Race me, Brighid!" Cuchulainn yelled as he sped past her on his gelding. The smile he threw over his shoulder was teasing. "Or at least try to catch me, old girl!"

Automatically Brighid gathered herself and surged forward, biting into the soft ground of the Centaur Plain with her hooves. Her long stride quickly ate up the distance between herself and Cu's horse. She pulled alongside him. Cu was lying flat over the gelding's neck, urging him on. Feeling her nearing, the horse found another burst of speed. With a fierce grin, Brighid lengthened her stride, easily keeping abreast of him.

Cuchulainn took his attention from the gelding long enough to grin at her.

"I'll show you what an old girl I am!" Brighid shouted into the wind. Then she tapped the deep reservoir of her vast centaur strength. She flew past the horse and rider as if they were a boy and pony team.

She ran for the sheer joy of it.

The prairie swished past with such speed it seemed she was floating over a sea of grasses. The wind was warm, but against her flushed skin it felt like a cool balm. The powerful equine muscles of her legs burned, but it was a feeling she welcomed. Her breathing deepened, as lungs that were stronger than a human's filled and expanded to support a body that was the perfect mixture of human beauty and equine strength.

By the Goddess, she'd forgotten how much she loved to run over the earth of her homeland! Partholon was a prosperous, beautiful country, but it didn't call to her soul as did the Centaur Plains. She felt like she could run forever, forgetting everything…everyone…

Perhaps if she ran long enough she would find a way to return home and to reconcile her beliefs with those of her family. If she did that she might be free from the nagging sense of living as an outlander, as if she had been a changeling switched not at birth, but at the moment when she'd found the young human girl after the accident.

Brighid's smooth stride faltered.

She wouldn't think of that. She couldn't think of that—not even in a dream. And anyway, wasn't she supposed to be focusing on helping Cuchulainn? She scowled and slowed. Where was the warrior? Brighid glanced back over her shoulder. The prairie was empty except for the tall grasses, which waved seductively, calling to her with their secret whispering melodies.

Brighid slid to a halt. Great. She was supposed to be helping Cuchulainn and she'd let herself get so wrapped up in her
own dream that she'd somehow lost him. She blew out a frustrated breath. *Think about Cuchulainn!* Brighid closed her
eyes, blocking the sight of her beloved prairie, and thought
about the warrior—or, more specifically, she thought about
the carefree, happy part of Cuchulainn's soul that visited her
dreams.

She heard laughter and splashing water before she opened
her eyes.

"Huntress! I wish you'd make up your mind about where
we are. It's dizzying to be pulled from one place to another."

Brighid blinked her eyes open and stared. She had gone
from prairie to forest within the space of a breath. The day was
still warm, but the indirect sunlight filtered through the green
canopy, so that the thick leaf loam of the forest floor was dap-
pled and hazy. It took a moment for her vision to adjust. More
splashing came from the other side of the moss-covered
mound of rocks directly in front of her. Totally confused, she
trotted forward and the waterfall-fed pond came into view. Cuchulainn was in the middle, water covering him to the waist.
His chest was bare, and he looked young and soggy with his
wet hair plastered to his head.

Brighid was just about to laugh at him when she recognized
where they were. It was the bathing pool she and Elphame and
Brenna had discovered during the early renovations of Mac-
Callan Castle. The three of them had bathed there often and
Brenna had told her it was a special trysting site for her and
Cuchulainn. Brighid's gut tightened.

Brenna had been killed here.

"You should know that I recognize your ulterior motive.
You were afraid of losing the race to me, so you dreamed us
here."

"Losing the race? With you and that fat gelding of yours?"
she scoffed, using annoyance to cover the uncomfortable tension that hummed within her. "Ridiculous."

"Ah, well then. That only leaves one reason why you would dream us here." He held his arms out, palms open, inviting her into a watery embrace. "You wanted to get me naked."

Brighid gave him a disgusted look. "Cuchulainn, you are deluded."

"Hey, it's your dream."

"And you're not naked. Or you won't be soon." She pointed at the clothes that had been haphazardly piled on the rocks. "Get dressed." With a flick of her tail she turned her back to him. "Did anyone ever tell you that you are entirely too preoccupied with sex?" she called above the noises of him emerging from the pool.

"El might have mentioned it a time or two. She's wrong, of course," he said as he used his kilt to dry his body.

"Really?" Brighid said sarcastically.

"Really. She doesn't understand that my passion for life and my passion for women are pieces of the same whole. I choose to live life fully, enjoying all of its richness and beauty. Women, or sex, as you and she put it, are a natural part of experiencing the fullness of a well-lived life."

His words prickled down her spine. "If you stopped desiring women—what would that mean?" she asked him.

"Goddess help me! That would mean I was dead!" He laughed heartily. "You can turn around now, Huntress."

Brighid turned to face him, a frown of worry creasing her brow. "Seriously, Cu. Are you telling me that your love for women is a reflection of how much you love life?"

"Yes." He used an edge of his kilt to wipe water from his face. "Why all the questions?"

"It's my dream. I can ask what I want," she muttered distractedly.

"Harrumph!" The warrior grunted. "You surprise me, Brighid. I would have thought you'd loosen up a little in your sleep. But I guess this proves that dreams are really only reflections of life."

"What is that supposed to mean?"

Cuchulainn shrugged. "You're always so uptight. You remind me of a sentry who is perpetually on guard."

"That is an absurd thing to say!" Brighid sputtered.

"Face it—" Cu sprawled on the ground, his back resting against the moss-covered boulder "—you never relax."

"Cu, we're not talking about me. We're talking about you."

"All right—all right." He held up his hands in mock surrender and grinned at her. "But I'd at least like to know why you're so set on talking about me."

"Because you're the one who keeps showing up in my dreams!" she blurted.

"And you think I know why?" He chuckled. "I have nothing to do with it. I admit that you are a rare beauty, Brighid, but if I were to purposefully enter a maiden's dreams I believe my choice would be less—" he hesitated, eyes sparkling mischievously, as they roved down her equine body "—hairy."

Brighid stiffened. "I am not hairy."

Cuchulainn laughed again. "You should see the expression on your face! You look like I just told you that deer had grown wings and you were going to have to track them through the air."

"I can't track something that can fly," she replied automatically.

Like a snuffed candle the open smile that was so naturally a part of Cuchulainn suddenly went out.

"I—I must go now." He stood and looked around him as if he wasn't sure where he was.

"What is it, Cu?" But she didn't need to ask—she knew what was wrong with him.

The joyful fragment of Cuchulainn's soul that stood before her was remembering.

"No…" Even as he shook his head in denial he was turning slowly, inexplicably away from the pool of water and toward the rough little path that led through the forest to the road to MacCallan Castle. He took two leaden steps forward before stumbling to a halt. When he looked back at Brighid his face was so pale that, for the first time, he looked more spirit than man. "This is all just a dream. In the morning I will wake at MacCallan Castle. We're preparing the Chieftain's Chambers for Elphame. You, Brenna and me."

Brighid approached Cu's shattered spirit slowly. The space in front of him was an ordinary enough part of the forest—just a small trail leading through a grove of umbrella-shaped plants and wildflowers. But she recognized it. It was where the mad hybrid, Fallon, had killed Brenna while the little Healer had been waiting to meet Cuchulainn. Two moons ago Brighid had led the rescue party from this very spot. She'd followed Fallon's trail, taking them deep into the forest until the creature's tracks disappeared because the hybrid had used her wings to catch the air currents and glide. As Brighid had explained to the distraught warrior that day, a Huntress could not track something that could fly…

"My friend, we—" Brighid began.

"No!" Cuchulainn cut her off. He lurched back from her, and then his horrified expression changed. He forced a laugh through bloodless lips that were twisted in more of a grimace than a smile. "This is a mistake…I haven't visited your dream…I've become trapped in your nightmare…"

"Cuchulainn!" Brighid held her hand out to him in a gesture meant to call him back, but instead he flinched away from her, backing even farther into the forest.

"No. I cannot. It's time to awaken, Huntress…"

The warrior's body faded as he blended into the shadows of the trees.

"Huntress…"

Brighid's eyes flew open.

"Cuchulainn, wait!" She reached out and this time she was able to grab him.

Acting on instinct, he whirled around pulling the throwing dagger from his belt and moving smoothly into a defensive stance, blade held at the ready. When he realized what had attacked his leg, he lowered the knife.

"By the Goddess, Brighid! You almost got yourself stabbed."

"Sorry," she muttered, struggling to orient herself. What had happened? Where were they now?

"You want to let go of me?"

She looked at her hand, which was still clutching the soft leather of his boot.

"Brighid?" Cu crouched down, peering into the tent at the prone form of the centaur Huntress. Her eyes were wide and round and her expression was stunned. "Are you unwell?"

"We're with the hybrids, not far from Guardian Pass?" Her voice sounded unnaturally breathless, like she'd just finished a marathon. "And we're awake."

"Yes, of course, to both of your questions! What's wrong with you?"

Brighid let loose his leg, rubbed her eyes, and then smoothed back the long silver-blond fall of her hair. "Nightmare. Just a nightmare. You woke me from it when you walked by."

Still groggy, she untangled herself from the thick pelts and escaped the small tent. She shook herself as if ridding her coat of water before glancing up at the sky. "You should have awakened me sooner. The moon is more than midway."

Cuchulainn gave her one last look of scrutiny before he shrugged. "I was just coming to wake you." He brushed past her and sat within the tent, pulling off his travel-dirtied boots. "The fire needs to be fed. All else is quiet and tended to."

"Did you talk to Ciara? Are the adults prepared for tomorrow?"

"Ciara and I spoke briefly. All is well."

Brighid strained to see Cuchulainn's expression within the dark tent. His voice gave away no hint of emotion. He sounded tired, but no more interested in Ciara than he had been in fueling the fire.

But part of his soul had clearly told her that for him love

of women and love of life were bound together. Knowing that, it didn't take the instincts of a Shaman to tell her that it would be a positive healing step for Cu to show interest in a woman—winged or not.

"So you talked with Ciara?"

Cuchulainn grunted an affirmative and then was silent.

Brighid rolled her eyes. "And she feels the camp is ready to enter Partholon?"

Another yes grunt.

The Huntress stood outside the tent listening to the sounds of Cuchulainn settling himself within the pelts. She should say something to him. Encourage him to talk with Ciara more often. Let him know—

"Brighid, why are you lurking out there?"

His gruff voice made her jump guiltily.

"I'm not lurking!"

"Then what is it?" He enunciated each word carefully as if she were one of the winged children.

"Ciara's dance was quite beautiful," she said, feeling awkward and obvious.

"She has many gifts from the Goddess," he said.

"I don't think I've ever seen a dance performed so well," Brighid continued.

Cuchulainn grunted.

"Have you?"

"It was a fitting tribute to Epona and Terpsichore." The words ended on a yawn.

"It was beautiful," Brighid said.

"As you already said." Cu yawned again. "Brighid, is this more of your attempt at soul-healing?"

"I'm not sure," she said miserably.

"Could I sleep while you decide?"

"Yes," she said. "Rest well, Cuchulainn."

Brighid retreated to the fire. As she fed the low-burning blaze she called herself several creative variations of a senseless, bumbling, muddle-headed fool.

CHAPTER
FIFTEEN

"It's weird how quiet they are," Brighid said to Cuchulainn.

The warrior glanced back over his shoulder at the subdued group of miniature travelers.

"I've never seen them like this," he said.

"They didn't sing once all morning."

"And hardly spoke a word during the midday meal."

"Do you think they're scared?" Brighid asked. It gave her a hollow feeling in her gut to think about the children being so afraid that their natural exuberance had been silenced.

"They don't need to be afraid. We won't let anything bad happen to them," Cu said shortly.

"You know that and I know that—but perhaps we should tell them," Brighid said.

Cu grunted and frowned. "I don't want to worry them."

She snorted and jerked her head back at the silent multitude. "They're quiet. They're never quiet. I think we can safely assume they're already worried."

"You're probably right," he said.

When he didn't say anything more she prompted, "We should talk to them. *Before* they're face-to-face with the warriors of Guardian Castle."

"Agreed. We'll gather them at the mouth of Guardian Pass. You can speak to them there," he said.

"Me?" Her brows arched up. "I'm not going to speak to them!"

"But you just said—" he began, but Brighid cut him off with a sharp motion of her hand.

"No! Not me. They've only known me for a handful of days. You've lived with them. The children idolize and trust you. If you tell them something, they will believe you. I'm just The Centaur Huntress—you're *their* warrior, *their* Cuchulainn."

Cuchulainn scowled.

"If you don't believe it's the truth, ask Ciara," she said.

His scowl deepened, but he stayed silent. *Like a big, grumpy bear,* Brighid thought. Being with the joyful part of his soul in her dreams had made her realize just how much she missed the old Cuchulainn. This warrior was so damned grim and silent and…

"…Uptight," she said aloud, meeting Cu's questioning look. "That's right, you're too damned uptight. And you said *I* never relax." The Huntress snorted. "You certainly got that all wrong."

"What are you talking about? I didn't say you never relax."

"Yes, you did. Last night."

"Last night we barely talked."

"Actually we talked quite a bit. And the night before." Brighid drew in a deep breath, hoping her instincts were leading her tongue because she certainly had no idea why she'd suddenly decided to tell Cu about the dreams. "You visited me. Twice. In my dreams."

Cuchulainn stiffened, his face a carefully maintained mask of indifference. "It wasn't me."

"Oh, it was definitely you. Or, more accurately, it was the you that existed before Brenna's death."

The warrior's expressionless face paled. "Then you found it—the shattered part of my soul." He glanced at her, barely meeting her eyes. "Aren't you supposed to bring it here? Tell it to return? Something?"

"First of all, Cu, it's not an it." She shook her head at him. "And it feels wrong for you to call him that. It's *you*."

"*I'm* me."

"No," she said quietly. "No, Cu, you're not. What you are right now is only a piece of you."

The warrior grunted, keeping his eyes focused on the rocky trail ahead of them.

Brighid sighed. "And the man who has visited my dreams is only a piece of you, too." She paused, not sure how much to tell him, then she puffed out a frustrated breath. She didn't know what was right or wrong. *Help me, Epona,* she prayed silently. *Just don't let me cause him any more pain.* "The Cuchulainn from my dreams thinks we're still at MacCallan Castle. He believes that it's the night after we first began readying Elphame's chamber."

At that, Cuchulainn's blank expression faltered, and his voice became rough with suppressed feeling. "He thinks Brenna is still alive?"

Brighid smiled sadly. "Not really. Some part of him knows she isn't—he's just denying it. Without the strength you have within you now, he is just an exuberant, fun-loving young man—completely unable to cope with disappointment or sadness or hurt. He's not whole—he's just a fragmented piece of you."

"And without him I can't seem to bear to live life."

"You have to want that part of you back, Cu. I can't reach him on my own. Every time I try, he fades away," she said.

"Maybe that part of me doesn't want to come back to reality. I can't blame him. If I could deny Brenna's death, I would, too."

"Would you?" Brighid said. "I don't think you would. That full-of-life part of you hasn't just denied Brenna's death, he's also chosen to forget the love you found with her. Is that what you want, Cu? To completely forget Brenna?"

"Of course not!" he snapped. "You know me better than that."

"Then you need to try harder!"

"I'm doing everything I can!" he roared.

The flutter of wings announced Ciara's arrival, and Brighid clamped her jaw closed. The Shaman looked from the Huntress to Cuchulainn.

"You two argue as if you had been mated for years," she said.

"Goddess forbid!" Brighid said.

Cuchulainn's grunt had considerably more animation than usual. The winged woman laughed.

"You even protest like a mated pair. But I didn't come to talk with you about your relationship. We're nearing the entrance to the pass. Before we begin crossing into Partholon we should take a moment and beseech Epona's aid and protection."

"How do you know we're near the pass? Have you been here before today?" Brighid asked.

"Of course not. I only know it from our mothers' stories." She opened her hand, gesturing in a wide sweep at the land around them. "We were told the rocks became redder, more bloodlike, as you neared Guardian Pass. Our foremothers warned us to stay away from the east. To flee from the scarlet rocks and the pass that spewed them from Partholon."

Cuchulainn looked around, chagrined that he'd been too busy arguing with Brighid to notice the change in the jagged rocks that flanked the mountains. He knew the deepening of color signified the pass was near.

"It makes sense," Brighid was saying thoughtfully. "Of course the women would tell you to stay well away from Guardian Pass. They would fear your capture."

"And our deaths," Ciara said softly.

"It will be different now," Cuchulainn said.

Ciara's bright, guileless smile returned. "Of course it will be! We have the two of you, and the sacrifice of your sister. All will be well."

Cuchulainn grunted, wishing she didn't look quite so naively confident. Partholon had spent over a century hating the Fomorians. It would take more than his sister's word and the presence of one warrior and one Huntress to win over a people who still remembered all too well the slaughter perpetuated by winged demons.

"Cu and I were just talking about the pass. We think Cu should talk to the children—reassure them—before we go any farther."

Ciara's smile was radiant. "They would love that, Cuchulainn! I'll pass the word." The winged woman squeezed the warrior's arm before hurrying away.

"Apparently that was the right decision," Brighid said with forced nonchalance. *Ciara's smile and the intimate way she touched Cu were good,* she told herself, *Cu needs the touch of a woman to feel the fullness of life.*

"There," the warrior said, pulling up his gelding. He pointed to a slash in two dark red rocks. No vegetation grew nearby. The sides were sheer, and the wind howled eerily through the gap. "It's the entrance to Guardian Pass and the way into Partholon."

Cuchulainn stood in the mouth of the pass facing the New Fomorians who watched him carefully. He glanced up at the sky. The sun had traveled past its midday position, but it still hung high in the blue-gray heavens. There would just be time for them to reach Guardian Castle before darkness. His gaze dropped to the silent crowd. He realized it was probably his imagination, but even the goats seemed subdued.

"Go ahead," Brighid whispered, moving to his side. "They're waiting, and we're running short on time."

He scowled at her, even though he knew what she said was

true. Actually the Huntress was proving to be annoyingly right about too many things. *The broken part of my soul has been visiting her dreams.* The knowledge of it astounded him. *So she'd been right about that, too. That's why I can't get past Brenna's death. That's why I feel so empty and lost.* Which meant if she was right about that, she was probably right about him healing when his soul was whole once more. Then he could live without Brenna. He might even learn to be happy again.

Is that what he wanted?

"Cu!" Brighid whispered.

By the Goddess! He'd been daydreaming while the entire group stared at him, waiting for him to speak. Broken soul or not, he needed to pull himself together—figuratively if not literally.

Clearing his throat, Cuchulainn stepped forward.

"You've done well on our journey. The Huntress and I are proud of your strength and endurance."

There was a happy rustling of wings and the children's bright eyes smiled up at him. He met those gazes, looking from child to child, making each of them feel as if he chose his words specifically for him or her.

"You know that Fallon went mad and killed Brenna?"

The children responded with vigorous nodding of little heads.

"And that Fallon is imprisoned in Guardian Castle, awaiting her execution." He barely paused long enough for their nods. "Then you must be prepared for the warriors at the castle to distrust you." Instead of the denials and various degrees of upset responses he expected, the children grew very still again. Their eyes never left him. "But I don't want you to be afraid."

Brighid had been studying the children while Cu spoke, but his last words drew her eyes to him. He sounded so gentle— so much like the old Cuchulainn—the man who was more than just a gifted warrior. He had so much depth, which was why Brenna had finally allowed herself to love him. And

Brighid surprised herself by thinking that when he looked so world-weary, yet sounded so gentle, she could understand why her friend had been unable to turn away from him.

"I will be with you," Cu continued, "as will Brighid. But you have more than that—more than our protection could ever command. You have the goodness within you that the warriors of Guardian Castle will see." Cuchulainn drew a deep breath and raked his hand through his disheveled hair. "I know it's true because I was once as they are—worse actually. When I came to you I was looking to place blame for Brenna's death. I wanted to find barbaric creatures on which to vent my hatred." His hard expression softened. "Instead I found you. And…" The warrior faltered, wiping his hand across his face as emotions he had been keeping at bay for weeks overwhelmed him. "And I…"

"Don't worry, Cu!" a little voice rang from the front of the group as Kyna jumped to her feet. "We understand. You didn't know us then."

"Yeah, you didn't know us then," Liam echoed.

Then, like tidewater breaking through barriers, all the children were on their feet surging toward the lone warrior. Brighid snorted and backed away quickly as they engulfed him, patting him with their small hands and offering childish words of comfort. Cuchulainn stood for a moment, a giant in the middle of young winged shapes, looking helplessly down at the throng. And then, with a deep sigh, he crouched and opened his arms to them. Disbelieving, Brighid watched as silent tears made wet paths down Cuchulainn's face.

"Thus it begins," Ciara said.

The Huntress wasn't sure if it was a good or bad sign that Ciara's eerie ability to sneak up on her had begun to feel normal.

"What begins?" Brighid asked.

"His healing. He's allowing himself to feel again."

"The part of his soul that is broken has been visiting me in my dreams," Brighid said, keeping her voice pitched low so that only the Shaman could hear.

"That doesn't surprise me. You and he have a strong bond. It would be easy for Cuchulainn to hear you calling to him, and natural for him to respond."

Brighid turned to face Ciara. "And what about you and him? What kind of bond do the two of you have?"

Ciara smiled. "I do not think you would call it a bond. Cuchulainn appreciates female grace and beauty—that is all."

Brighid narrowed her eyes at the flippant answer. "Don't hurt him."

Ciara's laughter was alluring and musical. "You need not worry about me hurting your warrior, Huntress, and someday soon you will realize it." Still laughing, the Shaman clapped her hands together and called the group of milling children to order. "Let us ask Epona's blessing."

The children parted and Ciara walked through, smiling at Cuchulainn as she took the warrior's place in the center of the circle. Cu nodded respectfully to Ciara before he backed away to stand beside Brighid. He wiped his face, and then ran tear-dampened hands through his hair.

"Are you all right?" she asked.

He looked at her and shrugged a little sheepishly. "I hadn't planned on getting emotional."

"I think it was exactly what the children needed."

He lifted his brows. "And me? Is this exactly what I needed, too?"

As Brighid opened her mouth to respond, Ciara lifted her face to the sky and evoked the name of the Goddess.

"Blessed Epona!"

The Goddess's name shivered through Brighid's body—like heat and ice filling her all at once. The Huntress gasped, and when she spoke she knew the words came more from Epona than from herself.

"Yes, what you need is here, too. In time you will see that."

Cuchulainn stared at the centaur. The power in her words was almost visible in the air between them. *Like when Elphame is touched by the Goddess.*

Suddenly like a magical tableau come to life, Ciara's arms
and wings raised over her head and she prayed in a voice that
was sweet and clear.

We enter Partholon today
through the strength of Epona;
by the light of Her sun,
the radiance of Her moon,
the splendor of Her fire,
the swiftness of Her wind,
the depth of Her sea,
and the stability of Her earth
we walk with our Goddess
surrounding us and touching us,
protecting us and loving us.
Hail Epona!

"Hail Epona!" the children cried. "Hail Epona!"
Cuchulainn could feel the heat from the magic against his
back, but he didn't turn to join the Shaman and her people in
their praise. Instead he continued to stare at the Huntress,
mesmerized by the silver-white light that colored her words
and settled around her body like a gossamer veil. Brighid returned his gaze, her violet eyes filled with wonder.

"I spoke Her words," Brighid whispered to Cuchulainn.

"I know. I can still see the Goddess's hand upon you," he said.

Brighid shivered, and then Epona's presence vanished.
"Why?" Brighid's voice was husky with emotion. "Why did
Epona use me and not Ciara to speak those words to you? I'm
not a Shaman, Cu!"

"I don't know, Brighid. I don't pretend to understand the
ways of Epona."

But deep within the warrior something stirred. The small
breath of a thought, more insubstantial than fog, whispered

through his shattered soul. *If I could, I would choose Brighid to speak Epona's words to me.*

Perhaps he was beginning to understand the ways of Epona...

CHAPTER
SIXTEEN

Though it was wider and easier to navigate than the secret entrance Lochlan and his people had discovered, traversing Guardian Pass was far from easy. Entering the great scarlet-colored maw had been like walking into a cave, or, Brighid thought uneasily, a blood-drenched tomb. The pass varied in width, from a narrowness through which a single horse could barely pass, to wider more spacious areas that could hold several mounted warriors. But narrow or wide, the pass was a challenge. It snaked like a twisting gorge. Jagged rocks littered the ground, which was made of shale—slick and hard enough so Brighid had to concentrate to keep from misstepping. And she found concentration difficult. She was still struggling with her shock. It was unbelievable that Epona had spoken through her. But there was no mistaking it. The words Brighid had said to Cuchulainn had not been her own—and the power that had rippled through her body had been the result of Epona's touch.

She wished Elphame had been with them. Her friend wielded the power of the Goddess easily, naturally. El could advise her—or, better yet—if El had been there then Epona would probably have used her as a conduit instead of a Huntress who had no desire to be the mouth of a Goddess.

Brighid frowned and looked quickly around her, worried that someone would overhear her blasphemous thoughts. She didn't mean to be unfaithful to Epona. But she could barely manage the problems in her own life. She'd be a poor choice for the gift of the Goddess's touch, she was too damned imperfect.

"The rocks are changing color. We must have crossed the halfway point," Cuchulainn said.

The pass had widened and the two of them walked side by side. Brighid looked up at the steep walls that flanked them. The blood color was giving way to marbled fingers of gray.

"This time I haven't been too busy arguing with you, so I actually noticed the color change," he said with a faint smile. "When all the red is gone, we'll have arrived at Guardian Castle."

"I hadn't realized the rocks changed colors again," Brighid said, glad to have something harmless to talk about.

"It's odd. There's so much red in the Trier Mountains, except in the area surrounding Guardian Castle. There everything is gray. I trained there for four years, and during all that time I never got used to the starkness of the castle or of the area surrounding it."

Brighid raised an eyebrow at him.

"Oh, I know, warriors are supposed to thrive in the austere setting. The official line is that it's conducive to honing concentration on the art of swordplay and the physical demands of battle." Cuchulainn grunted. "I found it bland and miserable, conducive only to making me work hard so that I was rewarded with frequent visits home where there were more aesthetically pleasing benefits." He barked a quick laugh. "I suppose I owe the foundation of my legendary abilities with the sword to my youthful distaste for dreary scenery."

Brighid tilted her head and gave him an appraising look. "That sounds like something the old Cuchulainn would say."

He blew out a breath. "I know. I'm…" He moved his shoulders. "After you told me about the dreams I've felt different." He lifted his eyes to hers. "You made the idea of a shattered soul more tangible for me. And if I believe in it, then maybe I can fix it. I mean *we,* maybe we can fix it." He paused again. "I would give almost anything to feel normal again. I had begun to believe that the only way to escape from this unending pain would be to give up my life. Today, for the first time since Brenna's death, I think there might be a way for me to live again."

Brighid's face flushed with her rush of relief.

"I'm glad, Cu," was all she could manage to choke out.

"Cuchulainn! Brighid!" Ciara called from behind them and they slowed, waiting for the winged woman to catch up with them. "I know that our time is short, but the children could use a break. They're tired today."

"One short break would be fine. But one is all we can afford. You can tell them that we're past the halfway point, that should bolster their strength," Cu said.

Ciara's sharp-toothed smile glinted bright and happy. "You tell them, Cu. Coming from you I know it would revive them."

"Go ahead," Brighid said quickly. "I'll scout ahead. I've noticed the spoor of wild goat. It would be nice if we could enter Guardian Castle with more than just hungry mouths to feed."

"Good idea," Cu said. As the Huntress turned to go, he touched her arm. "Be careful. The rocks are slick. My gelding has almost fallen several times today."

Brighid covered her surprise at his touch and his words with a delicately raised eyebrow and a frown. "I am not your fat, empty-headed gelding." She flipped her hair and trotted away.

"He is not fat!" Cu called after her, but the warrior was smiling.

"You are protective of her, Cuchulainn," Ciara said softly.

His gaze swung back to the lithe woman at his side. She was simply one of the most beautiful females he had ever seen. And he hadn't even really noticed her loveliness until she danced for them last night. Then his mind processed her words, and his reaction was automatic.

"Yes, I'm protective of her. She's part of MacCallan Clan. But that doesn't mean that the Huntress can't take care of herself. She's a fine warrior, too."

Ciara's smile widened. "And you respect that about her."

"Of course," he said.

"Good. I'm glad she has you for a friend. In the future, she will need her friends close about her."

Cuchulainn's eyes narrowed. "What are you telling me, Shaman? Have you seen danger for the Huntress?"

"My gift is not one of premonition. From what I understand when you were touched by the spirit realm, your premonition gift was strong. Many times you knew of events before they unfolded."

Cuchulainn grunted a rough yes. If her words about Brighid hadn't been so troubling he would have cut this conversation short. Beautiful or not, Ciara was a Shaman. And Cuchulainn wanted no traffic with the spirit world or its emissaries. It was difficult enough for him to cope with Brighid and the whole shattered-soul issue. But that was different. Brighid was like him. She wasn't comfortable meddling in the spirit realm, either.

Ciara was nonplussed by his gruff response and his instantly defensive demeanor. "My premonitions have never been as clear as yours have been. I only get vague Feelings, and sometimes instinct leads me to say or do things, the reasons for which only become clear in the future. I have had a Feeling about the Huntress—that the devotion of her friends will play an important part in the shifting sands of her life."

"So she's in trouble?"

"I cannot tell. I can only Feel that she will need friends, or at least one special friend, close beside her."

Cuchulainn nodded in a tight, controlled jerk. "I'll remember that, Shaman."

"I'm glad." Ciara's infectious smile was back. "I've come to care a great deal for your Huntress. She is an honorable centaur."

Cuchulainn grunted again.

"Come, let's return to the children. They will be overjoyed to hear that we are almost within the borders of Partholon."

Cuchulainn dismounted and led his gelding to the children. But his mind wasn't on what he would say to them. His mind was on the silver-blond Huntress. He would watch closely that nothing happened to her. His sister would string him up and gut him if he let her friend come to any harm.

A chill passed over his skin. No. Nothing would happen to Brighid. He would make sure of that.

Pebbles skittered down the side of the sheer wall on her right. The Huntress frowned. Too damned steep. The walls of the pass were riddled with narrow paths that snaked into crevices, forming cavelike hollows along the treacherous slopes. The goats were up there—her gut told her so—as did the spoor and tufts of fur she'd been tracking. But she couldn't get to them. It was extraordinarily frustrating.

The Huntress trotted doggedly down the pass, exploring each small side trail while her eyes scanned the walls searching for an access to the upper hollows and crests. More pebbles rained down the steep wall, only this time they were accompanied by a muffled *oof!*

It was not a goatish noise at all. Brighid stopped. Her sharp eyes scrutinized the shadows that deepened beneath each outcropping of gray-red rock, until she found the familiar shape. She sighed. This was just one of the many reasons Huntresses usually chose not to give birth. Children were bothersome.

"I see you, Liam. Come down from there. Now!"

His head peeked over the edge of one of the wider ledges. Within the gloom of the pass his grin looked childishly bright and impetuous. "I've been flanking you for a really long time, and you didn't even know! It's because I've been practicing my Huntress skills!"

Brighid snorted. She hadn't noticed him because she'd allowed herself to be preoccupied with Cuchulainn's problems, and Epona's unexpected touch, and bringing a herd of winged children into a country that wanted nothing to do with them.

"Lovely. Good job," she said awkwardly, shielding her eyes from the sun with her hand as she squinted up the west side of the pass. "Now come down. It's time for you to go back and join the rest of the children."

Not in the least bit discouraged, Liam leaned farther over the side of his ledge, looking very much like a baby bird bobbing over the lip of his nest. "I can't go back yet. I have to help you!"

Brighid's stomach tightened and she motioned the boy back. She hated heights. Just watching him perched on the edge made her feel vicariously uncomfortable.

"Liam," she said sternly. "Don't hang over the edge. You could fall."

"Don't worry, Mistress! I'm not afraid. And I can fly." Liam's gray-downed wings unfurled and he rocked forward, balancing easily as he caught the air currents and held himself erect.

"Nice. Good," Brighid said hastily, still motioning him back from the edge and trying to ignore that he had called her Mistress—the official title an apprentice used with a teacher. "I can see you're very good at balancing."

"And at being quiet!" he shouted.

"Oh, absolutely. So I think you've done enough for today. Climb down and run back to the others."

Liam's smile deflated along with his wings. "But we haven't got a wild goat yet."

"Well, one of the first lessons a Huntress learns is that she doesn't always get the goat." What was she saying? Babble. Babble was coming out of her mouth.

"Really?" Liam asked, studying her intently.

Brighid sighed. "The goats are up there. I am down here. Hence the fact that I will not be getting a goat today."

Liam's sparkling, pointy smile was back in full force. "I can make the goats come down!"

"No, *you* need to get down and—" she began and then clamped her mouth shut. It did make sense. He was up there. The goats were up there. She certainly wasn't going up there— even if she could fit she was not scaling those slick, steep walls.

"Yes! Yes!" The boy hopped up and down eagerly. "I can chase the goats down to you."

Brighid tilted her head to the side, considering. "Do you think you could find them?"

"Yes! Yes!" He peered down at her and in an exaggerated whisper said, "When the wind blows just right I can hear them. I have really, really good hearing. I can also smell them—they smell goaty." He started to hop again and then, with an obvious effort calmed himself. "They're that way." He pointed ahead of them.

Yes, it certainly seemed vaguely insane, and it was definitely an unorthodox way to hunt wild mountain goat, but it could work.

"All right. But only if you promise that you will do exactly as I tell you."

"I promise! I promise!" The boy's wings spread and he fluttered around the ledge, skipping and dancing happily.

"Liam!" Brighid's voice was sharp and the child froze. "A Huntress learns quickly to control her feelings. Especially in the middle of a hunt." Of course he wasn't a she, nor was he a centaur or a Huntress… She shook her head, more at herself than at the boy who was watching her so intently. "This is what I want you to do. Carefully and silently go forward along the path you found, listening for the sound of goats and looking for signs that they have traveled the same way."

"I'll be careful and quiet. I'll pretend to be a Huntress." His eyes widened and he lifted one small taloned foot, staring at it thoughtfully. "Except I'll pretend that I have magic hooves that don't make any clomping noise when I walk."

Brighid had to stop herself from rolling her eyes. The boy

thought he was a centaur. He had wings and talons, and he was pretending to have hooves. Magic hooves at that. He was clearly delusional, which couldn't bode well for his future development. Could it? It seemed the more time she spent with children the less she knew about them. They just didn't make good sense.

"Just pretend to be quiet. All you need to do is find the goats. When you do, come back to me—*quietly*. When I tell you I'm ready, then you quit pretending to have silent magic hooves. Jump out and yell at them. But stay away from the edge, or you'll make them run farther into the mountains." And it would make Brighid's stomach feel sick to see the small winged boy clinging to the edge of the steep chasm while goats ran pell-mell all around. "What you do instead is come around from behind them and then yell."

"I understand." He nodded his head up and down, up and down. "You want me to chase them to you."

"Yes. Exactly. I'll be following here, below you in the pass, slowly. If we're very lucky the goats will run away from you and down here." In theory it sounded like a good plan. She would certainly run away from the yelling, hopping, flapping boy. "And directly into me."

"And then you'll get one for dinner!" he said triumphantly.

"That's what I'm hoping."

"If that happens will I officially be your apprentice?"

"We'll see," Brighid prevaricated. "Being apprenticed to a Huntress is a complex procedure."

Liam chewed his lip. "I understand." Then he brightened. "I'll do my best, though. You'll see. I'll be the perfect Huntress!"

"Doing your best is always the best choice," Brighid said inanely.

And then, with a flutter of very uncentaurlike wings, the boy took off with his face pointed into the wind.

"Be careful and stay away from the edge!" Brighid called after him.

CHAPTER
SEVENTEEN

At least the child was being quiet. Except for the occasional spray of pebbles that his pretend magic hooves dislodged, the Huntress had to admit that Liam was moving silently along the narrow path above her. There was no giggling, no flapping of wings, no constant barrage of questions. Maybe keeping the young busy was the key to controlling them. Brighid glanced up in time to see the tip of one wing disappear ahead of her as the sides of the pass veered sharply to the right and Liam followed the goat trail along the turn.

No, she should know better. She wasn't in control of the boy. He was off in his own pretend world where he was a magic centaur Huntress. It was just dumb luck that part of his pretense included temporary silence. Had she been like that when she was young? Filled with fantasies and imagination while she chattered incessantly and hopped about? The Huntress sighed. She didn't ever remember being that young—it seemed like she'd been born old, weighed down by the responsibilities of tradition and her mother's expectations.

The breeze swirled around her, feeling suddenly several degrees cooler. Brighid shivered and looked up at the sinking sun. How long had she and Liam been hunting? The sheer sides of the pass were almost completely made of gray stone in this section of the tunnel-like trail. No wonder it looked darker here. At least the red brightened the shadowy gloom. The gray seemed to suck in the waning light of the sun as if the walls themselves wanted to steal the spirit of the day.

The Huntress shivered again and felt the soft hair at the back of her neck lift. Her eyes skimmed up the gray rock walls. Where had that boy gone? She couldn't see anything past the sharp turn. Damn it! He shouldn't be that far ahead of her. She stopped and listened to the wind. Was that the echo of a goat's bleat? She thought it might be and concentrated harder…

The screech from above had her pulling an arrow from the quiver slung across her back and notching her bow so quickly that had anyone been watching all they would have seen was the silver-blond blur of Brighid's practiced movement. She aimed the bow at the sound and the breath caught in her throat.

Circling above her was a silver hawk with gold-tipped wings. As if waiting for her full attention, it soared down on the air currents, folding its wings and diving directly at Brighid. The Huntress felt like a statue, frozen with the arrow notched in place, unable to do anything but stare at the beautiful bird as it rode the air. The bird's golden eye captured Brighid's gaze, and within its avian depths the centaur saw the reflection of her own soul.

Brighid Felt their connection. *Freedom…power…courage… a seeker of justice…a warrior…might used for right.* The words blasted through the centaur's consciousness in a clear, unfamiliar voice. *I belong to you and you to me. It is past time you acknowledge our bond, Sister.* The hawk screeched again as it skimmed above Brighid's body, so close that the wind under its wings caused Brighid's hair to move in response.

And like a bothersome black fly from the lowlands, something bit Brighid hard, squarely in the middle of her equine back.

A gift. Something that has too long been hidden…much like our bond and the power that is your heritage.

Utterly off balance, Brighid spun around and stared after the golden bird, her equine skin still twitching from the sharp bite. Had the damned bird clawed her?

Look down.

Brighid's gaze fell and she saw the stone. Its rich blue-green color stood out against the drab slate path, an oasis of color in a desert of gray. The centaur picked it up, intrigued by its brilliant coloring and the smooth, warm feel of it against her skin. It reminded her of something…

Above her, the circling bird screeched again, and Brighid's head snapped up.

He needs you.

"He?" Brighid called into the air.

The voice in her head was suddenly a shout. *Liam!*

Liam? Brighid kicked into a controlled gallop, placing the turquoise stone within her inner vest pocket. As she hurried forward she could feel its hard round shape press sharply against the softness of her breast.

The walls and the rising wind muffled the sound of her hooves as she slid around the abrupt turn, her eyes moving restlessly from the treacherous ground in front of her to the sheer sides of the rock walls. There was no sign of the winged boy.

"Liam!" she yelled. The boy's name bounced eerily off the walls and came back to her like a half-forgotten memory.

By the Goddess! She had a bad Feeling about this! She should never have allowed the child to be separated from the rest of the group. She and Cuchulainn had agreed on the importance of staying together. Who knew how many hidden dangers the rugged mountains held? Then there was the hawk and the voice that warned her Liam needed her. What, by the Goddess's silver breastplate, was that all about?

And where was the boy? How far ahead of her had he gotten? She'd had no idea he could move so fast. She vaulted over a heap of rock and rubble, stumbled, and then caught her balance. Gritting her teeth and silently cursing the Goddess-forsaken roughness of the trail, she increased her speed.

Once again the pass veered sharply to the right. She skidded around the curve, almost losing her balance as her hooves slipped on the slick rock floor. Here the pass was broader, opening to a width of several centaurs. Gray boulders dotted the ground haphazardly so that Brighid had to slow down to wind her way between them.

She Felt it. Someone was watching her. Instinctively she raised her bow along with her eyes, and was washed with relief. Above and ahead of her the unmistakable shape of Liam's little head and the tips of his wings jutted just over the edge of the chasm. When he saw the Huntress looking his way, the boy waved gaily at her. Brighid sighed and lowered her bow. He was too far away to hear her, so she lifted her arm and signaled for him to come to her.

What had been the damned bird's problem? Liam was fine. Or had the voice come from the hawk at all? She glanced warily down the dreary pass. Who knew what malevolence lurked within these mountains? Ciara had sensed something that made her wary. Perhaps the restless spirits of her people were prowling around. It seemed likely they would enjoy causing trouble. The turquoise stone pressed against her breast. Was she imagining its warmth?

She pushed the confusion from her mind. Later. When the children were safely deposited at MacCallan Castle, then she would have time to think about the oddness of this day, and the glimpses into the spirit realm she had been gifted with all too often during this journey.

Gifted…

The Huntress's skin twitched as if another stone had fallen from the sky. Realization made her suck in a breath. Ciara had told her to be careful what she asked of the spirit realm… The blue-green stone pressed warmly against her breast, sending a flush of knowledge through her body.

It was a soul-catcher, gifted to her through her spirit guide. The thought made her feel light-headed.

Later! She repeated the word sternly to herself. The Huntress shook herself and glanced up at the gray wall, trying to see Liam as he moved in and out of the deepening shadows. For now she should just forget about the wild goats and return Liam to the rest of the group. It was getting late; they would be worried about her and the boy's absence had more than likely been discovered. Brighid grimaced, imagining the scene with Cuchulainn when she returned with Liam chirping about being her apprentice and helping her hunt.

She squinted up at movement along the ledge. Liam was suddenly visible, his winged shape silhouetted clearly against the deep blue-gray of the sky as he scrambled toward her.

Brighid opened her mouth to call a reminder to him to be careful, even though it was obvious that the child was as comfortable scaling the heights as were the damned elusive goats. But she did not have a chance to speak the words.

The day exploded in violence.

She heard the familiar twang of an arrow being loosed. Instinctively she launched herself forward.

"Liam! Get down!"

The boy stood frozen, wings spread as he balanced on the edge. He was a panicked statue. An easy target. The black arrow tore through his right wing.

"No!" Brighid shouted, but the word was drowned out by the child's scream of pain. The boy crumpled. The wounded wing lay brokenly over the edge of the chasm, along with most of Liam's upper body. *Oh, Goddess! He's going to fall!* The Huntress's hooves bit into the gray shale shooting sparks as she cut through the maze of boulders, feeling more than seeing the way because she couldn't take her eyes from Liam. Fervently and silently she prayed to Epona that there would be no more arrows—that the boy wouldn't tumble to his death.

"Hold on! I'm coming! Don't move!" she called to him.

A hawk's shriek sounded from atop the opposite wall of the pass. Brighid wrenched her gaze from Liam to see the hawk diving like a golden arrow at a dark-clothed warrior. The man dropped his bow and used both arms to cover his head, trying to dodge the bird's talons.

"He's just a child, you fool!" Brighid screamed. She saw the warrior's head turn in her direction and his body jerk in obvious surprise, but she had no more time for him—she'd have to trust the hawk to keep him from firing another arrow. Liam needed her.

She slid to a stop beneath the boy.

"It's going to be fine," she called up to him as she frantically searched the rock wall for the narrow goat path. Liam's sobs echoed around her. *There!* Half an equine length up the wall was a roughly hewn trail. She bit off a curse as she approached it. The damned thing was two hand lengths wide! The centaur followed it up with her eyes. Yes, it got wider—by maybe another hand width. She'd never be able to climb the trail. Despite all of her strength and agility, it was physically impossible. She needed a human's body to scale the wall.

Brighid looked at the boy and her stomach rolled. He had managed to drag himself away from the edge, but his wounded wing still hung limply down the side of the rock wall, smearing scarlet stains against the gray stone.

Call the warrior. The voice was inside her head again. *Use your connection and call for him.*

Brighid didn't need to look up. She heard the angry cries of the bowman and the predatory shrieks of the hawk. She knew the voice came from the bird—her spirit ally.

"Brighid!" Her name was a sob.

"I'm here, Liam." The Huntress pressed her palms against the side of the pass, staring up at the wounded boy. "You're going to be fine. Just be brave a little while longer. You can be brave for me, can't you?"

Liam started to nod his head, but broke off with a moan. "It hurts," he said, biting his lip to keep from sobbing.

"I know, brave one, I know. I'm going to get help, though."

"Don't leave me!"

"I won't," she assured him. "I don't have to."

Liam's eyes met the centaur's steady gaze. "Magic?"

"Magic," she said. Oh, Goddess she hoped so. She closed her eyes and did the only thing she could—Brighid followed her gut instinct. He'd come to her in her dreams…dreams were only another part of consciousness…always there, just more elusive when one was awake…

She thought of her friend, the happy warrior with the ready laugh and the ability to draw people as bees to wildflowers.

Damn it, Cuchulainn! I need your help! Come to me!

Was it her imagination, or did she hear the whisper of Cuchulainn's laughter?

Ciara jogged alongside Cuchulainn's gelding. With her dark wings spread she used the gliding Fomorian gait to easily keep pace with the big horse. "Liam is not with the animals, and none of the adults have seen him since the last rest break," she said. "He seems to have vanished."

Cuchulainn grunted in annoyance and frowned down the stretch of pass that yawned ahead of them. "I have an idea where the boy might have gone."

Ciara's relief was obvious. "I didn't even think about that! Yes, he must have followed the Huntress."

"I wouldn't sound too pleased. Brighid is very unpleasant when she's angry." She's even prickly when she's not, Cuchulainn added to himself. "The boy is bound to learn a lesson in what it's really like to be apprenticed to a surly old Huntress."

"Old?" Ciara laughed. "Brighid is young and attractive."

Cu grunted. "She's old inside—old and prickly."

It was in the middle of Ciara's laughing response that he Felt it. He jerked his gelding to a rough halt. A sense of joy, of youthful unbound happiness flashed through him, making him gasp with surprise.

"Cuchulainn, what…"

The warrior heard no more of what the winged woman said. With the heady happiness came something else, something Cuchulainn hadn't experienced in many phases of the moon. The knowledge of what was happening settled within his mind like a nightmare as the vision slammed into him. Against suddenly blind eyes he saw Brighid. Her hands were pressed against the side of the pass and blood streamed down the stone walls all around her. *Damn it, Cuchulainn! I need your help! Come to me!* The words rang in his head.

"Brighid!" he cried. The vision disappeared. With it the fleeting sense of happiness evaporated and the world around him returned in a rush.

Ciara was grasping his arm and peering up into his face.

"What did you see? What's wrong with Brighid?"

"She's calling me." He shook loose from her. "Tell the adults to keep the children close and to be wary."

"Don't worry about us. Go to her."

Instead of answering, Cuchulainn dug his heals into the gelding's sides and gave the horse his head.

CHAPTER
EIGHTEEN

The moaning wind had stilled. Liam's small gasps of pain and Brighid's murmurs of encouragement seemed suddenly unnaturally loud in the echoing pass, so she easily heard Cuchulainn before she saw him.

"Thank the Goddess." Brighid's breath came out in a rush. "You're doing so well, brave one." She smiled up at Liam.

"I want to be brave. Huntresses are brave," the boy said.

"You are being an excellent Huntress, Liam." What else could she say? If pretending to be a centaur helped him bear the pain of his wound and kept him from falling over the edge, then he could damned well pretend away.

Before Brighid turned to meet Cu she spared a glance at the opposite side of the pass. It was empty. There was no dark-clothed warrior holding a black bow. No golden hawk diving in attack. Where had they gone? They couldn't be a hallucination, or even ghostly apparitions, Liam's wound was evidence that she had not imagined them.

Cuchulainn's gelding sprinted into the widened area of the pass. When he caught sight of Brighid standing so close to the wall—so disturbingly like the blood-drenched vision he had seen—the deadly sound of his claymore being unsheathed rang with metallic intensity against the rock.

"It's Liam!" she shouted, pointing up at the small, crumpled shape hanging precariously over the edge.

The warrior's hard, battle-ready face shifted and visibly softened. Quickly Cu reined the gelding around the boulders that separated them and galloped to Brighid's side.

"By the Goddess! What happened here?"

"Don't be mad at me, Cuchulainn," Liam said pitifully.

"Tell him you're not mad at him," Brighid whispered under her breath.

Cu frowned at her, but called up to the boy, "I am not angry, Liam."

"Cu's here to help, brave one," Brighid said. "Just rest quietly and he'll get you down." She turned to Cuchulainn, speaking fast and keeping her voice low. "An archer shot him." She gestured up at the place so recently vacated by the dark warrior. "From there. He's gone now. I don't know where."

"Did he see that you were with the boy?"

Brighid shook her head. "No, not until after he'd already shot him. He looked shocked when he saw me." The Huntress carefully avoided all mention of golden hawks and voices in her head.

Cuchulainn's gaze narrowed. "How was the archer dressed?"

"Dark," she said. "That's all I could see from here."

"Did you see the arrow?"

She nodded. "Black. It was dark like the—" Her breath caught with sudden realization. "He was a Guardian Warrior."

"Yes."

"What was he thinking! He could have killed Liam."

"He was probably thinking that he was protecting Partholon from a winged demon."

"But they know that we're bringing the children into Partholon!" Brighid said.

"They have no way of knowing that we are coming through Guardian Pass." Cu dismounted and walked over to the sheer wall, studying the narrow path that angled sharply up the side of it. "The last anyone knew we were leading the children through a hidden pass well west of here." He returned to his saddlebag for leather gloves. "The warrior was only fulfilling his duty."

Brighid snorted, but Liam's voice interrupted her retort.

"It's fire," he called down to the centaur and the warrior.

"I know, brave one. It must feel like fire." She automatically soothed the boy.

"No." He lifted his head and gestured weakly to the opposite wall. "There—it's fire."

Their eyes followed the boy's finger. Farther down the pass, on the same side from which the archer had shot Liam, yellow flames danced against the darkening sky.

"What is it?" Cuchulainn asked the boy. "Can you see?"

Biting his lip Liam pulled himself up straighter. Brighid opened her mouth to tell the boy to stay still, but Cuchulainn's firm hand on her arm stopped her words. Liam struggled a moment more, and then with a small moan he sat up, his wing fluttering brokenly across his lap.

"It's like a campfire, only it's the biggest campfire I've ever seen. And there's nothing around it."

"Good job, Liam. Hold tight. I'll be right up." Cuchulainn strode to the wall, pulling on his gloves. Then to Brighid he said, "It's the Guardian Warrior's signal. The pyres are lit to call the warriors. It means the pass has been breached."

"But we're not fighting the warriors of Partholon!"

"Not yet we're not. Boost me up. I need to get him down. It won't take them long to get here."

"I don't like this," Brighid muttered, bending to make a cradle of her linked hands for the warrior's foot. He stepped into it and she lifted him up to the path. "Be careful," she said to his back. "It's narrow."

He grumbled something unintelligible.

While Cuchulainn scaled the sheer wall Brighid's attention moved nervously from the warrior to the wounded boy who waited so patiently to the open end of the wide pass. The archer had been one of the famed Guardian Warriors. She should have known—she would have realized who he was if her thoughts hadn't been filled with broken children and talking birds. She'd never been to Guardian Castle, but she knew the warriors stationed there were ever-vigilant, and that they wore black to show their eternal mourning for mistakes of the past.

More than one hundred years ago the Guardian Warriors had become lax. Partholon was at peace, and had been for centuries. The demonic Fomorian race was no more than ancient history, faded into the bad dreams of children. No one guessed that the demons had been readying themselves for generations to return to Partholon as conquerors and masters. The Guardian Warriors were not prepared for the demonic onslaught, and were easily overrun, allowing death and evil to break into Partholon.

The black uniforms they now wore were their visible oath to Partholon that the warriors' vigilance would never again fail. They were formidable, and Brighid did not relish the idea of fighting them. Especially since her only allies were a depressed warrior and a wounded child.

Her brother would say they were damned stupid odds. She rarely agreed with her brother, but this time was a definite exception.

A cry from behind her had her spinning around. Ciara was at the head of the New Fomorians as they poured into the pass. Her lovely face was twisted into an expression of shock and horror as she stared up at Liam. Her cry was soon echoed by the distraught group surrounding her.

Brighid moved forward quickly to meet Ciara.

"Liam is fine." The Huntress pitched her voice so that it would carry above the children's cries. "He has been injured, but Cuchulainn is going to bring him down. Right now why don't we all take a little break while Ciara lights a campfire to warm everyone up?"

Ciara stood mute, staring over Brighid's shoulder at Liam.

"Ciara!" Brighid hissed. "Build the damned fire and get yourself together."

The winged woman snapped out of her daze, and with a nod to Brighid, called for fodder to be brought for the fire.

The Huntress's eyes searched the milling crowd of upset children until she found a familiar face. "Kyna, I don't think I remember the name of your Healer. Perhaps you could help me?"

The little girl blinked tears from her eyes and wiped at her wet cheeks. "Nara." The child looked around on tiptoes, until she spotted an adult figure who was working her way toward Brighid from the rear of the group. "There she is."

"Thank you, Kyna." *Keep them busy,* Brighid reminded herself. "And Kyna, I need your help. Could you and some of the children take charge of Cuchulainn's horse? Maybe you could rub him down so that he'll be ready to travel again soon?" Pitiful doggy whines reminded the Huntress of something else that needed tending to. "And take special care of Fand. You know how she gets when Cu's too busy to reassure her," Brighid added.

"Of course, Brighid!" Kyna nodded vigorously, and instantly began giving orders to several other children.

"I am Nara, the Healer." The New Fomorian was tall, thin, with pale blond hair and eyes that were an unusual shade of moss-green.

Brighid's attention still roved restlessly. She kept imagining hordes of black-garbed warriors descending upon them with drawn bows. She spoke quickly to the Healer, careful to keep her voice low so the children wouldn't overhear.

"Liam's wing has been pierced by an arrow. It didn't happen long ago, but even from down here I can tell he's lost more blood than is good for him. I couldn't get up there to stop the bleeding, and he was too weak to make it down by himself." She looked into the Healer's eyes. "He's in a lot of pain."

The Healer touched the centaur's arm. "I can help him."

Brighid glanced up at the top of the rock wall. Cuchulainn was there, crouching beside the boy. The warrior had his shirt off and was tearing it into strips to bind Liam's wing to his side.

"I will help the warrior bring the boy down," Nevin said, calling Brighid's attention back to the ground.

"As will I," Curran said.

"No, I need the two of you here," the Huntress said sharply. "Nara, help Cuchulainn with Liam, and hurry."

The Healer nodded and, with wings spread, she navigated the steep trail easily. Brighid turned to the twins.

"Liam was shot by one of the Guardian Warriors," she said bluntly. "The signal fire has been lit. The warriors are on their way here." Brighid's first response was to order the twins to arm the adults and bring them to the front of the group where they could best protect the children, but the thought of the winged people greeting Partholonians with weapons made her stomach tighten. That's not the way—it couldn't be *their* way. If they chose to greet the Guardian Warriors armed, how would they appear any different than their demonic forefathers? The Huntress drew a deep breath. *Epona, please let me be doing the right thing.*

"Spread word to the other adults. Have them stay scattered among the children. Tell them to sit, to blend in with the young ones." The twins nodded slowly at her.

"We understand. We are not our fathers."

"No, you're not. And this will not begin another war," she said firmly.

CHAPTER
NINETEEN

The children had fallen back into the unnaturally quiet state that Brighid was beginning to understand was their reaction to fear. They didn't whine and cry like most children. They became very still and attentive. The Huntress respected that about them, and thanked Epona for their maturity. They were composed and silent, sitting patiently in a semicircle around Ciara's hastily lit campfire, watching as Nara held Liam's wing carefully immobile while Cuchulainn carried the boy down from the ledge.

Brighid had to force herself not to shout at Cu to hurry, and she paced restlessly, keeping her keen eyes trained down the pass. She and Cuchulainn needed to go ahead to Guardian Castle and confront the warriors, explaining why they had decided to use this pass, and making it clear that the New Fomorians were not an invading force from the Wastelands— they were a group of children and hopeful adults who had been promised a home by the Chieftain of Clan MacCallan.

Surely the Guardian Warriors already knew most of that. Cuchulainn's mother had blazed the news of the deposed children of Partholon across the country. If not openly welcomed by the people, the New Fomorians should at least be expected. Etain was Epona's Chosen, and Elphame was revered as touched by the Goddess. Their acceptance would at the very least ensure that the Partholonian people would not raise arms against the hybrids. To do so would be an act of defiance against Epona herself.

Yet Liam had been attacked.

"Nara, I've made a pallet for him near the fire," Ciara called.

Brighid turned from her silent contemplation of the empty passageway to see Cu striding to the campfire with a pale Liam in his arms. The boy moaned when Cu laid him on the thick pile of pelts. Nara called for boiling water and began mixing herbs as she murmured reassuringly to the boy.

Cuchulainn moved to Brighid's side.

"We must intercept the warriors and diffuse this situation before it gets any worse," Cuchulainn said.

"Agreed. I want to speak with the warrior who mistook a child for a demon."

"Scolding a warrior of Guardian Pass is not the way to defuse this situation."

"Scolding is the least of what I would like to do to him," she said grimly.

Cuchulainn began to grumble a reprimand when a flicker of movement over the centaur's shoulder made his body stiffen. Brighid spun around and sucked in a breath. The end of the pass was no longer empty. Silently dozens of black-garbed warriors moved toward them.

"Stay beside me. Don't draw your bow," he said.

"Cuchulainn?" Ciara's whisper was a tremulous question.

The warrior spared a quick glance at the Shaman. "All will be well." Then his steady gaze went from child to child, and he repeated slowly, "All will be well."

Big eyes stared steadily back at him, bright with trust and belief.

Feeling the responsibility of their young idealism settling heavily on him, Cuchulainn nodded to Brighid, and centaur and human moved forward together to meet the line of dark warriors.

"Do you know any of them?" Brighid asked quietly.

"I can't tell yet. I should. I trained here, but that was several years—" His words broke off as the approaching line stopped moving. A single tall warrior stepped away from the others.

Brighid slanted a glance at Cu, and was relieved to see that the stern set of his face had relaxed. He intercepted the dark warrior and held out his arm for the traditional greeting of comrades.

"Master Fagan, well met," Cu said with genuine warmth.

The warrior hesitated only a moment before grasping Cu's forearm and returning the greeting.

"Well met, Cuchulainn MacCallan. We were apprised of your mission to the Wastelands. When the signal fire was lit I hoped that I would discover you and not an invading horde." Fagan's voice was as gnarly as his heavily lined face, but it was filled with the same familiarity Cu had shown in his greeting.

Cu chuckled. "An invading horde? Not hardly. I am simply leading children back to the land of their foremothers."

The old warrior studied the group of silent winged beings.

"So we had heard. But we expected you to guide them through a smaller pass that was discovered in the west. I wonder at your change in travel plans."

"The western pass was our original intent—before the blizzard two moons ago. The snow made the pass too treacherous for children, thus we decided to bring them through Guardian Pass."

"It is unfortunate that we weren't informed of your change in plans. I understand one of the Fomorians was wounded by my man."

"He didn't wound a Fomorian. He shot a child, not a demon. There is a distinct difference between the two." Brighid's voice was hard, and she thought—with satisfaction—that she sounded as imperious as her mother.

Fagan cocked his head back and studied the centaur down the length of his long nose. "You must be the Dhianna centaur who left her herd and joined the MacCallans."

Brighid's eyes narrowed dangerously but before she could speak Cuchulainn made hasty introductions. "Swordmaster Fagan, this is Clan MacCallan's Huntress, Brighid Dhianna."

"I assume the hawk belongs to you, Huntress?" Fagan asked.

Brighid ignored the surprised widening of Cuchulainn's eyes.

"The hawk doesn't belong to me, but I was grateful that Epona called her to my aid. She saved the boy's life."

Fagan gave her another long, contemplative look. "It would be a tragedy to kill an innocent youth. If the youth is, indeed, innocent."

"This particular youth is my apprentice," Brighid said firmly. "So when you question his honor, you question my own."

"Understood, Huntress," the Swordmaster said, holding Brighid's gaze unblinkingly.

Brighid did not like the tone of his voice, but before she could tell him so Cuchulainn was making a magnanimous, sweeping gesture with his arm.

"Come, Master! Let me introduce you to the New Fomorians and their children."

Reluctantly, the Swordmaster looked away from the Huntress. With obvious disbelief he said, "*New* Fomorians?"

Brighid was pleased to see Cuchulainn's face harden and his tone lose its warmth. "These are not the demons our ancestors fought and vanquished. They are innocent of those deeds. I would expect a man as wise as my old Master to know better than to prejudge them."

"And I would expect the warrior who so recently lost his betrothed to the madness of these creatures to be more careful in whom he placed his trust."

"Do not forget, Fagan, that I am no longer a young novice studying at your knee. The killing of my betrothed took place before my sister's sacrifice, which washed all vestiges of demon from the hybrids' blood."

This time it was Brighid's words that broke the simmering tension. "Master Fagan, you know Cuchulainn. You also know what he has lost. If he has forgiven them and accepted them, does that not speak well on their behalf?" she said. "Can you do any less than to show them the respect Cuchulainn's love has won for them?"

Cuchulainn's eyes met hers. He looked as surprised as she felt at her own words. Love was not an emotion she spoke of openly—it simply wasn't her way. But she Felt the rightness of what she had said, with the instinctual knowledge she was beginning to trust more and more easily. Cuchulainn did love the New Fomorians. They had quite probably saved his life.

And what of *her* feelings? She had just proclaimed to a Master Swordsman of the Guardian Warriors that little Liam, a winged hybrid Fomorian male child, was her apprentice. Could she have fallen in love with at least one of the children herself?

She'd never considered herself maternal—just the opposite actually. But she did know enough of the world to understand that blood did not automatically make a parent or a family. Love did. And trust. And bravery. And honesty. Liam had all of those things in excess. He also, she decided irrevocably, had her.

"Lead on, Huntress," Fagan said, with a sudden smile that transformed his gruff face. "Let me meet these so-called *New* Fomorians who seem to have bewitched not only my favorite pupil, but a famous centaur Huntress as well."

Brighid tilted her head in a small bow of acknowledgment, but her eyes flashed to the dark warriors who filled the pass and remained obviously armed and on guard.

"I have never before met a Guardian Warrior, but from the stories I have heard, it is a surprise they would stand armed against a group of children," the Huntress said with thinly veiled sarcasm.

"Guardian Warriors do not fight children," Fagan said.

Brighid lifted one mocking brow.

In response to Fagan's slight arm motion, the army rippled to a more relaxed stance. "My guard, to me!" Fagan barked and six warriors stepped from the front of the line to join them.

Brighid's smile was feral. "I, too, was nervous when I first met the children. Of course I am only a mere Huntress and not a Master Swordsman of the Guardian Warriors."

"What is the first lesson you learned as my pupil, Cuchulainn?" Fagan fired the question at Cu without breaking eye contact with Brighid.

"To remain ever vigilant," Cu replied automatically.

"My guard remains with me," Fagan said.

Brighid snorted.

"As you wish, Master Fagan," Cuchulainn said. "But direct them to keep their weapons sheathed. There's no need for your vigilance to frighten the children."

Fagan called a quick order to the somber men. Without another word, the three of them, followed closely by the Swordmaster's elite guard, walked toward the crowd of silent children.

Brighid and Cuchulainn's eyes met quickly with a look of mutual amusement.

"Perhaps you might want to prepare yourself, Master," Cu said.

Fagan's brows disappeared into the line of his thick graying hair. "A Guardian Warrior is always prepared."

"Under normal circumstances, one would certainly think so," Cu said.

"But these," Brighid said, sharing a secret look with Cu, "are not normal circumstances."

They approached the campfire. Nara knelt over Liam. They didn't need to see her face to read the taut concentration in her body. Her hands moved quickly, and Brighid caught a glimpse of a curved bone needle as it flashed up from the torn wing and then back down again. The Huntress's gut quivered as she realized Nara was sewing together the ragged edges of Liam's wing. The Healer hid most of the boy's body with her own, but Brighid could still see that Liam was lying too still, and she had a sudden moment of raw fear. Had he lost consciousness? Was he more severely wounded than she had believed?

"He is asleep, Huntress," Nara said without taking her concentration from the boy. "I have given him a dram to ease his pain and make him sleep. He will not wake until morning."

"Thank you," Brighid said, surprised that her voice sounded so normal because she felt like someone had hollowed out her gut. Then the Huntress turned to Fagan. In a low, angry voice she said, "This is the child your warrior shot. Take a good look at what you think might be a demon." Before Cuchulainn could stop her, the centaur grabbed Fagan's arm and pulled him roughly around Nara's body so he had a clear view of Liam. The six warriors of Fagan's guard moved menacingly forward and the Huntress whirled on them.

"Draw your weapons around this child and you will answer to my wrath!"

Cuchulainn stepped to her side, "And to the wrath of Clan MacCallan."

Fagan made a restraining motion and the six men warily stood down. But as they began to step back, Brighid's hard voice stayed them.

"No, come closer with your Master. You, too, should see what it is you wish to destroy."

Hesitantly the men crowded around Nara and peered down at Liam. The child looked fragile and pale and broken. His round young face was streaked with tears and dirt, and his blond hair had fallen over one of his closed eyes. One dusky wing was folded neatly against his small body. The other one lay open across Nara's lap. The tear in it was jagged, as if the arrow had taken a ragged bite instead of piercing neatly. Blood oozed freely from the gash, even though Nara was tying the wound tightly together.

"If the bleeding does not slow, I will have to cauterize it," Nara said, still keeping her attention focused on her patient, "but I would rather not. It would permanently injure the growing membranes of his wing. He is too young to bear the burden of being crippled."

"Will he heal?" Cuchulainn asked the question when it was obvious that Brighid could not find her voice.

"Only the Goddess knows. But he is young and strong," Nara said, then she did look up from her patient, into Fagan's eyes. Her voice was friendly. "Do you have children, warrior?"

"No. I have not been so fortunate," Fagan answered.

The Healer's gaze traveled to the other six men all dressed similarly in black. "Are any of you fathers?"

Four of the six nodded slowly.

"Sons or daughters?" The Healer asked in a warm, conversational tone.

The four men glanced at their Master, who nodded. His men answered quickly.

"I have two sons."

"I have a daughter."

"Three daughters and a son."

"I have three sons."

Nara smiled at each man as he answered.

"You have been richly blessed. Tell me, have any of you ever made a mistake?"

The men did not speak, but each of them nodded.

"Would it not pain you terribly if your children were blamed for your mistakes?"

"It would," the father of three sons said. The other men nodded again slowly.

"I pray to Epona that you will never know that pain," she said earnestly. Then the Healer turned her distinctive green eyes back to Fagan.

"Warrior, do you believe a child should pay the price for the sins of his father?" There was no malice in her tone, just gentle questioning.

"No," Fagan said. "I do not."

"Then let us hope this boy heals, because if he does not then that is exactly what will have happened—he will pay the price for the sins of a grandfather he never knew."

"We will beseech Epona that Liam heals and is whole again soon." Ciara's musical voice drew the gaze of each of the warriors. The Shaman walked gracefully to the group of men, and then with a fluid movement she curtsied deeply before Fagan. "Well met, Guardian Warriors. I am Ciara, granddaughter of the Incarnate Goddess Terpsichore. I am also Shaman of the New Fomorians, and I greet you on behalf of my people."

Clearly shaken by her introduction, Fagan's eyes widened as the beautiful winged woman rose and smiled radiantly at him.

"I—we did not expect—" He shook his head as if to clear it. "All of the Guardian Warriors are well versed in the history of the Fomorian War. It was reported that Terpsichore's Incarnate died after spreading the pox plague to the demon army."

"My grandmother did, indeed, infect the demons with the pox, but she survived it. She also survived the birth of my mother," she said in a sweet, clear voice. "Many of the Incarnate Muses and their acolytes survived with her."

"This is unexpected news," Fagan said.

"Perhaps you would like to meet some of the descendants of the Nine Muses?"

"I —" He glanced at Cuchulainn.

"Things are not always what you expect, Master Fagan," Cuchulainn said softly. "I think you should meet the children."

"Ah! You are a Master!" Ciara said. "What is your weapon?"

"It is the sword."

"The children will be delighted," she said with a joyous laugh. Then she turned to the silent group sitting patiently, their bright eyes trained on the strangers.

Brighid could hardly believe the children were being so good. She did notice a lot of wing rustling and she could almost see their nervous energy. But not one of them was chattering or leaping about. The Huntress felt a swell of pride.

Ciara's voice lifted and with it Brighid realized their temporary respite from the children's exuberance would soon be over. She glanced at the unsuspecting warriors. Well, at least four of them were already parents, and might be somewhat prepared for...

The Shaman made a grand, dancer's flourish and announced, "Let the descendants of the Nine Muses rise and be first to meet Swordmaster Fagan of the Guardian Warriors!"

Oh, Goddess, Brighid thought, *now she's done it.* The Huntress braced herself as children, all shouting at once, leaped to their feet like caged baby birds that had suddenly been set free.

With supreme satisfaction, Brighid watched Fagan take an automatic step back. She sought Cuchulainn's gaze and found the warrior watching Fagan with a knowing smile. He glanced at her and she had to struggle not to laugh out loud. Thankfully, Ciara clapped her hands and the children quieted.

"They do get excited when they meet new people," Ciara said apologetically.

"Are there no other adults except for you and the Healer?" Fagan asked.

"Oh, yes. But not many." Ciara looked into the crowd of children. "Adults, please make yourselves known," she called.

Sprinkled throughout the crowd the adult New Fomorians stood.

Fagan shook his head as he counted. "But this can't be right. There are so few of them."

"There are twenty-two adult New Fomorians," Cuchulainn said. "That is all."

"And how many children are there?"

"Seventy."

Fagan turned to him incredulously. "How can there be so few adults and so many children?"

"Master, if you offer us sanctuary tonight at Guardian Castle, we will be happy to explain everything to you," Cuchulainn said.

Fagan looked from his ex-student down to the pale boy with the torn wing and then out at the throng of eagerly waiting children.

"Guardian Castle will offer you and the New Fomorians—" he tripped only slightly over the people's name "—sanctuary."

CHAPTER
TWENTY

"I would rather carry him myself," Brighid told the Healer for the fifth or sixth time. She was walking beside Liam's makeshift litter that was lashed between two of the domesticated goats. Every time Liam's sleeping body was jolted the Huntress grimaced.

"It is better for his wing if he lies flat and immobile."

Brighid frowned in worry.

"Huntress." Nara touched the centaur's arm gently. "The bleeding has stopped. The boy will recover."

Brighid saw the truth in the Healer's eyes and allowed herself a small measure of relief.

"Brighid!" Cuchulainn's deep voice boomed back at her from his place at the head of the slowly moving column of people.

"You may rest assured that Liam will be well cared for. He will sleep through the night and wake in the morning supremely disappointed that he missed the first meeting with the Guardian Warriors," the Healer said.

Brighid snorted a laugh. "I'll have to remind him that he *was* the first meeting with the warriors." Before she left the boy's side she leaned forward and brushed the hair from his face. She didn't know why she did it, she just knew it felt right to touch him—to reassure herself that he was warm and breathing and living.

How could such a small boy cause her such a large amount of worry?

Children…little wonder parents, who were otherwise young and healthy, could appear so haggard and distracted.

She took one last look at Liam before trotting away to join Cuchulainn. She studied the mixture of warriors and children as she wound her way to the front of the group. All around her children chattered endlessly. They had been traveling through the pass escorted by the Guardian Warriors for the past two hours, and the children's questions had not slowed. They were like bright balls of impetuous curiosity wrapped in wings. Brighid thought the sound of their happy voices mixed with the warrior's much less exuberant answers was highly satisfying.

These warriors would not take up arms against the children. Not after marching with them and seeing them as living, breathing individuals. *True,* she thought, stifling another smile, *they might run from him if they came upon a winged child in a dark passageway, but they definitely wouldn't shoot him.*

"Brighid!" Cuchulainn called again, gesturing for her to join him.

The Huntress increased her pace, overtaking Cu's gelding easily. Brighid noted with a new wave of amusement that Fagan and Cu had pulled far enough away from the main group that they had outdistanced the questioning children.

"Guardian Castle is just around this next turn. Fagan sent runners ahead to prepare the castle," Cu said.

"Cuchulainn described the unique shelters the hybrids

carry with them. The courtyard of Guardian Castle should be a more than adequate place for them to set up camp tonight," Fagan said.

All vestiges of Brighid's humor fled, and she gave the Swordmaster a disdainful look. "Are you so unwilling to allow the New Fomorians into your guest quarters that you would leave children out in the cold?"

Cuchulainn started to answer her, but Fagan's raised hand stopped him. "You misunderstand, Huntress. Guardian Castle has no luxurious accommodations for guests. We are a military castle. Our sole purpose is the defense of Partholon. I simply thought the children would be more comfortable within their own tents, which they could erect inside the safety and warmth of the inner walls of the castle. My offer of sanctuary was genuine."

"So was the arrow that sliced through Liam's wing," Brighid snapped.

Instead of reacting to Brighid's words with anger, the Swordmaster gave her a long, thoughtful look. "Your anger is understandable, Huntress," he said. "The children are fortunate to have found such a fierce protector."

Brighid's hard gaze didn't waver. "They are just children, Master Fagan."

"And you are pledged to bring them safely to your Chieftain."

"We are pledged to do so," Cuchulainn said firmly.

"Understood," Fagan said. "No matter what the two of you think, I respect your pledge and the diligence with which you are fulfilling it."

The Swordmaster looked over his shoulder at his warriors who were still marching in formation, even though small groups of talking, laughing, question-asking children were sprinkled throughout their ranks. Fagan's rough voice rumbled with a dry laugh, which he quickly cleared from his throat.

"When word came that descendants of the Fomorians had

survived the war and had been discovered in the Wastelands, I instantly called the Guardian Warriors to high alert," he continued. "Warily, we waited to see if Partholon would need our arms. Then the murderess, Fallon, arrived at our castle." His jaw clenched as he carefully chose his words. "She is quite mad, a vile creature filled with hatred. You know her mate chose to join her in her imprisonment. Keir is not mad, but Fallon has poisoned him. He is a sad, withdrawn creature who cannot be trusted. The two of them were our introduction to what you call the New Fomorians. How could we expect anything except more creatures like the two of them? But these winged children." Fagan lifted his hands and let them fall back to his sides. "Their gentle Healer—" he shook his head as if in disbelief and wiped a hand across his brow "—and the beautiful winged Shaman." He shook his head again. "We did not expect such as them. I believe Partholon will be just as surprised as my warriors and I have been today."

"No one expected the children, Fagan," Cuchulainn said. "And the adults—they are honorable beings, who only wish to return to the land of their foremothers and live in peace."

"The future should prove—" the old Swordmaster paused as a torrent of giggles erupted from behind them "—interesting."

They followed the curve in the pass and pulled up short as Guardian Castle loomed before them. In the fading light of the setting sun it looked like a great gray ghost. A massive iron gate sealed the pass, and the thick walls of the castle, carved from the mountain itself, blocked the final entrance into Partholon.

"Ooooh! It's so big!" Kyna's exclamation carried easily across the silent crowd. Several of the warriors couldn't help chuckling in response.

"I like the color," another young voice said. "It reminds me of rainy days."

"I don't like rainy days. It would be prettier if someone painted nice pictures on the walls. Maybe flowers and girls,"

Kyna said, and her idea set loose another avalanche of childish jabbering.

Fagan quickly raised his arm, motioning for the gate guard to lift the iron barrier. His men began ushering the children inside the castle walls.

Once within Guardian Castle, Brighid and Cuchulainn stepped aside, encouraging the children to move between the rows of dark warriors and into the inner courtyard. Fagan took temporary leave of them so that he could gather the other Masters of Arms. Cuchulainn explained to Brighid that Guardian Castle's management was not set up like a typical clan castle. The position of chieftain was divided between the various Masters of Arms, as the castle's function was solely defense and training. Brighid listened to him, but kept a watchful eye on the archers who lined the walls of the castle. She'd felt their oppressive presence the moment she stepped past the iron gate.

"Fagan is trustworthy," Cuchulainn reassured her. "He has offered us sanctuary. He will not break his oath of protection."

"I'm not as worried about Fagan as I am about them." She jerked her chin up at the silent wall of warriors.

"Look more closely. Read their faces."

Brighid shifted her attention from their bows and swords to the warriors' faces, and felt a jolt of surprise. The men and women of Guardian Castle were staring in unblinking fascination at the children.

"They're intrigued by them," Cuchulainn said under his breath.

"Because they thought they'd be monsters," she retorted defensively.

"Isn't that what we both thought before we knew them?"

The Huntress opened her mouth to deny it, but found she could only snort her displeasure.

"If a jaded Huntress can accept a winged child as her apprentice, perhaps the warriors of Guardian Castle can see more than enemies within them, too," Cu said.

"You sound like your soul is feeling better," she grumbled. She didn't like being reminded of her very public proclamation that had officially made Liam her apprentice. She was sure that was going to come back to bite her.

"I'm better. Not whole, but better." His eyes swept over the crowd. "You didn't ask how I knew to come to you today."

"There hasn't been time. I assumed you weren't far behind us, and you heard me or Liam, and knew something was amiss."

"I did hear you, but only in my head."

"Your head? I don't underst—" But she *did* understand. "You were touched by the spirit world. It sent you a premonition."

His lips twisted in the parody of a smile. "More specifically than that, I believe the part of my soul that has been visiting your dreams touched me, and gave me what amounted to a friendly but firm shove down the pass."

Brighid's brow shot up.

"It…he…me." Cuchulainn blew out a hard breath. "Whatever I'm supposed to call that *other* part of me, didn't stay. And I don't understand why he didn't. It would have been so much easier if he had. You wouldn't have to make any journeys to the Otherworld, and you could be rid of the burden of being responsible for my spiritual health."

The Huntress shrugged. "It's really not a burden, Cu. Actually I've come to think of it like hunting for unusual prey. I just have to find the absent part of your soul, and then bring it back."

"So you're tracking it?"

The amusement that glittered in his blue-green eyes reminded Brighid of the carefree Cuchulainn who came to her dreams. *He's going to heal!* She suddenly believed it with a fierce surge of happiness. But it wouldn't do to let Cu know just how worried she had been about him—she didn't want him to look back and get trapped in a web of second thoughts and gloomy remembrances. So she kept a tight rein on her pleasure, and arched her eyebrow at him.

"A well-trained Huntress will take on any tracking job for her Clan, no matter how hideous or distasteful," she began in her best long-suffering voice. Thankfully Fagan interrupted them before Cuchulainn could work up a properly annoyed reply.

"The Masters of Arms would like to meet with the two of you and the leader of the hybrids," Fagan said.

"In the Great Hall?" Cuchulainn asked.

Fagan nodded.

"I'll get Ciara and meet you there," Cu said.

Of course he'd volunteer to get Ciara. Brighid frowned as she watched her friend weave through the crowd of children and warriors to find the Shaman. *He's healing, and to Cuchulainn life isn't truly whole without a beautiful woman.* The thought *should* please her—it was more proof that Cu would be himself again.

"Huntress?"

"I'm sorry, Master Fagan," Brighid said, quickly jerking her thoughts back to order and following the warrior's lead along the edge of the courtyard. "This is my first trip to Guardian Castle. I find myself distracted by your—" her gaze traveled up to the silent line of archers stationed along the castle's outer wall "—architecture," she finished.

"Ever-vigilant, Huntress. We are ever-vigilant," he said with a craggy smile.

When the centaur didn't respond with a like smile, the Swordmaster stopped and met her eyes.

"I give you my word that if your New Fomorians are what they seem, none of them are in any danger from the Guardian Warriors."

"They are exactly what they seem, but they aren't *my* New Fomorians," Brighid said.

"Well, one of them certainly is." Fagan's weathered smile was back, and he chuckled as he led her along the courtyard wall again. "A centaur Huntress taking on a male child as her apprentice, and the boy has wings."

Brighid clamped her lips together and said nothing. The damned Swordmaster was right. Her infant apprentice did have wings—and only one of them was currently in working order.

And she'd thought her life was going to get easier when she joined MacCallan Castle.

There were three other Masters of Arms awaiting them in the Great Hall. They sat in three of the four thronelike chairs atop a raised stone dais. Fagan left Brighid to take his place in the chair with the likeness of a claymore carved into its tall, regal back. Cuchulainn and Ciara joined her then Fagan began the introductions.

"Let me present our Masters of Arms." He gestured first to a thin, sharp-featured middle-aged woman who sat in a chair decorated with plunging horses. "Glenna is our Horsemaster." The woman nodded, her intelligent eyes curious and sharp on Ciara.

"Bain is our newly appointed Master of Combat," Fagan said. Powerfully built, Bain was clearly the youngest of the four. His thick black hair was untouched by any hint of gray.

"And Ailis is our Master Archer." The woman nodded briefly in acknowledgment of Fagan's introduction. She was of indeterminate age—her skin was weathered, but her body was firm and muscular. Her blond hair had been cropped short, accentuating the strong line of her jaw and her high cheekbones. All of the Masters were dressed in black like the warriors, only the air of command that clung to them differed.

Cuchulainn stepped forward, and bowed formally.

"It is good to see you again, Cuchulainn MacCallan." The Horsemaster's voice was pleasingly feminine and filled with warmth. Brighid found herself studying Glenna more carefully, and wondering just how well she had gotten to know Cu while he'd studied at the castle.

"Well met, Master Glenna," Cu said smoothly, then he bowed to each of the other two Masters in turn. Though the Masters were carefully polite, it was obvious everyone's attention was focused on the winged woman who stood silently at Cu's side.

"I am pleased to introduce MacCallan's Huntress, Brighid Dhianna," Cuchulainn said.

Brighid bowed formally to each Master.

"And I would also like to present to you Ciara, Shaman of the New Fomorians and granddaughter of the Incarnate Muse Terpsichore."

Ciara stepped forward and sank gracefully into a deep, formal curtsy. "I am honored to meet each of you, and I thank you for offering sanctuary to my people."

"Are you leader as well as Shaman of your people?" Glenna asked.

Ciara raised herself and turned her brilliant smile to the Horsemaster. "No, Master Glenna. The leader of our people is Lochlan, who is now mated to Elphame, the MacCallan Chieftain. I only stand temporarily in his position, and will be pleased to abdicate it to him when we join him at our new home."

"Where are the rest of the adult Fomorians?" Bain's voice, though flat and carefully emotionless, made the question sound like an accusation.

Ciara's smile did not falter, and she returned the young Master's gaze steadily. "The Fomorian race no longer exists, Master Bain. The last of them perished more than one hundred years ago. My people call themselves New Fomorians because we have broken from the ways of our demonic ancestors." Her gaze moved to each of the Masters of Arms, and her voice took on a musical quality. "Think of it, Masters. We exist because of love, the love our foremothers felt so deeply for us that they were willing to live outside of their homeland. And because of faith, the faith they had in our mothers and grandmothers—their winged children were more human than demon. And hope that Epona would some day allow us to be called home. How could a race born in love and faith and hope not be different than the demons that spawned it?"

"That may be so," Ailis said, "but our experience with your people has show us there is little difference between the 'new' and the 'old' Fomorians."

Ciara's smile faded, but her expression remained open and utterly non-defensive. "You speak of Fallon and Keir. They are not representative of my people, as Cuchulainn and Brighid, and even, I think, Master Fagan would tell you. Fallon chose madness, and not even Elphame's sacrifice could wipe the demon stain from her soul after she embraced it. Keir is her mate. He cannot help but be touched by the darkness within her. They are sad, twisted versions of what our foremothers dreamed for us."

"Do you ask us to ignore that they are your people?" Bain said, his voice flint-like.

"I ask only that you do not judge us based on their mistakes."

Before Bain could respond, Cuchulainn spoke. "Fallon murdered the woman who was my betrothed. I have every reason to distrust Ciara and her people, but over the past two moons I have come to know—and to trust—them. Give them the opportunity, and I believe you will agree with me."

The Master Archer turned abruptly to Brighid. "Huntress,

I hear you have accepted one of these New Fomorians as your apprentice."

Brighid raised her chin. "I have."

"That seems most unusual."

"They are a most unusual people, Master Ailis," Brighid said.

"We shall see…" the Master Archer murmured.

"Fagan tells us that there are far more children with you than adults. Can you explain this?" Glenna fired the question to Ciara.

Again, the winged woman did not hesitate in her response. "The other adults are dead. Some of them chose to end their own lives when the madness that lurked within their blood became too much to bear. Some, like Fallon, accepted the madness willingly. Those we drove from our settlement. They perished in the Wastelands."

"And you say that this madness has been cleansed from your blood?"

Brighid heard the disbelief in the Master Archer's tone, and she felt her own anger stir. Ciara needed to keep calm and oh-so polite. Not so with the Huntress. "My Chieftain's sacrifice washed the demon from their blood," Brighid said. "You know this. I believe you received word of it from Epona's Chosen herself. Are you questioning the word of Etain?"

"We do not doubt the word of The Chosen," Glenna said quickly.

"Then is it my sister's word you question?"

Brighid was pleased to hear the challenge in Cuchulainn's voice.

"Your sister's veracity is well-proven. She was touched by Epona before her birth," Glenna said, her tone much more conciliatory.

"Then there should be no more questions about the madness remaining within the New Fomorians blood. Question that and you question the honor of my mother and sister."

"And the rest of Clan MacCallan," Brighid added.

Fagan, who had been silently watching the interaction between the other Masters and their unexpected guests, finally spoke into the tense silence that followed Cuchulainn and Brighid's words. "How long do you require our sanctuary, Shaman?"

Ciara answered with a soft smile. "This one night only, Master Fagan."

"One night? Shouldn't the children rest longer than that?"

Ciara's magical smile widened. "We are eager to enter Partholon, Master. It is as if the joyous presence of our foremothers urges us on. We have been waiting more than one hundred years to return to our homeland, and we are impatient to wait even a day longer."

"Then one night of sanctuary it is," Fagan said.

Ciara's smile swept over the four Masters, touching each of them like the warmth of a friendly flame. "The Swordmaster and his warriors have already met the children. Would the rest of you like to meet them, too?"

Glenna was the first to stand. "I would, Shaman. I am curious to see these beings who have so easily won the protection of Cuchulainn MacCallan."

"I would not say that Cuchulainn was easily won, Master Glenna." Ciara's laughter drifted among them as the other Masters of Arms stood and descended the dais to follow the Shaman from the room. "Rather, the children are…well…as diligent and single-minded as worker ants when they focus on something or, in Cuchulainn's case, someone." More of Ciara's laughter brightened the room. "Come see for yourselves."

Brighid and Cuchulainn followed behind the group.

"See why she makes such a good Shaman, and I would not? I would have described them as insatiable irritants, like the biting black flies of the swamplands," Brighid whispered to Cuchulainn.

"Or fleas," Cu said under his breath. "Fleas are small and annoying and relentless."

Brighid smiled at Cuchulainn, noting that though he still had smudges of weariness beneath his eyes, his expression was animated and he walked by her side with the lithe, easy stride of a young warrior.

Ciara's voice drifted back to them. Brighid could hear her explaining how each adult New Fomorian was responsible for a group of children, and acted as parent to that group, whether there were blood ties involved or not. Deep in conversation with the Masters, Ciara emerged from the Great Hall into the inner courtyard. Brighid touched Cuchulainn's arm, holding him back from following the group.

"Let's let them go ahead without us. I think it would do the Masters good to experience the full force of the children's curiosity—without us fracturing their attention."

Cu's lips tilted up. "I had no idea you had such a capacity for cruelty, Huntress."

Brighid grinned. But her reply was drowned out by the sound of a terrifying shriek.

"No!"

As one, Huntress and warrior rushed into the courtyard. The huge open square was filled with winged children and dark-clothed guards. The two groups had mingled as the circle of tents was erected, but all work ceased at the sound of the unholy shriek.

"Not the children! It cannot be the children!"

The hate-filled words were screamed from above, and all heads tilted up, staring at the terrible winged form silhouetted against the barred window of a tower room.

"Fallon." Cuchulainn's voice had become cold and dead again.

"Embracing the enemy! Embracing the enemy! You sleep with the whore Partholon!" The words were filled with madness and loathing.

Several of the children whimpered, which seemed to thaw the frozen warriors.

"Take that creature to an inner room!" Fagan ordered.

A half dozen warriors jumped to obey their Master. As they rushed past Brighid, Cu moved quickly after them. Setting her jaw, the Huntress kept pace with him.

"This might not be a good idea," Brighid told him.

Cuchulainn gave no response, and Brighid had no time to prod him further. It took all of her concentration to navigate the winding hallways without knocking over the occasional man or woman. The Huntress frowned and fell behind Cuchulainn. The halls of Guardian Castle had definitely not been fashioned with centaurs in mind.

She slid to a halt at the entrance to the tower stairwell, snorting in frustration at the narrow, winding stone stairs where Cuchulainn had disappeared. If she went up there she might very well have to back all the way down—a potentially dangerous, as well as embarrassing, proposition. She'd wait.

Thank the Goddess she didn't have to pace past the tower entrance for long. Shuffling feet could be heard, as well as the clank and rattle of chains and deep, muffled voices. Then the laughter began. The sound of it walked up Brighid's spine and set the fine hairs on the nape of her neck stirring. Madness. The laughter was filled with madness. Brighid had heard it before, when Fallon had confronted Elphame at MacCallan Castle. It had shaken Brighid to her core then, and it had no less of an effect on her now.

A dark-clothed warrior appeared. His sword was drawn and he was gripping the end of a chain. Then another warrior stepped into view. He, too, was armed and holding a taut length of heavy chain.

Fallon emerged from the stairwell. Brighid became very still. She took in the changes in Fallon as if categorizing a new species she might soon be required to hunt. The creature was painfully thin, except for her distended abdomen. Her silver-white hair was in wild disarray around a face that belonged in nightmares. Fallon no longer looked more human than Fomorian. Even after she had been bound and battered at MacCallan Castle, she had been beautiful, but now that beauty had been twisted and sharpened and her pale, bloodless face had reverted to the feral, gaunt images drawn in the history texts. Her wings, though bound tightly to her body by circles of ropes, rustled and fought to unfurl. And her scent was all wrong. She was secreting a pungent, musklike smell that was raw with hatred and rage. Automatically, Brighid drew her dagger as the creature's red eyes lighted on her and she bared deadly fangs.

"Another MacCallan whore!" Fallon spat. "I should have known that where Elphame's brother was, there the centaur would follow, just as you did that day when you unjustly captured me." Fallon swiveled her head to look behind her in an insect-like movement. More mad laughter spewed from her mouth as she bared her teeth. "But you were too late, weren't you, warrior? Shall I tell you how sweet your Brenna's blood tasted?"

From the stairwell, Cuchulainn lunged forward, hurling himself at Fallon, but he was restrained by three of the Guardian Warriors as the entire group spilled into the hallway. Brighid quickly moved to Cu, pushing away the dark warriors. In their place she blocked her friend and used the power of her centaur body to keep him from reaching Fallon.

"Cuchulainn! You agreed to let her live until she gave birth to the child!" Keir shouted. He was still standing in the arch of the stairwell, and he, too, had been changed by Fallon's imprisonment. His eyes were sunken deep in his head and his hair was limp and matted. He still looked human, but he had aged markedly. His wings weren't bound as Fallon's were, but he kept them tight against his broad back. He was not chained, either, but a single warrior stood beside him, weapon drawn and ready.

"That's right. Don't forget that I am with child!" Fallon hissed, rubbing her abdomen with fingers that had become clawlike.

"We will not forget it!" Brighid snarled back at her, still carefully restraining Cuchulainn. "We will be here to welcome your child's birth because it will mark the day of your death."

Fallon's sly expression shifted and changed. She staggered like she was suddenly too weak to stand by herself. Keir rushed to her, wrapping his arms around her as she collapsed into him.

"Our child! Don't let them speak of our child, my dearest!" she sobbed.

"Get her away from here," Brighid said, feeling bile rise in her throat at the creature's theatrics.

The warriors dragged the two winged creatures down the hall, leaving Cuchulainn and Brighid to watch until they disappeared into a stairwell that led down to the bowels of the castle.

"I had forgotten her evil and her hatred," Cuchulainn said in a low, tight voice. "How could I have forgotten?"

"Such a creature is unimaginable." Brighid shook her head in disbelief. "No wonder the Guardian Warriors were willing to shoot anything with wings. I cannot blame them after seeing what Fallon has become."

"She is a Fomorian."

"She is the last of her kind. After she gives birth, we execute her and the evil of that race dies with her," Brighid said.

"I wonder..." Cu said, still staring down the hall.

Brighid watched his face. It had hardened again into the impenetrable, emotionless mask she hadn't seen for days. She rested her hand on his shoulder—a gesture of friendship she forced herself to make. He had turned into a cold and dangerous stranger, but she met his dead eyes when he turned to her.

"Don't let her take you back there, Cu. If she does that, she wins. Don't let her hatred win."

"We should return to the children," Cuchulainn said. He turned abruptly, pulling free of the warmth of Brighid's hand, and without another word retraced their path to the courtyard.

CHAPTER
TWENTY-TWO

In a way Fallon's disturbance had been a good thing for the New Fomorians. Not that Brighid liked having the children so visibly upset, but she had yet to meet a warrior who could remain detached and unmoved by the sight of helpless young ones who needed reassurance. And the children obviously needed reassurance.

When Brighid and Cuchulainn had returned to the courtyard it was to find little knots of children with big, frightened eyes clustered around the adult New Fomorians and, Brighid noted with surprise, around the dark-clothed warriors who had escorted them through the pass. The winged children weren't crying or showing any sign of childish hysterics, but there was a terrible, frightened silence about them as they kept close to the nearest adult.

The reaction of the Guardian Warriors—bows at the ready, their bodies in front of the children—relieved Brighid's mind immensely. No matter the doubts the Masters of Guardian Castle, the warriors seemed to accept the children's innocence, so much so that they were already protective.

"It's over. She's been taken to the dungeons," Cuchulainn said as he joined Fagan and the other Masters near the center of the courtyard. He turned on the Swordmaster. "Why was she not being kept there already?"

"She usually is," Fagan explained. "But the interior cells are cold and damp—terribly unhealthy—and she is with child. We allow her fresh air and exercise because of that."

"She deserves neither," Cuchulainn snapped.

"Of course she doesn't. But she is being kept alive for the sake of her child. If we cause her death or the miscarriage of the babe, isn't that negating the reason she was brought to us?"

"She is evil." Cuchulainn's voice was low and dangerous. "And she needs to be destroyed, with or without taking that demon spawn she carries within her."

Brighid moved quickly to Cuchulainn. This time the hand she placed on his shoulder was not the gentle touch of a friend.

"Enough, Cuchulainn!" she said, pulling him around to face her.

He jerked away, eyes narrowed, but before he could snarl a response she made a sharp, cutting gesture.

"Stop and think before you speak. You're scaring them. And they've already been frightened enough."

Cu's gaze blazed as he looked at the children. Those within hearing were staring at him with expressions that ranged from confusion to fear—and some of them, the older ones, were watching him with wide-eyed hurt.

Brighid stepped closer to him and spoke quietly. "What they do not need heaped atop everything else is to be burdened with the uncertainty of wondering if their warrior hero might actually hate them. *They* could very easily be considered the spawn of demons. Perhaps you would like them destroyed, too?"

Cuchulainn's gaze roamed over the children as Brighid spoke. She could tell the instant her words penetrated his wall of anger. His wide shoulders slumped and he wiped an unsteady hand across his brow.

"We have much work to do," Ciara said into the uncomfortable silence. "The children are hungry and tired."

"Yes, of course," Cuchulainn said in an unnatural, clipped voice. "We shouldn't waste time. Gareth! Cullon!" He called two of the oldest boys' names. He hesitated then added, "Kyna! Help me settle the animals while the tents are being erected." The fluttering of wings answered his summons as the three children and the half-grown wolf cub hurried to follow the stern warrior.

Then, as if Cuchulainn's departure was a signal for action, the hybrids, with the help of their Guardian escorts, resumed the job of setting up camp. Brighid smiled reassurance at the children who continued to glance her way, wondering silently when she had become an advocate for the young as well as unwilling healer to the spiritually infirm.

Ciara materialized silently beside the Huntress. "It is only a temporary setback."

"How can you be so sure?"

"The warrior has begun to feel the spark of life again. His body, his heart, even his spirit remember what it is like to be whole and to know the joy of really living. It will not be something from which he can easily turn away."

Brighid met the winged woman's eyes. She wanted to ask Ciara if she meant that Cuchulainn was falling in love with her, and she with him, but the words wouldn't come. They sounded ridiculously girlish and foolish in her mind. How much worse would they sound spoken aloud? And why was it any of her business? It wasn't. Not really. Let Elphame figure out her brother's love life. Brighid had taken on the job of helping him fix his spirit. That was it.

Ciara's smile warmed, and Brighid had the disturbing sensation the winged woman was reading her mind. Again.

"Ciara!" Master Fagan found his way to them through the throng of busy children and warriors. He had a well-rounded, middle-aged woman with him, who he quickly introduced as Kathryn, the castle's head cook, before he disappeared back into the throng of activity. The stout woman stared at the children with fascination and shock.

"We carried provisions with us," Ciara assured her, but the cook waved away the Shaman's implied offer.

"Guests granted sanctuary at Guardian Castle do not feed themselves," Kathryn said gruffly. "We will simply add a few more pots to the hearth." She scratched her double chins. "Exactly how many children are there?"

"Seventy," Brighid said, enjoying the cook's look of horror. "And twenty-two adults, plus Cuchulainn and myself."

"That is quite a solid number. By the Great Goddess! So many small mouths!" She rocked back on her heels, planting her hands on her thick waist.

Just then the Guardian Warriors began lighting the torches that rested snugly within wall sconces fitted around the inner courtyard. The area filled with the homey glow of dancing fire.

Brighid raised a brow at the cook. "It's dusk, and I do not know the territory, but that matters little. I should be able to track and kill something. Although probably not quickly enough to feed them dinner."

"Guardian Castle is amply provisioned!" Kathryn huffed.

"Would you consider Brighid's offer as our gift to you?" Ciara asked.

The cook's curious eyes swiveled from staring at the children to the lovely winged Shaman.

"A gift?"

"Yes, from our Huntress to yours."

Kathryn looked from Ciara to Brighid, obviously trying to decide if she could accept their offer without dishonoring her castle. Brighid caught the cook's eye and nodded encouragement.

"I suppose a gift of venison to cook up for the morning meal wouldn't be inappropriate. But it wouldn't be our

Huntress you would be gifting—it would have to be the castle in general. Our Huntress left us early several days ago."

Surprised, Brighid's mind cast back quickly for a name. "Isn't your Huntress Deirdre of the Ulstan Herd?"

"Yes, and sorely we miss her," Kathryn said. "Though that doesn't mean we are lacking." The cook straightened her spine with obvious pride. "Our warriors are not up to Huntress standards, but they will not let the castle—or its guests—go hungry."

They had been left with no Huntress? How could that be? No, she hadn't glimpsed any centaurs today, but a Huntress was not always at the castle. It certainly wouldn't be unusual for her to be out tracking game, even until well after dusk. Brighid shook her head as if to clear it. "I don't understand. Your Huntress left you? Without calling in another to stand in her stead?"

"Her departure was unexpected. One day she received a centaur runner carrying a message from the Centaur Plains. The next she was gone."

"When is she returning?"

"Soon, we hope. Though she didn't say." Kathryn shrugged off the question. "As I said, she is missed but we are adapting well. My pots have not been empty. Nor will they be."

"It would be my pleasure to gift Guardian Castle with a Huntress's catch," Brighid said formally, forcing down the warring emotions Kathryn's announcement had caused.

The cook hesitated only a moment longer before curtsying to her. "I accept your generous gift, Huntress of the MacCallan Clan."

"I'll get busy," Brighid said.

She nodded to Ciara and the cook, and made a hasty exit. Silently she thanked the Goddess for a reason to escape the controlled chaos of setting up camp. She needed time to think about what the sudden absence of the castle's Huntress could mean.

A Huntress did not shed her responsibilities and leave her

castle or village or herd without first making provisions for her absence. True, she'd left MacCallan Castle hastily, but the game in the under-hunted forests had been pathetically easy to take down. Even a sod-headed warrior could shoot an arrow through a deer that stood staring at him like a tame calf. She wouldn't have left the castle if that hadn't been so—not without first calling in the services of another Huntress.

But a message had come for Deirdre, and the Huntress had abandoned her castle instantly. Why?

Foreboding quivered down Brighid's spine. It smacked of centaur politics and intrigue. What was happening on the Centaur Plains that would require a Huntress to ignore her responsibilities?

The foreboding turned to fingers of ice.

Only the illness or sudden death of a centaur High Shaman could cause such a reaction.

No! Deirdre had probably received a message from her home herd. A family problem…something too personal to share.

Still, it didn't fit. A Huntress should make arrangements for her people, even during times of family emergency. It would have to be something far worse…far more disturbing…

"Huntress? Do you wish to leave the castle?"

From above her the deep voice echoed against the thick gray walls. Brighid stopped and stared blankly around her. Huge iron doors blocked her way. By the Goddess! She hadn't even realized she'd reached the entrance to the castle. Chains held the massive bolt that kept the doors securely locked. She looked up at the sentry and covered her disconcertment with annoyance.

"And why would I be standing here waiting for you to open the doors if I didn't wish to leave? Do you want fresh venison in the morning or not?"

"Of course, Huntress!" the guard called, waving apologetically as he motioned for his men to turn the wheel that would pull loose the bolt.

"I won't be long," Brighid said gruffly. "Keep watch for me."

"Yes, Huntress," he called after her as she trotted through the slim opening. But she hadn't gotten far beyond the thick walls before she pulled to a halt and took a deep breath.

Partholon…

For a moment the turmoil within her stilled. Even though she was tracking through strange territory, her hooves would once again tread the soil of Partholon. Finally, they'd left the Wastelands behind them. Her sharp centaur eyes drank in the land that dusk was washing in muted light.

As was to be expected, the land adjacent to the castle was cleared so no enemy could surprise the Guardian Warriors. But the ground beneath her hooves was noticeably softer than the desolate, rocky earth on the other side of the mountains. The forest of pine mixed with an occasional stubborn oak began almost a dozen horse lengths from the castle walls. Brighid cantered swiftly down the wide road, eager to enter the green forest. It wasn't as thick as the forest surrounding MacCallan Castle, but the trees were strong and straight and green. She drew a deep breath. She could swear the air was clearer here, too.

It felt like home, she realized with a small start. Not her childhood home of the Centaur Plains. It felt like the adult home of her choice…her own path. It felt right.

The Huntress scented the cooling breeze, and when she caught the clean liquid fragrance of water, she veered from the road. Moving quietly in the gloaming, she followed her instinct, and the hunt worked its magic on her frayed nerves. Brighid willingly embraced the familiar balm of her chosen life. Like scales, she shed the stress and worry of the past days.

Brighid slowed, scenting the verdant air again. She changed direction slightly, moving more to her left. She would find the stream there. She knew it. She could Feel it. And deer would be there, drinking in their shy way one last time before bedding down for the night. She could already Feel them. There were several, not far ahead of her.

By the Goddess, it felt good to be alone and hunting for a castle again! She needed the peace and solitude the hunt gave her—even if it was only a temporary reprieve.

The truth was that she missed the simplicity of the life she had carved for herself at MacCallan Castle. Years of dealing with the political manipulations within her family had made her long for a different way of living, and submerging herself within the rigorous Huntress training had taught her that she much preferred the silence of the land to the tumult of people—be they humans, centaurs, or New Fomorians.

Brighid moved liquidly between the pines. She could hear the musical sound of water as it tumbled over rock and ran merrily into Partholon. She grinned. She knew how the water felt. She was damned glad to be going home.

In the dimming light, she caught the crystal reflection of moving water, and she slowed, pulling an arrow from her quiver with a practiced, silent motion.

She'd been right. There were several of them. Brighid counted quickly. Three does. Two obviously pregnant, one thinner and larger than the others—she'd probably only recently given birth to her fawn. Standing some way off from the three females was a single buck. His small rack of mossy antlers said that he was too young to have won breeding rights of his own that spring, but the focused attention with which he watched the does said that he was old enough to be single-mindedly hopeful.

With a movement that was as deadly as it was graceful, Brighid sighted and then loosed a single arrow. The hum of the bow caused the young buck's head to rear up and his body to tense—just in time for the arrow to imbed itself neatly through the base of his neck, emerging through the wall of his chest. The hart staggered back two steps, then, as the does disappeared into the darkening forest, he crumpled to his knees, pitched onto his side and lay still.

Brighid let loose the breath she had been holding and made her way slowly to the fallen buck. She automatically whispered a prayer of thanksgiving to Epona for the kill. Her prayer was filled with respect and appreciation as she focused on the last moments of the young buck's life.

> I call upon You, O great Huntress of the summer sky
> Epona, my patron Goddess and inspiration.
> I thank You for the gift of this blessed hart.
> Speed his journey to You.
> Accept him—care for him—reward him.
> He is my brother and friend.
> Look favorably upon the hunt
> and upon Your people and their Huntress,
> as you have for ages uncounted.
> Let the ancient animal spirits of this land rest
> in the knowledge that their Huntress
> reveres them,
> honors them,
> and thanks them…

Brighid stood over the body of the slain buck and bowed her head.

> …as I revere, honor, and thank You,
> my beloved Goddess.

She stood silently for another moment, and took three deep, ritual cleansing breaths, before she bent to pull her arrow from the buck. As it slid free, the deer's chest exploded outward, showering her in gore. Brighid staggered back, reaching for the short sword she always carried at her waist.

Until she realized what had exploded from the young buck's chest. Circling around her, in a spray of black feathers and blood, was a single, all-too-familiar raven.

CHAPTER
TWENTY-THREE

"Mother!" She wiped blood from her face with the back of her hand and narrowed her eyes at the circling bird. "I don't know what game you are playing, but stop it! Even you know better than to interfere with a Huntress. You don't have to approve of my chosen career, but, by the Goddess, you will respect it!"

The black bird circled lower until, in a flurry of wings, it landed on the gore-encrusted body of the dead deer.

"Leave me alone," Brighid told it.

"Come home, daughter." Her mother's voice filled her mind.

"I am coming home. To MacCallan Castle. My home, Mother. My home!"

"That is not your home, foolish colt!"

"No," Brighid's voice was steel-edged. "I am not a child. Not anymore. I make my own decisions."

"Your herd needs you."

"My herd or your pride?"

"Insolence!"

"Truth!" Brighid countered. She paced two steps forward and glared down at the dark bird. "I will not be manipulated by you ever again. I am sworn Huntress to the Clan MacCallan. That is my chosen path."

"Your chosen path, but not your destiny…"

Her mother's voice faded as, cawing, the bird unfurled its ebony wings and, beating the wind, rose sharply into the night air, disappearing into the waiting darkness.

Grimly Brighid glanced down at the body of the deer. Except for her arrow wound it was clean. No exploded chest. No gore spattering the forest or—she touched her face and felt that it was clean—herself.

"Shaman's tricks and manipulations," she muttered between clenched teeth. Forget it. Focus on the job at hand. Brighid bent to gut the deer, readying it for the short trip back to Guardian Castle. She tried to lose herself in the familiarity of the task, but it was no use. The serenity of the forest had been shattered, as had the peaceful reprieve she had found. All around her she felt watchful, prying eyes.

It was full dark by the time the guards opened the thick doors to Guardian Castle. Eager hands met Brighid and relieved her of the deer while the people praised and thanked her. Brighid accepted their effusive show of gratitude uncomfortably. It made her even more aware of the sad state in which a sister Huntress had left her castle. Her mother should be paying attention to the habits of errant centaurs instead of focusing her time and energy on a wayward daughter.

Brighid frowned. Not that she was actually wayward. By the Goddess, why was her leaving the herd such an all-encompassing issue? Yes, it was Dhianna tradition that the eldest daughter of the High Shaman follow her mother in herd leadership, but that didn't always happen. There had been times when no daughter had been born to the High

Shaman, or when she had died without producing an heir. Why could her mother not see that her succession was to be one of those times?

It wasn't like Brighid didn't have any other siblings. Yes, her sister had shown little promise for leadership. Niam was golden and beautiful and perpetually happy because her mind was as empty as a broodmare. But Brighid's brother… Bregon's fondest desire would be fulfilled if he followed their mother. It wasn't forbidden for males to become High Shaman. The position of centaur High Shaman of Partholon was always held by a male. He was the centaur who mated with Epona's Chosen and led Partholon by The Chosen's side. Bregon would welcome the power that being Dhianna High Shaman would command, and perhaps then he would even believe he had attained that which he had struggled after his entire life—their mother's love.

Her brows drew together. Thinking of her younger brother always gave her a headache. They'd never been close. Or at least they hadn't been since…

"Brighid! Good, you're back in time for dinner."

The Huntress set her shoulders and let Ciara draw her toward the courtyard. *Another damned Shaman…another damned spying, meddling…*

"I've been watching for you. There is a place saved for you at fireside." The Shaman gave her a concerned look. "Is something wrong? You look—"

"No! Nothing's wrong." Brighid made her face relax and smiled at the winged woman. She would not let her mother poison her growing friendship with Ciara. This Shaman was not her mother. She was not spying; she was concerned. "I am hungry, though. I appreciate that you kept watch for me."

They entered the large, square courtyard, and Brighid's wooden smile became an authentic one. The tents were set up in a cheery circle, though not so tightly packed as they'd been in The Wastelands. Here they were already sheltered from the biting night wind by the walls of Guardian Castle. Children sat all around, talking to the Guardian Warriors in animated bursts between bites of steaming stew and hunks of fragrant bread.

"So the warriors didn't disappear with the night," Brighid said.

"Oh, no." Ciara laughed softly. "It seems the great warriors of Guardian Castle have been taken hostage."

"Hostage?"

"Yes. By curiosity."

Brighid snorted. "Or they're being slowly talked to death and have already lost the ability to escape."

Ciara laughed again. "You don't mean that."

"I do. You have no idea how dangerous those little voices can be to the uninitiated."

"You mean one of them could even cause a centaur Huntress to take on a new apprentice?" The Shaman smiled knowingly at Brighid.

"That is exactly what I mean," she said.

Ciara touched the centaur's arm lightly. "Liam is resting comfortably inside the castle infirmary. Nara will stay with him through the night. She assures me he can travel in the morning, but it will have to be on a litter."

"Thank you. I…" Brighid paused and swallowed around the knot that had suddenly risen in her throat. "I find that I have developed an affection for the boy." The Huntress stopped short. Shaking her head, she said, "I don't know what's wrong with me. I announced formally that Liam was my apprentice before going to his parents."

She sighed, thoroughly annoyed with herself. It was bad enough that she had broken with tradition by taking on a male apprentice—one with wings who was decidedly not a centaur. She had also completely disregarded proper protocol. For a child as young as Liam, his parents should be consulted and their approval obtained. Of course, she had been young when she had begun her Huntress training, and her mother had definitely not given her approval—not that that had stopped Brighid, but…

"Rest your mind. Liam's parents are dead. If Lochlan was here you could go to him for his permission, which I feel certain he would give." She shrugged her smooth shoulders, causing her wings to rustle. "I am acting as our leader in his absence, and I gladly give consent that he be apprenticed to you."

"I still should have thought of it. I don't know why—"

"Be a little easier on yourself. You accepted the boy under unusual circumstances—you were facing the warriors who had tried to kill him. I think even Huntress protocol can be loosened in a case such as this. Come," Ciara said. "Eat and rest. Tonight you can sleep soundly knowing that an army of warriors guards our back."

Brighid snorted and muttered, "You mean the same warriors who shot my apprentice?"

"That was then," Ciara said, making a sweeping gesture toward the campsite where Guardian Warriors and winged children intermingled, "before they knew us. You can relax tonight, Huntress. The only malice I sense within these walls comes from one of our own, and she is securely locked within the bowels of this great castle."

Silently Brighid followed Ciara into the circle of friendly firelight. The Shaman led her to a centaur-size empty space. With a sigh that came close to being a moan, Brighid folded her knees and reclined on the thick pelt someone had been thoughtful enough to prepare for her. She accepted a hot bowl of stew and a hunk of fresh bread gratefully from the human woman who offered it. It was simple fare, but tasty and satisfying. *Excellent food for warriors,* she thought. *Warriors and hungry growing children.* As she ate she watched the firelight play across the children's faces. She had never known a group of people—especially people who had overcome so many hardships—who were so filled with joy.

And the Guardian Warriors! Those staid, well-trained soldiers, men and women who lived to protect Partholon, were smiling and answering the barrage of childish questions.

At least for this evening, hope glimmered along with the campfire. Perhaps enough time had passed for the wounds of war to heal. Perhaps Partholon would accept these disinherited children of mothers long dead.

Kyna's familiar laughter drew her gaze. Fand lolled beside her, licking the little girl's fingers, as well as her face, causing the child to dissolve into giggles. Brighid couldn't help smiling in response. What an odd mixture they were—a wolf cub that should never have survived the death of her mother, winged children whose births should have killed their mothers, a centaur who had escaped from her mother…

No—Brighid clamped down on her negative thoughts. She hadn't run away. She'd left and found a new people. She belonged with Clan MacCallan. So much so that the Clan Chieftain had sent Brighid on this quest to bring her beloved brother safely home. Brighid would complete her Chieftain's charge—and she would figure out some way to get Cuchulainn's stubborn soul to rejoin him in this world. She had been making definite progress. She had to remember Cuchulainn had been devastated by his loss and…

…And where was the damned man?

The Huntress's keen eyes searched through those gathered around the campfire. Worry tightened her gut. What if he'd decided he couldn't wait for the birth of Fallon's child before carrying out her death sentence?

The warrior would be stripped of his rank and cast from Clan MacCallan.

Brighid sought Ciara's winged figure, and found her not far from her tent, involved in an animated discussion with two female warriors. Grimly the Huntress made her way to Ciara. She did not wait for a lull in the conversation. Apologizing hastily, she pulled the winged Shaman to the side. "Cuchulainn?"

"I wondered when you would notice his absence," Ciara said.

"Where is he?" Brighid struggled to keep her voice low and

told herself it wouldn't do to cause a scene by picking up the winged woman and shaking her.

"I heard him asking Fagan about the castle's graves. I assume he's there."

"You assume! You mean you don't know?"

"See for yourself." Ciara nodded toward a wide, grassy passageway that intersected with the square courtyard. "Fagan sent him in that direction not long before you returned from your hunt."

Before Brighid could start after him, the Shaman's hand stayed her. "He is not going to kill Fallon. His thoughts are elsewhere."

"Oh, now you can read his thoughts, too?"

"No. I can read neither his thoughts nor yours. But I do know that Cuchulainn's honor prevents him from killing Fallon. You should know it, too."

Scowling, Brighid pulled away and hurried down the torch-lit passage. The damned Shaman was right. Now that she really thought about it, she knew Cuchulainn would never dishonor himself or his Clan by breaking his Chieftain's sentence. Still, Cuchulainn shouldn't be left alone with his dark emotions. Not after the incident with Fallon. He would just withdraw back into that hard shell of his. Ciara knew that!

The passageway spilled into an area that looked like an herb garden. A woman crouched down clipping sprigs of early mint gave the centaur a curious glance.

"I'm looking for the castle's grave sites," Brighid said.

"Follow the wall, Huntress. When the path splits, take the branch to the east. The graves are easily found near the wall, in the raised area that looks down upon the rest of the castle."

Brighid nodded her thanks. Except for the ever-present sentries atop the thick walls, this part of the castle was deserted. Torches from the warrior's walk above shed pale, shadowy light. When the wall turned to the right she felt the earth beneath her rise until it peaked in a rounded corner. The area was raised, and small tors had been mounded all along the wall. There were no effigies or carved tombs. Instead the Guardian Warriors had chosen to lay their dead to rest within man-made burrows.

Curious, Brighid slowed and approached the first hill-like mound respectfully. An arched doorway had been set into the side of it, and its gray stone was beautifully carved with knots in intricate forms.

"Fagan says that in the summer they are covered with blue wildflowers."

Cuchulainn's deep voice startled her. "Could you give me a little warning? What is it with you and Ciara? Do you enjoy scaring the sense out of me?"

"Sorry," Cu said gruffly. "I thought you knew I was here."

"I knew you were here, but not here." She pointed to where he had stepped from the dark shadow beside one of the larger tors. "And just exactly why are you here?"

"Because of them."

Cuchulainn moved aside. The grave's door was decorated with a single carved design that Brighid instantly recognized as the Healer's Knot—that of a huge oak interwoven with knots. Its branches reached high into the sky. Its roots dug deep into the earth. Yet all were woven together, signifying the interconnectedness of all things: earth, sky, life, death. And she suddenly realized what had drawn Cuchulainn here.

"Brenna's family," she said. "I had forgotten that she'd lived at Guardian Castle. I'm ashamed to say that I had even forgotten her parents were dead."

"I never asked her about their deaths, or about the accident that scarred her. I was curious, and I meant to ask, but it didn't seem as important to look back as it did to focus on our future. It seemed we had forever to unearth the past…" Cuchulainn's words faded and he touched the symbol of the tree. "Did you know it was Brenna's accident that caused the death of her parents?"

"No," Brighid said softly, feeling a wave of sadness for her dead friend. "Brenna didn't talk about the accident. I didn't even know her parents were dead until the two of you became formally betrothed and you had to go to Elphame for permission to post the bans because Brenna had no living family."

"I didn't know, either. Just as I didn't know that Brenna's mother had been a Healer, too. Fagan told me the story. Brenna was ten years old, not much older than Kyna. She'd been helping her mother prepare poultices for a particularly nasty cough that was making its rounds through the castle. Fagan said she was a smart, happy child—but that she was always daydreaming and rarely paid close attention to her mother's words." Cuchulainn paused, swallowing hard as he remembered the shy, serious woman the gregarious child had grown into. He had seen only glimpses of the child still within her—especially after she'd accepted his love.

"You don't have to tell me this, Cu," Brighid said. "Not if it's too hard."

His gaze caught hers, hot and intense. "Yes I do! You're the only one here I can tell, and maybe if I say it aloud some of the pain of it will go away."

Brighid nodded, understanding his need to purge himself.

"Brenna mixed up the buckets. She was to put water in one and oil in another. It had been a cold day, and she had been standing too close to the hearth. The end of the shawl she tied around her head caught on fire. Brenna screamed and her mother instinctively reached for the bucket that was supposed to hold water and tossed it on the shawl."

"Oh, Goddess…" Brighid breathed, horrified at the image of a mother setting her own child afire.

"Her mother blamed herself. Brenna was her only child, and her only child was dying horribly because of what she had done. Fagan said she went mad. That same day her mother doused herself in oil and set herself aflame. She left a letter saying she had chosen to join her daughter."

Brighid felt her head shaking back and forth, over and over.

"Her father fell into a deep depression. He didn't eat. He

didn't drink. He didn't sleep. He refused to visit Brenna. One morning not long after his wife's suicide, they found him dead."

"Poor Brenna, that poor child. To have gone through that terrible fire, and then to recover only to find that her parents were dead," Brighid said. She shuddered. "What awful knowledge to have as a child—that your mother…and your father—"

"Died of a shattered soul," Cuchulainn finished for her. He met Brighid's gaze. "That's what happened to him. I know it. It was happening to me."

"Was?"

Cuchulainn ran his fingers lightly over the Healer's symbol on the tomb's door. "Was," he said firmly. "It won't happen to me. I can't let it. Can you imagine the pain it would cause Brenna for me to meet her in the Otherworld, and for her to realize she had caused the deaths of two men she loved?" He shook his head. "No. You're going to have to make the broken part of my soul return."

"I don't think I can actually *make* him do anything, Cu. He's too damned much like you—well, only decidedly happier. You're going to have to invite him to return, and make sure he believes it's a true invitation."

Cuchulainn grunted. "I'll work on it."

"You have until we reach MacCallan Castle. That is when I'll make the Otherworld journey, may the Goddess help us."

"So, a few more days," he said. Then he stroked the Healer's knot one last time. "I'm ready to go back."

Did he mean back to MacCallan Castle, or to life? When he stopped to look at the graves one last time, she stayed respectfully silent. This was something Cuchulainn would have to work out. She could help him find the shattered piece of his soul, but the rest was up to him.

"Blue wildflowers."

Brighid cut her eyes at him, surprised by the laughter in his voice. "Why are blue wildflowers funny?"

His eyes were filled with unshed tears, but he was smiling. "Brenna loved blue wildflowers. She said they reminded her of my eyes. She even collected things that were the exact shade of my eyes long before she met me."

"Really?"

"She kept them on her altar to Epona. There was a feather from a bluebird, and a turquoise stone of the same shade, she even had a pearl that…"

A turquoise stone of the same shade. In the pocket of her vest she felt the weight of the blue stone pressing against her breast.

"What happened to the turquoise stone?" She interrupted him.

"I put it, and the rest of the things from her altar, in the tomb with her."

Slowly the Huntress reached into her pocket and drew out the stone. Placing it flat on her open palm, she held it out to Cuchulainn. As soon as he saw it the warrior's face paled. With shaking fingers, he picked it up and turned it over and over, studying it.

"Where did you get it?" His voice was thick with emotion.

Resigned, Brighid spoke the words aloud that she had barely admitted to herself. "A gold hawk, who I think is my spirit guide, dropped it on me. I—I think it's supposed to be my soul-catching stone," she finished in a rush.

"It came from the spirit realm?" he asked in a shaky voice.

"Is it the same stone you entombed with Brenna's body?"

"Yes, I'm sure of it," he whispered, staring at the stone.

"Then it definitely came from the spirit realm."

"Do you think that means Brenna is somehow here, watching us?"

"I can't answer that, Cu. But I do think it means your spirit is meant to be whole again, and I am meant to help you make that happen."

Cuchulainn handed the stone back to her, and she slipped it into her vest pocket.

"We are a confused pair, Huntress," Cuchulainn said.

"We most certainly are, my friend."

Cuchulainn's grunt of response was somewhere between a laugh and a sob. Brighid quickly changed the subject.

"Ciara doesn't think we need to keep watch over the camp tonight. She says the only malice she senses is from Fallon. She trusts the Guardian Warriors."

"Let us just say that we're tending the campfire then. We are within walls, but it's still a cold part of the world. I would prefer the second watch," Cuchulainn said.

Brighid's eyes met his in perfect understanding. "Then I will take the first. That way our campfire will never be in danger of dying out."

"Agreed."

As they walked back to the campsite Brighid felt the warmth of the turquoise stone near her heart. Surprisingly it comforted her.

CHAPTER
TWENTY-FOUR

Brighid didn't want to dream. Not in Guardian Castle, home to too much ugly history. As she made herself comfortable within the pelts that were still warm from Cuchulainn's body...still smelled of him...the Huntress took firm rein of her mind.

Not tonight, she ordered herself. She took three cleansing breaths and focused. *Not tonight!* She powered the thought with every bit of innate Shaman instinct in her blood and sent it hurtling out into the Otherworld—aimed directly at Cuchulainn's shattered soul. Tomorrow, under the open skies of Partholon she would be better prepared to deal with the charismatic missing part of Cu. Tonight the story of Brenna's tragic life was too fresh, and the castle surrounding her too filled with ghosts.

She fell asleep hoping the happiness Brenna had found at the end of her life had made up for the pain and tragedy of her youth.

* * *

At first Brighid didn't realize she was dreaming. She was just happy to be back at MacCallan Castle. Home! And everything was heartbreakingly real. It was early, not yet dawn, so the Main Courtyard was deserted. The statue of the famous MacCallan ancestor, Rhiannon, poured musical water into a graceful marble fountain surrounded by benches and potted ferns. The ceiling—newly restored by MacCallan hands—had been left partially open to the sky so that predawn light mixed harmoniously with the wall sconces creating a soft, rose-colored glow.

The scene was familiar and dear. Normally Brighid woke before most of the castle, broke her fast, and hunted early. She smiled at the beauty of the mighty marble columns of the courtyard, marveling anew at the delicate knot work that meshed the plunging MacCallan mare with animals of the surrounding forest. From habit, she made her way through the spacious heart of the castle to the Main Hall.

The enticing fragrance of freshly baked bread wafted from the hall that served as both dining room and general meeting chamber. The room was usually empty this early—unlike the kitchen. But Brighid was used to breaking her fast alone. She enjoyed the solitude and the chance to order her thoughts for the hunt that day. Through the wall of etched beveled glass between the Great Hall and the Main Courtyard, Brighid was surprised to glimpse someone already seated for breakfast. Probably one of the cooks taking a much needed break. No matter, she liked the cook staff and wouldn't mind the company.

The Huntress entered the chamber and stumbled to a shocked halt. Brenna sat at what had been her usual place at the Chieftain's smooth pine table. Brighid had the sudden urge to blink and rub her eyes, but there was no mistaking the Healer. Her thick dark hair hung over her right shoulder, partially obscuring the latticework of deep scars that covered the right side of her body.

"I am dreaming," was what blurted from Brighid's numbed lips.

"You are, my friend."

Brenna looked up at the centaur and smiled, and Brighid felt her heart squeeze. That dear, familiar lopsided smile! Tears filled the Huntress's eyes, spilling over and running down her cheeks.

"Oh, Brighid, no! Please don't do that."

Brighid wiped quickly at her cheeks. "I'm sorry, Brenna. I didn't expect...I didn't even realize that I was dreaming until now. And I've missed you."

"I've missed you, too, Brighid."

The Huntress wiped at her face again and drew a deep breath before approaching the spirit of the little Healer. Brenna looked so much the same! So real! Brighid mentally shook herself. Brenna was real—she was just spirit instead of body.

"No more tears?" Brenna said.

"No more tears."

"Good. Our time is too short to waste." Brenna sighed and let her gaze roam wistfully around the Great Hall. "It turned out so beautiful—just as I pictured it would when Elphame was describing it to us."

"You haven't—" Brighid hesitated, unsure how to frame the question "—been here since..." She trailed off awkwardly.

"You mean have I been haunting MacCallan Castle?" Brenna laughed, a shy, sweet sound. "No. Tonight is a special night. I felt compelled to come here...and to talk with you..." Her eyes took on a faraway look, as if she could see something beautiful through the stone walls. Then Brenna laughed again, and her eyes turned back to her friend. "MacCallan Castle already has one ghost. It doesn't need another."

"I didn't know there was a limit," Brighid said.

"There isn't. But it wouldn't be good for me, or for Clan Mac-Callan, if I lingered here. It's important for all of us to move on."

"You mean Cuchulainn."

"Yes, I mean Cuchulainn." When Brenna spoke his name her voice softened to a verbal caress. "But not just him. El, you, me—we all have our destinies. I met mine, and it would not be just if I stood in the way of the rest of you meeting yours."

Brenna's words chilled Brighid.

"Is there something I should know, Brenna?"

"I didn't come to your dreams as a harbinger of doom. You are fated to live a long life, my Huntress friend. I just want to make sure it is a long and happy one."

Brighid blinked in surprise.

Brenna smiled. "You didn't expect that, did you?"

"I thought you were here because of Cuchulainn."

"I am, in a way. What I want you to know will help both of you."

"What is it, Brenna?"

"The turquoise stone was my gift to you. Use it to heal Cu."

"I will, Brenna. He's already better. He visited your parents' grave today after Master Fagan told him what had happened to your family. He vowed that he would not—" Brighid broke off, horrified by what she had almost blurted. Where was her mind? Would she never get control of her habitually too-honest tongue!

The Healer's spirit form reached out and laid a cool, almost weightless hand on Brighid's arm. "You can say it, my friend. Death has healed that old wound. The past cannot cause me pain."

"Cu vowed that he would recover so that you would not be responsible for the death of another man you love," Brighid said softly.

"Good. If learning of my past did that for him I only wish that he had known it earlier. Perhaps he could have begun healing sooner."

She straightened her shoulders and pushed back her hair. Brighid could only stare. The terrible scars that had given the right side of her face a melted appearance had faded, leaving her skin whole and astonishingly beautiful.

"Oh." Brenna lifted her hand to her smooth cheek. "They're gone. It's odd. I don't take a physical form often, and when I do sometimes the scars are there, sometimes they are not. I find that it matters little."

"That's how Danann carved your image, without scars," Brighid said. "He said he didn't even realize he was doing it, he just did as his memory directed him."

Brenna's smile was bright. "I always thought that old centaur was more spirit than body." Then the little Healer's eyes took on a faraway look and her body wavered and became less substantial.

"Brenna?"

The spirit blinked and pulled her attention back to the Huntress. "I don't have much more time. The most important thing I came to tell you is that I want your oath that you will keep an open mind."

"About what?"

"About everything that may seem impossible."

"Brenna, can't you be a little more specific?"

"I can, but you're not ready for that. Yet. And anyway, it's something you're going to have to discover on your own. I can't help you any more than I already have. So, just give me your oath, please."

Brighid frowned. "All right. You have my oath."

Brenna looked relieved. "Thank you, Brighid."

"Do you want me to tell Cuchulainn anything for you?" Brighid said quickly, concerned that, like a beautiful sketch slowly being erased, her friend's form was fading.

"You can tell him about this visit, but not now. It's not the right time." Brenna's voice was taking on the breezy quality of an echo.

"Wait! When will it be the right time?"

"You'll know. Freely, and without any hesitation, I leave him to you, my friend. Remember that…freely… Sleep now, Brighid, and may your future be richly blessed…" The spirit faded into nothingness.

Brighid slept deeply. For the rest of the night she dreamed only of the fresh scent of pine trees on an early morning hunt.

* * *

The children had eaten a morning meal of venison sandwiches and hunks of goat cheese and, with the help of the
Guardian Warriors, had broken camp before the sun had seen
fit to peek above the horizon. Brighid couldn't blame them.
She was in a hurry to be on her way, too. Not that Guardian
Castle hadn't been hospitable, but she was more than ready
to exchange the thick gray walls for the ancient forest that covered the northeastern part of Partholon. The Huntress needed
to think through her dream, and ponder the message from her
unexpected visitor.

The New Fomorians were lined up like little warriors behind Cuchulainn and Brighid, waiting semipatiently as they
finished the business of thanking their hosts.

"We do so appreciate the loan of the cart," Ciara was saying to the four Masters, who shrugged off her thanks.

*As well they should. It was their fault the boy needs to be car-
ried in it,* Brighid thought, glancing over at Liam who reclined
comfortably on pelts and down-filled pillows—all gifts from
the Guardian Warrior who had wounded him. The boy's face
was pale, but he was wide-awake, and when he caught Brighid
looking his way he grinned cheekily at her. She smiled back
at him but mouthed the word, *rest.* Liam nodded, but the
happy smile stayed on his face and his wide, curious eyes took
in everything around them. As they had anticipated, the boy
had been completely annoyed that he had missed what he
called "all the fun" with the Guardian Warriors, and was only
slightly mollified by the news that Brighid had formally proclaimed him her apprentice.

Brighid snorted softly to herself. The young imp had said
he'd known all along he was supposed to be a Huntress; he
had just been waiting for Brighid to admit it. By the Goddess,
what was she going to do with the boy!

"Your apprentice looks well this morning," Cu said, following her gaze and nodding in response to Liam's grin and wave.

"Don't remind me," Brighid grumbled.

"Don't remind you that he looks well?" Cuchulainn raised his brows.

"No, don't remind me that he's my apprentice. The boy thinks he's a centaur Huntress."

Cuchulainn tilted his head to the side, and scratched his chin with an exaggerated, considering gesture. "Would that make him gender or species confused?"

"Both," Brighid grumped.

Cuchulainn laughed, a full, heartfelt, joyous sound. If taking on such an unusual apprentice had prompted Cu's open, infectious laughter to return, Brighid thought it might very well be worth it.

"The Masters would like to join us for our morning blessing ceremony," Ciara said. Her beautiful dark eyes sparkled as she smiled sweetly up at the laughing Cuchulainn.

"Excellent." Cu returned the winged woman's smile. "I think it would do them good to witness one of your rituals to Epona."

Brighid watched their friendly exchange with a quiver of irritation. Of course Ciara would materialize the instant Cu laughed. The two of them obviously had some kind of connection. But watching them beam foolishly back and forth at each other was damned annoying. It also made Brighid feel more than a little invisible.

"I would like to offer our thanks to the Goddess outside of the walls of Guardian Castle—on the soil of Partholon," Ciara said.

"Excellent idea. You lead, and we will be close behind."

Ciara smiled again, this time at both of them, before hurrying back to bring the Masters with her to the front of the castle. Cuchulainn clucked to his gelding and kneed him forward. Brighid moved with him.

"You don't think a ceremony outside the castle walls is a good idea?" Cu asked.

Brighid slanted a quick, sideways look at him. "It's fine."

"Then what's wrong?"

"Nothing."

"I wish you wouldn't do that," he said quietly.

"Do what?"

"Shut down like that. You've chastised me for it often enough, but now you're doing the same thing."

This time she let his gaze catch hers. His turquoise eyes were warm and concerned. "Sorry," she mumbled.

"Not a problem. That's why we make such a good team. Neither of us is perfect."

He squeezed her shoulder, and suddenly something besides irritation quivered through her. It felt hot and slick, and it lodged low in her gut, making her draw in a quick, surprised breath.

"Now, want to tell me what's wrong?"

"I was thinking about the trip," she lied. "It's maddening that it's going to take us at least four or five more days, when if we had wagons and horses we could get there in half that time."

"Well, we discussed it with Fagan. They had a couple wagons they could spare, but they aren't a typical castle. Partholon gives them provisions in payment for their vigilance. The castle doesn't trade goods, so they don't keep wagons for hauling." He shrugged. "You know they offered to send word to Laragon Castle and ask them to bring enough wagons for us."

She shook her head, wishing she could rattle back into place whatever part of her mind had suddenly come loose. "By the time the wagons got here we would be halfway to Mac-Callan Castle," she answered him absently.

"So we travel as we are. Keep your chin up, Brighid. You might be surprised at how quickly the next days pass. And I don't mind admitting that I am damned glad we're finished with the Wastelands—" he lowered his voice "—and Guardian Castle. I find it no less oppressive than it was during my school days, and the ghosts of the past feel too…" He hesitated, searching for the right word.

"Alive?"

"Yes, alive," he said.

She nodded and mumbled a vague affirmative. Goddess

knows she'd been too immersed in ghostly visits of her own lately.

"This should be interesting." Abruptly Cu changed the subject, pointing his chin in the direction of Ciara and the four Masters. "She was pretty subdued last night when she said the evening prayer and lit the campfire. I don't expect such a tame performance for the first time she enters Partholon."

"Uh-huh," Brighid said, wondering just how much Cuchulainn had come to care for the Shaman. Could he be falling in love with her, or was he just infatuated with her exotic allure? Was accepting their relationship what Brenna had meant last night when she had made Brighid swear an oath to keep an open mind about the future? No…it didn't fit. Brenna had said to keep an open mind regarding the *impossible*. Once the warrior was healed, Cuchulainn falling in love with Ciara didn't seem impossible at all. Actually it was logical. His sister had been handfasted with the leader of Ciara's people. The New Fomorians were going to settle at MacCallan Castle, which is where Cuchulainn had chosen to live, too. It would make for a cozy little arrangement.

Then why did the thought of it make Brighid feel so damn annoyed? It was almost as if she was jealous of the Shaman. Ridiculous. Completely, utterly, ridiculous. Why should she feel jealous? He was her friend. It wasn't like he was a centaur male and she and Ciara were vying for his affection.

The sudden inhalation of awe behind her broke into Brighid's tumbling thoughts. The great iron gates of Guardian Castle had been pulled completely open, and Partholon stretched before them, green and magical in the soft light of the blush-colored morning sky.

Ciara rushed down the wide, well-trodden road until she came to the tree line. She stood very still then walked purposefully to the east until she stood before a lone oak whose mighty branches were covered with the slick green of spring leaves. She sank to her knees, pressing her palms against the earth and bowing her head. The children didn't wait for her cue. With a glad cry, they surged forward forming a familiar circle around their kneeling Shaman. Brighid and Cuchulainn moved to join the four Masters, who stood a little way apart from the circle. With a slight movement, Cu motioned back to the castle. Brighid glanced over her shoulder. The wide walls were filled with dark warriors, all silently watching. Then Ciara began to speak and all eyes were riveted to her winged form.

Magnificent, loving Goddess
today Your people have been richly blessed.

The instant Ciara said the word *Goddess* the air around her shimmered. Not with the tame, earthy light Elphame evoked, or even the golden, flame-kissed glow of Ciara's other blessing ceremonies. This morning the winged Shaman blazed with a vibrant, powerful light that crackled and pulsed like fire. As she continued to speak, the brilliance of the light grew, and Ciara brought her hands out, away from her sides, palms open, rapturously embracing the living presence of her Goddess.

Mother of animals, She who listens to our pleas
Epona, Great Goddess, I call to Thee.
Guardian of horses strong and free,
Epona, Great Goddess, I worship Thee.
Thine are the blessings of liberty and peace,
Thine are the gifts of happiness and grace,
And whenever I ask a blessing of Thee,
its burdens I do fully embrace.

Unexpectedly Brighid felt a chill run over her skin that contrasted sharply with the flamelike warmth radiating from Ciara. *The Goddess's gifts all come with a cost...*whispered the memory of her mother. She knew that—she did not take

Epona's gifts for granted. *Remember,* she told herself, thinking of how power had corrupted and changed her mother, *remember that with great blessings come great responsibility.*

Epona, Mother Goddess, today we celebrate with Thee,
through Thy power we return to Partholon, finally free.
For long, cold years You guarded us as if we were a rich treasure,
through our exile You kept alive within us a joy beyond measure.

Ciara stood and the New Fomorians rose with her. They did not obstruct the sight of the shining winged Shaman, if anything they were like a frame that accentuated the beauty of a master's piece. Ciara's wings unfurled and her graceful hands and delicately rounded arms lifted to trace mythical patterns in the magic that licked like tendrils of flame through the air surrounding her.

Epona was present. The power of the Goddess was thick and tangible and unforgettable. No one who witnessed the New Fomorians' entry into Partholon would ever say otherwise. Brighid tore her eyes from Ciara to look at Cuchulainn. He stared unblinking at the Shaman. The Huntress looked from him to the four Masters. They, too, were staring at the winged woman. The Horsemaster, Glenna, had one hand pressed against her mouth, as if to hold back a startled cry. The pessimistic Master of Combat, Bain, had fallen to his knees. Tears streamed unheeded from his eyes. Brighid glanced over her shoulder at the wall of the castle. Many of the warriors were kneeling and reverently bowing their heads.

Shining Goddess, Thy promise has been fulfilled.
Never again shall Your children roam outcast.
With Thy loving hand a new home we shall build.
And by Thy flame of love our frozen years are past.

Ciara flung her arms up over her head and, as if she had called it into the sky, the sun burst over the eastern tree line, blazing with a fierce, joyful glory that spoke eloquently of Epona's presence among them.

"Hail Epona!" Ciara cried.

"Hail Epona!" The New Fomorians echoed their Shaman.

"Hail Epona!" Brighid joined Cuchulainn and the warriors of Guardian Castle in the joyous shout.

And then, miraculously, a voice was heard above theirs as, over the rise in the wide road poured wagon after wagon led by a stunning redheaded woman on a prancing silver mare. The same fire crackled in the air around the pair, except it was smoother. No less powerful, it was more focused and controlled, with an aura of maturity and experience.

"Hail Epona!" the woman cried again, her voice magically magnified by the Goddess.

With a loud cry of gladness, Ciara ran to the woman and knelt before her. The woman slid gracefully from the mare and without hesitation, lifted the Shaman into her arms.

Brighid could hear the murmurs of the warriors and the Masters, murmurs that turned into shouts of welcome as they recognized their new visitor. Cuchulainn clucked to his big gelding. "Will you join me in greeting my mother?" he asked Brighid.

Brighid gave him a surprised look, and he shrugged his shoulders.

"Don't you know her? I assumed she visited MacCallan Castle shortly after I left."

"She did, and, yes I have had the honor of meeting your mother," Brighid said.

"Well, then come with me," he said, kneeing his gelding forward.

The Huntress jogged at his side. "I thought you might like to present Ciara to your mother alone."

The warrior's brows drew together. "Why would you think that? This isn't exactly a private setting." He waved a hand at the group of children descending upon his mother, Epona's Beloved Incarnate Goddess, and the silver Chosen mare.

Feeling more than foolish, Brighid clamped her lips together. She sounded like a petulant schoolgirl.

"Anyway, I'll need your help rescuing her," Cu said.

Brighid looked from the shining Beloved of Epona to the long line of wagons that stretched down the road behind her.

"How did she know we were here and that we needed the wagons? There was no way a message could have arrived at Epona's Temple in the space of one night," Brighid said.

"There's one thing you should learn about my mother—between her, that mare and their Goddess, she literally knows everything. Or at least, as she has often told me, she knows everything that is important."

As they pushed their way through the group of laughing, talking, singing children, Brighid sent silent and semiblasphemous thanks to Epona that her own mother didn't know everything—whether it was important or not.

CHAPTER
TWENTY-FIVE

"I've always thought that being in the company of children makes time seem to pass more quickly."

Brighid snorted with even more than her customary sarcasm, causing Etain to toss back her head of glorious hair and laugh with full-throated exuberance. Brighid tried to maintain a sober expression, but quickly gave it up. It was impossible not to laugh with Etain.

"I suppose they keep us busy, because there never seems to be enough time for…for…*anything* when they're around, so they do appear to make time pass more quickly," Brighid conceded.

"There. I knew I'd get you to admit that the past two days have flown by."

It was true. If they kept up their brisk pace, by dusk they would reach MacCallan Castle.

Now, the High Priestess of Partholon grinned, looking more

like a fresh-faced young bride than a woman who had seen the passing of sixty springs. The Beloved of Epona laughed again. "Flown by! Those are well-chosen words. Would it not be a wonderful thing to experience? Whenever I see one of the children running by with that amazing, gliding gait of theirs I wish I could grow wings and join her."

Brighid could only stare at Etain in shock. Was it blasphemy to imagine Epona's Beloved with Fomorian wings?

"Oh, I know. Your look reminds me far too much of my husband. You must be another centaur who can not abide heights."

"Heights and equine limbs are not compatible."

Etain's silver mare blew heavily through her nose, as if she had been listening and was agreeing with the centaur. Actually the mare probably *was* listening—and understanding— Brighid reminded herself. She was the Chosen equine incarnation of Epona, and much, much more than an ordinary horse.

Etain stroked the mare's slick neck fondly. "No, I won't be taking you near any cliffs, my beauty. I do remember how you rebelled the last time." The High Priestess glanced at Brighid and lowered her voice to an exaggerated, conspiratory level. "You might say that the Chosen is deathly afraid of heights. You might say it, but don't say it too loudly. She is usually utterly fearless."

Brighid smiled back at the beautiful priestess. "I'll consider it our secret."

"Then you, my fine Huntress, will have the eternal thanks of Epona!" Etain's tone was teasing and light, but by simply mentioning her Goddess's name, the air around her filled with the sweet scent of lavender and violet-winged butterflies appeared, circled the priestess, and then disappeared into the dense forest.

Brighid just smiled and watched, taking it all in. Etain was simply incredible. And now she knew where Cuchulainn, or at least the part of his spirit that was nothing but joy, had inherited such a strong sense of happiness. Etain's passion for life was infectious. Traveling with Epona's Chosen for the past two days had been a much more pleasurable experience than Brighid had anticipated when the High Priestess of Partholon had arrived so unexpectedly at the gate of Guardian Castle with her fleet of wagons, handmaidens, and palace warriors who had temporarily been relegated to the job of wagon drivers.

The truth was, Brighid had been rather nervous and uncomfortable around Etain at first. She hadn't had the opportunity to get to know Epona's Chosen during Etain's short visit to MacCallan Castle. Etain had spent most of her time closeted with her daughter and Elphame's new mate, Lochlan. Brighid had been busy hunting for the suddenly increased number of mouths to feed. Not that her impression of Partholon's High Priestess had been negative—in fact it had been just the opposite. Brighid had been awed by the presence of the Beloved of Epona, and impressed by the obvious love she showed for Elphame. Brighid knew what it was like to have a powerful mother, and she had been surprised by the tenderness Etain had shown her daughter and Lochlan. Several mornings Brighid had even seen Etain praying alone at Brenna's tomb, in obvious mourning for her son's lost love.

And then there was the devotion Etain showed Cuchulainn. Brighid had watched closely when Cu had first approached his mother, waiting for Etain's reaction to the physical changes that grief had caused in her son. Brighid's mother would have chastised her, probably publicly, for allowing herself to appear less than perfect. Etain had simply opened her arms and embraced him, then laughed and wiped away what she called tears of joy at seeing her beloved son again.

Etain had to notice the difference in Cuchulainn. It didn't matter that Cu was obviously trying to put on a happy facade. The warrior had probably smiled and talked more in the past two days than he had in the past two moon cycles.

He'd made a good effort to cover his pain, but there was no doubt that the High Priestess and Beloved of Epona was completely aware that her son's soul was shattered and that he had come precariously close to giving up on life. Brighid kept waiting for Etain to lecture him, or to purposefully let slip little comments about how he should be doing this…or thinking that…or to show that she was disappointed in him for being broken and battered by something that was over and done with. But it didn't happen. Etain loved her son, completely and without judgment or conditions.

How different would Brighid's life have been if her own mother had known how to love her children, as well as be High Shaman of the Dhianna Herd?

"That's a serious look, even for you, Huntress," Etain said.

Brighid made herself smile at the woman she had come to like as well as respect. "I was just thinking about—" She hesitated, surprised at the sudden desire to tell Etain the truth.

"About?" Epona's Beloved prompted.

Brighid noticed that even the silver mare had pricked her delicate ears as if she, too, was waiting for Brighid to finish her sentence.

"I was just thinking about my childhood," Brighid said softly. "It's hard for me to talk about."

Etain's green eyes were wise and kind. Instead of questioning her further she simply nodded and continued to ride easily at the Huntress's side. Slowly, Brighid relaxed again. Their surroundings helped ease the tension that thinking of her mother had automatically triggered. She and Etain were at the head of the long line of wagons, which were filled with laughing, singing New Fomorians. For the moment they were alone. Cuchulainn had ridden back to check one of the wagons reputed to have a loose wheel, and Ciara was…

Goddess only knew where Ciara was. All of the New Fomorians were excited by the beauty of Partholon and the thick wildness of its eastern forest, but since Ciara had stepped into the land she had been utterly enamored. It was as if she had been deprived of water for days and Partholon was her cool stream of salvation. Etain had said the winged Shaman was a spiritual conduit for her people, so it was only natural that the entry to Partholon had affected her more dramatically than it had the others. Brighid noticed that the High Priestess took special care with Ciara, and that Etain encouraged the Shaman's exploration of her new land.

And the morning and evening rituals of blessing! Brighid felt a surge of joy just thinking about them. Etain and Ciara had performed them together. Once again, the Beloved of Epona had shown herself to be a kind and gracious High Priestess. She could have very easily excluded the winged Shaman, or patronized her and made her abilities look immature or inconsequential. Instead Etain had shared the ritualistic words of some of Partholon's most ancient blessings, weaving her calm, experienced voice with that of the young Shaman's. She had even praised Ciara excessively and publicly when she used her affinity with the spirits of fire to light the campfire.

Etain's benevolence and love for her people, be they humans, centaurs or even hybrid Fomorians, was a deep commitment between herself and her Goddess. She truly was the Incarnation of Epona's love.

Brighid was as drawn to Etain as she was amazed by her, but the Huntress said little. She just observed and made mental notes. She watched and waited for Cuchulainn to show his mother that he was beginning to have special feelings for Ciara. Brighid expected Etain to be thrilled to learn of her son's affections. But nothing of the sort happened. Cuchulainn spent very little time with Ciara. He was always kind to her, but he definitely didn't make a point to spend any extra time alone with her and, as far as Brighid could tell, he had spoken to his mother about her only in the polite terms he would use when discussing any Shaman.

Of course, none of them had time for much privacy or many prolonged personal discussions. Brighid hadn't been exaggerating when she'd said the children left no time for anything except their care. While they were in the Wastelands, so much of their lives had been spent on survival that the youngsters hadn't had the freedom to get into much mischief. The trip through the Partholonian forest was a different story indeed. Brighid was just glad they had been able to take small, rarely used roads and skirt the larger towns and most of the villages. The Huntress internally shuddered when she thought about the horde of exuberant, questioning, ceaselessly moving winged children descending upon sleepy, unsuspecting Partholon villages. The children didn't understand that not everyone was as pleased to meet them as they were to meet Partholon.

"I don't think I've told you this, but you remind me very much of Elphame," Etain said, breaking the easy silence that had fallen between them.

Completely surprised, Brighid stared at her, wide-eyed.

"Oh, don't look so shocked. The two of you have become close friends, haven't you?"

"Yes, but…" Brighid gulped nervously. "Yes, Elphame and I have become close friends."

"You know you and Brenna were the first friends she had outside our family."

Brighid hesitated, thinking before she blurted something inappropriate. "I don't think El ever told us—that is Brenna and me—in those words, but we knew it without her saying anything." The Huntress drew a deep breath and met the priestess's eyes. "I don't think many people wanted to get too close to a living Goddess."

"That's what El said. More times than I care to count. But you were willing to get close to her. Why?"

"She accepted me as I am," Brighid said without hesitation. "That's why Brenna became friends with her so quickly, too. It wasn't that El didn't see Brenna's scars—it was impossible not to. Just like it was impossible not to see that joining Clan MacCallan was an escape for me. It's not that the scars and the radical centaur family didn't matter to your daughter, it's just that she accepted them. Easily. Without conditions."

"And in return you accepted her—Elphame—not the Goddess the rest of the world sees."

"Oh, I saw the Goddess. I still do. So did Brenna. It's just that we mostly saw *her*. And Elphame is a mixture of both—woman and Goddess, centaur and human. And now she's friend as well as Chieftain." Brighid sighed, frustrated by the inadequate words. "Does that make sense? When I say it, it sounds…I don't know…not enough."

"I know exactly what you mean, child," Etain said. "Which is why I said that you remind me of her. You and Elphame view the world the same. You're both strong, logical females who don't tolerate nonsense and don't want to waste time on pretenses and excuses. I like you, Huntress. I like that you are friends with my daughter. And I believe that very shortly I will owe you a debt of gratitude."

"I am honored, my Lady," Brighid said roughly around the knot of emotion that had lodged in the back of her throat. "But you owe me no debt. I hold no voucher for my friendship with your daughter."

"The debt is not for Elphame. It is for Cuchulainn."

"Cuchulainn? But I haven't really done anything—" Etain's candid turquoise eyes met Brighid's and the Huntress clamped her lips together, ending her protestation. "Of course you know that his soul has been shattered."

"I've known since the day it happened."

"The day Brenna died," Brighid said.

Etain nodded. "It's been maddeningly frustrating for me—knowing of my son's pain and not being able to use my powers to fix it…to make it better for him."

Brighid opened her mouth to question Etain, but couldn't make the words come. How does one question the Beloved of Epona?

"Brighid, I am Partholon's High Priestess, and the Chosen Incarnate of Epona, but I am also a mother and a woman who laughs and cries and loves like any other woman. There is no need for you to be afraid to ask me questions."

Brighid looked at the beautiful, regal woman who rode beside her and was, again, amazed at Etain's honesty and accessibility. No wonder the people of Partholon were so wholly devoted to her. Brighid drew in a deep breath before she spoke.

"Why can't you fix Cu? Why can't you retrieve his shattered soul?" she asked quietly.

Etain sighed. "First of all, I am not a Shaman. Yes, I can travel to the Otherworld—I do so regularly, but I do so to be in the presence of Epona and to do the Goddess's business. I rarely interact with the spirits that inhabit the different realms. Not that I haven't ached to search for Cu's shattered soul. That was my initial reaction when I realized what had happened to him." The priestess's smile was small and quirked a little to the side. "Epona had a very different view of what I should do." She looked at Brighid and moved her shoulders that were draped in luxurious golden fabric. "I have a tendency to want to rescue my children, even though they are no longer children. My logic tells me this is not good for them. My heart tells me something else entirely. I am grateful that my Goddess stays near to my heart, even when she forces me to keep to my logic."

Brighid frowned. "So Epona kept you from fixing Cu?"

"At first. Then I realized that this was not a pain from which a mother could protect her child. He needed to grieve for his lost love, even if his grief was tearing his soul asunder. Grief is part of the healing process. And I believe you've witnessed the alternative for yourself."

Brighid blinked in surprise. "You mean the shattered part of Cu's soul."

"Yes. He's come to you in your dreams, hasn't he?"

Brighid snorted. "Cu said you know everything."

Etain laughed. "Just everything important."

"Yes," she admitted, "he's come to my dreams."

"And what did you learn about him except that he is a terrible rogue?" Etain's eyes sparkled at the Huntress.

"That he's singled-minded about his pleasure and…"

"…And?"

"And endearing and charismatic and boyish," she muttered.

Etain smiled. "*That* he certainly is. But what did you learn about him that was not so endearing?"

"He's completely in denial. He can't, or won't, face any emotional difficulty. The instant I mention Brenna or try to talk to him about what's really happening in the world—versus the happy pretend place he's retreated to—he disappears."

"Exactly. If I had stepped in and scooped Cuchulainn up after Brenna's death, and had done what my heart was begging me to do—cushion him from pain and surround him in the power I have to duplicate Epona's love—he would not have grieved and he would be eternally as the shattered part of his soul is now, unable to face reality. He would have become a weak, emotionally bereft man who spent a sad life running from his problems. He had to grieve."

"I understand that. But he has grieved. He's even begun to work through his pain."

"Which is why your soul retrieval will be successful," Etain said, quickly shaking her head when Brighid began to protest. "This is not the job for a mother. Nor is it a job for Ciara. He needs you to do this for him, Brighid. But more than that, Epona has decreed that it is part of your destiny."

Brighid felt jolted by the Goddess Incarnate's words. "Epona has spoken of me?" She didn't realize she'd said her thought aloud until Etain answered her.

"Of course. Why would that surprise you? Epona's presence is very strong in your family."

"But my family…" Brighid floundered, not knowing what to say about the Dhianna Herd's radical beliefs that centaurs and humans should not interact.

"Brighid, you do not need to feel such guilt. Epona has

given her people free will—all of her people. Even those who have been richly blessed by her. Along with the gift of free will comes the possibility of mistakes. Rest assured that the Goddess knows your heart is clear of hatred. Epona does not hold a daughter responsible for her mother's sins."

Brighid tried to speak, but could not. The relief that poured through her was almost too much to bear. Epona did not blame her. She had not been branded or rejected by the Goddess.

Then Etain touched Brighid's arm, and into the tumult of Brighid's emotions flowed a soothing balm of kindness and love. The Huntress drew a long, shuddering breath.

"Thank you," she told Etain, speaking to the woman and the Goddess she represented.

"Don't let it haunt you, child." With Etain's words there came a swirling of the air around her, and suddenly within Brighid's mind she heard the echo of a thought, so filled with power and warmth that it filled her eyes with tears,

Know that I am with you, precious one.

Brighid gasped. Then the swirling air and the whispering voice were gone.

"I—I think Epona…" Brighid stuttered, "She—she…"

"Her touch is breathingtaking, isn't it?" Etain asked kindly, as if she hadn't been feeling the Goddess's presence for most of her life.

Brighid blinked and swiped the back of her hand across her wet cheeks. "Yes," she whispered. "Yes it is."

"Here, child." Etain turned and dug through one of the butter-colored saddlebags strapped behind her and pulled out two silk handkerchiefs. She handed one to the Huntress and kept the other so that she could delicately dab at her own eyes. "I'm always prepared for a good cry. It cleanses the soul."

Brighid wiped her face, still in awe of the voice that had sounded through her mind. *Epona had spoken to her! Her! And she was not being rejected because of her mother's choices.*

"Better now?" Etain asked.

"I think so," she said.

"Good! I should go back there and find Ciara. She should pass the word that the children can break out their finery. It never hurts to look ones best."

"Wait!" Brighid cried, and the silver mare stopped midturn. "I don't know how to retrieve a soul."

Etain smiled at her. "You're doing just fine. You've already called him to you in your dreams."

"But not recently. He stopped coming to my dreams the night we got to Guardian Castle."

"I wouldn't worry about that. He'll come again. When you're home, with your Clan about you, ready yourself for your spirit journey, just as you would use your powers to track new prey."

"You—you know about that?" As soon as the words escaped Brighid felt ridiculously foolish. Again. Of course Epona's Chosen would recognize her affinity with the spirits of animals.

"Using gifts granted to you by Epona is nothing to be ashamed of," Etain said firmly.

"I'm not ashamed of the gift," Brighid insisted, anxious that Etain understand. "I've been ashamed of how my family has used its gifts. I didn't want to be like…" She paused. The priestess's gaze was kind, motherly, understanding.

"Go on, child. You can say it."

"I don't want to be like my mother," Brighid said in a rush.

"Did you ever consider that it is possible for you to be like her in that you have been gifted greatly, and be unlike her in the way you choose to use those gifts?"

"Yes! That's why I only use my affinity with the animal spirits. The rest of it—I didn't even really realize I had more until recently."

"But you do have more than a simple affinity for the spirits of animals. Isn't your denial a victory for your mother?"

"I've never thought of it that way." Brighid could almost

hear her mother's hard voice, *You will follow me as proper High Shaman, or you will be nothing.*

"Perhaps you should think of it. And don't worry about not being able to find Cu's spirit. When you're ready, he'll come to you."

"And then what?" Brighid blurted, mind whirring with Etain's words.

"You'll know, child. You'll know what will bring him back. I'm sure of it. I have faith in your abilities, Brighid." Etain smiled, turned the mare so that she was pointed back down the wagon line, and trotted jauntily off, leaving Brighid with a silk handkerchief and unanswered questions.

CHAPTER
TWENTY-SIX

She liked the quality of light that filtered through the forest just as the sun was rising, or as it was now when it was almost ready to set. The connection between dawn and sunset was like a coin with two faces. Alike, yet separate. Similar, yet not the same. There was a simplicity and rightness to thinking of the two as reflections of one another…beginning and ending…and then beginning again…just another part of the great circle of life. The thought brought Brighid peace, and it was one of the many reasons she preferred to hunt during the shifting of the day.

"Brighid!"

The Huntress sighed.

"Brighid!"

She rolled her head, trying to relieve some of the tension that was settling in her neck.

"You'd better see to him. You know he's not going to leave you alone," Cu said.

"He's injured. He needs to be still and stay where he is," Brighid said firmly.

"Brrrrighiiiiid!"

Swathed in golden silk and draped with jewels, Etain definitely looked the part of Epona's Chosen as the silver mare trotted up to join her son and the Huntress at the head of the line. "Your apprentice is calling for you."

"I know that," Brighid ground out between clenched teeth, trying hard to keep her tone civil.

"Take the word of a mother. Ignoring him will not make him go away," said the Beloved of Epona. The Chosen mare blew firmly through her nose in agreement.

"Go back and talk to him," Cu said. "It's the only way we'll get any peace. Just remind him that we're almost there. Soon he should have a lot more to think about than you."

"Easy for you to say," Brighid grumbled. "You don't have an annoying winged apprentice shrieking your name day and night."

"He's just restless. He'll be fine when he can move about again on his own," Etain said.

"Huh," Brighid snorted. "You didn't know him before. He was just as annoying." Setting her jaw, she fell out of the forward position and cantered back to the first wagon, sure that she heard Etain's musical laughter floating behind her.

Like small flowers following the sun, all of the little heads in the first wagon turned in her direction. She met the gaze of the haggard-looking wagon driver. He nodded politely, even though his eyes said he'd rather be just about anywhere else, including the heat of battle, than cooped up with the cluster of chirping, laughing, chattering children.

Brighid gave him an understanding smile.

"Brighid! Brighid! Brighid!" Liam started to hop up and down while he clutched the edge of the wagon's frame, but one sharp word from Nara, who was sitting beside the wagon driver, was enough to make him hold himself very still. All of himself, Brighid thought, except for his mouth. "Can I come up with you? I really should come up with you. I'm your apprentice. I should be with you. Don't you think? Isn't that right?"

Brighid wasn't sure if she wanted to scream or groan. How did mothers do this?

"Liam! Enough." She held up one hand and the boy went blissfully silent. Then she turned her attention to the New Fomorian Healer. "Is he well enough to ride?"

The Healer tried unsuccessfully to stifle her smile. "Not far and not fast. But, yes, he is well enough to ride."

She looked at Liam. His eyes were big and round with surprise, but his lips were carefully clamped together.

"If I let you ride with me you must carry yourself with the dignity of a centaur Huntress. Can you do that?"

"Yes! Yes! Ye—" Unbelievably the boy stopped mid-yes. Carefully, he drew himself up, holding his bandaged wing close to his body, and nodded. Once.

Before she could think better of it she edged up to the side of the wagon. "Help him on," she told the children who were sitting around him. All talking at once, they boosted him onto her equine back. "Hang on," she said, putting one hand back to hold his leg. She hoped he wouldn't fall, but if he did she could at least keep him from hitting the ground. Maybe.

"Hang on to what?" he asked in a little boy's voice.

"Put your hands on my shoulders," she said, then sighed and added. "If you're scared, you can wrap your arms around my waist."

After a slight hesitation, she felt warm little hands on her shoulders.

"I'm not scared," he said. "You wouldn't let me fall."

Not having a ready answer for his blind faith, Brighid kicked into a smooth canter, quickly rejoining Cuchulainn and his mother at the head of their company.

"Not a word," Brighid told Cu as the warrior opened his mouth.

"It's good to see you looking so well, Liam," Etain said, with a motherly smile. "You should be back to hunting form soon."

Brighid could feel Liam quiver with pleasure at Etain's words, but when the boy spoke his words were polite and brief.

"Thank you, Goddess."

Pleased, Brighid squeezed his small leg before loosening her grip, and then she smiled secretly to herself when Liam squeezed her shoulders back and whispered, "See, I'm a good centaur."

"There," Cuchulainn said, pointing to where the small rugged trail forked to join a much wider road that was obviously well traveled. "This is the road that runs between the castle and Loth Tor."

"Finally. I was beginning to think we would run out of daylight before we got to it," Brighid said, trotting onto the well-packed road and turning to her right.

"Is the castle close?" Liam asked.

"Very," she said. "Tonight you will be sleeping at MacCallan Castle."

"Will they like us?" the boy asked in a small voice.

Brighid looked over her shoulder at him. He was so young. His eyes watched her, waiting for her answer as if she held the keys to all the mysteries of the universe.

"Of course they will like you," she said firmly. As she turned her head back she caught Cuchulainn's eye and wasn't reassured by the sober look he gave her.

"It will all work out. You'll see." Etain's voice was filled with her usual confidence, and the silver mare snorted agreement.

Brighid looked beyond Cuchulainn at his mother. The Goddess Incarnate was smiling at Liam. She didn't look at all worried. The Huntress glanced back at Cu. The warrior gave her a half smile and shrugged.

"Everything important?" Brighid mouthed silently to him.

"Yes," Etain said without looking at either of them. "Absolutely everything important."

Liam whispered, "She does know everything."

Cuchulainn grunted and Brighid decided to turn her attention to the darkening roadway.

A fluttering of wings announced Ciara's arrival, and the Shaman glided into the space between Cu and Brighid.

"They're ready." Her smile trembled and her eyes were riveted on the road ahead of them. "I think I'm nervous," she said with a little laugh.

"We all feel a little nervous when we return home after a long absence, but it is a happy nervousness," Etain said gently. "Remember, this is your homeland. The prayers and blood of your foremothers made that a certainty. It will all work out. You'll see."

"You can believe her. The Goddess tells her everything that is important." Liam spoke in an awed, uncharacteristically serious voice that made the three adults smile. "Well, she does," Liam said, and then—thankfully—the boy was too busy staring around them at the giant pines to chatter.

The caravan of more than a dozen wagons, all filled with New Fomorians, followed the Huntress, the warrior, their Shaman, and the Goddess Incarnate onto the road that would be the final leg of their journey. The four leaders trotted in silent anticipation, each of them deep in their own thoughts. When Fand padded beside Cu's gelding, Brighid glanced at the warrior. He looked tense and grim. Had they been alone she would have reminded him that he was only coming home, not heading into battle. But she was reluctant to speak in front of Ciara, not sure if calling attention to the struggle taking place within him would embarrass or maybe even annoy Cuchulainn. And part of her understood that this homecoming was a type of battle for her friend. Soon he would be fighting to regain his soul and his life—and it was at MacCallan Castle that both had been irrevocably altered.

The road made a familiar bend to the west, climbed up, and

suddenly they spilled out of the pine forest and in to the carefully tended castle grounds. The sun was setting into the ocean behind the castle, serving as perfect illumination for the imposing edifice that was already fully lighted from within. Its cream-colored walls were tinted by the bold colors of the evening sky, so it seemed that firelight danced within and without, welcoming them with the warmth of flame.

"It's so pretty," Liam breathed.

"It's beautiful and perfect and…" Ciara's voice choked and she couldn't go on.

"And it is your home," Etain finished for her.

Home…Brighid's heart echoed. It wasn't the open grasslands of her youth, but seeing it again made her feel settled and safe.

"They've done a lot the past two moons," Cu said, working hard to keep his voice flat and emotionless, as if he was afraid that if he let any feeling leak into his words he would not be able to stop the tide and it would overwhelm him. "The four towers are completed, and much of the sentry's walk."

A shout helloed at them from the outer wall of the castle.

"Shall we let our Elphame know we're here, my beauty?" Etain said, patting the silver mare's neck.

Understanding perfectly, and without needing any further guidance from her rider, the mare pranced forward for several paces and then she reared gracefully, trumpeting a sharp greeting that was unmistakably amplified by the power of Epona's presence.

The response from the castle was immediate.

"Hail, Epona!" called the sentry, and a moment later the newly installed iron gate was raised and figures rushed through the opening.

With a glad cry, Elphame sprinted forward. Her two powerful equine legs made her faster and stronger than the rest of her people, and she outdistanced them easily, reaching the group of travelers even before her winged mate.

Cuchulainn slid from his horse and just had time to open his arms for his sister as she rushed into them.

"Cuchulainn!" She hugged him tightly, burying her face in his shoulder.

"Shhh," he murmured, stroking her head. "Don't cry, sister-mine. Don't cry…"

Elphame pulled back a little so that she could take his face in her hands and kiss him soundly. "I've missed you so much."

"And I you."

"And what about your mother?" Etain asked through her own tears.

Elphame stepped out of her brother's arms and approached the Goddess Incarnate and the silver mare. "Oh, Mama—" her eyes shining happily "—who wouldn't miss you?"

The mare bowed down so that Etain had only to step gracefully from the horse's smooth back to take her daughter in her arms. "Don't cry, precious one. Your brother has returned, and all will be well."

Elphame kissed her mother on both cheeks. Then she turned to Brighid, and, smiling, was moving to hug her enthusiastically too, when she realized Brighid carried something…someone, on her back. The Clan Chieftain's eyes widened as the scene expanded to include more than her brother and mother.

"Oh, Goddess…" Elphame gasped.

Without looking behind her, Ciara walked forward, knowing her people would follow. When she stood directly in front of Elphame, she knelt and placed her hands, with wrists crossed, over her heart, in an ancient gesture of respect and homage.

"Goddess, there will never be adequate words with which to thank you for the sacrifice you made. By accepting the madness of our forefathers you freed the humanity within us. You saved us." The Shaman's passionate voice filled the castle grounds.

Brighid watched her Clan Chieftain's face carefully. Was she the only one who noticed the shadow that shivered through Elphame's eyes, dark and malignant? Then Lochlan moved to one side of his mate, and Etain, the Beloved of Epona, moved to her daughter's other side. Elphame seemed to take strength from their presence, and to draw herself up straighter. Like shadows retreating from light, the darkness in her gaze cleared. She reached down, took Ciara's hand, and raised her to her feet.

"It is not me to whom you owe your debt of gratitude," Elphame said. "Without Epona's strength the curse could not have been lifted from your people."

"And your debt to Epona has been repaid many times over by the fidelity of your foremothers," Etain said.

"So we have no debtors here, only friends and comrades," Elphame finished.

Then Lochlan stepped forward, and his deep voice rang throughout the Clan.

"Elphame, my Chieftain and my love, and Clan MacCallan—" he looked behind his mate, smiling at the humans and centaurs who crowded behind them "—this is Ciara, Shaman of the New Fomorians, granddaughter of the Incarnate Terpsichore abducted by demons more than one hundred years ago."

Elphame returned Ciara's elegant full curtsy with a regal tilting of her head.

"Chieftain, my Lord Lochlan, and Clan MacCallan, these are my people, who are now your people—the people your Chieftain saved—the New Fomorians." With a graceful, sweeping flourish, Ciara stepped aside so that Elphame had an unrestricted view of the winged children and adults who still knelt, filling that part of the grounds like a beautiful flock of exotic birds.

Elphame's eyes traveled over the silent group, and as her gaze touched each of them, face after face broke into tentative smiles. Then one little voice spoke from the front of the group.

"We are so glad to be here, Goddess!" And then a torrent of young voices joined hers.

"Yes, Goddess!"

"Oh, yes!"

"It's so green here!"

"Everything is growing!"

Elphame raised her hand and the barrage of youthful exuberance was stilled.

"First," she said slowly, "I am not a Goddess. I am simply touched by one. You may call me Chieftain, or my Lady, or even Elphame. Understand?"

Lots of bright little heads nodded ardently.

"Good. Now that we've gotten that out of the way." Elphame's face broke into a joyous smile. "Stand, New Fomorians and be welcomed to MacCallan Castle—your new home!"

Taking their cue from their Chieftain, Clan MacCallan surged forward, greeting the children and adults until soon the groups were so co-mingled Brighid could no longer tell where MacCallan plaid ended and the wings of the New Fomorians began.

"Is this someone special I should meet?" Elphame asked Brighid.

Before she could respond Liam chirped a quick, "Yes!"

Brighid slipped a hand onto the boy's leg and squeezed. With obedience that the Huntress was beginning to find surprising, the boy instantly quieted.

"Elphame, I would like to formally introduce you to my new apprentice, Liam."

To her credit a small twitch of her lips was all that betrayed the Chieftain's surprise and—Brighid was sure—amusement.

"Well met, Liam. A clan can always use another good…" She hesitated, and at Brighid's inconspicuous half-nod she finished, "Huntress."

"Thank you, my Lady! MacCallan Castle will be needing an extra Huntress with all of us here now."

Brighid thought he sounded very mature, and she would

have been fooled into thinking he had suddenly aged several years, had she not felt him squirm with barely suppressed excitement.

"That's a very wise thing for you to say, Liam," Elphame said without a hint of the smile Brighid knew she had to be struggling to conceal—knew it because her friend was studiously avoiding meeting Brighid's eyes. "I can see why Brighid chose you to be her apprentice."

"Oh, she didn't choose me," Liam said gravely. "I chose her. From the first time I met her I told her that I was supposed to be a centaur Huntress, just like her."

Elphame pressed a hand against her lips, as if gravely considering the boy's words. She carefully cleared her throat before answering the boy. "You know, you remind me of my brother. He knew from a very early age just exactly who he was going to be."

Brighid could feel Liam sucking in a mighty breath with which to sustain what she felt certain would be a long barrage of very young and very excited words, when she saw Nara approaching them.

"Elphame, please meet the New Fomorian Healer, Nara," Brighid said quickly.

Nara curtsied respectfully to the Clan Chieftain. "We're so pleased to be here, my Lady."

Elphame smiled. "I'm pleased to add a Healer and another young Huntress to our ranks."

Nara frowned up at her young charge. "This is one Huntress who has done enough riding for today."

"I think we all have," Brighid said under her breath as she helped Liam slide reluctantly from her back.

"You are absolutely right, Brighid," Elphame said. She clapped her hands together, drawing the attention of the crowd. "Supper is laid. Let us retire to the castle and our cooks' excellent fare."

The children responded with a jubilant shout, and soon they were following Clan MacCallan through the wide open gates of their castle. Elphame stood beside Brighid, watching as the last of the wagons pulled within the castle walls.

"Lochlan told me how many children there were. We've been preparing and planning for them. But to see them…all of them…well, it's much different than talk," Elphame said.

Brighid snorted. "At least he prepared you."

Elphame grinned at her friend and then hugged her warmly. "I have missed your honest tongue, Brighid."

CHAPTER
TWENTY-SEVEN

With a sigh of relief Brighid stretched and rolled her neck, feeling the tight knots in her shoulders relax. Stepping carefully so that her hooves made as little noise as possible, she walked from the now empty Main Courtyard, through the open doors of the inner walls. Goddess be praised, she was finally alone! And the children, all seventy of them, including her precocious apprentice, were tucked snugly in the newly restored warriors' barracks. Dinner had been an exhausting mixture of chaos and control, and Brighid thought she would probably be eternally grateful for the women of Clan MacCallan. They'd spread out amongst the children and hadn't even seemed to mind the endless chattering and ceaseless questioning. Actually, Brighid mused silently, there had been a lot of laughter and very little openmouthed staring or suspicious looks. Of course that only made sense. Unlike the warriors of Guardian Castle, Clan MacCallan had had more than two complete cycles of the moon to prepare for the arrival of the New Fomorians.

And then there was Lochlan, the Chieftain's chosen mate. He was a noble example of his people. She had been wrong to mistrust him, Brighid realized that now. Obviously the majority of Clan MacCallan had not been so reticent in accepting him. Brighid shook her head. Through the hybrid children, she had come to accept the goodness within the New Fomorians, and she was able to see Lochlan with new eyes.

But it wasn't only the New Fomorians she saw differently. A part of her had begun to stir…to beckon. She didn't want to think about it, much less admit it, but she was no coward. It was her nature to face things head-on. She was changing. Now that she was home, back to the one place in the world she felt most accepted, most secure, the difference within her was undeniable.

It intrigued her almost as much as it worried her.

The outer walls of MacCallan Castle loomed suddenly before her, and she quickly reoriented her thoughts, smiling at the newly constructed sentry walk that ran along the inside of the smooth stone walls. At Elphame's insistence, the wide staircase and high steps had been built to specifications large enough to accommodate a centaur's added bulk. Centaur friendly—that definitely described MacCallan Castle. Brighid wondered briefly if visiting a castle such as MacCallan, where centaurs were not only respected because of their hunting skills, but were truly accepted as a part of the Clan, a part of the Chieftain's family, would change her herd's isolationist views?

Probably not. The Dhianna Herd kept to itself, ferociously proud that they did not deign to mingle with humans. One visit to MacCallan Castle would not change what had been imprinted within them for…

How long had it been? With a start Brighid realized that the last time the Dhianna Herd had left the Centaur Plains for more than brief trading must have been during the Fomorian

War, and that had ended disastrously for the herd. More than half of the centaur warriors who had fought in the great battle at the Temple of the Muse had been butchered. Many others had been horribly wounded and had limped back to the plains vowing never to leave again.

She was the first of her herd to choose to leave the Centaur Plains in more than one hundred years. By the Goddess, it was a daunting thought!

"Well met, Brighid!" The sentry's voice echoed down from the archer's post.

Brighid patted the banister of the wide staircase, nodded her head and grunted as if she had been standing there studying the workmanship and not standing there lost in depressing thoughts of the Dhianna Herd. Shaking off the shadows of the past, she climbed up to the archer's post, and returned the sentry's formal salute.

"We're pleased to have you home, Huntress."

"It's good to be home." She smiled a greeting and then covered the short distance to the edge of the wall. "Nice night," she said, looking out on the dark, silent forest, and up at the cloudless sky that was alight with countless stars.

"It's been a dry spring. That's why we've been able to complete so much work on the castle." The sentry chuckled. "Of course Wynne and the rest of the cooks are already complaining that we're going to be hauling water for her gardens if we don't get rain soon, but the weather suits me just fine—even under the threat of water hauling."

Brighid smiled absently. Her attention had been caught by a ring of torches near the forest tree line. The sentry followed her gaze.

"Brenna's tomb." His voice sobered.

Brighid grunted and nodded her head, remembering. "The monument has been completed."

"Yes, just three nights ago the permanent torches were lit for the first time. Now every evening they're lit. Every dawn they're extinguished."

"Three nights ago?" Brighid's stomach tightened. Three nights ago Brenna had visited her dream. What was it the little spirit said? That she'd been compelled to visit that night? "How far does the walk extend?" she asked the sentry abruptly.

"It's been completed more than halfway around the castle wall." He gestured to their right. "Go ahead and see for yourself. There are torches posted throughout." He grinned. "No need to worry about tumbling off, Huntress."

"Well, that's comforting," she muttered, wished the sentry a good evening, and walked around the sturdy wooden walkway, annoyed that it seemed to be common knowledge that she disliked heights. At the next archer's turnout, she moved onto the balcony and leaned her forearms against the smooth stone balustrade. From there she had a clear view of Brenna's tomb. A simple, elegant structure had been erected over it—a domed roof standing on four columns. Into each of the columns had been placed carved sconces from which torches blazed, illuminating the large marble sarcophagus and spreading gentle fingers of light over the shape of Brenna's effigy.

"I wonder if she likes it," Elphame asked softly as she stepped from the shadows.

Brighid considered it a reflection of how many times Ciara had materialized soundlessly beside her over the past several days that she didn't jump out of her skin—or fall from the balcony. She did close her eyes briefly and take a deep breath to still the pounding of her heart.

"El, make some kind of sound, would you?"

She squeezed in beside the Huntress. "Did I scare you?"

The Huntress scooted over so that her friend had more room and gave her a disgruntled look.

Elphame grinned. "Sorry."

Then they both gazed out at the tomb.

"It looks peaceful, even from here," Brighid said.

"It's not quite finished. I've begun to look for an artist to paint the ceiling with the Healer's Knot. And I'd like to expand the blue wildflowers out farther and have them blanket that part of the castle grounds. Cu said they were her favorite flower."

"Because they're the color of his eyes," Brighid said.

Surprised, Elphame smiled at her friend. "I never thought of that before, but I'll bet you're right."

"I think Brenna would like what you've done to remember her." As Brighid spoke the words she Felt the rightness of them, deep within the part of her that had recently begun to stir.

"I think you're right. She was too important to become a forgotten piece of the past."

"She won't be. There are seventy winged children who will pass on her story. The New Fomorians seem to have a very long memory." Brighid raised a brow contemplatively. "And I don't think you'll need to look any farther for that artist. Has Lochlan mentioned how many of the hybrids are descendants of Incarnate Goddesses of the Muse?"

"I don't recall him saying anything specific about any of the foremothers, except his own," El said. "I was as surprised as the rest of the Clan to find out their Shaman was Terpsichore's granddaughter."

"Wait till you see the talent that's been hidden in the Wastelands all these years. The walls of their Great Hall were covered with spectacular artwork. Even the legs of the tables were carved into blooming flowers. You, my Chieftain friend, have inherited a group of artists."

"That is excellent news. I wonder why Lochlan didn't mention it."

Before meeting the New Fomorians Brighid would have second-guessed Lochlan's silence, reading ulterior motives and sly evasion into his omission. Now she thought she knew better. She smiled at her friend.

"Men—be they human, hybrid, or centaur—are essentially alike. They tend to say too little about important matters and too much about the obvious."

Elphame laughed. "That, my Huntress friend, is the truth."
She leaned against the stone of the castle and studied the centaur. "So, you want to tell me about your apprentice?"

Brighid gave a long-suffering sigh. "The boy is obviously
confused."

"And?" Elphame prompted.

"And for some mad reason I find I care about him. He's…"
She sighed again. "He's endearing. And he has no parents."

"He needs you," Elphame said.

"I supposed he needs me, and, in some way I might need
him, too. Or at least taking responsibility felt right after he
was wounded."

"What happened?"

"The Guardian Warriors were not as eager to welcome the
New Fomorians as was Clan MacCallan. All they knew of the
hybrids was what they had learned from Fallon. She has…de-
teriorated even further." Brighid shook her head. "She mocked
Cuchulainn. It was ghastly and disturbing."

"I should have ignored her child and killed her. For Cuchulainn. For Brenna. For all of us."

"No!" Brighid turned to her Chieftain. "You did the right
thing. Anything less would have been uncivilized and unjust."
The Huntress's gaze went back to their friend's tomb. "Fallon
did kill Brenna—and that was a terrible act. But she committed the crime out of a desire to save her people. In return for
choosing the only path she thought open to her, she was rewarded with madness, imprisonment and soon death."

"Are you saying she should be forgiven?" Elphame asked,
incredulous.

"Not forgiven. But perhaps understood and pitied." Brighid
pressed her hands against the balustrade. "Some things in life
can't be placed tidily on sides of good or evil. We are often in
the midst of a balancing act, where the scales are hopefully
tipped toward the good and away from the evil. But sometimes
evil wears the face of friends and family. And good looks like
the outlander."

Elphame studied her. "Are you well, Brighid?"

She met her Chieftain's clear gaze. "I'm relieved to be home."

"I missed you. Having you and Cu gone at the same time—" Elphame drew in a ragged breath "—I hope it doesn't happen again soon."

"I have no intention of going anywhere except hunting—on rich MacCallan soil."

"Good. Now if we can just convince Cu that he should stay." Elphame turned to face her friend. "Thank you for bringing my brother back to me. I will always be grateful to you."

"You don't have to thank me, El. He's my friend, too, and he belongs here. With you—with Clan MacCallan. Here he can heal."

Elphame sighed. "He looks so old and tired. I could tell that it was hard for him to be here."

"It is, but it is also where he needs to be. It's time for his self-imposed exile to end," Brighid said.

Elphame shook her head. "It was so unlike him to leave like that. Cu doesn't run from problems, and he's always found strength in family."

"Cuchulainn left because he lost a part of himself," Brighid explained. "The joyous, life-loving part of his soul couldn't bear the grief of losing Brenna. It shattered and has remained in the Otherworld. That's why Cu has acted so unlike himself. That's why it has been so difficult for him to heal."

"Oh, Goddess!" Elphame breathed. "What are we going to do? There has to be a soul retrieval." She looked desperately around them. "Mama! She can fix this! We have to—"

Brighid's hand on her arm broke off Elphame's rant.

"Your mother already knows. There is going to be a soul retrieval, only she's not going to perform it."

Elphame's brows drew together. "Then who? Da? Is he coming?"

"No, El." Brighid drew a deep breath. "Your father's not going to perform the soul retrieval either. I am."

Elphame blinked. "You are?"

Brighid shrugged her shoulders, feeling decidedly uncomfortable. "So it seems. Your mother agrees. Cuchulainn agrees."

"But you're not a Shaman."

"No, but apparently that makes little difference. I—I have a..." She paused, trying to decide how to phrase it. "I have a power in my blood. Your mother calls it a gift. I'm just learning about it. I think—" she took another deep breath, feeling a little like she was plunging into a pool of icy water "—I think it's the same gift my mother has in her blood. You know I'm the daughter of Mairearad Dhianna."

Elphame nodded.

"I'm the *eldest* daughter of Mairearad Dhianna."

Elphame sucked in a breath. "And you left the herd to become a Huntress! All this time I assumed you were just one of the High Shaman's younger daughters." The Chieftain shook her head, a slight smile tilting her lips. "I'll bet your leaving caused quite a bit of—" El broke off. "That's why we understand each other so well. We're both daughters who have chosen to break tradition. I was to have followed my mother as Epona's Chosen. You were to have followed yours as High Shaman of the Dhianna. Little wonder the Goddess caused our paths to cross."

"Except your mother supports and accepts your decision. Mine does not. She is not like Etain." Brighid stared out into the night. "When I left my mother I was determined to leave that unwanted life behind me, which included the power in my blood that tied me to her. I felt I had to deny it and suppress it to prove that I was different—that I was committed to another destiny." Brighid rubbed at her face. She wanted to explain herself to Elphame, she needed to. But it was difficult. Would it always be this hard to talk about herself and her life before she came to MacCallan Castle? "But there were parts of my powers, or gifts—as your mother puts it— that I couldn't deny. You know I'm a Master Huntress. Perhaps even so adept at finding and capturing prey that I could vie for Lead Huntress of Partholon."

"Yes, of course. I've often marveled at your skills, as has the rest of our Clan. We're fortunate to claim you as our own."

"It's because my gift is an affinity with the spirits of animals." Brighid spoke quickly as her friend began to protest. "I'm not saying that I don't have the skills of a Huntress. Of course I do. I've gone through the training. I understand the ways of animals and I can track anything that moves over the earth. But I have more than a normal Huntress's abilities. I Feel the spirits of the deer and elk, boar and bear. I know them in a way that is only possible because of the powers gifted to me by Epona."

They were silent, the two friends, both gazing out at the sleeping forest, considering the weight of Brighid's words.

"Had I been more experienced in the ways of the spirit world, I would have guessed your truth. Now that you tell me, it seems obvious," Elphame said. She glanced at Brighid. "Mama knows, doesn't she?"

"Your mother knows everything," Brighid said with a smile.

"Everything important," Elphame added.

"No, I'm beginning to think she knows *everything*." Both women laughed softly.

"That's Mama," Elphame said. "She's scary and amazing and wonderful."

Brighid hesitated for a moment, then said, "Today she told me that I remind her of you."

Elphame grinned. "That doesn't surprise me."

"I have to tell you that after traveling with her and getting to know her that I am envious of you, El. I can only imagine what it would be like to have a mother who loved me selflessly."

Elphame tilted her head and looked up at her friend. "It is a priceless gift," she said simply.

"One I will never know."

"You don't have to be born someone's daughter to share in her love."

Now it was Brighid's turn to blink in surprise at her Chieftain. Elphame grinned at her. "Mama has two daughters, but she has said over and over that she wished Epona had gifted her with more."

The Huntress felt a rush of hot emotion. Acceptance. This was what it was like to be truly accepted and loved and honored for herself. And Elphame wasn't jealous of her, or angry, or shocked. She was clearly pleased at the prospect of sharing her mother's love with Brighid. It was miraculous.

Then guilt washed over Brighid. She had a mother. True, Mairearad was selfish and manipulative, and clearly cared more about herself than her offspring, but she was her mother nonetheless. How was it possible to have two mothers at once?

It wasn't. By the Goddess, she wished it was possible. But it wasn't.

"Brighid," Elphame said softly, touching her arm. "Don't let it tear you apart. Can you not accept one mother's love without negating the other?"

"Isn't that a betrayal?" Brighid asked, trying unsuccessfully to keep her voice from trembling.

"No, sister. You are not capable of betrayal. Look elsewhere for that."

"I'll try…" she whispered. Turning her head away from Elphame, she wiped at the wetness that had leaked onto her cheeks. And a flicker of movement caught her eye. She refocused her vision. Two figures moved between the torches that illuminated Brenna's grave site. One was a man, the other a wolf cub.

"It's Cu," Elphame breathed.

The warrior walked to the head of Brenna's tomb. He stood very still, and then he cupped her stone cheek with his hand. Slowly he bent. Brighid thought he would kiss the effigy's lips, but he simply rested his forehead against the unyielding marble. Then he turned, and stumbled into the darkness, with the wolf silently trailing him.

"I denied the Shaman power within my blood," Brighid said softly. "Then I found your brother in the Wastelands—shattered and despairing, and somehow I have come to understand that I can help him. But that's all that I really do understand. I don't know why, but Epona has made you and your brother a part of my destiny."

Elphame turned to her. "Our Goddess is wise. There is no one I would rather trust my brother to than you."

"I hope I'm worthy of your trust."

"You are, my sister." Elphame smiled, and the hair on Brighid's forearms prickled and lifted as motes of power swirled suddenly, unexpectedly in the air around them.

CHAPTER
TWENTY-EIGHT

Her chamber had been aired and made ready for her. It had been built as an addition to the warrior's barracks, an extension of the long, narrow room that currently housed the New Fomorians. Elphame had ordered a thick wall constructed between the traditional barracks and the Huntress's quarters, and she had even insisted the spacious room have a private entrance. Brighid didn't need all the fuss, but her Chieftain had shrugged off Brighid's protestations and created a chamber befitting the Mac-Callan Huntress. It was private and well appointed. And, Brighid noted with pleasure, in the days she had been gone someone had hung a tapestry depicting the Centaur Plains, flush with spring wildflowers and dotted with dark bison, along one of the walls.

"May the Goddess bless her," Brighid whispered, knowing that it was Elphame who had covered Brighid's walls with scenes from her childhood. Elphame understood her well.

One of the housekeepers had been considerate enough to start a cheery fire in the hearth, as well as light the sets of tall candelabrum that stood like iron sentinels around the room. The long, narrow chamber was sparsely furnished with a large dresser, a sturdily built table—constructed to centaur proportions—and an enormous down-filled mattress, which rested directly on the marble floor.

Brighid drew in a long breath, loving the familiar scent of the MacCallan candles, which were made by crushing oily leaves of local lavender into the wax. Then she smiled. May the Goddess bless Wynne and her bevy of cooks! On the table sat a basket filled with cold meats, cheeses, bread, dried fruit and—best of all—a skin of—she uncapped it and took a long, deep pull—excellent red wine from Etain's own vineyards.

Brighid popped a piece of cheese in her mouth. They knew her habits. They understood that she enjoyed a snack during the night and that sometimes she rose even before the cooks. They wanted to make sure she had provisions. They cared.

She hadn't lived here for more than three full cycles of the moon, yet every scent, every face, every touch, spoke to her of safety and acceptance. *I think I've finally found my place.*

It was a unique, wondrous experience to have a castle filled with people who worried after her and cared about her comfort. What would her mother think if she could see this? Brighid shook her head. Her mother wouldn't ever see this, even if she were to stand in this very room. Mairearad Dhianna could see only shadows, never the light that cast them. She would find fault with Clan MacCallan and belittle their affection for Brighid.

Why was she thinking about her mother? That part of her life was over.

It was because she was so damned tired. The trip had been exhausting. She just needed to sleep. She'd be herself in the morning. Tomorrow she'd be sure the New Fomorians were settled—there was talk of building a village for them on the plateau south of the castle. Perhaps she would take Liam there.

She sighed, methodically blowing out the scented candles, until the only light came from the flickering hearth fire. What was she going to do about Liam? She'd proclaimed him her apprentice. She'd have to begin training him. *Tracking,* she thought with satisfaction, *set him at scouting out different tracks—identifying…following…naming…categorizing.* Tracking took most apprentice Huntresses years to master. She'd just keep him busy.

If she got lucky, he'd lose interest.

Ignoring the hard lump of the turquoise stone in her breast pocket, the Huntress shrugged out of her vest, and poured fresh water from the pitcher to the bowl that waited atop the dresser. Using the thick linen towel she found hanging from a hook shaped like a dagger, she freshened herself, and then she sighed deeply as she settled on her bed. Tonight she would sleep soundly. Tomorrow she would consider all the ramifications of the turquoise stone and the soul retrieval and the damned golden hawk she had conveniently been too busy to mention except to Cuchulainn. Tomorrow would be soon enough…

She wasn't aware of dreaming. She was just content, drifting on a cloud of serenity. There were no children in her dream…no dead friends…and definitely no damned men, soul shattered or otherwise.

The sound of her door slamming shut and the feel of a rough hand shaking her awake dissipated her contentment like smoke in the wind.

"Brighid! Wake up!"

The Huntress opened one eye. The fire had burned down to glowing embers, but the man held a taper in his hand. She opened her other eye.

"Cuchulainn?" Her voice was rough with sleep.

"There, I knew you'd be awake," he said, and set about lighting the candles that she'd all too recently blown out.

She sat up and brushed long, silver hair from her face. "Is it morning?"

Finished with lighting the candles, he crouched in front of the hearth, feeding the fire logs and coaxing it into life. He glanced over his shoulder at her. His eyes slid down to her naked breasts before snapping back to her face.

"No. It is not morning. Get dressed." He turned his back to her and resumed poking at the fire.

Brighid's cheeks warmed as she rose from her bed and retrieved her vest. But even as she put it on her mind raced. What was wrong with her? Centaurs often went naked. There was no shame in baring her breasts. And even fully clothed in the traditional beaded leather vest, her breasts were often at least partially visible. Why was she blushing like a youth? He had burst into her chamber, waking her and causing her to feel…naked. It was ridiculous.

"Cuchulainn, what is this about?" she snapped. "I'm tired. And I didn't give you permission to come in here and—" she gestured at the lighted candles and the hearth "—wake everything up."

He stood and faced her. His tangled hair was wild around his head like the mane of a great beast. He brought his hands together, interlocking his fingers in a grip that was so tight it whitened his knuckles, and then lifted them to his brow and closed his eyes, as if he meant to beseech her with a prayer.

"Cu?" She was worried now. The man before her looked haggard and broken.

"Help me," he said, keeping his eyes closed. "I can't do this anymore. Can't live like this for one more day."

"Of course I'll help you. We've already talked about this."

"No more talk." He opened his eyes. "Now or not at all."

Brighid felt a little flutter of panic. "Cu, be rational. Now is not the time."

"It has to be." He unlocked his hands with a violent cutting motion. "I can't be here and not be myself."

"You know it won't change your pain, Cu. It won't make it go away."

"I know that!" He raked his fingers through his hair and

paced back and forth in front of the hearth. "I'll have to learn to live without her, but I can't do that unless I'm whole, and I can't stand being here—home—back where I met her and loved her and then lost her. I'm breathing, so I'm living, but not really. I—I can't explain it any better. You just have to believe that I'm ready. Either you help me tonight, or in the morning I will ride away."

"Running won't solve this."

"I know that, too!" He rubbed his forehead, and then he lifted his eyes to hers. "Help me, Brighid. Please."

"I don't know if I can do it!" she cried.

He almost smiled. "Is that all that's bothering you? You're worried that you can't get to the part of me that's missing?"

"What do you mean, is that all that's bothering me? Of course that's bothering me! Cuchulainn, I am not a Shaman," she said clearly and distinctly, as if he was a thickheaded child.

"But it—" He broke off at her frown. "I mean him, or me, or whatever you want to call that missing part."

"He," Brighid said.

"*He* has already come to you. He will again."

"You seem sure."

Then he did smile. "I am sure, Huntress. We like you—he and I. You're prickly and too tightly wrapped for your own good, but we still like you. He'll come to you. Just call."

Brighid ignored the skittery way his words made her gut feel. Of course Cuchulainn liked her. They were friends—comrades—members of the same clan.

"Either help me, or go with me right now to explain to my sister and mother that I will be leaving again first thing in the morning."

She frowned at him. "That sounds vaguely like a threat."

"It's not vague and it's not a threat. It's clearly blackmail."

Brighid met his turquoise eyes again, all kidding gone from her voice. "I'm scared, Cu."

"Of what?"

"Of failing…and of succeeding."

Surprising her, he nodded slowly. "It's the spirit realm. You don't want to go there. I understand that, and I'm sorry that I have to ask you to do this for me. If there was another way…"

"No," she said quickly, "It's not the going that bothers me. I'm afraid of what I might discover there." She ended the sentence on a whisper.

Cuchulainn's face paled, but he didn't look away from her gaze. "You know what you'll discover. It's just me, Brighid. Shattered or not—bodiless or not—it's still just me."

"This is changing me, Cu," she said. "I can Feel it."

"I know…I…" His jaw tightened. "Forgive me for asking this of you."

She stared into his eyes and felt suddenly ashamed of herself. Cuchulainn was pleading for his life. She needed to push aside her childish fears and get this job done. She carried the blood of a powerful Shaman in her veins, as she had for her entire life. The only difference now was that she was going to tap into that heredity and use it to her advantage.

"There's nothing to forgive. I'm being foolish. Let's get this done." She glanced around the room. "Build up the hearth fire, but I think you should blow out these candles."

Cuchulainn quickly moved from candle to candle, then he returned to the hearth and added more wood to the fire, prodding and coaxing until the flames danced and crackled. Then he stood, rubbing his hands together nervously.

"What's next?"

Brighid had the urge to yell at him. His guess was as good as hers—she didn't have any idea what to do next. But the look in his eyes stopped her. He was counting on her. She didn't know why, but she was destined to help him. She sighed.

"We have to lie down," she said, retreating back to her soft pallet. The centaur folded her legs and reclined, in almost the same position she had been in when he burst into her room. She glanced up at him. He was still standing in front of the hearth. "Cu, you don't have to travel to the Otherworld, but you have to be relaxed and ready to accept the return of your soul. My guess is that's easier to do lying down."

"Where?"

She rolled her eyes and pointed to the empty place beside her. "I'm going to retrieve a piece of your soul. You can't be afraid to lie next to me."

"I'm not afraid. I'm just..." He raked his fingers through his wild hair. "By the Goddess, I'm nervous. I don't know what to do!"

"Try lying down."

He nodded, grunted, and strode to the other side of the Huntress's pallet. He lay back, crossing and then uncrossing his arms.

"I don't know what to do with my hands," he said without looking at her.

"I don't care what you do with them as long as you hold them still."

"Sorry," he said.

She turned her head so she could look over at him. "This is what I'm going to do. I'm going to relax and take myself to the same place I go to when I'm preparing for a hunt. Then I'm going to go deeper into...well, into wherever the trail takes me."

His brows shot up.

"The only way I can do this is to compare it to a hunt," she said in exasperation.

He started to hold his hands up, like he was fending off an assault, but then he stopped and held them tight to his sides.

"However you want to do it is fine with me," he said carefully.

"Oh, stop it!" she snapped.

"Stop what?"

She raised herself up on her elbow and jerked her chin at his stiff arms and motionless body. "You're acting like you've never been in bed with a female before."

This time only one eyebrow went up and his lip twitched like he was trying to hide a smile. "Is *that* how you'd like to relax me?"

She frowned at him. "Of course not." She wouldn't think about how having him there, so close beside her made her stomach tighten. She wouldn't think about it, and she certainly wouldn't mention it. She reclined back on the mound of bedding. "But you sound more like yourself now."

"You're a wily one, Huntress."

"Just close your eyes and concentrate on being open. Remember, I can't force your soul back. He has to want to come, and you have to accept him."

"I'm ready."

By the Goddess, she wished she was.

CHAPTER
TWENTY-NINE

She reached into her vest pocket and pulled out the turquoise stone. Holding it tightly in her fist, she closed her eyes. *Think of it as a hunt,* she ordered herself. *It's not that different. Today it's a shattered spirit I'm tracking instead of an animal.* Brighid drew in a deep, slow breath and centered herself. As she did each day before a new hunt, she imagined a powerful light originating deep within the base of her spine, and as she breathed out, the power flowed around her. When she drew her next breath she imagined breathing in the light and letting it fill her body; then she breathed out again, again filling the space around her with the brilliant, powerful light.

As she continued to center herself, she imagined where she would begin the hunt—and for a moment she faltered. Where was her prey? Usually she would cast her thoughts out to the surrounding forest, seeking the flitting spark that she could always Feel as distinctly different for each animal. Finding the creature's light always showed her where to seek her prey. But Cu had looked exactly like himself—she had no idea what color his spirit light would be, or even if it had a light at all. Consequently she had no clue as to where Cu's habitat would be.

Should she break her meditation and ask him about his favorite places? No…he'd come to her before. She hadn't had to seek him. He'd visited *her* favorite place—the Centaur Plains. Feeling suddenly more confident, Brighid focused her mind on the homeland of her youth.

She didn't know her spirit had left her body until she felt the warm breeze on her cheeks. Even before she opened her eyes she knew she was there—the breeze had told her. It smelled of tall grasses and freedom.

Brighid smiled, and opened her eyes. She had returned to the crosstimbers near her family's summer settlement. She could hear the Sand Creek tumbling lazily through the shady grove of oak and ash and hackberry trees directly in front of her.

In her dream she had heard Cuchulainn's laughter, and that had led her to him, so she stood quietly, listening to the caressing breeze. Hearing only birdsong, she sighed in frustration.

Track him, she reminded herself. The Huntress studied the ground. Nothing. How was she supposed to track a spirit?

Ask for help, child…

Etain's voice whispered on the wind. Brighid started, and looked around her. She saw no one, but her instincts told her she was not alone. Etain's presence was watching, and Brighid couldn't decide whether that made her feel better, or even more nervous. *Stop worrying and think!* she told herself.

Ask for help…

She squared her shoulders and, feeling a little foolish, the Huntress called into the wind. "I'm out of my element in this particular hunt, and I could really use some help!"

The familiar cry came from above her, and she looked up,

shielding her eyes against the bright spring sun. The golden hawk circled over her head. Brighid felt a rush of excitement. The bird must truly be her spirit ally.

This time no words formed in her head, but the hawk dipped its wing and changed direction, heading away from the Sand Creek and out into the grassy plain. Without hesitation, Brighid cantered after it, trying not to get lost in the sensual experience of moving through the waving grass. The plains called to her blood. She could run there forever. Dividing her attention between the land and the hawk, she increased her pace, moving from canter to gallop and taking fierce pleasure in the bunching of her equine muscles and the satisfying way her hooves struck the rich earth.

She would have galloped past him if he hadn't called her name. Cuchulainn stood on a gentle rise. Hands on his hips, he watched her slide to a stop and then gallop back to him.

"So, I see you took the gelding away from me. Why? Afraid that he would beat you in a race this time?" Then his gaze purposefully lingered on the slick equine muscles of her hindquarters. "Are you slowing up, old girl? You are looking a little…healthy. What have you been eating?"

Brighid opened her mouth in shock. Was the scoundrel saying she was old and fat?

Cuchulainn tipped his head back and let his laughter roll, which caused the Huntress to scowl darkly at him. "Oh, Goddess!" He held his side, gasping between chortles. "You should see your face!"

"You should see yours. You look ridiculous laughing like a village fool," she grumped.

Still chuckling, he flopped down on the ground, looking boylike and terribly young, especially when she contrasted this carefree warrior with the haggard, world-weary man whose body rested beside hers at MacCallan Castle.

"What shall we do today, Brighid? Go back to the creek and fish? Or, if you'd produce my horse we could track some bison. I've always wanted to hunt bison. Tell me, are their tempers as evil as my father says?"

Instead of answering, the Huntress studied him. She had been wrong when she had thought Cuchulainn didn't have a light of his own. How could she not have seen it before? The warrior shone like a young, golden god. He was filled to overflowing with life and joy.

Cu needed this part of himself, and the young godling needed the strength of the mature warrior who had stayed with his body and chosen to cling to life and try to survive the pain of loss.

Undaunted by her silence, Cuchulainn smiled at her. "Fine. We'll do what you want to do. It is your dream."

"It's time to come home now, Cu," she said.

The warrior shrugged and jumped lithely to his feet. "It's your decision—your dream. Of course there aren't any bison there, but the deer are amusingly suicidal. Want to see who can bring one down first?"

"No hunting. No dreaming. No more pretending. It's time to come home."

He huffed out some air on a strangled half laugh. "I don't know what you're talking about, Brighid. Like I said before, it's your dream. I'm just along for the ride."

"Stop it," she snapped, surprising them both with her vehemence. "This charade dishonors her memory. I understand grief. I understand loss. But I do not understand dishonor."

Cuchulainn's face lost some of its golden glow. "You're not making sense."

"Enough, Cuchulainn. You remember, I know you do. It's time to face the real world. Back there we're not rebuilding Elphame's chambers. That was almost three cycles of the moon ago. Your sister's chamber is finished. Much of the castle has been rebuilt, but you haven't been there to see it. You've been in the Wastelands in self-imposed exile, grieving for Brenna."

He shook his head. "You're wrong."

"No," she said wearily. "I wish I were wrong. I wish I could undo it. But I can't. You loved Brenna, and she was killed."

"Why are you doing this?"

She continued as if he hadn't spoken. "When Brenna died, it shattered your soul. Since then part of you has been living and breathing and trying to cope with grief and guilt and pain. Trying to go on with everyday life. And I can tell you it has been damned hard for him because the part of his spirit that loves life—that's filled with joy and hope and happiness—is here," she spoke softly. "That's what you are, Cu. A piece of a whole. Look inside yourself. You're incomplete and you know it."

He kept shaking his head back and forth. "No…"

He took a step away from her, but she moved quickly, covering the space between them, and put a restraining hand on his shoulder, surprised that he felt so real, so solid and warm.

"Not this time," she told him. Brighid reached into her pocket and brought out the turquoise stone. She held it out to him on her open palm. "Whose is this, Cu?"

His face drained of the last of its color. He stared at the stone.

"Whose is this?" she repeated.

"It's Brenna's stone." His voice had lost all of its youthful exuberance and he sounded like the warrior back at MacCallan Castle. "She said it was a gift from Epona." He looked up at Brighid, his expression that of a lost boy. "She said it's the same color as my eyes."

"It is, my friend," Brighid said.

"I loved Brenna," he said slowly.

Brighid nodded. "Yes, and she loved you."

"Brenna is dead."

"Yes." Brighid wasn't sure what she had expected, but the calm resignation that settled over Cuchulainn's face surprised her.

He was staring at the stone again. "I remember."

"I knew you would." She squeezed his shoulder. "Are you ready to come home now?"

He lifted haunted eyes to hers. "Why should I?"

"He needs you. You need him. And it's the right thing to do, Cuchulainn."

"Why doesn't he come here? It's nice here. There's no pain. No death. No—"

"Have you seen Brenna here?" she interrupted him.

His body jerked. "No. Not yet. But maybe if I were whole again, then she'd come."

"She wouldn't come, Cu. This place isn't real—not even by the Otherworld's standards. It's flawed, fake, pretend. Nothing here really exists."

"How do you know?" His voice edged on desperation.

"You'll just have to trust me, Cuchulainn. I would never deceive you. The man whose body lies beside me at MacCallan Castle knows that. Don't you, too?"

His gaze stayed on hers, and she could see him considering. Slowly, he nodded his head. "I do trust you. Enough that I believe you'll give me an honest answer to one last question. What is there for me to return to other than grief and pain and the pieces of a broken life?"

The importance of her answer pressed down upon her soul. *Oh, help me...Etain...Epona...someone.* Frantically her mind struggled for a well-worded, logical answer that would make her friend whole again. Should she mention his sister? The people of Clan MacCallan? How about the children he had obviously grown fond of?

Stop thinking, child, and Feel. You'll find the right answer.

The words in her head were unmistakably Etain's. Blindly, like a drowning man, she clung to them, plunging through the flotsam in her mind. When she spoke, the answer came from her heart.

"You will love again. That's why you have to return. I think you might already be a little in love." Brighid's eyes filled with tears as her emotions overwhelmed her. "It's not going to be easy, and it's come from an unexpected place…" She thought of the beautiful winged Ciara and realized that "unexpected" was a definite understatement, but she took a breath and kept talking to the stricken warrior. "I don't claim to know much about love, but I do know that it can make life worth living. Trust me, Cuchulainn. Your life will soon be filled with love and it will be well worth living again."

As she spoke a change came over the warrior. The sadness in his turquoise eyes remained, but the despair lifted from them, and when he smiled his whole face warmed.

By the Goddess, he was handsome!

Her hand still rested on his shoulder. Not taking his eyes from hers, he covered her hand with his own and raised it to his lips. Shocked beyond words, Brighid could only stare at him. His gaze was intense, and it seemed the blue in his eyes had darkened. When he spoke his voice had deepened.

"Have you become a High Shaman, Brighid?"

She shook her head, wondering how she could feel numb and hot at the same time.

Cuchulainn laughed softly, a sublimely male sound that reverberated low in Brighid's gut.

"I would say that a human man loving a centaur who cannot shapeshift is perhaps a little more than unexpected, but I do trust you, my beautiful Huntress. And I am now ready to come home."

He believed that she was the woman he was falling in love with! Brighid opened her mouth to deny it—to explain—to correct his misconception and—

Bring him home, child.

Etain's voice in her mind caused her mouth to clamp shut and her cheeks to warm. The priestess was right, of course. Now was not the time to explain to Cu that he was mistaken. Now was the time to get him home. Explanations wouldn't be needed once he joined his body. Cuchulainn might not be ready to admit that he could love Ciara, but he knew the attraction was there. Just as he knew there was none between the two of them.

"Are we going, Brighid?"

She blinked and reordered her thoughts. Cuchulainn was standing very close to her, and he was still holding her hand in his. He smiled, looking suddenly shy. *Oh, Goddess! He actually believed they were falling in love.* She felt her heart compress and her stomach tighten, and for just a moment she let herself wonder what it would be like to have this warrior as her own, to forget that he was an unattainable man. She found that it wasn't very difficult for her to do. Maybe it was because of his centaur father, maybe it was the fact that his mother was Epona's Chosen, for whatever reason this man called alive feelings within her that no other male, be he human or centaur, had ever stirred.

It was just a dream—fleeting and impossible—but it tempted her…intrigued her… And she let it. For a moment, she let it.

Breathe him in, and bring him home, child.

Etain's voice jolted her, and she felt her face heat again. She was supposed to be retrieving his soul, and instead she was indulging in ridiculous childlike fantasies. All while his mother was watching.

Cuchulainn laughed softly and laced his fingers with hers. "What is it? You look terrified."

"I—I have to bring you home," she blurted.

He nodded. "I'm ready. What's next?" he asked, sounding eerily like the Cuchulainn who had burst into her bed chamber.

"I'm supposed to breathe you in." Her voice was almost inaudible.

He cleared his throat and his hand tightened on hers. She thought that he looked suddenly, obviously, nervous. "I think there's only one way to do that."

"How?" she asked, but she already knew.

"Kiss me, Brighid. Breathe in my soul. Take me back to the land of the living."

Her stomach clenched and she felt like her heart would explode from her chest.

Cuchulainn smiled. "Now you look like *you'd* like to run away."

"No, I'm just... It's just..." she sputtered.

His brows went up. "We haven't kissed? Ever?"

She shook her head.

He sighed. "Of course we haven't. Part of me is here—part's there. And I'm still in mourning for Brenna..." He passed the hand that wasn't holding hers through his hair. "I don't imagine this thing between us has been easy for you." Then he moved even closer to her and touched her cheek. "I apologize for being so broken. For making things even more complicated than they already are. Kiss me, Brighid, so that I can heal for both of us."

He was a tall man, with a warrior's honed muscles and breadth of shoulder. She only had to bend a little to meet his lips. Brighid stopped thinking. Cuchulainn's golden light was back, and even when she closed her eyes she could see the brilliance of it, bright and burning. The kiss started as tentative. His lips were warm, and the taste of him reminded her of the grasslands that surrounded them—welcoming and sensuous. She opened her mouth and let her arms go around him as the kiss deepened. His body was hard and he seemed to fill not just the space around her and within her arms, but his aura enfolded her, just as his hands cradled her face. His tongue met hers and she felt an indescribable shiver of need ripple across her skin and lodge deep within her. His hands left her face to splay into her hair. When he moaned against her lips she felt the breathless, masculine sound like it was a caress.

I want him. I want all of him.

The instant the thought passed through her mind, she felt the change. The golden light against her closed lids disappeared. The warm, fragrant breeze was gone. The only thing that remained was Cuchulainn. His lips against hers—his hands in her hair—his body straining to meet hers.

Brighid opened her eyes. She was back in her chamber at

MacCallan Castle. They were on her bed, facing each other. Cuchulainn was kissing her. Her body tensed, and the warrior's eyes shot open. Abruptly, he broke the kiss. His hands fell from her hair at the same instant she disentangled her arms from around him. Mortified that she was breathing so heavily, she wanted to hurl herself off the bed and rush from the room, especially when the warrior made no move to pull farther away from her. With a shaky hand, she smoothed her hair back from her face. Her lips felt wet and bruised. Hesitantly, she met his eyes. They were as blue as the turquoise stone she still clutched in her hand, and just as impossible to read.

"Are you back?" she asked, surprised she sounded so normal.

"Yes." His voice was rough. He sat up and looked down at his hands and arms, as if they were new to him, and then he ran his fingers through his hair. He stopped, feeling the length and tangle of it, and touched his face, which was rough and unshaven. "It's such an odd sensation. I know that I've let my hair grow and that I need to shave. Or at least a part of me knows it. Another part of me is surprised."

"I don't think the feeling of being disconnected will last long," she said, rising quickly from the bed and walking over to the table on which the wineskin slouched in the basket of food. She forced her hand open, and let the turquoise stone roll out of her palm, noting that it had left an almost perfectly round indentation on her skin. Moving methodically, Brighid reached for the wine, eager to give her hands something to do, and took a long drink. Then she glanced over her shoulder at him. He was still sitting on the bed, but he had quit studying himself. Unfortunately, now all his attention was focused on her. "You need to eat and drink to ground yourself. So do I." She turned back to the food, breaking a hunk off the fragrant bread and chewing it between swallows of wine.

She could feel his eyes on her. She took another long drink

and then, without looking at him said, "I'm sorry for the misunderstanding back there."

"Misunderstanding?"

She heard him leave the bed and approach her. She busied
herself with slicing off a thick piece of cheese.

"The misunderstanding about us. You—he—assumed that
I was talking about us falling in love. You, the whole you,
knows that's ridiculous. I wasn't talking about myself, I was referring to Ciara." She glanced at him and looked quickly away.

"I'm not falling in love with Ciara." His voice was carefully
neutral.

"Love is probably too strong a word. I suppose lust or attraction or—" she faltered, shrugging her shoulders "—something else would probably have been more accurate, but love
seemed like the right word at the time."

Cuchulainn took the wineskin from her and drank from it.
He wiped his mouth with the back of his hand and said, "I'm
not lusting after Ciara. Of course I've noticed that she's beautiful, but that's where my notice has ended."

"Oh." Brighid had no idea what to say.

"Look at me, Brighid," he said.

Reluctantly she met his gaze. Physically he didn't look
changed. Or at least not much. Maybe he stood a little
straighter, as if whatever had been pressing on his broad
shoulders had been lifted. There were no fewer lines creasing
the edges of his eyes, and his hair, which was too sandy to
match the auburn shade of his sister's fiery mane, was still
sprinkled with premature gray. The noticeable difference was
in his eyes. They were no longer haunted and empty. And it
felt to her like they looked into her soul.

"My feelings for Ciara did not bring me home. My feelings
for you did."

"We're friends, clan members. We've hunted together
and—"

The touch of his hand on her arm cut off her rush of words.

"Don't deny what happened between us."

"We kissed. That's all."

Slowly his hand moved from her arm to touch her cheek. "Why are you trembling?"

"I don't know," she said.

"I think you do."

"There can be nothing between us except friendship, Cuchulainn," she said, wishing her voice wasn't shaking.

He caressed her cheek. Then he let his fingers trail lightly down the side of her neck. "That is exactly what my mind is telling me, too."

"Then you shouldn't be touching me like this," Brighid whispered.

"The problem is, my beautiful Huntress, that right now I'm finding it difficult to think with my mind." He moved closer to her and she could feel the heat of his body. "You see, what you restored to me was filled with passion and joy for life, and at this moment that part of me feels young and strong and very, very willful."

Brighid forced her voice to be steady. "But that part of you will recede, and return to its proper place. And then where will that leave us, Cuchulainn?"

He blinked, and his hand dropped away from her body. He stepped back. She could see the struggle within him as his jaw clenched and he brought his breathing under control.

"I should leave," he said abruptly. Before he turned away he looked down at the table—at the turquoise stone that rested there. With a jerky movement, he scooped it up and stumbled away from her. He stopped at the door and bowed his head. "Forgive me, Brighid," he said without looking at her. Then he opened the door and was gone.

Brighid closed her eyes and tried to still the trembling within her soul.

CHAPTER
THIRTY

Cuchulainn hadn't expected to sleep, but he'd returned to his quarters to find privacy. To think, to reacquaint himself with…himself. And to understand what had happened between Brighid and him.

He sat on the edge of his bed and stared into the dying firelight. By the Goddess, it was a bizarre feeling! He knew the events that had taken place during the past several cycles of the moon. He remembered loving Brenna and the tragedy of her death. He remembered traveling to the Wastelands and being snowbound with the New Fomorians. He could recall everything that had happened to them on their journey into Partholon and their return to MacCallan Castle. And yet a part of him marveled at the memories like they were foreign tales told by a visiting bard.

The strangest thing was that he felt inexplicably light with joy. The thought made his hands tremble as he sipped slowly from the goblet of rich red wine he'd poured himself. It wasn't the kind of joy he'd known in Brenna's touch—or the youthful exuberance he'd felt at breathing in life and knowing that the world was waiting for him. It was more the possibility of joy than the unbridled emotion itself. It was something he'd thought he'd never experience again, and the part of him that had been bereft of it felt more alive than he'd been since the terrible day Brenna had been murdered.

He still grieved for Brenna. She was his lost love. Part of him would always miss her and even yearn for her, but he knew he could go on. He knew he could live—and even love—again.

Brighid…

The Huntress had shaken him to his core. Was it because she had literally touched a part of his soul? Had she been right to say that as soon as he became accustomed to being whole once more his feelings for her would go back to their proper place? What exactly was their proper place?

In his twenty-four years he had seduced many women, but had been in love with only one. His love for Brenna had been new and young and easy. Their life together would have been full—their children many. He would have happily grown old by her side. She would have been the only one for him. The first and last woman he would have loved.

And he would never have known the flame that had been ignited when he touched Brighid. When she'd kissed him his soul had rejoiced. He'd been consumed by her, and in return he wanted to possess her. His desire had been insistent and engulfing. Just the remembrance of the taste of her, the feel of her body against his own, was mesmerizing. It had been like nothing he had ever before experienced, and so overwhelming that while they touched she had become his world, as if he had been created to love her.

Surely that was just a side effect of the soul retrieval.

Regardless, they couldn't be lovers. Brighid Dhianna was a centaur. A *centaur.*

He stood and paced back and forth in an attempt to relieve the energy that pulsed through his body. It was, of course, not impossible for a centaur and a human to fall in love and mate. He was a product of such a union. But that was a unique situation. His parents were lifemates because Epona always fashioned a centaur High Shaman as mate for her Chosen Incarnate. And a centaur High Shaman had the ability to shapeshift into human form so that their love could be fully consummated.

Brighid was not even a Shaman—and a High Shaman? Definitely not. To be gifted with such power was a rare and fantastic thing.

She is the eldest daughter of a High Shaman. Had she not left the herd she would have been expected to one day take her mother's place.... The thought teased him.

"But she's chosen the life of a Huntress!" He argued aloud with himself. "Centaur Huntresses do not love human men. They rarely even form permanent bonds with centaur males. And they cannot shapeshift."

Then why had she responded to his touch with a passion so fierce it had seemed to consume him?

What was he thinking? It *had* consumed him. She had breathed in his soul and then returned it to his body. That's all there was to it. That had to be all there was to it.

There was only one word for anything else between them—impossible.

He drained the last of the wine, and then set the goblet on his bedside table. Feeling suddenly, thoroughly exhausted, he stretched out on top of the thick, down-filled linens that covered his bed. As sleep pulled him under, he could still taste her on his lips.

Cuchulainn liked waking early. It was a habit that had taken root during his warrior training. He often was up honing his skills before any of his peers had begun to stir. So rising early the next morning had nothing to do with knowing that Brighid often left the castle at dawn. He wasn't trying to chance a meeting with the Huntress. He was just falling back into a comfortable habit.

He was hurriedly washing his face in his small private bathing chamber when he caught his reflection in the wall mirror. He looked like a gnarled old man. His hair was long and matted and wild. He frowned at his reflection. How long had there been gray in his hair? His beard was rough. He rubbed at his chin. And it itched. Cuchulainn glanced down at his kilt. It was stained and threadbare. He expelled a long breath. Little wonder Brighid had had such a startled look in her eyes last night, and had so rapidly rejected him. Not only was he a human—he was a pathetic-looking human. He sniffed. He even smelled bad.

First, he'd bathe. Then he'd shave and…he shook his head at the mess that was his hair. It needed to be washed and cut. Warriors of Partholon usually wore their hair long, but he'd never liked the mess of it. When he was younger he'd had many an argument with his mother over it. He'd told her over and over that he wasn't less of a warrior with less hair—and then set about to prove it to her. When his skills had become almost legendary, she'd capitulated, and he'd even managed to coax her into trimming it for him herself from time to time…

He grinned at his rumpled reflection. His mother was currently lodged down the hall from him. After a bath and a shave perhaps he'd be a considerate son and join her for breakfast.

Humming to himself, he began to strip.

The door to the guest suite opened before Cu could knock on it. A striking young blonde dressed in a mostly see-through robe of diaphanous pink material giggled at his raised fist.

"Your mother has been expecting you, warrior," she said.

"Of course she has," he said. Then he felt himself returning the maiden's flirtatious grin. "And it's nice to see Mother still believes in surrounding herself with beauty."

The maiden's cheeks flushed an alluring shade of pink that perfectly matched her gown, and she dropped into a lithe curtsy, which gave the warrior a clear view of her shapely breasts. Automatically Cu looked, with a long, hot gaze that had his body tightening.

He was, after all, still alive.

"Cuchulainn! Come in—come in," Etain called from within the chamber.

He winked at the handmaid before she moved aside so he could greet his mother. Etain was sitting on a chair which was opulently upholstered in gold velvet. Another attractive young woman brushed the priestess's mass of red curls sprinkled with silver-gray. Cuchulainn smiled at her, noting that she had covered the walls of the guest suite with tapestries depicting herself, bare breasted, riding the Goddess mare as young maidens frolicked about showering their path with rose petals. Etain had also filled the suite to overflowing with luxurious furnishings and a silk-canopied bed on—of course—a dais.

His mother never failed to travel in a style befitting the Beloved of Epona. The part of his soul that had been absent so long stirred, and Cuchulainn felt a sudden rush of love for the flamboyant, powerful woman who was his mother. Laughing joyously, he strode to her, pulled her into his arms, and kissed her soundly. Her musical laughter joined his own as she hugged him.

Then she pulled back and looked into his eyes. Her smile widened and she laid her hand against his newly shaven cheek.

"It is so good to see you whole again, my son."

"You knew, of course," he said.

"Yes." She paused and made a slight, graceful motion with her hand, dismissing the maidens. "I knew the day it happened," she continued after they were alone. She kissed his cheek and smoothed back his long hair. "I would have helped you if I could have, but some things are beyond even a mother's reach."

"I wish you had known Brenna."

"Epona has spoken to me of her often. Your betrothed was an exceptional young woman. She was—and is—very dear to the Goddess."

Cuchulainn closed his eyes on the bittersweet pain. "Thank you, Mother."

She patted his cheek. "Let her go, my darling. Think of her—remember her—but let her go. It is time you moved forward with your life."

He nodded. "As always, you are right."

"Of course I am." She stood on tiptoe and again kissed him softly on the cheek. Then she ruffled his hair. "I had the handmaids fetch my scissors. Shall we get started?"

He grinned at her. "It's a good thing that I've never tried to keep anything from you. It would certainly make life damned difficult."

She raised her eyebrow at him, reminding Cu of his sister. "You know it's blasphemy to keep secrets from your mother."

"Blasphemy?" He laughed, but let her lead him to the golden chair. With the scissors in one hand, and a slim comb in the other, she began to work on his hair, sighing as she combed through the thick mass of it.

"I don't suppose I could talk you into leaving it long. I could just take a little off here and there…"

His eyes met hers in the vanity mirror and she sighed again and began cutting. Under her familiar touch he relaxed, letting his memory sift back through all the times in his youth that his mother had willingly set aside the business of the Goddess to care for him, as well as for Elphame and their twin siblings, Arianrhod and Finegas. His father, too, High Shaman of Partholon, had never failed to make his children's needs a priority.

What kind of man would he have become if he had been raised without parents? Poor Brenna—to have had to go through the most difficult part of her life without the love of her mother and father.

Brighid's father was dead, too, he remembered with a

sense of surprise. He'd died years ago. Strange that Cu was just now thinking of that. Brighid had berated him for allowing grief to make him give up on life. She'd spoken as if from experience, but when he'd challenged her she'd only spoken of the loss the New Fomorians had survived. Odd that the Huntress so rarely spoke of her family. Yes, her herd was known for their radical beliefs, but her mother was High Shaman. Surely such a powerful dam had had a profound and lasting effect upon her daughter. Yet Brighid had broken tradition and left her family. He wondered why...

"Have you seen her this morning?" His mother's soft voice seemed to come directly from his thoughts. He jerked, and she thumped his shoulder. "Be still or you'll be even more unpresentable than you were when you arrived all wild and shaggy."

He cleared his throat. "Who?"

His mother looked down her regal nose at him.

He sighed. "No, I have not seen Brighid this morning. I came straight here."

"After bathing and shaving—Goddess be thanked."

He grunted.

"Soul retrieval is a very intimate act," she began in a smooth, conversational tone. "For the soul to be successfully returned to the body, the Shaman must build a bridge of caring and understanding between herself and the patient. If I am not mistaken, you and Brighid had a strong friendship before the shattered piece of your soul began visiting her."

"Yes," he said.

"It was Brighid who tracked Elphame the night she was injured and almost killed by the wild boar?"

"Yes."

"And Brighid who led you to Brenna's body?"

"It was," he said. "Mother, I don't—"

Her raised hand stopped his words. "Wait. Let me speak, and then you can ask me all the questions you wish."

He nodded slightly, feeling expectant as well as nervous.

What did his mother know about what had happened last night? Was she preparing to chide him about being infatuated with Brighid?

Was he infatuated?

"So you and she had already established a friendship. If I'm not mistaken, you have quite a bit of respect for the Huntress?"

"You are rarely mistaken, Mother."

She smiled at his reflection. "That is a truth. Now let me share with you another one. After a healing of the soul takes place, the patient—" She shook her head at his scowl. "No, there is nothing wrong with being a patient. Your spirit was broken and in need of healing. That makes you a patient. There is no shame in that. Now may I continue?"

He nodded, still hating that it sounded like he had become an invalid.

"After a soul retrieval takes place the *patient,* who would be you, is spiritually changed."

Cuchulainn sat up straighter and blinked in surprise.

His mother's voice lost its clinical detachment, and her hand rested warm and maternal on his shoulder. "You may notice that you feel sensitized, as well as energized. Your perception of reality might expand." When she felt him tense beneath her hand she patted him gently. "The effect can be temporary, but often it is not. And you will be forever linked to the Shaman who guided your soul home."

"But Brighid isn't a Shaman."

"It is true that she has not made the Otherworld journey to drink from Epona's Chalice, but the centaur carries Shamanistic power within her. If she didn't, she would never have been able to bring the lost part of you home."

Cuchulainn met his mother's gaze in the mirror.

"Ask," she said.

"Could Brighid become a High Shaman?"

"Only Epona can answer that, Cuchulainn."

"I'll take your best guess, Mother." He tried to smile at her, but the tension that radiated through his body drew his face into hard, sober lines.

"Then my best guess is that she could, but that it would not be an easy journey for her, and that it might lead her to a life of extreme loneliness." She ran the comb through his hair, smoothing and trimming while she talked. "You know that her herd's views are radical, perhaps even dangerous?"

"Yes," he said shortly.

"If she were to become High Shaman she would have to take her place as the leader of the Dhianna Herd. Brighid has chosen a different path, and I believe she has found a measure of peace and happiness in it. If she were to deviate from that path she would be thrust back into the world she purposefully departed, even though her beliefs differ drastically from theirs. That would be a very lonely life for her."

"What if she were not alone?"

Instead of answering, his mother continued to carefully and methodically trim his hair.

Undaunted by her silence, Cuchulainn continued. "What if she had someone by her side who was willing to fill in the lonely space—to support her beliefs. Someone who respected her and…"

"And loved her?"

He turned so that he could look directly at his mother. "Is what I'm feeling just a result of the soul retrieval?"

"What are you feeling, my son?"

"I am so drawn to her that I can hardly bear being away from her! I would have rushed to find her this morning—" he barked a humorless laugh "—if I hadn't realized that I looked like a wild mountain hermit."

"Centaurs are magical and alluring beings," she said noncommittally. "They are passionate and beautiful. The soul of a human enhanced by the strength of an equine is something that can be a very powerful draw."

"Mother! You must tell me. Is what I'm feeling temporary

obsession because she touched my soul, or is it something more?"

"Only you and Brighid can decide that. For all of my knowledge, I cannot predict love. The bond caused by soul retrieval is rarely more than deep understanding and respect." She smiled at him. "It seems that you feel considerably more for the Huntress."

"Considerably," he said under his breath.

"Enough that you are willing to ask her to change her life and her future so that the two of you can be mated?"

"I don't know!"

The priestess touched her son's cheek. "I wish your father were here."

"He wouldn't tell me that I have gone mad?"

"He might." She laughed.

He put his hand over hers. "I don't know what to do."

"Of course you don't. You can't decide that on your own—not really. Talk with Brighid. You've already shared your soul with her, how much more difficult could it be to share the secrets of your heart with her?"

"It feels like it's happening too fast. Too soon after Brenna."

"The world is turning quickly, Cuchulainn. I Feel a great restlessness approaching. Perhaps now is the appropriate time for fast actions." She brushed her hands through his hair and gave him a considering look, then she smiled again. "You are finished here."

He turned to the mirror, smoothing his newly shorn hair back from his forehead. Then he took his mother's hand and kissed it.

"Thank you," he said.

She squeezed his hand and gave him a little push toward the door. "Go find your future, my son. And know that whatever you choose, my blessing, as well as Epona's, goes with you."

CHAPTER
THIRTY-ONE

At dawn when Brighid cleared her mind to concentrate on searching for the light of wild boar the first light that blazed before her subconscious was golden and not situated in the surrounding forest. It was coming from the quarters Elphame had prepared for her brother during his absence.

No! Brighid closed her mind's eye, turning away from the beckoning golden light. *Find the blood-red light of a boar.* The searching power within her spun away from Cuchulainn and MacCallan Castle—out into the forest. It sifted through the glimmering soul lights of animals, small and large, until it focused on a single red shaft. Automatically Brighid's infallible sense of direction locked on the boar. Northeast of the castle. Not far from where Elphame had been attacked by one of the beasts those many moons ago. Brighid knew where she needed to go.

She took a skin of water and a healthy portion of the bread

and meat that was left over from the night before, filled her quiver with arrows, strapped her long sword across her back, fitted her short sword in its sheath around her waist, and slid her throwing daggers within the hidden pockets of her vest. Then she silently made her way to the front gate. As they had done so many times before, the sentry saluted her, opening the iron doors and calling luck to her for the morning hunt. She was so intent on getting free of the castle that she hardly took time to return the sentry's salute before she kicked into a swift gallop. Even after she was well within the concealing northern woods she barely slowed her pace.

It felt good to push herself, to keep her mind so busy with dodging trees and underbrush, ravines and rocks, that she couldn't think…couldn't remember. She ran a long time before her sanity returned.

When she finally slowed, and then stopped, she realized that she had passed the boar's territory. Brighid wiped the sweat from her face and reoriented herself. She wasn't far off. She scented the slight breeze and caught the unmistakably clean smell of moving water. When she found the stream, she would follow it to the boar's wallow. Then she would take the animal down with one clean shot, dress it out, and return the meat to the castle. Simple. Clear. Uncomplicated. Exactly the way she liked her life.

And exactly the opposite of what her life had usually been. When she started toward her prey again, she did so slowly. It was time to think. Here, surrounded by the forest she knew so well, she would sift through the intricacies of last night. She'd work it out in her head—figure out how she could go on living at MacCallan Castle with Cuchulainn and the knowledge of what had passed between them. She would do it because she had to find a way to make this work—to turn back time and have things be simple between the two of them again. She didn't want to leave MacCallan Castle. The thought of it made her immeasurably sad.

Of course she didn't want to leave—to displace herself

again so soon after she had begun to take root—but perhaps she should, temporarily. Guardian Castle was missing a Huntress. She could honestly say they needed her presence until their own Huntress returned. It was likely she wouldn't be gone long. Surely Guardian Castle's Huntress would not desert her post for more than one moon cycle. But even a few days should be enough for Cuchulainn to...

To what?

"To stop thinking with his passion," she said aloud to the ancient pine trees.

That's how he'd explained it last night. His mind had known that he shouldn't touch her with such desire, but his passion and his joy in life had been too newly restored to him. Its voice had drowned out the sound of reason. It made sense. She knew the part of Cuchulainn that had shattered. He had been all heart and passion and impetuosity. He really couldn't help it. She had been there, breathing his soul back into him...kissing him... He had been raw and newly whole, and a part of him had believed the two of them were falling in love. There had been credible reasons for his behavior, but what about hers?

Brighid rubbed a hand across her face and picked her way over a fallen log. When she looked at the soul retrieval logically, there had been nothing wrong with her behavior. She hadn't meant to mislead Cuchulainn about their relationship. That had been an honest miscommunication, which had, when she looked at it frankly, without emotional strings, worked out well. Cuchulainn's shattered soul had returned to his body. She had performed the complicated task of a Shaman, and had been successful at it.

Unfortunately, that wasn't all there was to it.

Emotional strings... If they had been visible Brighid had no doubt that she would be covered with them, like a ball of wool waiting to be woven into a garment. But her emotions weren't visible, and Cuchulainn wasn't the only one who could hide his feelings. But she wouldn't lie to herself. Not here, in the middle of the forest she considered sacred. She hadn't meant for Cuchulainn to misunderstand their relationship, but when he had, she had been glad. And when he kissed her, she had been filled with more than his soul. She desired him. The memory of his touch, his scent, his taste, still made her gut clench with a tension that was definitely sexual.

By the Goddess, what was she going to do!

Even if his desire for her was more than a temporary reaction to an extraordinary event, the facts still remained the same. He was human. She was centaur.

Yes, she knew human men found her attractive, even alluring. And though she had never before thought of them in a particularly sexual manner, she was no foolish young virgin. She knew how human anatomy worked. She could give Cuchulainn satisfaction with her hands and mouth. Brighid stumbled to a halt. What was she considering? Any centaur from the Dhianna Herd, and many from the other herds that shared the Centaur Plains, would consider the mere thought of a Huntress pleasuring a human man repellent, abhorrent behavior. It would make her even more of an outcast than she already was.

"But I don't find the thought of pleasuring him abhorrent." She whispered the words aloud, and then put her face in her hands. Was she turning into some kind of horrid freak of nature? Or… Oh, Goddess! Could it be that she had fallen in love with Cuchulainn?

She wasn't entirely sure which would be worse.

If she loved him that would certainly explain why her reaction to what she'd thought was Cuchulainn's growing desire for Ciara had been so completely negative. She hadn't been prejudiced against the winged woman—she'd been jealous of her! And then there was the ease with which she'd called his shattered soul into her dreams. With a groan she remembered Cuchulainn's almost nonstop ribald teasing. Did some part of the warrior recognize her innermost feelings? It was possible—he had been in her dreams, which meant on some level he'd had access to her subconscious. Didn't it?

She didn't know enough about this...this world of spirit and emotion. Trying to understand it was like trying to capture smoke and shadows! She was sure of very little except that the most damning evidence against her was the kiss, or more precisely, her reaction to it. His touch had made her forget who and what they were. Human...centaur... none of it had mattered when their lips had met and she'd inhaled him.

She groaned again. Etain had been there! In some way the High Priestess had been with her during the soul retrieval— encouraging and advising. Did she know what her son's touch had made Brighid feel? Heat rushed into the Huntress's face.

Think logically! Etain's lifemate, fashioned for her by Epona, was a centaur. Etain would not be shocked to learn that a centaur desired a human. And she must know that her son was a passionate warrior. Everyone knew that before Cuchulainn had fallen in love with Brenna he had rarely slept alone. Etain would not judge Brighid harshly for enjoying the kiss that restored her son's soul to his body.

But what would Epona's Chosen think if she knew that the Huntress's desire for her son hadn't ended there?

There was no sense in thinking about it. It had to end there.

So Brighid made her decision. If Cuchulainn still thought he desired her, she would seek and gain Elphame's permission for a temporary sojourn to Guardian Castle. By the time Brighid returned, the warrior's passions would be back under control, and he would, doubtless, have found a human woman eager to share his bed.

Actually, there was an excellent chance that when she returned to the castle today Cuchulainn would be back to himself, and probably worrying about how she would react to seeing him again. She'd focus on putting his mind at ease. She'd assure him that what passed between them last night would not affect their friendship. She would simply pretend that she'd felt nothing more for him than fleeting desire while they had been caught up in the intimate act of the soul retrieval. Maybe they would even laugh about it together over a goblet of Etain's excellent wine.

The thought of carrying on such a pretense made her feel sick. She loathed dishonesty. It was against her nature to lie. But she damned well was not going to lose her home and the peace she had found at MacCallan Castle because of an impossible love.

A twig snapped and the Huntress instinctively slowed her movements and tested the wind that blew softly into her face. She grimaced—boar. The beasts were always rank with mud and anger. She drew an arrow from her quiver and felt the stillness of the hunt blanket her tumultuous thoughts. This was something she knew she could control. She would take the boar, thank Epona for its sustaining life, and then be too damned busy dressing it out and hauling it back to the castle to obsess over Cuchulainn. She'd made her decision. There could be no future with the warrior, so she would protect herself and her place at MacCallan Castle. She would deny her feelings for him. Someday the denial would become truth.

As she'd predicted, the boar had made a wallow near the bank of the small stream. With the eerie silence of an experienced Huntress enhanced by the power inherent within her blood, Brighid crept closer without the boar detecting a single sign or scent of her. When it lolled half up in a sitting position, she notched the arrow and took sight. The arrow twanged and sped to its bloody bed, and as it pierced the boar the forest exploded with an unearthly shriek of pain. The Huntress was rushing forward before the sound died. She surged through the stream to where the boar's body should have been and gasped in horror.

The raven lay on the muddy ground with a bloody arrow piercing its chest.

"Mother!" she cried, sinking down to her forelegs beside the twitching bird.

Avenge me! The words screamed through Brighid's mind, and then the bird lay still, its eyes turning milky with death. Brighid's hand did not tremble as she stretched it out to touch the blood-soaked feathers of the dark bird. The instant her fingers made contact with the raven its body vanished, and Brighid found herself kneeling beside the dead boar.

"Oh, Epona, what does it mean? What has happened?"

There was no answer from the Goddess, and, feeling lost and alone, Brighid made herself bow her head and speak the traditional words to honor the spirit of the fallen boar. As she dressed the corpse and readied it to be carried back to Clan MacCallan she was filled with a terrible, unspeakable sense of dread.

CHAPTER
THIRTY-TWO

"Brighid! Brighid! Brighid! I've been watching for you!" Liam began chattering at her as soon as she passed through the front gates of the castle.

"The boy's been waiting all morning," the sentry called down.

Brighid tried to shake off the sense of unease that had followed her from the forest. She flashed a strained smile up at the man. "But has he been waiting quietly?"

The sentry's hearty laugh was answer enough.

"I didn't know I had to be quiet *inside* the castle," Liam muttered as he fell into step beside the Huntress. Then his eyes went big and round as he inspected the well-wrapped carcass she had strapped securely to the tether lines she dragged behind her. "What did you get?"

"You tell me," she said. "No!" She spoke sharply when he started to pull up a flap in the leather skin in which the boar was wrapped. "Use your sense of smell."

"But I don't—" he began, but one look from her silenced him. "I'll use my sense of smell," he said.

"Good. Use it all the way to the kitchen."

"I like the kitchen. It always smells good in there, and I like Wynne. She's really pretty with all that red hair and—" Another pointed look from Brighid made him clamp his lips together. "I'll scent the animal."

Brighid returned the friendly hellos from clan members as she followed the grassy path to the rear kitchen entrance. She didn't worry about unexpectedly meeting Cuchulainn. She knew he wasn't inside the castle walls. How she knew it she didn't damn well understand—but she could Feel his absence.

More good news, she thought, feeling like she was coming to the end of her tolerance for mysterious signs from the spirit world. The centaur's jaws clenched. She just wanted to be a Huntress—to live and hunt and have a secure, predictable life.

Just as she entered the gate to the kitchen gardens, she noticed several of the older winged children bent over wilted-looking rows of herbs and vegetables, digging, weeding and watering. She only had a moment to wonder how they had convinced the overprotective Wynne to allow them into her precious gardens, when Liam's voice bubbled up like an irrepressible spring.

"It smells like…like…like—" Liam took another big, audible sniff "—like mud and anger!"

Brighid stopped and looked back at him. "What did you say?"

He scuffed his taloned feet in the grass. "It smells like mud and anger?"

"How do you know that?"

He looked up at her with big eyes and shrugged his shoulders, wincing only slightly as the movement made his bandaged wing stir. "I don't know. It's just what it smells like to me. Is that wrong?"

"No," she said. "That is exactly right. Boars always smell

like mud and anger." Before he could begin hopping around in victory, she took his arm. "Be still and close your eyes."

Amazingly enough, the boy actually obeyed her. He froze and closed his eyes. She glanced around. The winged children were so busy prodding and pampering the plants that they hardly spared her a glance. For the moment, at least, she and Liam had some measure of privacy.

"Breathe deeply in and slowly out. Three times," she said, watching him closely.

He did as she commanded.

"Now, picture a boar in the forest."

"I don't know what a boar looks like," he said hesitantly.

"It doesn't matter. You don't have to picture the animal. Just think about the way it smells. Can you do that?"

He nodded his head vigorously.

"While you think about the way it smells, imagine the forest and imagine that you're looking for an animal that smells of mud and anger. Tell me what you see."

Liam's brow wrinkled as he concentrated. Then his brows shot up. "I see a bright red splotchy light!"

She couldn't believe it. The boy had the soul of a Huntress. She smiled. She had a winged apprentice who seemed more centaur than Fomorian, and she was in love with a human man. The smile grew into laughter. And she had wanted an uncomplicated life? Obviously Epona had other plans for her.

Liam peeked one eye partially open at her. "Did I say something funny?"

"No, my young apprentice. You said the exact right thing. Again. I'm just laughing at life."

"Why?" he asked, opening both his eyes.

"Because sometimes it's either laugh or cry. I prefer laugh. How about you?"

He grinned. "Laugh!"

"Och, there ye are!" Wynne stood, hands on hips, legs planted wide, in the rear doorway of her kitchen. The cook's smile flashed. "I can tell ye honestly, Huntress, that I am greatly pleased that yer back home where ye belong."

Brighid's laughter still danced in her eyes. "Thank you, Wynne." She nodded her chin in the direction of the busy winged children. "I was just wondering how they managed to win their way into your sacred gardens."

"The bairns seem to know a thing or two about plants and herbs and such, and I thought to keep their wee hands busy. Besides, it has been a long, dry spring, and my herbs need the extra pampering." Her imperious gaze swept over the gardens and the children. "But donna fash yourself. I'm keeping my eye on them."

Little heads turned up with toothy smiles. Brighid was surprised to see Wynne's face soften in response.

"You like children," she said, more than a little shocked.

Wynne's emerald gaze came back to the Huntress and her full lips tilted up. "I canna deny it. I like the life bonny young ones bring to a castle."

"Huh," Brighid said, thinking that Wynne wouldn't like it so much if she'd been alone with seventy of them.

"Donna use that tone with me, lassie, not when I see what is following ye around." She pointed at Liam.

Brighid cleared her throat. "Wynne, have you met my apprentice?"

"No, but I've word of him." She gave the boy an appraising look. "Another good Huntress 'tis always welcome in a kitchen."

"He'll be a good Huntress," Brighid said, causing Liam's chest to swell. "Someday," she added before the boy exploded.

"Well then, young Liam," Wynne said, moving out of the doorframe to join them. "What is it ye have brought me?"

"Boar!" Liam said proudly.

"Did ya now?" Wynne clapped her hands together. "Wild boar! Goddess 'tis good to have ye home, Brighid! Bring it in— bring it in." Her gleeful tone changed quickly to that of a warrior in command. "But mind where yer walkin'! Have a care with the young mint and basil shoots. This horrid dry weather has practically shriveled my garden to death." When the Huntress and boy moved too slowly, she tapped her foot impatiently. "I dinna mean for ye to turn to molasses! Get the beastie in here. 'Tis none too soon for the dinner meal."

"Are we to move carefully or quickly?" Brighid said.

"Both, of course!"

Smiling at Wynne's familiar bossiness, Brighid pulled the carcass into the kitchen, soaking in the warmth of the enthusiastic greetings called by the army of scullery maids. The rich smells and the bustling activity chased from her mind the last vestiges of the unease brought on by the vision of the fallen raven. By the Goddess, she loved this part of her life! It Felt right to provide for the Clan—and to be a part of a family unit. Liam was an unexpected element, but the boy had a gift. He could actually see animal spirits. So she'd just weave him into the fabric of her life.

And Cuchulainn? He was equally as unexpected. Perhaps there was a way to stitch him into her life as well.

No. She was being foolish. Cuchulainn was already a part of her life. He was her Chieftain's brother and her friend. That was the role fate had relegated to him. Simple. Logical. Predictable. Just the way she liked it.

But wasn't there even the smallest possibility that he could be more?

"Brighid? Can we go, too?" Liam's expectant question broke through her tangled thoughts.

"Go?"

"Aye, aye." Wynne made rapid shooing motions with her hands at them. "Be gone. We donna have time to step 'round ye."

Brighid snorted at the cook, but before disappearing out the rear door she snagged something that still lay with the great carcass.

"Come, Liam." She headed to the door. "Getting in the way of a busy cook can be more dangerous than tracking wild beasts." Out in the garden she tossed the lump she had been holding to her apprentice, who caught it neatly. "Speaking of tracking, do you know what that is?"

Liam sniffed it before he answered. "A hoof."

"Of?"

"The boar, of course," he said.

"You know that now. You can smell it, and you know that I pulled it from the carcass. But would you know it as a boar's hoofprint if you saw it in the forest?"

Liam stared at the grisly relic of Brighid's hunt. "I don't know."

"Well, let's go find out," she said. Then paused as they left the kitchen gardens. "How is your wing?"

"It feels good," he assured her. "I'm not tired at all."

She narrowed her eyes at him. "What would Nara say if I asked her the same question?"

"The same thing, I promise." At her doubting look he added. "Ask her for yourself. She's out with the rest of them."

"Out? Where?"

"Where Wynne said, remember? That way—" he pointed to the south "—outside the castle. Everyone's there setting up camp and trying to decide where to build the new buildings. I'd be there, too, but I thought I should wait for you."

"You did well," she said absently. Already her senses were reaching, tendril-like, to the grassy plateau southeast of the castle. Easily, clearly, she Felt the brilliant golden light that was Cuchulainn's spirit. *Get it over with. You can't live here and avoid seeing the man.* "Yes, let's join the others. And I'll give you your first lesson in tracking." She glanced down at the boy. He did look better, and he seemed to be moving more easily. But his wing was still bandaged securely to his back, and his color was paler than she would have liked. The centaur sighed and reached down to him. "Come on. Climb up."

His smile tugged at her heart. She lifted him to her back and felt one of his warm little hands rest on her shoulder. She knew without looking that the other hand still clutched the bloody hoof stump. His weight was slight and easy to bear and she found that she liked the feel of his hand on her shoulder and how he chattered about boars and hooves with the same excitement she had felt when she had been a young apprentice. She didn't even mind the surprised smiles and stares the sentries gave her as she trotted back out the front gates.

"Can we go fast?" Liam asked, leaning his chin on her shoulder and talking directly into her ear.

She probably should have said no, that his wound was still too raw to be jostled, but she Felt the lure that was coming from the golden light. She would certainly surprise everyone if she galloped up with a laughing Liam astride her back. No one would expect such behavior from her.

Perhaps it was time that she did a little of the unexpected.

"Hold tight," she said over her shoulder and launched herself forward. She did, of course, keep one hand on the boy's leg to steady him, but she was pleased to feel the child settle into a deep, firm seat and hold tight to her. He didn't bobble around and flail his arms annoyingly. Actually the boy stuck to her like a particularly persistent tick, an image that made her smile. When she pounded around the bend in the land and the southern plateau opened up before her, she ignored the workers, and widened her stride, cutting in and around the clumps of humans, centaurs, and New Fomorians, and was rewarded with Liam's whoop of excitement.

She didn't slow until she caught sight of Elphame's distinctive figure. The Chieftain was part of a small group standing near the cliff which fell dramatically down to the shore far below. Their heads were bowed over a large wooden table situated under an awning meant to serve as protection from the crisp sea wind. Brighid recognized Lochlan's tall, winged shape, as well as the old centaur Stonemaster, Danann. Beside him stood a wide-shouldered, amber-haired warrior who made her heart squeeze in her chest.

Once she saw Cuchulainn she didn't have to tell herself sternly to go over there and get this first meeting over with.

The truth was, she was drawn to him, as if his golden light was a beacon guiding her home. The Huntress galloped up to the small group in a rush of pounding hooves and boyish giggles. She slid to a stop beside Elphame, who laughed in surprise.

"Brighid, Liam, I was wondering when the two of you would join us," Elphame said, eyes glittering with humor.

"Brighid got a boar! It smells like mud and anger. And I got its hoof!" Liam proudly held up the bloody stump like a trophy.

"Mud and anger, huh? That doesn't surprise me. I don't particularly like boars," Elphame said.

Lochlan's arm went around her waist, and she automatically leaned into her mate. "I'm rather fond of them. Isn't that true, my heart?" He and Elphame shared an intimate look, remembering that it was the attack of a wild boar that had brought them together for the first time.

"Well, I am fond of eating them," Danann said. The old centaur moved to clasp Brighid's forearm warmly. "Well met, Huntress. I missed greeting you last night."

"Well met, Stonemaster." Brighid gestured to the grounds before them, filled with clan members and New Fomorians, all busily erecting tents. "In this horde, it's easy to miss one another." She drew in a fortifying breath and finally allowed herself to look directly at Cu. She'd opened her mouth to wish him a friendly good morning, but the sight of him made her words catch in her throat.

He was so different from the Cuchulainn who had stumbled from her room the night before that the nonchalant greeting she had prepared vanished from her mind. Goddess! He looked vibrant and powerful—like the warrior he had been; only now the boyishness that had always seemed such a part of him had been forged into the maturity of a man. Where was the grief-stricken, broken Cuchulainn she had traveled with and shared quarters with in the Wastelands? Like her flippant greeting, he too had vanished. In his place was a warrior whose hair was washed and neatly cut short. The reddish beard that had covered his face was gone. The lines that had formed at the corners of his eyes were still there, but he had lost that weary, dark-shadowed look. And he was watching her carefully, with those knowing turquoise eyes and lips that were just beginning to tilt up.

"You're looking at me as if you don't recognize me. I didn't look that bad before, did I?"

Her first coherent thought was that he didn't seem nervous to be around her at all. His deep voice was full of good humor, and his smile looked mischievous.

Elphame answered while Brighid was still trying to find her voice. "Brighid's obviously being polite, so I'll say it. Yes—" she punched her brother's arm playfully "—you did look that bad."

"Well, I like your hair short," Liam chimed in from her back. "I like Brighid's long, and yours short. Of course Brighid's is prettier, though."

Cuchulainn laughed heartily and strode over to sweep the boy from the centaur's back. "I'll tell you a secret." Plopping Liam down on the ground near Brighid, he bent and, with an exaggerated whisper said, "I like her hair long and I think it's prettier than mine, too." Then his eyes met hers with a heat and intensity that was in direct contradiction to the light tone of his words.

Brighid felt like someone had knocked all of the air from her lungs.

"Oh, Cu." Elphame rolled her eyes at her brother. "You are incorrigible." But the happiness on his sister's face clearly showed how pleased she was that once again she had reason to banter playfully with her favorite brother. "Come on, Brighid, let's leave these males, and I'll catch you up on what we've decided for the New Fomorian village."

"But Brighid has to teach me about tracks," Liam said.

"Your first lesson is this one," Brighid said firmly. "When your Chieftain asks you to accompany her, you change your plans and obey." The boy instantly looked chagrined, and the Huntress had to stop herself from reaching out to run a consoling hand through his fluffy hair. She couldn't expect him to grow if she coddled him, and he needed to understand that Elphame's word was MacCallan law. "The second lesson is one that you must learn on your own. Take the hoof and go over to the tree line. Brush aside the pine needles until the soft earth of the forest is exposed, then press it firmly into the ground. Learn its shape. Touch the indentation it makes. Memorize everything about it. I'm counting on you to help me track the next boar."

Liam's face instantly brightened. "I won't let you down!" And off he went, scampering across the grassy plateau toward the line of pine trees.

"He's healing quickly," Cuchulainn said.

"Yes, he's a strong boy," she answered without looking at Cu.

"Riding on your back he looked happier than I've ever seen him," Lochlan told her.

Brighid's gaze shifted to the winged man. "I should have waited to ask your permission to accept him as my apprentice. Forgive me for overstepping."

Lochlan's smile was warm. "Huntress, I believe now is the perfect time for many of the old traditions to be overstepped. But if you need my permission, know that I grant it to you readily. With or without my blessing, the boy obviously belongs to you."

"I couldn't agree more, Lochlan. It's time we make traditions of our own," Cuchulainn said, still gazing steadily at the Huntress.

"Good," Elphame said with satisfaction. "Then you won't mind explaining to Lochlan and Danann the ideas you and I discussed earlier for where the longhouse and cottages should be built." Without waiting for her brother's reply, she linked her arm familiarly through Brighid's and guided the Huntress away from them.

Brighid could still feel Cuchulainn's eyes on her.

The women walked together, staying to the seaward side of the busy plateau. It was only when they were well out of the group's hearing range that Elphame spoke.

"How will I ever be able to thank you for healing Cuchulainn?"

"You owe me no thanks," Brighid said quickly. "I'm just relieved that it worked. Last night he still seemed…" She hesitated, struggling to choose the right thing to say. "He still seemed shaken. He may not seem quite himself for some time to come," she explained carefully, hoping to give Elphame a rational reason for Cuchulainn's lingering looks.

Elphame gave her a fast hug. "I'll take him just as he is. Of course he's still missing Brenna. He probably always will, but he's ready to move forward now. He's whole again. You've returned my brother to me. If there is anything I can ever do for you, know all you need do is ask, my sister."

"I might need to ask that you allow me to return to Guardian Castle—temporarily, of course."

Elphame's brows pulled together. "I don't understand. You just got home. How can you want to leave again so soon?"

"It's not that I want to leave," Brighid explained as they resumed their walk around the plateau. "It's just that Guardian Castle's Huntress returned to the Centaur Plains suddenly, without appointing a replacement. I couldn't help but notice that their need for a Huntress was great. I thought I might, perhaps, give them aid. With your permission," she added.

For a moment Elphame didn't speak. She just studied her friend. Then she looked over Brighid's shoulder at Cu. Brighid turned and saw his strong body silhouetted against the clear spring sky. He was turned in her direction, just standing. And staring.

"Harrumph," Elphame said, abruptly taking her friend's arm again and continuing their walk.

"So," Brighid continued, trying to hide her discomfort. "If I need to leave, temporarily, would I have your permission?"

"Are you running away?" Elphame asked.

Brighid began the denial, and then closed her mouth. She looked her friend in the eye. She didn't want to lie to her Chieftain, and she realized that she couldn't lie to her friend. "Yes. I think I might be."

Elphame's brow wrinkled. "I want to ask you something, but I need you to know that you may answer me honestly without jeopardizing our relationship. You have my word as your friend, as well as your Chieftain, on that."

Stomach clenching, Brighid nodded.

"Does the fact that Cuchulainn desires you repulse you?" When Brighid drew in a shocked breath, Elphame hurried on. "I mean, it would be understandable if it made you uncomfortable. It's hard to totally set aside the teachings of our childhood. The Dhianna Herd does not mix with humans, so it wouldn't be surprising if—"

"No!" Brighid cut her off. "By the Goddess, no! Humans don't repulse me. Cuchulainn doesn't repulse me. But what makes you think he desires me?"

"I have eyes. I know my brother. You're very beautiful, Brighid, and my brother has always been interested in beautiful women."

"I'm not a woman," she said flatly.

Elphame brushed aside her objection with a restless motion of her hand. "Men find you beautiful and desirable, just as centaurs do. You must know that. And it's obvious Cu desires you. He's not trying to hide his attraction." Elphame shook her friend's arm as if to shake some sense into her. "The two of you experienced something very intimate. I'm not sure about the details of how a Shaman brings a soul back to the land of the living, but I do know that you had to have been joined with him, spirit-to-spirit, for the retrieval to have been successful. And it was decidedly successful."

"El." Brighid drew a deep breath and guided her friend closer to the edge of the cliff so the sound of crashing waves would ensure they wouldn't be overheard. "Cuchulainn does not repel me. At all."

Elphame's eyes widened and she grinned. "You desire him, too! Someday you're going to have to tell me what does happen during a soul retrieval."

"Elphame—do not get all doe-eyed and romantic about this. Keep it in perspective. What Cuchulainn is feeling for me is simply the residue of an unusually intimate experience." She gave her friend a stern look. "And, no! I will not tell you the details."

El sighed. "I suppose I could ask Cuchulainn…"

"Goddess no!" Then the Huntress's eyes narrowed as she understood her friend was only teasing. "This is not a matter for jesting."

"Sorry," Elphame said insincerely.

Brighid frowned at her. "As I was trying to explain— Cuchulainn just thinks he desires me because of what we experienced together. That will fade. That's why it would be best if I absented myself from MacCallan Castle for a little while. To give him time to return to himself."

"I understand your reasoning. It's highly logical and realistic." Elphame smiled slyly at her friend. "And it doesn't take into account my brother's stubbornness."

"Of course it does."

Elphame laughed. "Do you remember when Cu first realized his feelings for Brenna were serious?"

"Yes. His actions were far too annoying to easily forget. He made a complete ass of himself pursuing the poor girl relentlessly until she…" Brighid suddenly ran out of words.

Elphame arched one brow. "So you didn't take into account his stubbornness. I also couldn't help but notice that you've said Cu's feelings were caused by the soul retrieval. But you've failed to mention much about your own."

"Your brother and I are friends. I like him and I respect him," she prevaricated.

"You are friends who care about and respect each other.

Now add to that your beauty and the legendary centaur passion." Elphame raised her voice and talked over her friend's sarcastic snort. "*Plus* my brother's definite flair with females, and then mix into it a soul-touching, intimate experience. Seems to me that unless you're repulsed by humans it could all add up to much more than temporary infatuation."

Brighid stared down into the frothy ocean. She was incredibly moved by what Elphame was saying. Her friend was making it clear that she would accept any kind of relationship Brighid had with Cu. Her heart tripped around in her chest. If only…

"It's not that easy," she finally said.

"Love rarely is," Elphame said.

"El, I can't love him! I can't shapeshift."

"After what you've just experienced in the spirit realm I shouldn't have to remind you that love has more to do with the soul than it does the body."

"Then I phrased it wrong," Brighid said wearily. "The problem isn't that I can't love him. The problem is that if I do, I'll forever desire what is absolutely and utterly *impossible*."

"Look, I know you don't like to talk about it, but your mother is—" Elphame broke off at her friend's look of shock. "I'm sorry, Brighid. I didn't mean to cause you pain by bringing up your family."

"It's not that." Brighid wiped a shaky hand across her face. "It's Brenna."

"Brenna?"

"She—she came to me in a dream. Here, at MacCallan Castle. Oh, Goddess! I didn't even realize until just now…"

"What is it, Brighid?"

The Huntress pressed her hand to her heart where it beat wildly against her chest. "She wanted my oath that I would keep an open mind to things that seemed impossible. She used that word exactly, El."

Elphame's eyes were bright with tears. "Did Brenna look happy?"

The Huntress nodded and her eyes filled, too.

"Did she say anything else?"

Brighid nodded slowly. "She said I could tell Cu about her visit, but not right away, that I'd know the right time. She also said that…" She hesitated, emotion choking her words.

Elphame took her friend's hand.

"Oh, El—she said that she was leaving Cu to me. Freely, and without any hesitation. I—I thought she was talking about the soul retrieval. I never thought… I didn't realize…"

"She was telling you that you have her blessing to love him," Elphame said.

"I think she was."

Elphame wiped at her cheeks. "Do you still think you should run away to Guardian Castle?"

Brighid smiled through her tears at her friend. "I can't. I swore an oath to be open to the impossible. I have to stay and face it."

"Well, my brother would certainly qualify as impossible."

"And there you, Brenna and I are in perfect agreement."

CHAPTER
THIRTY-THREE

"So what are you going to do about him?" Elphame asked, sniffling happily and wiping her eyes.

"I don't really know. I suppose I'll just have to stay open to the possibility of…" She trailed off, feeling awkward and uncomfortable and extraordinarily out of her element.

"You're going to stay open to the possibility of having a relationship with my brother."

"Yes."

"Well, he'll be glad to hear it."

Brighid gasped. "I'm not going to tell him!"

"But—"

"And neither are you. Please."

"Fine. I'll stay out of it."

"Can we change the subject now?"

"If you insist," Elphame said.

"I insist."

"Just know that I'm here if you need to talk to me. As your friend, or as your Chieftain, or as Cuchulainn's sister if he doesn't behave himself."

"Changing the subject?" Brighid reminded her.

"I just wanted you to know."

"Thank you, now I know." Brighid smiled fondly at her friend. "And I still want to change the subject."

"I suppose you actually want to know what we're planning for the New Fomorian village."

"Absolutely."

"Would you like to return to the blueprints so that I can show you what Cu and I drafted this morning?" Elphame's eyes glittered at the possibility of taking the Huntress back to her brother.

"Why don't you show me from here," Brighid said dryly.

Elphame huffed an exaggerated sigh, but began pointing and explaining that she and Cuchulainn had decided to— once again—break tradition. Because of the lack of a typical family structure, they would build one large barracks-like building to house the majority of the children. The structure would be situated not far from the southern wall of the castle. Radiating from it would be a few small cottages, where the adults, as well as the older children, could have privacy. The rest of the plateau would be tilled and planted with a variety of crops, which the New Fomorians could tend and use for trade as well as tithe to MacCallan Castle.

"My hope is that eventually what happened between you and Liam will happen with more of the children and the clan," Elphame continued.

"You hope that the children will almost pester the clan to death?"

Elphame laughed. "You know better than that. That boy belongs to you. I'm hoping many of the children find a place in the hearts and homes of my people. But I want to be careful not to force them. It has to happen naturally, and that could take some time."

"Exactly like your brother and me," Brighid muttered.

El smiled. "Not exactly, but I get your meaning." She hesitated, and her smile faded. "You've been busy, so I'm sure you haven't noticed, but we're missing several members of Clan MacCallan."

"How?"

"The first group left the same day you did. I didn't like it, but it didn't surprise me. I released them from their oaths, and said that if any more of the clan would like to join them to step forward." Elphame shook her head sadly. "It still grieves me to think of it, but I do understand them. What we are proposing, to accept the return of a people who carry the blood of Partholon's sworn enemies, is a radical thing."

"They also carry the blood of Partholonian women—innocent women who lost their homes and their lives, and whose children deserve to be given a chance," Brighid said.

"Not everyone believes that. Some people believe that anything with wings is a demon, despite what lives within his heart."

Brighid snorted. "I'm glad those people are gone. We're well rid of them. You are The MacCallan. They should have trusted that you would never put them in jeopardy."

"I'm also mated to a man who carries the mark of his demon father's blood."

"And who proved his loyalty to you!" Brighid said furiously, even as she remembered her own instinctive mistrust of Lochlan. But she hadn't let her doubts cause her to desert her Chieftain. Those who left had been wrong. They should have stayed close to Elphame and kept watch to be sure she wasn't in danger.

"He proved his loyalty, and he still does—both to me and to Clan MacCallan, but that might not be enough to overcome more than a century of hatred." Elphame met Brighid's eyes. "You know that prejudice isn't logical, which is why it is so hard to overcome." She sighed. "And more left than just that first small group."

"How many more?"

"The next morning a dozen more men and three women left."

"Fifteen more people? Just like that?" Brighid snapped her fingers, incredulous.

"They said that now the time was at hand, they, too, could not stomach the acceptance of the New Fomorians," Elphame's voice had gone flat.

"But you'd given them their opportunity to leave. They'd chosen to stay. They were sworn to you."

"They are now forsworn," Elphame said the word as if it had a bitter taste.

Brighid stared at her Chieftain, thoroughly shocked, as her friend's expression changed. Elphame's face hardened. Her eyes became shadowed, and Brighid Felt the echo of a presence that was dark and sticky with evil intent.

"El!" she cried, taking her friend's arm. Goddess! Her skin was cold.

Elphame clenched her jaw, closed her eyes, and drew a deep breath. Her lips moved in a nearly silent prayer, and Brighid could see the shimmering of Epona's power shiver in the air around them. Her friend's hair lifted, swirling in an almost invisible wind of energy that, with an audible crackle, settled into Elphame's skin. Brighid's hand tingled from where it had been Goddess-touched.

"El?" Brighid said, this time more tentatively.

The Chieftain gasped and opened her eyes. When she looked at her friend the shadows within her had, once again, retreated.

"It stirs," she explained before Brighid could decide whether or not to ask. "Especially when something has made me angry, or when I feel despair. The madness is always within me, lurking silently…waiting. It is only love and truth, along with Epona's mighty touch, that keep it at bay."

"Faith and fidelity," Brighid whispered the motto of Clan MacCallan.

"Faith and fidelity," Elphame echoed her.

Brighid wanted to ask her more, and she was trying to formulate the right words when they both were distracted as a rider pounded onto the plateau. Though the area was seething with sound and activity, there was something about the man that drew their attention. He slid to a halt in front of Cuchulainn. Brighid could hear his shouts, but couldn't make out his words.

"Stay with me," Elphame said, not waiting for her brother's raised arm to signal that she was needed. Her powerful equine legs were so quick, that in a sprint Brighid was hard-pressed to match her Chieftain's speed. As the two of them raced up to Cuchulainn, he had already mounted the rider's horse, and had his head pointed back in the direction of the castle.

"A centaur has just arrived from the Plains. She has an urgent message for Brighid."

As one, Elphame, Brighid, Lochlan and Cuchulainn rushed to the castle.

"She waits in the Main Courtyard," the sentry called as they reached the castle's open gate.

Stomach tightening with tension, Brighid slowed. The centaur stood with her back to them, as if she was consumed with looking at the fountain of the MacCallan ancestor. Brighid was surprised that she could hear the centaur's labored breathing, and her surprise expanded into astonishment when she realized the centaur's coat was lathered with flecks of white foam and her body was trembling. It was unheard of for a centaur to show such obvious signs of fatigue. She must have raced nonstop for days to put her in such a state. Then she turned and Brighid gasped.

"Niam!" She hurried to her sister, who stumbled forward and almost fell into her arms. "What has happened?"

"Thank Epona that you're here," she said between heaving breaths. "It's Mother. She's dead."

The shock of her sister's words imploded in Brighid's mind and she felt her head shaking back and forth, back and forth, as if she had no ability to control it.

"Help me get her to the Great Hall." Elphame's voice cut through the white noise of disbelief that ran in Brighid's head.

Suddenly Niam was no longer in her arms, but being half led and half carried by several of the men of Clan MacCallan, along with their Chieftain and her mate, into the Great Hall. Brighid could only stand there, staring after them, completely unable to move.

A strong, warm hand slid under her elbow and Cuchulainn's presence registered. "Remember to breathe," he told her.

She sucked in air like a drowning woman, blinked, and was finally able to focus on the turquoise of his eyes.

"Stay with me," she said.

"I'm not going anywhere except in there with you," he told her.

Still holding her arm, he moved forward with her. She stumbled, but he helped her catch her balance and through his touch she could Feel the warmth of his golden light flowing into and around her, surrounding her with a warrior's strength.

They entered the Great Hall together and moved quickly to the long, low centaur bench Niam had collapsed upon. Wynne ran out of the kitchen, carrying a heavy skin, which she passed to Elphame. The Chieftain uncorked it and held it to Niam's lips when the centaur's quaking hands couldn't support it.

"Drink slowly. Water first, then we'll get you some wine and something to eat." Elphame spoke in quiet, soothing tones to Niam. While the centaur drank Elphame turned to one of the wide-eyed clansmen. "Get my mother," she ordered. And then to another, "Get towels and blankets. Lots of them."

Brighid felt a stab of panic as she knelt beside her sister. Steam was rising from the equine part of Niam's foam-flecked body, which quivered and twitched spasmodically. Niam's human torso was slick and flushed an unnatural scarlet. Her blond hair was darkened with sweat and plastered against her delicate head. She had run herself dangerously past the point of exhaustion.

Suddenly Niam pushed the water skin away from her

mouth, choked and coughed. Brighid brushed the wet hair from her sister's face, murmuring to her.

"Shhh, you're here now. Focus on being calm…on cooling the heat within your body."

"No! Brighid, you have to listen!"

Niam clutched her hand and Brighid almost cried aloud at the heat that radiated from her sister.

"Later, Niam. When you've rested."

"No, now!" The centaur spoke frantically, and then more violent coughs consumed her.

"Let her speak."

Brighid looked up at the sound of Etain's voice. The people who had gathered in the Great Hall parted so the Chosen of the Goddess could approach. The priestess's face was serene, but when Brighid met her eyes she saw within them a terrible sadness that made her heart turn cold.

My sister is going to die.

Brighid turned back to her sister and held her flushed hand between both of her own, trying to will strength into her.

"I'm listening, Niam," Brighid said.

"Mother died this morning, but the accident happened four days ago. She fell into a bison pit. The stakes pierced her." Niam closed her eyes and shuddered with the horror of the memory. "I knew she was dying. We all knew it. I had to come for you."

"No! No—that can't be. We don't hunt bison in pits. We don't use stakes." Brighid shook her head, feeling awash in confusion.

"It wasn't a centaur pit. It was a pit of human design."

A terrible, foreboding chill skittered through Brighid's blood. "But humans do not hunt the Centaur Plains, not without the permission of the herd's High Shaman." Which the Dhianna Herd never gave.

"They trespassed and poached, causing the death of our mother."

Niam had to stop again to cough. This time when she gasped for air afterward her lips were wet with blood-tinged spittle.

"Her dying has driven Bregon mad. Before I left the Plains

he had already sworn to take up the Chalice of High Shaman and to lead the Dhianna Herd against any human who dared step foot on the Centaur Plains."

Horrified, Brighid could only stare at her sister. Her brother was willing to begin a war over a dreadful accident?

Niam clenched her sister's hands. "It's not just the Dhianna Herd. Since word reached the Plains that the winged creatures were being accepted back into Partholon, the Shamans of other herds have joined us. They mean to make war, Brighid."

Niam broke off, retching painfully and Brighid held her while blood spewed down her sister's chest and ran in crimson rivulets to the floor.

"Mother didn't send me for you. She wanted the war. She told Bregon over and over again to avenge her. I had to try to stop it. I had to come for you."

Niam didn't have to explain how she knew that their mother had died. The truth of it settled over Brighid as her mind flashed back to the stricken raven and the hate-filled words of its death rasp.

Avenge me!

As her spirit left her body, Mairearad Dhianna would have sent the same message to each of her children, hoping that even her death wouldn't end the manipulative hold she considered the one true bond of motherhood. Even at the end of her life, her mother had still been plotting...trying to force them to bow to her will. In Brighid's brother's case, Mairearad seemed to have been victorious.

"Shhh now, Niam." Brighid took the linen cloth Elphame silently passed to her and wiped the blood from her sister's face. "We'll figure this out. Shhh."

Niam shook her head and gave a little half sob, half laugh. "You always thought that I was stupid." When Brighid began to deny it, Niam just tightened her grip on her sister's hand and kept speaking. "That part doesn't matter now, but I wanted you to know that I wasn't what you thought—I just wasn't strong like you. I couldn't stand up to her, so I made her believe that I wasn't worth her notice." Her lips trembled as she tried to smile. "And I fooled everyone. No one watched me, especially not Bregon. No one thought that I would be the one to come for you." With surprising strength, Niam pulled her hand from her sister's so that she could grip Brighid by the shoulders. "You must return. Even those who have been most corrupted by Mother would not dare to stand against the power of the Dhianna High Shaman. Take the Chalice. Make sure that Mother doesn't win. Bring an end to the madness."

Niam's next cough was a bloody sob, and she slumped down onto the bench. Through the blood that was trickling steadily from her nose and the corner of her mouth, she smiled at her sister.

"I always envied you, Brighid. You got away from her. But maybe now I have finally gotten away from her, too…"

Niam's eyes rolled so that only their whites showed, and her body convulsed so violently Brighid was knocked from her side. Through a haze of despair Brighid watched Etain. The Goddess Incarnate's arms were spread wide, and as she spoke a pure white light emerged from her open palms, engulfing Niam.

Niam, sister to our Beloved Brighid, in the Name of
our Great Goddess
I bid you to forget your broken shell
It can serve you no longer.
I bid you in the Name of Epona,
Goddess of things wild and free,
To go beyond this pain…
To rest within the bosom of Epona's Summerland.
Child of the Goddess, I release you!

Etain pressed her glowing hands against the centaur's heaving flank, and Niam's body went still. With a small, relieved gasp, Brighid's sister breathed her last breath.

CHAPTER
THIRTY-FOUR

In the stunned silence Elphame's voice sounded calm and authoritative. "Lochlan, go to Ciara. Tell her what has happened. Have the adults keep the children away from the castle until I send word that they may return."

The winged man hesitated only long enough to touch Brighid's shoulder and murmur, "I am sorry for your loss, Huntress," and then was gone.

"Mother," Elphame continued. "Will you—"

Before she could finish the question Epona's Chosen was already responding.

"Of course. Have her brought to me." But like Lochlan, before she left the room she approached Brighid, who knelt on the floor near her sister's body, head bowed. The Goddess Incarnate lifted one of the layers of her silk robe, and used it to wipe the blood and tears from Brighid's face. She bent and kissed the Huntress on each cheek, as a mother would a daughter.

"Epona knows your pain, child, and the Goddess weeps with you."

Then Etain hurried from the room, her clear voice echoing from the Main Courtyard as she called for her handmaidens.

Danann, the centaur Stonemaster, with the help of several men, took Niam's body to Etain's chamber.

When Cuchulainn and Elphame were alone with Brighid, he crouched down so that he was level with her eyes. He heard the clip of his sister's hooves against the marble floor as she joined him.

"Brighid." He pitched his voice so that it was calm, as his mother's had been, even though his emotions were raw and bleeding. He understood too well her look of shock and grief. "Brighid," he repeated, and she finally moved her eyes to his. "Come with El and me. Let's leave this place of death."

"But it's my home," she said numbly.

"It is still your home," Elphame said quickly. "It will always be your home. Cuchulainn doesn't mean for you to leave MacCallan Castle. Just this room." Elphame took her friend's limp hand. "Let's go to your quarters and leave the cleansing of this to Wynne and my mother."

Brighid stared at Elphame, her eyes wide and round with shock. "Is that what you want me to do?"

"Yes," El said.

Brighid nodded her head twice in an unnatural, jerky movement. Still holding tight to Elphame's hand, she lurched up.

"Cuchulainn?" Her voice was hesitant and soft.

"I'm here." He took her other hand firmly. "El and I won't let you go through this alone."

She lifted her eyes to his. "You'll have to forgive me. Right now I can't pretend that I don't need you close to me."

He raised her blood-spotted hand to his lips. "By your side is exactly where I want to be."

"You couldn't get rid of either of us," Elphame said.

Linked by love and loyalty, Brighid walked with heavy, somnambulistic steps to her chamber. When Elphame and Cuchulainn let loose her hands she stood in the room, waiting for whatever would happen next. It suddenly seemed that she was unable to continue the forward motion on her own.

"There's blood all over me," she said, surprised at how strange her voice sounded.

"I'll take care of that," Elphame said, moving to the pitcher and basin that waited on the table. "Cu, get Nara." In response to his rebellious look, she grabbed his arm and pulled him close to her, whispering, "Brighid won't thank you later when she remembers that you stood and stared as I cleaned her sister's blood from her body."

Cuchulainn closed his mouth and nodded understanding.

"Brighid needs a dram to make her sleep."

"Yes. You're right, of course," Cu said.

While his sister poured clean water into the bowl, he took Brighid's hand again. He looked into her pain-filled eyes and remembered how she had been beside him when they had discovered Brenna's body, and then, as if his mind was just now truly processing it, he realized Brighid had always been beside him in those bleak days after Brenna's death while Elphame had been in a coma and it had seemed that everyone he loved had deserted him. Brighid hadn't, and he'd been too distracted by grief and then by selfishness to realize it.

Well he realized it now, and he would not let her be alone, either.

"I'm going to get Nara. But I won't be long. Elphame will be with you until I get back."

"But you're coming back?"

"Always," he said. Cuchulainn pressed her hand against his lips, and then he strode from the room.

Before Brighid could feel his absence, Elphame was back at her side. With a wet cloth and soothing words, her friend cleansed the scarlet spatters from her body. Days later, Brighid would not remember what Elphame had said to her. All she knew was the gentle touch of Elphame's hands, and the cool feel of the clean water as it washed away Niam's lifeblood.

"Come, lie down."

Brighid clung to her friend's voice. Obeying it as if she had no will of her own, she let Elphame lead her to her thick sleeping pallet. In slow motion, she folded her knees and let her body drop down. Elphame took a wide, soft brush from the top of Brighid's dresser, and while she hummed a wordless lullaby, she stroked the Huntress's long, silver-blond hair. It was in the midst of that simple, loving gesture that Brighid returned to herself.

She drew in a deep breath. Her muddy thoughts sifted through the refuse of pain, settled and then finally cleared. Swiftly she reoriented herself.

Her first coherent thought was that she was whole. Her soul had not shattered. Briefly, she wondered how she knew it with such certainty, and the answer came to her simply. Her blood told her. Her heart told her. The Shaman instinct inherent within her soul told her.

Her next thought was like a cold knife piercing her body. *My mother is dead.* It sounded impossible, but her heart— and now her mind—knew it was true. And then, like a flash-flooded gorge, her memory was swept with painful images.

Her sister was dead. *She gave her life for me. I was wrong about her, and now it's too late to fix it. I can never make it right.*

"If you blame yourself for her death, you will be as wrong as Cuchulainn was for blaming himself for Brenna's murder." Elphame continued to brush Brighid's hair as she spoke.

"How do I not blame myself?"

"Your sister chose to give her life so that you—and through you the rest of Partholon—would be forewarned. She didn't blame you, she made that clear. If you blame yourself when she didn't it will be disrespectful to her memory."

Brighid drew in a shaky breath. "Niam was strong and brave."

"Yes…yes she was."

"No one has ever brushed my hair for me," Brighid said.

"When I was a child Mama used to brush my hair whenever I was feeling particularly lonely. I never understood why, but it always seemed to help." Her voice hitched on a sob. "I—I didn't know what else to do to make you feel better."

Brighid turned her head so that she could gaze at her friend. "You did the right thing."

There were two rapid knocks on the door, and then it opened. In a rustle of agitated wings, Nara hurried into the room, followed by Cuchulainn. The Healer was carrying a steaming pot in one hand and a heavy leather pouch in the other.

"Stoke the fire, warrior," she ordered, passing the pot to Cuchulainn. "I need this to brew."

With no-nonsense gestures, she settled to the floor beside Brighid's pallet. With hands that were infinitely gentle, she quickly touched the pulse points at the centaur's temples, neck and wrists, and then ran her hands gently down Brighid's equine body.

"I'm not injured," Brighid told her.

Nara glanced up while she dug through her leather pouch, pulling out bundles of dried herbs.

"I wasn't worried about a physical wound, Huntress," Nara said. "And now I'm less worried about your spirit, though I still want you to drink my brew." The Healer stood and moved to the table, mixing herbs into a small, tightly woven strainer.

Brighid started to shake her head, remembering Brenna's potions. She didn't want to sleep—she was sure that there was something she needed to be doing. But before she could stir, Elphame was back at her side.

"Mama is caring for Niam. There is nothing more for you to do today."

"I should go to her. I have to…" Brighid ran out of words and could only gaze brokenly at her friend.

"Epona's Chosen is anointing the body of your sister. She and her handmaids are saying prayers over her and guiding her spirit to the Goddess. Wynne and her cooks are cleansing the Great Hall. Soon I'll call the children and they will return and fill the castle with life and laughter."

"But what can I do, El?"

Elphame took Brighid's hand. "You can sleep and heal so your mind will be clear to make decisions that will honor your sister's sacrifice."

"Is that all I can do?" Even to her own ears she sounded defeated.

"That's enough for now," Elphame assured her.

"I knew she was dead," Brighid said, her voice more resigned than sad.

"Niam?" Elphame asked.

The Huntress shook her head. "No. My mother. She came to me this morning when I killed the boar. She said..." Brighid paused, swallowing around the thickness in her throat. "Her spirit shrieked at me to avenge her.

"I thought—" Brighid paused again, drawing in a deep breath. "I thought that it was just another of her tricks, just another attempt to pull me back to a place where she could change me...control me...use me." Brighid shook her head. "But I think deep inside I knew she was dead. I didn't want to face it. But I should have. If I had started back to the Centaur Plains at that moment, maybe I would have met Niam and stopped her before she—" Her voice broke, and she couldn't go on.

"No!" Cuchulainn knelt, touching her face, wiping away her tears. "Don't do this to yourself, Brighid. You could not have changed your sister's fate any more than I could have changed Brenna's. Let her go, my strong, beautiful Huntress. Let Niam go."

"Drink this." Nara handed Brighid a steaming mug that smelled of lavender and spice.

Suddenly yearning for oblivion, Brighid emptied the cup, not caring that the fragrant herbs didn't quite mask the bitterness of the brew.

"You'll sleep now, and when you awaken your mind will be clear," Nara said. "I cannot heal your heart, but I can give you a rested body for wise decisions while your spirit mourns."

"Nara," Brighid called to the Healer before she could slip quietly from the room. "Don't let Liam worry about me. Tell him that all will be well."

For the first time, the Healer smiled. "Do not fret, Huntress. I will put your child's mind at ease."

"I must go, too," Elphame said, kissing Brighid on the cheek. "Don't worry about anything. Mama and I will take care of the pyre. Rest. I'll come back and check on you soon."

Brighid's eyelids were already beginning to feel heavy when her gaze met Cuchulainn's.

"I'm not going to leave," he said.

"Good." Her eyes fluttered shut. Then, with a gasp, she forced them open.

"What is it?" Cuchulainn said, smoothing her hair from her face.

"I'm afraid to sleep. What if part of her spirit comes to my dreams, like yours did?"

Cuchulainn knew it was her mother's twisted soul to which she referred. "That won't happen," he said, settling back on the down-filled pallet so he could pull her torso into his arms. "I won't let it."

She rested her head on his chest and tried to fight the drug. "How? How can you stop her?"

"I've been in your dreams before. I'll go there again, and I'll make certain nothing harms you." He kissed the top of her head. "Sleep, my beautiful Huntress, and I'll watch over you."

Unable to fight it any longer, sleep pulled her into darkness.

CHAPTER
THIRTY-FIVE

When she opened her eyes again it was dark except for the low-burning hearth fire. For a moment she didn't move—she just remembered.

Her mother was dead. Her sister was dead. Her brother was bent on beginning a bloody war of vengeance.

Tentatively she tested the knowledge within her. Her mother's death made her feel relief, which was instantly followed by a rush of guilt. Brighid mentally drew herself up. She had no reason to feel guilty. Mairearad Dhianna had been her mother, but she had also been a mean-spirited, manipulative centaur. Power had corrupted her until she had eventually misused gifts granted to her by Epona, and used and discarded even her own children. The world would be a lighter place without the shadowy presence of Mairearad Dhianna, and Brighid would not mourn for something that was truly more of a gain than a loss.

But the knowledge of Niam's death was profoundly different. It made her feel bruised and sad. All these years she had been blind to her sister's true character. There had been a time during their youth when Brighid had been close to her brother, but not even then, before the years of dissension began, had she paid much attention to her little sister. She had believed Niam was a beautiful shell—witless about anything that did not focus on beauty and entertainment and luxuries. Niam had been right. She had fooled them all—even their powerful mother. In the end she had shown more heart than any of them. Brighid would be sure her sister's memory was venerated, and that her strength was told and retold in the ballads sung around MacCallan campfires for years and years to come. Brighid only hoped she would be there to hear them. Her brother's choices could make that impossible.

A shadow disentangled itself from beside the hearth, causing Brighid's heart to hammer wildly. Was it an apparition? Had her mother's spirit followed her here to deliver another hate-filled message? The Huntress was gathering herself to repulse the Otherworldly attack when the shadow became a man.

"You'll want to drink this. Nara said you'd be thirsty when you finally awoke." Cuchulainn handed her a goblet filled with cool water.

Relieved, her hands trembled only a little as she took the goblet and drank thirstily. Cu prodded the fire alive and then moved around the room, lighting several of her candelabrum, effectively chasing the lingering shadows from her chamber. Then he grabbed the basket of food and wine from the table, and brought it to Brighid, sitting down on the pallet beside her.

The Huntress unwrapped a cold sandwich of thick sliced cheese and bread from the basket and dug heartily into it.

"I feel like I haven't eaten for days," she said between bites.

He smiled at her and brushed a crumb from her chin. "You haven't."

She narrowed her eyes as she realized that his face was shadowed with what must be at least a day of stubble.

"How long have I been sleeping?"

"It's not long after dawn of the second day since your sister's death," he said gently. "I worried that your sleep was unnatural, but Nara assured me that you would wake when your spirit was ready."

Slowly she lifted her hand to touch the roughness of his unshaven face. "You've been here the whole time?"

"I told you I wouldn't leave you." Without taking his gaze from hers, he cupped his hand over hers, turned his head slightly, and kissed her palm.

"Cuchulainn…" she began, pulling her hand from his face. "This thing between us—it doesn't have to be any more than friendship," she said awkwardly.

"Doesn't it?" His smile was slow, and it made his turquoise eyes sparkle.

"You should know that after a soul retrieval—"

"The Shaman and the patient are bonded," he finished for her. "Yes, I know that. But usually that bond isn't more than respect and understanding. Usually." He took her hand back and lifted it to his lips again. Then he held it, palm down, against his heart as he continued speaking. "The Shaman and the patient aren't drawn together by desire, or if they are it quickly fades." He could feel the beat of his heart against the warmth of her palm. "Remember when we awoke, and you were kissing me…breathing my soul back into my body?"

She nodded, transfixed by his deep voice and the impossible blue of his eyes.

"I told you that my mind understood that I shouldn't desire you, but that my passion was overruling the logic of that understanding. You told me that my passion would recede. It hasn't receded, my beautiful Huntress. Now where does that leave us?"

"I don't know," she whispered.

"In the Great Hall, after the horror of your sister's death you asked me to forgive you because you couldn't pretend that you didn't need me by your side."

"I remember," she said.

"You were in shock then, numb with grief and confusion. Now that your thoughts are clear, once more I have to ask you if you still need me by your side."

It's impossible, her mind told her. Then echoing from her memory drifted Brenna's sweet voice: *The most important thing I came to tell you is that I want your oath that you will keep an open mind…about everything that may seem impossible.*

"I do. I know it's impossible but I do," Brighid said in a rush, before common sense and logic could stop the words.

"That's what I needed to hear. Now all we have to do is discover how to overcome the impossible."

"Oh, that's all?" Brighid said with a hint of her normal caustic humor.

He smiled charmingly. "My mother seems to think it's possible. And you know she knows everything important."

"Your mother?" Brighid shook her head and reached for the wineskin. "You told your mother about us?"

He lifted a shoulder. "Do you think I had to?"

"By the Goddess! Have you ever been able to keep anything from her?" She felt flushed with embarrassment as she remembered that Etain had been with her during the journey to retrieve Cuchulainn's soul. And then the flush changed to pleasure. Etain, the Chosen of Epona and High Priestess of Partholon approved of them!

"No one keeps anything from my mother." Cuchulainn laughed at her stunned expression. "You'll get used to it."

"Maybe…I don't know…" She looked away from him as her thoughts caught up with her. "It must be a great blessing to have a mother who loves you unconditionally."

The warrior's face instantly sobered. "It is." He took her hand again. "Have you decided what you're going to do?"

She nodded and her eyes turned slowly back to meet his. "I've known what I must do since the moment I saw Niam." The centaur sighed. "Before that, actually. I think I've known it my whole life. I've just been trying to run from it."

His hand tightened on hers. "You don't run from things, Brighid."

"What else would you call it?"

"Survival—bravery—independence. I would call it any of those things. Cowards and fools run." His tone was acrimonious. "I should know. I ran from the grief of Brenna's death."

Brighid tried to smile. "You're no coward."

His bark of laughter made her soul feel considerably lighter. "And hopefully I've reached my limit of foolish actions."

Brighid looked down at their joined hands and quirked a brow. They both laughed.

Which is exactly when Elphame rapped softly on the door and peeked into the room. Her eyes widened at the two of them, sitting on the centaur pallet with food spread around them, holding hands and laughing.

"Well, it's good to see my brother is making some use of himself." Her words were teasing, and her eyes sparkled with pleasure.

"El! Just in time. Come join us," Cuchulainn said.

"Actually I was coming to fetch you—both of you. Da's here."

"Good," Cuchulainn said, standing up and brushing crumbs from his kilt. "If anyone can make sense out of what's going on with the centaurs, it'll be our father." He held out a hand to Brighid, and she took it, rising reluctantly to stand beside him. He smiled. "Don't worry. You'll like him."

"I'm not worried about not liking Midhir! By the Goddess, Cuchulainn, your father is centaur High Shaman of all of Partholon!"

"You don't need to be nervous, Brighid. Our father will like you," Elphame assured her, shooting a frustrated look at her brother. "Da's wonderful. You'll see."

Brighid felt like she was moving through a dream as the three of them made their way around the back of the castle to the rear entrance to the family quarters. Before they entered the family wing, the Huntress stopped and stared at the young sun where it had just risen over the eastern castle wall.

"Where is Niam?" she asked quietly.

"After Mother anointed her body I ordered that she be kept in the small room off the infirmary. Her funeral pyre has been built on the extreme southern edge of the castle grounds. I thought that you would want it facing the direction of the Centaur Plains," Elphame said.

Brighid nodded. "After we speak with Midhir I would like to light the pyre."

"Of course. I'll send word to the Clan to make ready."

"The Clan?" Brighid asked woodenly.

"*Your Clan.* They would not let you stand beside your sister's pyre alone."

Brighid said nothing, only let out a long breath. Her eyes were sad and resigned. Then she straightened her shoulders. "Let's go speak to your father." She led the way into the castle, her hooves making a lonely, muffled sound against the smooth marble floor.

The first thing Brighid noticed about the opulent guest chamber was that the bed that usually sat atop the huge circular dais had been replaced by a large centaur pallet. The second thing she noticed was the imposing centaur who stood behind Etain's chair, talking in a low voice to the Chosen as she was being properly coiffured for the day. He was tall and had the thick, magnificent build of a mature centaur warrior. His coat was a deep bay, shading to black around his hocks. His thick dark hair was worn long, and tied back with a leather thong. As soon as they entered, Etain waved her handmaidens away and stood to greet them. She took Brighid's hands in her own, and the Huntress felt a surge of warmth and comfort pass through the High Priestess's gentle touch.

"I knew you would recover and be stronger than you were before," she said, studying the Huntress carefully. "And now let me introduce you to my beloved." She stepped to the side and the centaur moved to stand next to her. "Midhir, my love, this is Brighid Dhianna, MacCallan's Huntress."

Brighid placed her fisted hand over her heart and dropped

gracefully into the low bow of respect centaurs showed for their High Shaman.

"I have been eager to meet you, Brighid Dhianna." Midhir's voice was deep and powerful, and it reminded her very much of Cuchulainn, as did the strong, handsome lines of his face and broad shoulders. "The death of your mother was a shock, and the loss of your sister a tragedy." Then he turned to his son and pulled the warrior into his embrace. "It has been too long since last I saw you, my son." He smiled sadly at Cuchulainn. "Your loss, too, has been great. I ached for your pain and for the shattering of your soul—and I rejoice now that you are whole once again."

"You have Brighid to thank for that," Cuchulainn said, after returning his father's warm embrace.

"I think before it is all over, we will all be much indebted to this young Huntress," Midhir said.

Brighid thought the *all over* sounded disturbingly ominous.

"What news have you of the Dhianna Herd?" Cuchulainn asked.

"It is not good. I hear nothing."

Elphame sucked in a breath of surprise. "Nothing, Da?"

The centaur High Shaman shook his head, his face as grim as his deep voice. "The Dhiannas have severed trade lines with Partholon, as have the Ulstan and Medbhia Herds. I know that they have gathered far in the southwestern part of the Plain."

"The Dhianna winter grounds," Brighid said.

"Yes, and I can get no word of their activities. The herds' High Shamans apparently have banded together and are expending quite a bit of power to keep their activities private, although it doesn't take much guesswork to realize that they must be, at the very least, arming themselves against outsiders. From the Otherworld all I can receive are disjointed images of anger, death, paranoia—all oddly wrapped in smoke, and an unclear, flame-colored light." The great Shaman shook his head and looked visibly disturbed. "Smoke and shadows… I get nothing more clear than that and an occasional glimpse of a lone centaur." Midhir paused and his eyes widened with sudden understanding. "He is a young, golden warrior, who reminds me very much of you, Brighid."

"It is my brother, Bregon." Brighid's stomach felt ill.

"Yes, I see that now. He is the impetus behind their actions." His kind eyes met Brighid's. "What your mother began, he is trying to finish."

"Can you tell if he's become a High Shaman?" Brighid asked.

"I don't sense that power in him. Not yet. But Shaman blood runs thick in your herd's veins."

"Da, what do the centaur runners say about the herd activity?" Elphame asked.

"This is what is most disturbing," Etain said, twining her arm through her husband's. "We have no word at all. None of them have returned from the Centaur Plains."

"Several Huntresses have also left their posts, avoiding me and any of my warriors," Midhir said grimly.

What he left unsaid hung heavy in the air around them. A centaur would not lie to Partholon's High Shaman. No matter his or her allegiance, their bond of respect for Midhir would not allow it. Obviously the centaurs who were joining Bregon's revolt were judiciously leaving Partholon so as not to be confronted by the High Shaman of all centaurs. And the fact that none of Midhir's loyal runners had returned from the Centaur Plains meant that they were either being held there against their will. Or they had been killed.

Centaur against centaur…centaur against human… It was those nightmarish thoughts that swam through Brighid's tumultuous mind. This was her responsibility. She was a Dhianna centaur. With her mother's death, leadership of the herd shifted to her shoulders, and the weight of it seemed to press into her soul. It didn't matter now that she had yearned for, and then chosen, another path in life. Brighid swallowed down the bitter taste of fate that rose thick in her throat.

"Midhir, will you help me journey to the Otherworld and drink of Epona's Chalice so that I may become a High Shaman?" she said grimly.

CHAPTER
THIRTY-SIX

"He cannot." Etain's clear voice was a spark that sizzled in the silence following Brighid's request.

"What do you mean he cannot?" Cuchulainn said. "A High Shaman always guides another on his or her quest to find Epona's Chalice."

"You should have paid more attention to your teachers when they attempted to educate you about the Otherworld, my son," Midhir said, tempering the harshness of his words with a quick smile.

"Mairearad should have guided Brighid on her Otherworld journey," Etain said.

"But my mother is dead."

"She could still guide you," Etain said softly.

"No! I won't accept her guidance. It won't come without a price, and I know it will be too costly—for my soul as well as for the Dhianna Herd."

"The spirit guide must be one who is closely tied to you, through blood or lifemate bond," Midhir explained. "Though I am Partholon's High Shaman, I cannot usurp that position."

"I will have to find the Chalice on my own," she said slowly. And as she spoke the words she felt a chill of despair at the prospect of the lonely, dangerous ordeal ahead of her. "My brother is the only blood relative I have left to me, and it is his position I will assume if I become High Shaman. He would not aid me in taking it from him." *This is impossible,* Brighid told herself. *Becoming a High Shaman is difficult enough. Alone I will have little chance of success. But I have no choice, and I must get used to being alone. If I succeed I will return to a life that breeds loneliness.*

"Then your guide must be your lifemate," Cuchulainn said.

All eyes turned to the warrior, but his attention was focused on Brighid. "I admit that, as my father has already said, I did not mind my lessons on the Otherworld. It is well known that I have never wanted any traffic with that realm, but it seems my fate must lie in that direction. I've tried to deny it—it will not be denied. I've even run from it—I will not be foolish enough to do so again. I can't guide you, but what I can do is give you my oath that I will not let you walk that shadowy path alone. My strength will be yours if you are in need. My sword arm will always be raised to protect you. Perhaps together we can finish this quest and claim your birthright."

She could hardly believe what she was hearing. Didn't he understand that—?

"But you're not my lifemate!" Brighid blurted.

"I will be if you accept me."

She shook her head, wondering if everyone could hear the painful pounding of her heart. "You don't have to do this just to help me. I'm not afraid to travel to the Otherworld alone," she lied. "A lifemating is not something that should be undertaken to help a friend in need."

Cuchulainn's smile was intimate and knowing. He stepped close to her and took her hand. "We have been friends. But, my beautiful Huntress, we have become much more. My soul tells me that I am willing to gamble on a lifemating with you. What does your soul tell you?"

She shook her head. "What my soul tells me is not important if I cannot become a High Shaman. Think, Cuchulainn! If I can't shapeshift you have shackled yourself to someone who cannot truly be your wife."

His hand tightened on hers, and even though his next question was directed at Etain, his gaze never left Brighid's. "Mother, if Father lost the ability to shapeshift, and could never come to you in human form again, would you still be his wife?"

"Of course. It's not your father's form that binds me to him," Etain said firmly.

"But they've had years together," Brighid said. "They've had children and shared each other's lives and bed for decades."

"I'm willing to bet that we will, too," Cuchulainn said.

"You're willing to bet your life and your future?"

"I am, because I'm willing to do something I've not allowed myself to do until now—I'm going to listen to my own spirit. I'm done running from my fate." He shrugged and smiled at her. "I also believe that you will make a very fine High Shaman. So, Brighid Dhianna, what does your soul tell you?"

She looked into his turquoise eyes and felt lost—and found. "It tells me that this is an impossible dream, but one that I don't want to end."

His smile was filled with promise. He kissed her quickly and then turned, and dropped to one knee before Elphame.

"Elphame, as Chieftain of Clan MacCallan, I ask your permission to make your Huntress my lifemate." He grinned, and for a moment he looked every bit the rakish warrior of his youth. "I would ask her brother's permission, but I believe, all things considered, that would be rather unwise."

Instead of returning Cu's smile and automatically awarding her blessing, Elphame's expression was strained and sober. "You said it yourself, Cu. You have shunned the Otherworld and the Realm of Spirits. Will you help or hinder Brighid?

More rests upon this mating than a life bond. If this joining is the wrong choice, all of Partholon will suffer the ramifications." Elphame looked from her brother to their mother. "I cannot give Cuchulainn my permission unless Epona approves of this mating." She ignored her brother's grunt of annoyance, along with Brighid's sharp, questioning gaze, and continued to beseech Etain. "Would you ask Epona's blessing on them? If the Goddess grants it, I will gladly give my permission."

"Elphame, what—" Cuchulainn began, but his mother cut him off.

"You are a wise and responsible Chieftain, Elphame. I am proud of you." Etain crooked her finger at her frowning son. "Come." And then while he got to his feet, she held a hand out to Brighid. "And you, too, child."

Feeling her stomach tighten with nerves, Brighid took Etain's hand. Cuchulainn took her other.

The Beloved of Epona smiled at them. "You must link hands, too, and complete the circle."

Cu's frown softened when he laced his fingers with Brighid's. He squeezed her hand and she held tight to him. Then the High Priestess lifted her face and evoked the presence of her Goddess.

My Epona, Goddess of shimmering beauty
for whom the stars are shining jewels,
and the earth Your sacred trust,
weaver of destinies
and protectress of things wild and free.
As your Chosen One, Beloved and touched by You,
I do ask now if You will grant
Thy blessing upon this mating.
Show us through sign, or vision, or word
Your wisdom and Your will.

Instantly the air above the circle made by their linked hands began to swirl and shimmer. Two forms took shape within the brilliance. Brighid gasped as she recognized Cuchulainn's torso, naked and muscular, shining with his golden light. And then another torso took shape from the diamond-sparked mist. It shimmered with a bright silver light. It was her own naked body wrapped within Cuchulainn's strong arms. When the apparitions' lips met, Brighid was filled with the liquid heat of newly awakened passion. She heard Cu's deep intake of breath, and knew he felt the joining of their spirits, too. Then the air spiraled, whirlpooling into a mass of glittering sparks before the vision dissipated with the sound of rain-soaked wind.

Etain smiled. "You have the Goddess's blessing, my son."

Cuchulainn lifted Brighid's hand and pressed it firmly to his lips before he broke the circle and returned to kneel in front of Elphame.

"Now, sister-mine, do I have your permission to take your Huntress as my lifemate?"

Elphame smiled down at her beloved brother. "Gladly, Cuchulainn."

Cu stood and hugged his sister, lifting her and making her laugh. Brighid still felt flushed by the hypnotic vision, and was more than a little overwhelmed as Partholon's High Shaman and Epona's Chosen congratulated her warmly and welcomed her to their family.

"Mother, will you honor us by overseeing the oath-giving?" Cuchulainn asked.

"Of course, my darling." Etain smiled fondly at her son.

"It will have to be today." Brighid thought her voice sounded out of place, and too serious. It wasn't that she didn't want to celebrate and laugh and revel in the magical and unique surprise with which Epona had gifted her, but her Huntress's mind was too aware that the trail she and Cuchulainn must follow would be difficult, and the track was already growing cold.

Cuchulainn moved back to her side, and touched her face gently. "Then it will be today."

She smiled at him, grateful that he seemed to understand— that he wasn't put off by her brusque, unromantic manner.

"And Niam's pyre will need to be lit," Brighid said.

"Yes, it is as it should be. Today we will make it a celebration of one life, ended in honor and love, and the beginning of another, rooted in the same. It is the circle of the Great Goddess. Life cannot exist without death, one cannot be fulfilled without the other," Etain said solemnly. "But first we will break our fast and fortify our bodies for the day to come."

"To the Great Hall, then," Elphame said.

The Great Hall was noisy and crowded—filled to overflowing with small winged shapes and the Clan MacCallan. The air was thick and sweet with the smell of freshly baked bread and the dark, lumped sugar the children had already become so fond of adding to their morning porridge. Brighid paused in the arched doorway. The hall looked so alive, so different now from how it had appeared two days before when her sister had breathed her last breath. But she could still see Niam there, collapsed on the long, low centaur bench, retching blood and delivering her dire warning.

Before the shades of the past could overwhelm her, a small winged shape detached itself from a nearby table and hurled himself at her.

"Brighid!" Though the top of his head reached no higher than her equine chest, he clutched her with a strength that was surprising.

She bent and ruffled his hair and patted his back.

"Oh, Brighid." He tilted his head up to look at her. His eyes were large and luminous with tears he was trying bravely not to shed. "I was so worried about you! I wanted to come see you, but no one would let me."

"I'm all right now." She stroked his head, thinking that his hair was as soft as duck's down. "I just needed to rest."

"I'm sorry about your sister. Curran and Nevin have already begun telling tales about how brave she was."

Brighid's heart squeezed painfully. "They're right. She was very brave."

"Come on, Liam, you can sit with us and tell us everything you've been doing for the past two days." Cuchulainn lifted the boy to Brighid's back, winning himself a narrow-eyed look from his betrothed. He winked back at her, the Huntress snorted, and Liam launched into a breathless explanation of all the different tracks he had discovered.

As they moved through the Great Hall to the head table, Brighid was stopped often by kind words and sincere condolences. Her first reaction was discomfort. She rarely garnered such concentrated attention, but she wasn't halfway through the room when she felt herself relax. They cared for her. Her family, Clan MacCallan, was surrounding her with their love and concern. Brighid drank it in. She would remember it, so that later, when she was far from here she could relive what it felt like to be accepted and at peace.

As they joined Lochlan and Ciara at the Chieftain's table, Brighid sat very still while life moved around her. Liam chattered ceaselessly. Elphame and Etain discussed the full moon ceremony that was only days away, and Epona's Beloved kindly included Ciara in the conversation. Cuchulainn was talking with Lochlan about how to expand the barracks for the children since it had been decided that until they received word that the strife with the centaurs was over, the New Fomorians should be housed within the protective walls of MacCallan Castle.

It was all so natural—so normal. And Brighid couldn't help but compare it with the morning meals that had been "normal" for her before she left the Centaur Plains. Mairearad Dhianna had set a sumptuous table, but the quality of the food had always paled in comparison to the intrigue and power-plays that surrounded their High Shaman. Her mother had served manipulation and passive-aggression as the main dish, and Brighid clearly remembered how she had always been on guard during meals when her mother was present. Who would Mairearad target? Would she be open in her attack, or would it be veiled innuendo and seemingly harmless comments meant to cut and destroy will and independence and freedom...

Brighid was going back into that. It would matter little that Mairearad was gone. After almost five decades as Dhianna High Shaman, her ghost would not easily relinquish its hold.

Brighid jerked only a little when Cuchulainn slid his warm hand within hers. He didn't break his conversation with Lochlan. He made no showy public production of intimacy with the proud Huntress. No one knew their hands were linked and that his touch warmed her.

The warrior understood her.

How had this happened? It seems I'm a world away from my beginnings, yet somehow here, with this man, I have found my true home and family. Please don't let me lose it, Epona.

They had chosen a beautiful spot for Niam's funeral pyre. The enormous mound of dry pinewood timbers had been erected on a sliver of land located at the southernmost area of the castle grounds. It jutted like a slender finger over the swirling ocean far below, as if Niam's burning pyre was meant to be a beacon for lost ships. The centaur's body was high atop the mound, and it had been draped in a heavy shroud woven with intricate knots of power, as would a warrior's body.

Brighid approached the pyre with Cuchulainn and Elphame flanking her. Etain, Midhir, and Lochlan were already present, standing near the mound. Epona's Beloved held a flaming torch in her hand. As Niam's closest kin, the lighting of the pyre was Brighid's responsibility, but instead of taking the torch from Etain she turned and faced the group that had assembled around them. Clan MacCallan spread out before her. Human and centaur, they had come dressed in their finest, and the warm, cloudless morning was alive with the bright lime and sapphire blue of the MacCallan plaid. Interspersed between Clan members were small winged shapes standing respectfully silent with big eyes focused on the Huntress. She searched through the crowd until she found the twin storytellers. When she spoke her voice was strong and clear.

"Her name was Niam Dhianna. Beauty was her shield. It kept her safe from manipulation and intrigue, hiding her until she was needed. I only wish that I'd had the wisdom to see beyond her ruse, and that her body had been as strong as her heart was valiant. I ask that you remember her with me. Do not let her story die with her body." Nevin and Curran bowed their heads in acknowledgment, and Brighid paused, drawing in a steadying breath. When she looked up again, her eyes easily found the winged Shaman. "Ciara, I ask that you join me at my sister's pyre."

The winged woman looked surprised, but she moved quickly to Brighid's side.

"Your affinity is with the spirit of fire, and you carry within you the spark of the Goddess Incarnate Terpsichore. Niam loved beauty and dance. But I have chosen to ask you to call upon the spirit of fire to release her body from this earth not simply because of the outward beauty you and your grandmother represent. In the short time I've known you I have learned to appreciate your ability to see within a person's soul. If I had developed that ability as well as you, I might have understood Niam's worth before she was lost to me. So I ask you to use the spirit of flame to light my sister's pyre."

"I accept, Brighid Dhianna. You honor me greatly."

Wordlessly, the group stepped with Brighid away from the pyre, leaving the winged Shaman standing alone. Ciara turned to the south, facing the pyre. She bowed her head, obviously collecting herself. Then with the grace of a dancer she approached the mound with slow, elegant movements that flowed smoothly like water over pebbles. Her long, dark hair swirled around her, as if it was a curtain parting to allow her access to another realm. As she spoke, she traced delicate patterns with her hands, calling awake bright specks of tiny sparks in the air around her.

O Epona, I do call upon Thee.
Goddess of things wild and free,
today it is the lovely, somber Goddess of the Declining Moon
to whom I speak.
Strong and somber, Goddess of the Far Realms and beyond,
be with us here at this time of loss.

The winged Shaman's voice was hypnotic—a perfect mixture of music and magic.

There is a time for life
and a time for death.
Your Summerland is warm, pleasing, beautiful
with all ills gone and youth renewed.
Joyous it is, to walk with the Goddess in Her fields of clover.
So let us rejoice, for Niam rests in Epona's bosom
safe, happy, replete.

She danced ever closer to the pyre. Raising her hands over her head her dark wings began to unfurl, spreading around her like a living veil.

O spirit of fire
grant release from pain.
With Your purifying flame
heal those who remain in this realm
and speed and cleanse the soul of this one

who is loved
into the beautiful realm of our Goddess.
I call upon Thee—
Alight!

From Ciara's palms silver sparks rained, setting the pyre to flame with a glorious white light that caused Brighid to shield her eyes from its brilliance. Gasps of awe sounded from the watching crowd as the fire burned high and bright. As it consumed Niam's body Brighid felt the healing heat that radiated from the pyre. It lifted the chill from that sad place within her soul that had been so dark and cold since the raven had shrieked at her in her mother's dying voice.

She looked at Cu. He pulled his eyes from the blaze and met hers.

"We've honored death. Are you ready to take the next step with me and honor life?" she asked the warrior.

"I've had enough of death, my beautiful Huntress." He pitched his voice so that the words were for her ears alone. "I am more than ready to honor life."

Her tense expression softened just a little. "Thank you, Cuchulainn." She looked from him to his mother, but as was usual with Epona's Beloved, few words were needed for her to understand.

"You want it to be here and now," Etain said.

"We do." Brighid nodded.

"Then let us make it so." Etain stepped forward, replacing Ciara before the blazing fire. The instant the Beloved of Epona raised one slender hand the crowd became absolutely silent.

"Today death has been purified by flame and prayer. Now we will celebrate the full circle of life through the purity of the sacred handfast ritual. Cuchulainn and Brighid, please come forward."

The crowd stirred with a surprised rustle as the warrior and Huntress joined Etain.

Etain smiled. She spoke directly to the two of them, but she projected her voice so that it carried across the castle grounds.

"You begin a long journey today. In some ways it is a journey familiar and ancient—the joining of two who love and pledge themselves together. And in some ways you begin the quest for something totally new and unique—a love that is built more on spirit than body, and depends upon courage as well as the cooperation of the Otherworld for its consummation." Her smile grew and warmed. "You already know that you have Epona's blessing. Know that you have mine, too."

She nodded to her son and the warrior turned to face Brighid. He held his hands out to her, and without hesitation she pressed her palms against his. Their eyes met and held.

"I, Cuchulainn MacCallan, do take you Brighid Dhianna, in handfast this day. I agree to protect you from fire even if the sun should fall, from water even if the sea should rage and from earth even if it should shake in tumult. And I will honor your name as if it were my own." His deep voice was strong and true.

"I, Brighid Dhianna, do take you, Cuchulainn MacCallan, in handfast this day," Brighid began, wondering at the fact that her voice sounded so calm when everything inside her was shaking. "I agree that no fire or flame shall part us, no lake or seas shall drown us and no earthly mountains shall separate us. And I will honor your name as if it were my own."

"So has it been spoken," Cuchulainn said.

"So shall it be done," Brighid said the words that completed the ritual.

Cuchulainn pulled gently on her hands so that she took a step closer to him. Before their lips met he murmured, "Now we're truly in it together, my beautiful Huntress."

The youthful cheer that sounded as they kissed caused them to start and break apart. All of the New Fomorian children were shouting and clapping and jumping around with much rustling of wings and waving of arms.

"Children…" Brighid sighed and shook her head, though

she couldn't keep the smile from her face. "They can never be still."

"Isn't that the truth," Cu said, sliding his hand in hers again. "May the Goddess bless them."

Clan MacCallan was definitely not as enthusiastic in their reaction to the handfast as the children. They weren't rude. They didn't withdraw from the new couple—congratulations were duly given. The right sounds and motions were made, but Brighid noticed that few Clan members would actually meet her eyes. She was the only female MacCallan centaur, but several males had joined the Clan. None of them spoke to her, although she noticed that Cuchulainn approached each of them, and they did offer congratulations to the warrior—albeit with little warmth.

So it begins. Get used to it. It will be far worse with the herd.

She shuddered, not wanting to think that far ahead. The night to come was daunting enough.

Brighid drifted away from the small group that had been gathered around Cu, his sister, their parents, and Lochlan. It was easy enough to slip away. Not many of the humans were talking to her anyway. Moving with heavy steps she made her way to stand before her sister's still smoldering pyre.

Goddess, what have I gotten myself into?

"You're very quiet," Cuchulainn said.

She glanced guiltily at him, not sure what to say—or what not to say.

"Tell me," Cu said. "We've always been honest with each other." His smile was quick and endearing. "Even when we didn't particularly like each other."

"The only reason I didn't like you was because you were so damn arrogant," Brighid told him.

"Me?" Cuchulainn pointed in mock innocence to his chest. "I think you have me confused with my sister."

Brighid snorted, but she did smile at him.

The warrior—who was now her husband—took her hand. "Tell me what you're thinking," he said.

"I'm wondering what I've gotten myself into," she said bluntly.

Cuchulainn laughed. "I know exactly what you mean."

She frowned at him. "Are you sorry we did it?"

His laughter instantly sobered. "No, Brighid. I am not sorry."

She sighed and looked down at their joined hands. "The Clan doesn't approve."

"I think the Clan is more surprised than disapproving. We're doing something that's never been done before. The only centaur and human who have ever mated are the High Shaman and Epona's Beloved. It will take people—and centaurs—time to get used to us."

"If they ever do."

"Would it bother you so much if some people never approved of us?"

"Yes. More than I thought it would," she said. "I've come to think of MacCallan Castle as my home, and I find that it bothers me a great deal to think of being rejected yet again."

"They're just surprised, maybe even shocked. I think eventually they'll get used to us. You'll see."

"That's part of the problem," she said. "I won't have time to see."

"We must leave that soon?"

Brighid drew a deep breath. "Today."

Cuchulainn opened his mouth, and then closed it. She saw his jaw tighten, but instead of arguing with her, he nodded.

"I have to—*we* have to," she corrected at his sharp look. "I don't know how much you know of the quest for the High Shaman's Chalice…" She paused. He looked uncomfortable. He ran his fingers through his hair, and blew out a short, ir-ritated breath.

"I know nothing about it. All my life I've focused on mas-tering things I can see…feel…best with the strength of my body or my sword. It is a frustrating irony for me that now all of my hard-won mastery seems to be of no use to me whatso-ever."

"Except for tapping into the spirits of animals, I, too, have avoided the Otherworld. As with the soul retrieval, I know lit-tle more than you of dealings with the spirit realm. The Oth-erworld has always meant my mother to me—and I have spent my life avoiding her dominance, so I avoided it, too. I do know something of the High Shaman's Quest, though, be-cause she intended for me to drink of the Chalice. She edu-cated me, probably thinking she could tempt me with the lure of power. She failed. I would never have touched the Chalice on my mother's terms."

"You'll drink of the Chalice, Brighid. But it will be on your own terms," Cuchulainn said.

Brighid's gaze drifted back to her sister's funeral pyre. "I'm going to use what my mother told me, and then do what I did with your soul retrieval—try to think of it as a hunt."

"We'll track the Chalice?"

"We'll try," she said. "But we can't begin from here. A High Shaman's Quest is three parts spirit, one part body. We must travel away from the castle where we can be physically separated from this world and the problems of those who populate it, men, centaurs and Fomorians, new and otherwise. Once we're more isolated, entering the Otherworld will be—" her lips twisted into what she knew was a parody of a smile as she stared at the pile of burned pine timbers "—well, I won't say it'll be easier, but at least if we separate ourselves from all of this the Otherworld should be more available to us."

"I suppose that makes sense," Cu said. "And you want to begin today?"

"I don't *want* to!" she cried, and then took a tighter hold on her emotions. "I don't want to," she repeated more calmly. "But I can think of nothing else to do except ride the tide of events to their conclusion, and it feels to me that the tide is swelling with an oncoming flood. All of the time my mother was wounded and dying my brother will have been questing for the Chalice, probably with at least some measure of aid and guidance from her. He has many days on us, and the help of a High Shaman. We have catching up to do."

"We also have Epona's blessing. I cannot believe he does," Cu said.

"Because we have the Goddess's blessing does not mean that I will be granted her Chalice before Bregon, or even that I will be granted it at all."

"We have catching up to do," Cuchulainn agreed grimly. "We'll leave today."

"Cuchulainn," she said as he began to turn away, stopping him. "If there was some other way, you know I would take it. This place…this Clan…it has been more of a home to me than I have known for most of my life."

"This will always be home to us. Elphame will make sure of it."

"But we won't be able to live here, not if I become Dhianna High Shaman. We'll have to stay with the herd, at least until things are settled. And even afterward. A High Shaman does not leave her herd for long."

"I knew that when I handfasted with you, Brighid," Cuchu-lainn said.

"And you were willing to leave your home for me?"

"I don't think of it as leaving my home for you. I think of it as making a second home with you." He smiled and raised her hand to his lips. "And we will return to MacCallan Castle, even if it's just to let our children play with their cousins."

Brighid felt a nervous thrill at his words. "You're awfully sure of yourself."

He grinned. "That I am, but I'm more sure of you, my beautiful Huntress."

In his eyes she saw the truth of his words. She could depend upon his trust and belief and honesty. Before she could stop and think herself out of it, she kissed him quickly on the lips, and was rewarded with his brilliant smile.

"Don't be so cocky. I'm going to make you tell El that we're leaving," Brighid said, trying to cover how breathless his touch made her feel.

Cuchulainn's smile didn't waver. "Excellent idea. And while I'm doing that, you'll be telling Liam the same thing." He kissed her hand again, and then strode over to his sister.

Brighid looked across the castle grounds. Liam stood beside the Stonemaster Danann, talking in animated little bursts to the patient old centaur.

"Damn…" she breathed. Squaring her shoulders, she made her way to the boy. She'd just get it over with. Quickly. No point in putting it off.

"…And then I saw the bright red splotchy that was all angry and I knew it was the boar and Brighid told me that I was right that it really was a boar because it smelled like mud and anger and then she—" The boy broke off his breathless recital when he caught sight of his Huntress. "Brighid! Brighid! I was just telling Danann about the boar and how its tracks smelled and he said I did a really good job and then I was saying that—"

Brighid's raised hand ended his chatter, thank the Goddess.

"Excuse me, Danann, but I need to speak privately with my apprentice," she said.

The old centaur smiled indulgently at the boy. "I bow to your Mistress, child." Then he turned his smile to Brighid. "And I have yet to congratulate you, Huntress. Cuchulainn is a mighty warrior and a good man. My wish for you is that the two of you have many years of happiness together."

"Th-thank you!" Brighid stuttered, taken completely off guard by the old Stonemaster's kindness.

He bowed respectfully to her and left her alone with the boy.

"I'm so glad you handfasted with Cuchulainn!" Liam chirruped. "He's very strong and honorable and I think he might be almost as good with a bow as you are."

Brighid quirked an eyebrow at the child. "Almost as good with a bow as I am?"

Liam grinned impishly. "Well, *almost*. But no one's as good as you are, Mistress!"

He was, quite simply, adorable. By the Goddess, she didn't want to leave the boy! She wanted to hurt him even less.

"One day," she said, "you will be as good as I am, Liam."

The boy's face lit with happiness. "Do you really think so?"

"I do," she said solemnly. "But first there is much you have to learn, and many difficulties you must endure."

"I'll work hard. I promise."

"I know you will, Liam. I'm already proud of the Huntress you will become." As the boy wriggled and beamed under her praise she realized that they weren't just empty words. The boy had a gift. No, he obviously wasn't a centaur, but if he wanted to title himself a Huntress, what harm was there in it? He could learn the ways of the hunt. She would be proud to claim such a brave, loyal child as her own.

But she wasn't here to praise him. She was here to tell him she was leaving.

"Liam, you know that my sister died bringing news to me."

His jumping about stilled at her serious tone and he nodded. "Yes, I know that."

"The news she brought was not good. My mother is dead."

"Oh! I'm sorry Brighid," the boy said, blinking his eyes quickly.

Oh, Goddess! Please, no crying, she thought and went hastily on. "My mother's death has caused many problems with my herd. I am the eldest daughter, and my mother was our High Shaman. Do you know what that means?"

He screwed up his forehead in thought. "You're supposed to be High Shaman next?"

"Yes."

"But you can't be! You're a Huntress!"

"I know. I never wanted to be High Shaman. That's why I left my Herd. I've never wanted to be anything except a Huntress." She smiled gently at him. "Just like you. But sometimes we don't always get exactly what we want."

Liam started to shake his head from side to side, and Brighid bent to cup his small shoulders with her hands.

"I have to go to the Centaur Plains and put things to order. I have to take my mother's place or terrible things will happen."

"Then I'll go with you!"

She squeezed his shoulders, feeling his body trembling beneath her hands. "You cannot."

"But I don't want to be away from you," he whispered, trying desperately not to cry.

Brighid felt her chest grow hot and heavy. She wasn't a mother; she didn't know what to say to the boy to make his hurt better. Her own mother had never comforted her. How was she supposed to know how to deal with this? Maybe it would be best if she was short with him, or angry with him. Then he might not be so sad without her.

No. That sounded like something Mairearad Dhianna would do to a child—use anger instead of facing the pain of love. Brighid would not be her mother. She would not repeat her mistakes.

She touched the side of the child's face gently. "I don't want to be away from you, either, Liam. And I'll make you a promise right now. When I set order to the Dhianna Herd I will send for you. You will always have a home with me."

One small tear spilled over and ran down his cheek. "But what do I do until then?"

"If your Mistress will allow, we would be honored to have you join us at Epona's Temple," Etain said.

Brighid glanced up as Etain and Midhir approached. The Goddess Incarnate crouched down beside the boy and wiped a soft hand across his cheek, drying the tear.

"We have a Huntress there, too," Etain said.

"But maybe she won't think that I can be a Huntress. She might think I'm just a boy with wings," Liam said, biting his lip as he tried to keep from crying.

"You are apprenticed to the MacCallan Huntress." Midhir's deep voice boomed from above the boy. "If anyone questions your right to follow the path of the Huntress, they will have to question me."

Liam stared up at the massive centaur, his wide-eyed expression clearly saying that he didn't think anyone would ever dare to question Midhir. Then his gaze turned back to Brighid.

"I'll do what my Mistress wants me to do," he said, and his voice shook only a little.

"I think going to Epona's Temple is an excellent idea," Brighid said. "Moira, the Lead Huntress of Partholon is there." She glanced quickly at Midhir, who nodded encouragement. "I'm sure she will help you study your tracking until I call for you." Then Brighid ruffled the boy's hair. "And remember, Epona's Temple borders the Centaur Plains."

"So we won't be too far apart?"

"No. We won't be too far apart."

Brighid took the boy's hand firmly in her own and together they started to walk back to the castle.

CHAPTER
THIRTY-EIGHT

Brighid had wanted to get on the road before midday, but the sun was beginning its path down the western part of the sky when they finally left MacCallan Castle. They took the wide, newly restored road that led from the great front gate to Loth Tor, the town that nestled at the bottom of the plateau. She and Cu spoke very little at first. Brighid set the pace. Cuchulainn rode beside her on his big gelding, leading an extra mount, who would spell his buckskin when the horse tired, as he would inevitably do. No normal horse could keep pace with a Huntress for long. And the road they had begun was going to be a long, wearying one.

Cuchulainn let Brighid pull a little ahead of him, though he kept his gelding close to the centaur's rear flank. It had been difficult to leave MacCallan Castle. Not like the last time, when he had been so shattered from Brenna's death that he was only going through the motions of living. It was an irony that this time his soul was healed, and he was newly married, but his departure had been much more wrenching. His sister had been stoic. There had been no weeping. El hadn't tried to convince them to stay another night—she had understood the need for haste. But in her eyes Cuchulainn had seen the sadness that losing him again so quickly had caused. He understood it; he felt it himself. Etain had, of course, been loving and offered Epona's blessings on them. It had been his father's idea to take the extra horse so Brighid would not have to slow her pace. He had also suggested their initial destination—the Blue Tors.

"You're right! I wouldn't have thought of it, but it's a natural physical entry to the Underworld," Brighid had said with more animation than she'd shown since they had separated at her sister's pyre.

His father had nodded and given her what Cu thought of as his Shaman look—one that was serious as well as kind. "But beware, Brighid. You will not find the Chalice in the Underworld. It will be in an upper level of the spirit realm."

"But all of the spirit realms are interconnected," the Huntress had said.

Midhir had nodded again. "They are. Just remember that…" His voice had trailed off and he'd sighed in frustration as he checked his impulse to aid the centaur. "I should not say more, though I wish I could give you more guidance."

"I understand," Brighid had quickly assured him. "I—" She hesitated only a moment before adding, "Cuchulainn and I must discover our own way. This does help us, though. It gives us a clear direction in which to travel, rather than just aiming toward the Plains and praying that we somehow find the Chalice along the way. I appreciate it."

Cuchulainn frowned as he thought back to their departure. It had been heart-wrenchingly obvious that Brighid had been holding her emotions in tight check. She and his sister had whispered only a few parting words to one another and embraced. She had hardly spoken to Etain. But he'd seen the pained look on his new wife's beautiful face when they finally turned away from the castle. Her usually graceful body had moved woodenly, as if her hooves had become mired in mud.

They'd passed through the little village of Loth Tor, barely hesitating to return the greetings called to them, and then the Huntress had kicked into a ground-eating canter that had Cuchulainn settling deep in the saddle and concentrating on coaxing the gelding to match. Grimly he realized that Elphame had been right when she'd insisted that Fand remain behind at MacCallan Castle. He would miss the wolf cub. She had become a part of him over the past several moons. Her presence was warm and familiar, but the wolf had become attached enough to the hybrid children, especially the little girl Kyna, that he was fairly sure that even after they untied the howling cub she would remain at the castle. At least he hoped she wouldn't try to follow them. Fand wouldn't catch them—or if she did, there was no way the young wolf could maintain the grueling pace the Huntress was setting. It was a pace meant to cut the time it would take to get to the Blue Tors by at least a full day. It was also a pace that was not conducive to conversation, and Cuchulainn wondered if that might not be part of the reason Brighid had chosen it.

He'd handfasted with her. She was his wife—his lifemate. Had they chosen to keep the ceremony private, between only the two of them and simply speak the words before Epona, the mating would have been legally binding for the space of one year. But he had negated that condition when he had asked the ritual to be witnessed by his mother. Handfastings presided over by the High Priestess of Partholon were lifetime bonds. Of course no two people would be forced to stay together if either or both truly wished to part from the other, but the breaking of a lifemating was rare.

He watched the beautiful Huntress pushing her pace. What was she thinking? Just the thought of losing his sister and his mother in the space of one day chilled him to his marrow. Should he try to get her to talk about it? He thought of how he felt after Brenna had been killed. He'd refused to speak of her. He'd run away from his memories of her. But he'd also been broken…shattered. Brighid was whole. So wouldn't she need to vent? To remember?

His thoughts had so totally eclipsed his concentration that Cu's mind didn't register the darkening of the sky or the slowing of Brighid's pace, until his gelding broke from their steady canter into a jarring trot. Reorienting himself, Cu nudged the big horse up beside the Huntress.

Brighid glanced over at him. "It's almost full dark. I thought we should start looking for a place to camp." She hesitated, not meeting his questioning gaze. "Or we could just slow our pace and keep going. The road is wide and well-marked. Maybe we'll come to a village. I traveled up from the Centaur Plains on this road, but my trip was…" Her eyes narrowed in painful remembrance. She hadn't allowed herself to think during the hasty trip from her old life. She'd pointed herself toward the promise of a future and not let anything get in her way. Now she was heading into another future, only this one was filled more with pain and danger than promise and contentment.

"It's fine, Brighid."

Cu's deep voice was so normal—so ordinary—so in complete contradiction to what was going on within her head. He was just a man, talking to a woman. Not a human warrior who was freakishly mated to a centaur Huntress. Not a man joining his mate in a futile quest that would either be successful and lead them blindly into deep waters, or unsuccessful and strand them to flail about in unconsummated shallows. He was just a man—*the* man who cared about and accepted her. It calmed her and anchored her heaving emotions. Perhaps it shouldn't—perhaps she was being foolish—but it did.

"Brighid," he repeated. "We can keep traveling. The moon is nearly full, and after it rises the road will be easy to follow. But the day has been long." He smiled. "Honestly, I'd prefer camping and beginning renewed at dawn."

She returned his smile gratefully, feeling the ice that had been holding her emotions in check all day begin to thaw. "Do you know if there are any villages close by?"

"Mostly between here and McNamara Castle there's nothing but vineyards and forest." He jerked his chin to the right of the road. "We could climb to the top of the plateau. Should still be grassy up there and a decent place to camp."

"Lead the way," she said, relieved that she could mindlessly follow him for at least a little while.

Slowing considerably, Cuchulainn nosed his gelding between a break in the trees that lined the road. Almost immediately, the land became an incline, angling up and up until they finally emerged from a scattering of oaks and pines onto the plateau that eventually gave way to the imposing cliffs over the B'an Sea. The sun had already set, but the ocean horizon was still stained with the burned colors left by a dying sun. For a moment they simply stood quietly watching the close of another day. Then Cuchulainn dismounted and tossed the reins of the extra mount to Brighid.

"I'll gather some firewood if you unpack the supplies. I don't think we'll need the tent up tonight. Sky looks clear and it's been warm enough."

Before she could answer, he and the buckskin gelding disappeared back into the trees. At least unpacking and setting up a temporary camp would keep her occupied. She was hungry. When had she eaten last? That morning before she lit Niam's pyre and handfasted with Cuchulainn. Had all of that happened just this morning?

Oh, Goddess. She stopped suddenly in the middle of untying a pack. *Tonight is my wedding night.* The thought made her fingers slow and clumsy. *Breathe, just breathe.* She pulled the last pack free from the horse and gave the mare a quick, perfunctory wipe down before she hobbled her and then began pulling supplies from the packs, silently thanking Etain when she discovered the generous skins of rich red wine.

She was taking a long pull from one of the skins when Cuchulainn dropped the load of dry branches near her.

"I've made you turn to drink already, and we haven't even been married one full day," he said, smiling boyishly.

"Just thirsty," she said.

His chuckle was more of a grunt.

"Want some?" she asked.

"Definitely—as soon as I unsaddle the gelding and settle him in. I think I'm *thirsty*, too." He grinned at her and led the gelding over to where the mare was already grazing.

Nervous and uncomfortable, Brighid busied herself with building the campfire. By the time he rejoined her she had thick slabs of salted pork frying and cheese and bread laid out on a blanket.

"By the Goddess, that smells good!"

She told herself to relax and smile at him. "You wouldn't believe the supplies wrapped away in those packs. I won't have to hunt for days."

"Wynne's doing," Cuchulainn said.

"Not the wine." Brighid tossed a skin to him. "This has your mother's touch all over it."

Cuchulainn uncapped it and drank. Then he sighed in pleasure. "May Epona bless my mother for her love of fine wine."

"And her willingness to share."

Cu grunted his agreement before taking another drink. Then he sighed and reclined next to the Huntress near the campfire. Before long, they were both busy forking hot pork onto bread and relishing the sharp tang of the well-aged cheese. Cuchulainn was almost finished with his third helping, and was feeling relaxed and replete, when he gave a little half laugh of remembrance.

"These sandwiches will always remind me of El."

"El? Why?" Brighid asked, clearing her mouth with another long drink of the excellent wine.

"Well, she was a loner—liked to go off by herself, especially in the years before she studied at the Temple of the Muse. Mother didn't want to restrict her, so she let her explore, even allowed her to go all the way up to the fringes of Ufasach Marsh, under only one condition."

"That you accompany her?"

Cuchulainn grinned. "You guessed it." He raised the small piece that was all that remained of his last sandwich. "These were a favorite of hers whenever we went camping. I imagine she was behind making sure that Wynne included them in our provisions."

"Nice of her to think of that," Brighid said.

"She's like that. She remembers small things—always has," Cuchulainn said, his voice and face softened as he thought of his sister.

"So you two have always been close? Even when you were young?"

Cuchulainn nodded. "Always. It was just us until the twins were born when I was six and El was seven. Arianrhod and Finegas were so much younger." He shrugged. "And they had each other."

"Like you and El had each other," Brighid said.

"Yes." His smile didn't reach the sadness in his eyes.

"I'm sorry that I've taken you away from her," Brighid said slowly.

"You haven't taken me anywhere. I handfasted with you willingly. I don't want you to ever think otherwise. And this—" he gestured absently around them "—isn't your fault. Neither you nor I wanted to leave MacCallan Castle, but it was the right thing to do. It was what we had to do."

She almost blurted that it was what she had to do, not him, but the stubborn set of his jaw had her sipping from the much depleted wineskin and keeping quiet instead.

"So tell me about what you were like when you were young," he said, motioning for her to pass him the wine. "My guess is that you were much like El—you liked to be off by yourself."

Instead of answering him right away, she fed the fire more branches and they were both silent as the logs popped and cracked.

"Brighid," he said her name and waited for her to shift her gaze to his. "You made me talk to you when I wanted only to crawl into a dark hole and lick my wounds. You wouldn't let me give up on life."

"And now it's your turn to do the same for me?"

"I don't know. Maybe. Right now, though, I'd just like for my wife to be able to speak easily with me about her past."

Wife…the word was heavy in the night air. Brighid took another long drink of wine, welcoming its warmth and its ability to loosen the bonds she kept carefully in place around the past.

"It's hard," she began haltingly. "I'm not used to talking about it."

"Well, take your time. We have all night." He popped the last of the bread and meat into his mouth and then shifted the saddle that he'd propped behind him as a backrest, using the same movement to edge closer to her. Looking comfortable and settled, he leaned back, bringing himself within touching distance of her. "It's just us. Fand's not even here to listen in."

"Or to yip annoyingly," Brighid said.

"Wolves don't yip. They growl."

"Whatever you want to call it, the cub is annoying."

"Which is one of the reasons I left her at the castle," he said. "And the children like her. They'll keep her occupied."

"They're equally as annoying."

Cuchulainn laughed. "I won't even begin to deny that."

Brighid smiled at him, captured by his infectious laugh. "Just like the cub, they never stopped making noise."

The warrior chuckled and stretched. "There are definitely some good points about being off by ourselves. One is that our ears aren't constantly bombarded with the voices of the young—be they winged or furred."

She sighed and took another pull from the wineskin. "On that point you and I are in complete agreement."

The wine and Cuchulainn's good humor had worked its magic. She wasn't feeling so self-conscious and nervous; actually, she was relaxed and a little sleepy. So she started talking.

"You were right. I was alone a lot when I was young, but it wasn't because I was a loner. It was because it seemed that everyone around me wanted something from me. It was just easier for me to be alone."

"Everyone?" Cuchulainn prompted when she fell silent. "Even your brother and sister?"

"Like Elphame, I'm the firstborn. Niam was several years younger, and she and I were never close. She cared about luxuries and gazing at herself in any and all reflective surfaces. I cared about avoiding our mother." Brighid's brow wrinkled. "I didn't understand then that what she was doing was finding her own way to avoid Mother."

"It was always like that with your mother?" he asked.

She sighed. "Almost as far back as I can remember, though when I was very young, and my father was still alive, she was less controlling and more—" she struggled to find the right word "—more normal. After he died it was like the coldness that had always shadowed her took over completely."

"What about your brother?"

"Bregon and I were nearer in age, like you and El. As children we were close, even though it used to confuse him that I didn't want to spend time with Mother. He idolized her. In turn, she ignored him. I always expected him to sour toward her, to see what a user she was, but he never did. Instead he began resenting me. Especially after…" She stopped talking, like her words had run out. Brighid stared into the fire, remembering. In the crackle of the flames she could almost hear the small, frightened voice from her past, and see the terrible red sunset of that long ago day.

Cuchulainn's touch on her arm made her jump, and her

eyes swung back to his, wide and dark in her suddenly pale face.

"What happened?"

She opened her mouth and words that had remained unsaid for years rushed out. "It was near the end of my training as a Huntress. I was about half a day away from the herd's campsite. No one knew I was there. When I saw the wagon tracks I thought I'd use them as a training exercise. I'd follow and see what they led me to, all the while reading the story they told. I was already unusually good at tracking animals." She moved her shoulders apologetically. "I was drawing on my affinity with animal spirits, though I wasn't consciously aware of it. So I was particularly interested in tracking the wagon. It was pulled by animals, but technically *it* wasn't an animal. I thought it would be more difficult to read. Plus, it had left the road and was cutting through a crosstimbers area of the Plains, which was rugged and harder to track. Then it started to rain. Just lightly, but I remember that I liked the added element of difficulty. When the hoof prints mixed with those of the wagon's it was easy to tell that they were the tracks of centaurs. Five of them."

Brighid met Cuchulainn's eyes and she gave a dry, humorless laugh.

"I'd wanted a story to read in tracks—something difficult—and that was exactly what I was granted. Only it wasn't the reading of it that was difficult. That was clear, at least to me. I suppose Ciara would say that I should thank the ability that runs innately through my blood for that clarity. That day I didn't feel much like giving thanks." She stopped speaking, and tilted the wineskin against her lips.

"What story did the tracks tell you?" Cuchulainn asked softly.

She glanced at him, and then looked away, back into the fire. "They told me that the five centaurs had chased the wagon. That the horses that were pulling it had panicked, and that the centaurs purposefully herded the stampeding team toward the timberline and the cliff that the creek and time had eroded. Then I didn't need to read the tracks anymore because I heard her. I followed the sound of her cries as I slid down the side of the cliff to where the wagon had overturned, spilling out its driver, as well as the bolts of brightly colored cloth that she had been bringing to the centaur herd for trade. I remember that most of the cloth was dyed rich jewel tones— reds, blues, emerald greens—so when I found her at first I thought that the bottom of her body was swathed in yards of ruby-colored linen."

Brighid shook her head, her eyes far away, seeing that day in the past.

"The wagon had rolled over her, crushing her body just below her rib cage. She lay there on the ground, the rain mixing with her blood, and she was still alive. She was crying. When she saw me she tried to drag herself away, begged me not to hurt her anymore. I told her I didn't want to hurt her. I don't think she believed me, but when she moved the bleeding got worse. A lot worse. Like something within her had snapped and broken loose. She knew she was dying and she didn't want to be alone, even if it meant breathing her last breath in the arms of a centaur." Brighid lifted her eyes from the fire to the warrior beside her who was so silent and attentive. "Oh, Cu, she was just a girl. She said she'd snuck away from her merchant train and come alone to trade with the Ulstan Herd to prove to her parents she could do the work of an adult, but she'd gotten lost. Then the centaurs—young males, she said, had surrounded her and scared the horses and laughed and whooped while they ran her over the cliff. Then they'd left her alone in the rain to die."

Brighid took another long pull from the wineskin, forcing the trembling from her voice. It was important that she tell the story clearly—that he understand everything.

"She clung to me. There was nothing I could do for her except hold her and be with her at the end. She kept saying, over and over again, 'Tell Mama not to be mad at me. Tell her I'm sorry that I'm late.' Afterward I cared for her body quickly. The rain was heavier, and I didn't want to lose their tracks."

"You followed them?" Cuchulainn asked.

She nodded. "Yes, I followed my brother and his friends back to our home. In my heart I'd known it had been his tracks from the moment I'd found them. But I didn't want to believe…I didn't want to think that…" Her body shuddered and she spoke between gritted teeth. "I tracked him home and I watched them laugh and make merry, as if nothing had happened. When I dragged him before my mother and confronted him with what he had done he said that the silly human girl should have controlled her animals better. That's what he said, Cu. In front of my mother, the High Shaman of our herd— the centaur who should have been exemplifying honor and integrity."

"She did nothing?" Cuchulainn's voice was rough with emotion.

"She *said* nothing. She *did* much more than that. From that day on her attitude and actions toward my brother changed. She no longer ignored him—she went to the other end of the extreme. My mother petted and spoiled him outrageously. His friends were awarded her favors, too." Brighid's lip curled in disgust, making it clear what kind of favors her mother granted her brother's young friends.

"I went back the next day to get the girl's body. I was going to try to find her parents…take her back to the mother she'd died crying out for…but all I found was a burned shell. My mother wouldn't speak of it, but I knew she'd had it done. It wasn't long afterward that I left the Dhianna Herd. Since then I have wandered the Plains, staying as far away from my herd as possible. When I heard Elphame wanted volunteers to rebuild MacCallan Castle I turned to the north and let the call carry me to her."

"Goddess…" Cuchulainn choked out the word.

Brighid wiped a shaky hand over her face. "I should have told you before. I should have told someone before…I just didn't…" She looked wildly at his face as if she could find redemption there. "All I could think to do was to get away from that life. To change my future and to try not to look back. But I understand. Now that you know you might…might not be able to stay with me…might not want to care about me and—"

"Stop!" Cuchulainn's voice was sharp as he grabbed her arm. "I'm not going to leave you. What they did was not your fault. What they are today is not your fault. By the Goddess, do you think I'd let you go back into that alone?"

"I don't know what I think. I've never told anyone. Didn't think I ever could. And now I've told you. My husband. My husband who is a man." Her breath hitched on a sob. "What dream were we living when we thought we could be together? How can this possibly work?"

In an instant Cuchulainn had swiveled to his knees and was facing her. He reached out and pulled her into his arms. She stiffened, feeling the oddness of his torso against hers—the unfamiliar sensation of the muscular width of him that was just man and not melded with the equine body of a centaur male. He ignored her stiffness and didn't relinquish his hold on her. When he spoke he turned his head so that his voice was a warm breath against her ear.

"It will work because we are bonded, the two of us. Because somehow, miraculously, Epona fashioned your soul to match mine. We are not defined by our bodies alone, Brighid. You and I know that only too well."

"It seems impossible," she said.

"No. It's not impossible—it's just difficult."

She pulled back, and this time he loosened his hold on her so that she could look into his eyes. "How can you be so sure? I'm from a different world. We're different species. We can't even consummate our mating tonight."

"My father is a centaur, Brighid. Don't forget that I have his blood running thick in my veins. We're more alike than we are different."

"But your body is human."

"That it is." He sighed and rested back on his heels, letting his hands slide down her arms. "Does that repulse you?"

Brighid frowned at him, hearing the echo of his sister's words in his voice. "Of course not! How could you even ask me that? I wouldn't have handfasted with you if you repulsed me."

"There are many different reasons to handfast. Physical attraction is not always one of them," he said. "You mated with me. That does not automatically mean that you're attracted to me."

Her frown deepened. "I'm attracted to you. You're not like most men."

His brows shot up. "I can assure you that I am very much like most men."

Brighid felt her cheeks heating. "I didn't mean that you're not…uh…not…"

"Yes…" He drew the word out. "Go on. I'm not what?"

Her frown turned into a scowl. He certainly wasn't making this any easier for her. "Most men seem too small."

His brows disappeared completely into his hairline. She shook her head, trying to figure out how to explain it to him without sounding patronizing or offensive.

"Remember the first day we met? You were with El and Brenna in the Main Courtyard of MacCallan Castle. You'd just uncovered the fountain."

"I remember," he said. "You said you were of the Dhianna Herd and I may have reacted badly to that."

"May have?" She snorted. "You wanted El to kick me out. You were defensive and overprotective of your sister." Before he could protest, she hurried on. "And I thought you were intriguing. You weren't some small, weak man. You were a warrior, and everything you said and did was filled with such confidence and power that I never thought of you as just a man. From the first I've thought of you as a warrior, without the label of 'centaur' or 'man.'"

"So you didn't hate me on sight?"

"No. I just disliked you." His amused expression made her smile. "But part of me agreed with you. Had I been another member of my herd, you would have been wise not to trust me."

"I learned to trust you," he said.

"And I you."

"Don't you see that that's it, Brighid? Our relationship is based on trust and respect, which grew into friendship." Slowly he took one of his hands from hers and lightly, just using the tips of his fingers, retraced the path up her arm to the roundness of her shoulder. He felt her skin prickle under his fingers and he heard the sharp intake of her breath. "And then that friendship changed. I'm not even certain when." In a long, slow caress, he drew his hand across her shoulder until he found the softness at the base of her throat. There he let his thumb trace a light, sensuous pattern along her delicate collarbone. "I remember how the part of my soul that came into your dreams teased and kidded with you. You thought I was playing...only pretending desire for you..." His thumb moved to the hollow of her neck and he felt her pulse beating fast and hard against the smoothness of her skin. "It was no pretense. You are the most beautiful creature I have ever seen. And I don't care what form your body takes. I will always desire you."

CHAPTER
THIRTY-NINE

All Brighid could do was stare at him. She was trapped by his slow, intimate caress. For all the strength of her body, this one gentle touch had completely unnerved her.

"May I ask you something?" he said, stroking his thumb up and down the sensitive skin of her neck.

"Yes," she whispered.

"After we kissed in your room when you breathed my soul back into my body, did you ever think of touching me? Of me touching you?"

"Yes."

"What did you think?"

She wet her lips with her tongue and saw his eyes go hungrily to her mouth. "I thought about your hands on my body, and I wondered what it would be like to touch you in return."

"If you touched me now you wouldn't have to wonder," he said.

Hesitantly she lifted the hand that he had so recently been holding, and touched his hair.

"I'm glad you cut it again," she said. "I like it short."

"Then I will always keep it short."

She touched his cheek, and quickly pulled her hand away. Then, with a self-conscious little laugh she touched it again, rubbing the back of her knuckles along the roughness of his day-old beard.

"Centaurs don't have facial hair," she said.

"I know. I've told my father many times that I envy the fact that he doesn't have to bother with shaving."

"It feels strange," she said. Her eyes lifted hastily to meet his. "Not bad strange, just different strange."

He smiled. "You've already told me that I don't repulse you. You're not going to upset me by telling me that there are things about my body that seem strange to you. I don't want you to be afraid to tell me what you're thinking."

"Agreed. But you have to tell me what you're thinking, too."

"Right now I'm thinking that your skin is so soft and smooth that it feels like water—hot water. I can feel the heat of you from here. Logically I know that's because you're a centaur and your body generates more heat than mine. But when I get this close to you, logic leaves my mind and all I can think is that I want to be consumed by your heat."

She knew he could feel how his words made her pulse leap under his fingers. His voice was as seductive as his touch and she couldn't stop her hand from moving to his chest. He was wearing a simple white linen shirt and a kilt made of the familiar MacCallan plaid, the end of which was thrown over his right shoulder. Her hand strayed to the plain round brooch that held it in place. Before her skittering thoughts could stop her, Brighid took her other hand from his and unpinned the brooch. Carefully, she pulled the plaid from his shoulder. Then she unlaced the front of his shirt, so that it fell open, exposing his muscular chest.

Except for the thumb that continued to caress her neck,

Cuchulainn held very still as she splayed her hands over his bare chest and up to his shoulders where she lifted the shirt. In a few quick flicks of her hands, he was naked from his waist up. He shivered.

"Are you cold?" she asked, her voice barely louder than a whisper.

"No!" He half laughed, half moaned the word.

She met his eyes and saw that their turquoise depths had darkened to the azure of a turbulent ocean. "I like the feel of your chest. It's hard and powerful." She paused, running her fingertips purposefully over his puckering nipples, which caused him to suck in a quick breath. "Ah." She breathed the word. "Your centaur blood is showing. Did you know—" she continued to circle his nipples with her fingertips "—that a centaur's nipples are one of the most sensitive parts of his— or her—body?"

"No, I—" His body jerked and his words broke off in a moan when she bent and flicked her tongue across one of his nipples.

When she raised her face he met her lips with his own, surging up on his knees so he could press his naked chest against her. She opened her mouth willingly and welcomed his tongue. He had said that the heat of her body drew him to her, and his bare skin felt alluringly warm and hard against hers, too. She explored his broad back as they learned the secrets of each other's mouth. Then the roughness of his palm was under her vest and pressing against her naked breast, and it was her turn to moan and fight for breath as he teased the sensitive bud of her nipple. When his lips moved to her breast she arched against him, closing her eyes and thinking of nothing except his lips and tongue and teeth.

When their mouths joined again she shrugged out of her vest, pressing her hot breasts against his chest. Both of their bodies were slick with sweat. By the Goddess, she wanted him! More than she'd wanted anyone in longer than she could remember. He made her feel alive and liquid and she wanted more and more. Her hand slid down his back to his waist, and then beyond. Her eyes jerked open in surprise at the alien feel of the hard swell of his buttocks.

What was she doing? She'd actually forgotten that he wasn't a centaur male—forgotten that there was little he could do to quench the raging fire that his touch was igniting within her.

Feeling the instant change in her body, he broke their kiss and pulled back to look into her eyes. What he saw there had him running a shaky hand through his hair as he made an obvious effort to slow his breathing.

"I'd forgotten that you're not…that you can't because you're only a…that we're…" She sputtered to silence at the clear look of hurt that flashed over his face.

"I'm sorry. I didn't think," he said, his voice as flat and expressionless as his face had suddenly become.

"No, Cu. I meant—"

He didn't let her finish. Instead he pushed himself to his feet and grabbed his shirt from the ground, pulling it on with quick, jerky movements.

"The fire's almost out. We'll need more wood. I'll get it." Without looking at her he turned and walked into the forest.

Brighid pressed her hand against her chest where her heart battered itself like a caged bird against her ribs and cursed herself sincerely and fluently. Wonderful. As if the situation wasn't difficult enough—now she'd insulted him.

Cuchulainn took his time in coming back to camp. He felt like a fool. Worse than a fool actually—a randy, frustrated fool. What, in all the levels of the Otherworld, had he thought he was doing? Had he thought he was going to actually make love to a centaur Huntress? No. That was the problem. He hadn't thought at all. Her skin…her heat…the taste and scent of her…it had all worked on him like a hypnotic spell and he'd stopped thinking. He'd only meant to get her used to his touch—like she was a wild filly that had needed to be tamed. Fool was too simple a word for what he'd been. Brighid was no filly. She was a passionate Huntress and she needed the power of a centaur male to match that passion.

But he was just a man, as she had made abundantly clear. Now what? The only thing he knew for sure was that he wouldn't leave her. He searched his heart. He wasn't staying with her only because he'd given her his oath before his mother, their clan, and the Goddess. He wanted to stay with her. Truly. Beyond his physical desire for her was a loyalty that had been founded in friendship and respect—just as he'd told her—and that had grown into something more...something richer. He loved the Huntress. It was that simple. And that complicated.

And it was so different from what he'd had with Brenna.

Brenna... The thought of her still had the power to sadden him. He had loved her—he still loved her, but it was a different feeling than his love for Brighid. The physical part had been easy with Brenna, at least it had been easy once he had overcome her shyness. But, he admitted to himself, it had never been as easy to talk with her as it was with Brighid.

Compassion had drawn him to Brenna. Respect had drawn him to Brighid. Respect and passion. From the first the Huntress had fired something within him. Even when he used to mistrust and argue with her, she always drew him. He just never let himself think of it—admit it. And now he was handfasted to her and he could think of little else. And do nothing about it.

Brighid had called their relationship impossible. Maybe she had been right.

If he had been gone any longer she would have gone after him. Instead she felt sick with relief as he tromped back out of the forest with his arms filled with firewood. She'd been pacing nervously, trying to figure out what she was going to say to him. Then when he was finally there she felt her mouth grow dry and her words evaporate. Without speaking, he fed the fire and then stacked the rest of the wood not far from where he'd left his saddle and packs. Silently, he dug through the larger of the saddlebags and retrieved a woolen blanket, which he wrapped around himself like a cocoon. With a sigh he settled onto his side, facing the fire. Unbelieving, she watched as he closed his eyes.

The damned man was going to sleep!

"Cuchulainn, I want to explain—" she began, but he cut her off.

"There's no need," he said without opening his eyes. "We're both tired. It's late. Tomorrow will be a long, hard day. Get some sleep, Brighid. We can talk later."

And just like that he went to sleep. She thought seriously about throwing something at him—something heavy like a piece of the wood he'd spent such a damned long time collecting. Or, more satisfyingly, maybe she should kick him. Hard.

Eventually her Huntress nature took over and she did neither. The truth was that he'd been right. Tomorrow would be a long, grueling day and she needed to sleep. Since he hadn't left her, and apparently he wasn't planning to any time in the near future, they could discuss what had happened between them later. So she went back to her own place near the fire—not far from where her husband slept—and settled down for the night. She knew she wouldn't have any trouble sleeping. A Huntress was accustomed to shutting off the world and catching sleep when and where she could. Brighid blocked out the frustration and confusion in her mind, closed her eyes, and let the weariness of the day pull her into darkness.

In her dream the blackness of sleep swirled, lightened and turned to fog. The fog brushed against her skin, caressing her nerve endings awake as it pulsed against the naked flesh of her torso. Like a knowing lover, it teased her breasts, making her nipples harden and ache. She moaned and arched restlessly against the mist…and the dreamy fog solidified and became lips and tongue and mouth. Her arms automatically wrapped around her lover. Even before she could actually see him she recognized the feel of Cuchulainn and somewhere in her sleeping mind she was surprised that he already felt so familiar against her body. His head lifted from her breasts and he smiled slowly.

"Where have you taken us now?" he asked.

"I don't know. I'm dreaming."

"Yes you are." His eyes blazed. "I've come to your dreams before, only this time I won't keep my hands from you," he said fiercely. "Whatever happens when we wake, in your dreams I will touch you and hold you and make you my own."

Then his mouth was on hers, insistent and hot. She gave herself over to him, letting him tease and nip her tongue while his hands busied themselves at her breasts. She moaned into his mouth, needing the touch and taste of him. She was sleeping—it was only a dream—so there was no reason to hold to the inhibitions and fears of the waking world. Embracing the abandon of the erotic dream she let her hands search his body, finding the hard heat of him that lengthened under her touch.

Tell him…the soft voice whispered through her mind. *Speak your heart to him.*

"Cuchulainn," she said against his lips. "I want you. I want all of you. Please know that."

He cupped her face in his hands and smiled. "You have me, my beautiful Huntress. All of me."

When he kissed her again it was as if she melted into him. They were no longer centaur and man—they were only sensation and spirit—and the shock and glory of the joining sizzled through her with such an intensity that she woke, shivering with emotion in the aftermath of pleasure.

Her eyes instantly found Cuchulainn. He still lay on his side, facing the fire, just as he had been when she'd fallen asleep. She couldn't see his face, but his breathing was deep and regular. She wanted to touch him, wanted to wake him, but instead she resettled herself and closed her eyes.

Tomorrow night will be different, she promised herself.

Before she fell asleep her last thought was that she hoped he would come to her dreams again—even if who he was in them was only a piece of her own imagination.

Cuchulainn waited until he heard her breathing shift, telling him that she had fallen back to sleep. Then he rolled over so that he could look at her. They'd awakened at the same time.

By the Goddess, the dream had shaken him! When he'd materialized from the mist all he'd been able to see of her was her naked torso. The silver curtain of her hair had been falling around her shoulders parting only to expose the sensitive nipples of her breasts that drew his touch…his mouth. It had seemed so easy, so right, to take her in his arms. And she'd touched him—all of him. His body felt hard and heavy at the remembrance. Then in the midst of the wet heat of passion he'd heard the woman's voice asking Brighid to speak her heart to him, and the Huntress had told him of her desire. When he kissed her it had been like she was drinking in his soul again—only this time the experience had been intensely physical. The jolt of his orgasm had awakened him—at the same instant he'd heard Brighid gasp and awaken.

Was it possible they had experienced the same dream? Had their souls truly met in that nebulous realm of sleep? Had she really given herself to him?

Impossible…

CHAPTER
FORTY

The smell of frying pork had her mouth watering before she'd rubbed the sleep from her eyes. The sky was just lightening with predawn and the air was already warming with the coming of morning. Cuchulainn's back was to her as he bent over the fire, stirring the sizzling meat. She got up, shook herself, and stretched. As she joined him she noticed the gelding was already saddled, and that, except for the few cooking utensils, everything was packed and ready to go.

"Good morning," he said without looking at her.

"Good morning. I can't believe I slept through you packing up and making breakfast."

He glanced up at her and gave her a little half smile, which held only the shadow of his usual warmth. His tone was carefully neutral. "You didn't move. I hope you slept as well as it seemed you did."

She looked into his eyes, remembering the erotic dream and what had prefaced it.

"I slept well," was all she said.

"Good," he said briskly. Cu turned back to the fire and forked the pork between two slabs of bread and cheese, which he handed to her. "Do you mind eating as we travel? I think we should move from dawn to dusk today. We really didn't get a full day in yesterday."

"I agree," she said.

"Good," he repeated. Setting his sandwich on the one saddlebag he'd left unpacked, he put out the campfire.

"Cuchulainn?"

He gave her a quick look over his shoulder.

"Is it going to be this awkward between us all day?" she asked.

His lips twitched. "Looks like it might be."

"Is there anything I can do to change that right now?"

"Probably not," he said, and turned back to the fire.

She sighed. It wasn't even full light and it already felt like it had been a long day. And that feeling held through the endless hours of the morning and then midday. At least the grueling pace she forced herself to set left little opportunity for conversation, though she would have welcomed the respite of talking with him. It was usually so easy between them— ironic that now they were mated everything felt so complicated.

The silence between them did give her time to think. The dream stayed with her, so that her thoughts of Cuchulainn were tinged with an erotic quality, which she knew was silly and unrealistic. Then she'd remember how his hard body had felt against her and the explosion of sensation that had flooded her dream...

"We'll stop here and I'll switch mounts. The gelding is played out." Cuchulainn's deep voice carried above the pound of hooves.

She blinked, rousing herself from the trancelike state induced by endless travel. The sun was just beginning its descent toward the ocean, and the little village they were approaching looked cheerful and welcoming in the bright afternoon light.

"Do you know where we are?" she asked.

"A little over half a day's hard ride from McNamara Castle."

"Which means if we keep up this pace we'll be at the edge of the Blue Tors tomorrow night."

"Can you keep up this pace?"

She saw his eyes flick down her body and was sure he was noting the sheen of sweat that had begun to darken the blond of her flanks. She raised her brow and gave his gelding a pointed look. The horse's coat was drenched and flecks of white foam spotted his chest and flanks.

"I think you better worry about your mount. I'm fine."

Cu grunted. "That's why I'm changing to the bay. This old boy's had it." He smiled at her then, and the wry humor even touched his eyes. "You know you could probably run any horse into the ground."

"Of course I could," she said, giving him a slow, knowing look. "Centaur Huntresses are known for their power and stamina as well as their beauty and passion." Purposefully, her lips curved into a sensuous smile and she watched, amused, as his eyes widened in surprise at her flirtation. *There*, she thought, *let's see what he makes of that*.

"I can see there's no need to worry about you if you have enough energy to be sarcastic," he said.

Again, she sent him that slow, dreamy smile. "I wasn't being sarcastic."

Before he could answer Brighid broke her gait and slowed so they could enter the village at a more sedate pace. For such a small settlement, Brighid was surprised by the number of people crowding the streets around the open air market. The village was neat and prosperous, and she didn't remember it at all from her blind rush from the Centaur Plains. She did notice that there were no other centaurs visible, and that several of the people stared openly at her.

"If I remember correctly there should be an inn just around this corner." He pointed ahead of them and to the left. "We can each get a quick bowl of hot stew, I'll change mounts, and we can be off."

She nodded, preoccupied with the looks she was drawing. She knew she was a beautiful Huntress. It was a fact and had nothing to do with vanity or ego. She was used to being stared at—especially by males. But these looks felt different. They weren't appreciative or inviting. They were speculative, narrowed, distrustful. By the time they halted in front of the crowded little inn, Brighid's skin was jumpy. She had to force herself to keep her hand from the bow that was always strapped to her back.

Cuchulainn dismounted with a grunt and stretched.

"I'll take care of the gelding and switch your saddle to the bay while you go in and get us the stew." At his questioning look, she added, "It'll save time."

He shrugged his shoulders and nodded, walking into the inn with an easy, confident grace. As she loosened the gelding's sweaty girth, she could hear a delighted female voice crying Cu's name, which was soon followed by other greetings.

"Like they're welcoming home a damned hero," she muttered to the gelding, who was still blowing hard. She sighed and pulled off the saddle, leading the exhausted horse to the watering trough, where he sank his muzzle and drank deeply of the cold, clear water. Under normal circumstances she would have joined him, splashing some of the water on herself, but she could feel watching eyes and instinctively she decided against making any move that could be mistaken for bestial.

She was a centaur Huntress, not a mindless equine.

She was just lifting the saddle onto the new mount when Cu came back through the door. She glanced up, frowning at the spryness of his step and the annoying gleam in his eyes.

What was it Elphame used to call him? An incorrigible rake.

"Here, let me do that." He took the saddle from her hands and put it on the bay's broad back. "The stew will be right out. Or we could go in and eat."

She gave the narrow door a dismissive look. "It's not centaur-size."

"There's plenty of room inside," he said.

"I prefer a more open space," she said. Ignoring the question in his look she set about securing the saddlebags on the buckskin gelding, double-checking the horse's breathing... anything to keep from meeting Cuchulainn's eyes.

Was she being overly sensitive? Was she imagining the tension around her? Before she could decide, a plump, attractive blonde rushed from the inn. She was carrying a wooden tray laden with two bowls of steaming stew, bread and fruit, as well as goblets brimming with what smelled like mulled cider. Giggling coquettishly she wiggled up to Cuchulainn. Brighid wondered at the balancing act she managed—with all that wiggling and giggling, she didn't spill one drop of food or drink. The girl was truly talented.

"When you didn't come back in I thought you might like it if I brought your meal to you, my Lord Cuchulainn." She batted her eyes ridiculously.

Brighid felt her jaw setting.

"That was kind of you." Cu smiled absently at the woman as he gave the girth one last pull. "I think we're going to eat—"

"Right out here," Brighid interrupted, pointing to the little porch. "You can just leave the tray there. We're in a hurry to get back on the road."

The blonde's eyes slid to the Huntress and Brighid saw her acknowledge and then quickly discount her. She did set the tray down, though, being sure that she afforded Cuchulainn a deep view of her ample bosom. Brighid narrowed her eyes at her husband, who was obviously pleased at the additional scenery. The Huntress was contemplating how satisfying it would be to kick the blonde on her very round behind when a couple of men emerged from the doorway, pewter mugs of ale in their hands.

"Cuchulainn! It's always a pleasure to see you," the taller of the two said.

Cu nodded pleasantly before he took a bowl of stew from the platter and passed it to Brighid.

"Will you not come in and join us?" the shorter, more florid man asked. Then his eyes flicked to Brighid and stayed. He licked his liver-colored lips. "We could make room."

Brighid took some pleasure in the fact that Cu's voice flattened at the man's obvious interest in her. "Afraid we don't have time."

"Little wonder you're in a hurry. I hear there's some trouble in the Centaur Plains," the short man said. He couldn't seem to keep his eyes from Brighid. She frowned at him, but realized that her dark look did no good. The man wasn't staring at her face.

"It's those Goddess-be-damned Dhianna centaurs. That herd never could act right, not since the Fomorian War," the first man grumbled. "Like they were the only ones to suffer losses? Maybe you can teach them a thing or two about respect, Cuchulainn."

Brighid felt her gut tighten as her initial reaction was to come to the defense of her herd. But she clamped her jaws closed. She couldn't defend them. They didn't deserve it. But that didn't mean it was any easier for her to hear this man's slander. She lifted her eyes to Cu's and knew he could read the turmoil and hurt there. She heard his voice again, echoing from the night before... *We are bonded, the two of us. Because somehow, miraculously, Epona fashioned your soul to match mine.*

And she knew it was true. No matter what else might come between them, their souls completed one another.

Cuchulainn turned away from her and faced the men again,

this time he was not smiling. "Funny that you would mention the Dhianna Herd. I was just about to introduce you to my traveling companion, Brighid Dhianna."

Brighid enjoyed how the men and the plump blonde suddenly looked decidedly uncomfortable. She tilted her head in quick acknowledgment of Cu's introduction.

"It's charming to meet you," she said, keeping most of the sarcasm from her voice.

"Of course she's not just my traveling companion. She's also MacCallan Castle's Huntress." He paused and took a purposeful step closer to her. When his gaze shifted to her his expression changed and lost its dangerous edge, turning warm with open affection. "And as of yesterday, she is my wife."

The blonde burst into a gale of breathy giggles. "Oh, Lord Cuchulainn! You do so love to jest."

Brighid leveled her gaze on the woman. "He's not jesting."

"But that's impossible!" sputtered the short man, who had finally managed to pull his eyes from the Huntress's breasts.

"Do you mean to insult me by doubting my word?" Cuchulainn's voice was low and dangerous.

"No!"

"Of course not!"

"I—I should get back to the rest of our patrons," the blonde said, throwing nervous looks over her shoulder at Brighid as she scampered, amidst much jiggling of flesh, back up the stairs, and disappeared into the inn.

"Well then," the tall man said, not looking directly at the warrior or the Huntress. "Good luck with your journey."

"Yes." The florid man wiped the sweat from his upper lip. "Luck be with you."

Both men retreated hastily into the inn, whereby the easy sounds of conversation died and soon Brighid saw several pairs of wide, shocked eyes peering through the single window.

She wanted to forget the rest of her food and bolt from the village, but when she glanced at Cuchulainn he had moved to lean against the edge of the porch and was leisurely wiping the bottom of his bowl with a thick piece of the bread.

If he wasn't going to let the stares and the shocked whispers bother him, she damned well wasn't going to, either. They ate the rest of their meal slowly, and only after they had finished every drop of the cider and eaten every speck of the fruit, did Cuchulainn toss a few coins onto the tray and then mount the bay. Side by side they trotted from the inn.

"I think that went well," Cuchulainn said pleasantly.

"Oh, definitely. I don't know why I ever thought people would be shocked at the news of our marriage," she said in the same nonchalant tone.

Cuchulainn turned his head and looked at her—and they both laughed.

CHAPTER
FORTY-ONE

Their laughter broke the last of Cuchulainn's uncomfortable silences. This time when Brighid swung into her traveling pace he kept his mount beside her.

"You should do that more often," he said.

"Do what? Offend and shock small groups of people?"

He grinned. "I meant laugh. You don't laugh enough."

"I think I've laughed more since I came to MacCallan Castle than I have since I was a child." She smiled at him. "Did you know that your laughter was one of the things I missed most about you when your soul was shattered?"

"It was a dark time for me," he said. "I don't think I realized how dark until I was whole again."

She studied his strong profile, not wanting to remember how close he had been to ending his life. The thought upset her then—now it sickened her.

"You surprised me back there," she said, needing to change the subject.

"Did I?" His grin was back. "Surprised that I announced that you're a Dhianna centaur?"

"No, not really. Just yesterday you vowed to cherish my name as if it were your own. You're not a man who would take such vows lightly."

"Right you are, my beautiful Huntress."

Her lips tilted up at the familiar endearment. "I was surprised that you announced our marriage."

"Did you think it was something I would hide?"

"I hadn't really thought about it, but hearing you say it was…well…nice," she said. "I wanted you to know that."

"I'm proud that you are my wife, Brighid. Things have happened so quickly, I don't think I've done this properly."

"This?" She arched a questioning brow.

"This wooing of you—courting you." His voice deepened and his turquoise eyes met hers. "This ritual of lovemaking."

"Oh." The way he was looking at her reminded her of her erotic dream. She pushed down the nervous flutter that threatened to mix up her words. By the Goddess, he was so damned handsome! "You were doing fine last night."

She saw his jaw tighten, but he didn't turn away. "I should have talked to you when I came back to camp. The truth is you hurt my pride, and I didn't handle it well."

"The truth is," she said quickly, "that I shocked myself and I didn't handle it well."

"Shocked yourself?"

"I forgot you're not a centaur."

"You forgot?" He tried unsuccessfully not to smile.

"So you can imagine that it was a shock for me to feel your…"

"Butt?" he provided.

"Exactly," she said.

"Harrumph." He studied her, obviously trying to decide what to say and what not to say. "Then you were just surprised. You weren't disappointed and—"

"If you ask me again if I'm repulsed by you I'm going to use part of this centaur body you seem to be so fond of and kick you squarely in your very manly butt."

"That would be hard to do while I'm sitting on this saddle."

"One of the first virtues a Huntress learns is patience." She smiled sweetly at him.

"I should have kissed you back there while the entire inn was watching," he said, grinning at her.

"Yes," she said, flipping her silver-blond hair over her shoulder. "You should have."

When they came to the creek, twilight was shading the roadside vineyards with the colors of evening.

"The horses are done in—it's almost dark. I think we've pushed enough for today," Cuchulainn said.

Brighid nodded and eased her ground-eating canter to a trot and finally, with a sigh, she slowed to a walk. Even the echo of her hooves crossing the small, arched bridge sounded tired. She noticed the two horses pricked their ears at the moving water.

"Might as well camp down there." She gestured to the bank of the creek. It was flat and lined with delicate weeping willows and the emerald green of water-loving grass.

"Anywhere that's not moving looks good to me right now," Cu said.

Brighid noted the shadows under his eyes and the two-day-old beard. The warrior definitely looked tired. "If you get the firewood and take care of the horses, I'll get out the pork and the wine."

"You have a deal," he said.

Brighid thought about how well they worked together as she unloaded the saddlebags and got out the cooking implements. Since the tension between them had broken, the day had been a pleasure. Yes, they had been traveling at a difficult pace, but he had been beside her, talking and laughing, and then, later, as evening had fallen and they'd been too tired to speak he'd just been there, beside her. He was a good companion—a good man—and in spite of their obvious differences, they fit well together.

Cuchulainn dumped a load of broken branches in the middle of the ring of rocks she'd gathered to mark their campfire. "I'm taking the horses to the creek." He sniffed at himself, making her smile. "And I do believe I'll take myself to the creek, too."

"Good idea. You smell like a horse."

His laughter drifted back to her on the warm night breeze. It was different between them tonight. Easier. They'd soldered their bond.

When he led the horses back from the creek she glanced up from the frying slices of pork to smile at him, and her stomach tensed. His hair was wet. He'd put on a fresh linen shirt. A new kilt was wrapped haphazardly around his waist. And his face was clean shaven. He grinned and rubbed his chin.

"Rumor has it you prefer your men clean-shaven."

"There is only one man I prefer," she said, holding his gaze. "And I like him exactly as he is—shaven or un." She tossed him the wineskin. "It's my turn in the creek."

He watched her move out of the firelight and into the gentle glow of an early moon, thinking she must be the most graceful creature in all of Partholon. He was supposed to be minding the pork, but he could see her as she took off her vest and entered the creek. He couldn't take his eyes from her. She found the same spot in which he'd bathed, an area that had been beaver-dammed into a nice-size pool. The water was up to her withers. He watched as she turned to face him. In the silver moonlight she looked like a lake goddess—part human, part divine. She made his body feel hot and heavy, and his soul feel incredibly light.

She belonged to him, and he to her. And anyone who didn't like it could just be damned.

They spoke very little as they ate, but the silence wasn't uncomfortable. They sat close to each other, so that when they passed the wineskin back and forth it was easy for their bodies to brush against one another. No words were needed for what was happening between them—only looks and touches.

When they were finished eating, instead of reclining beside her against his saddle as he had the night before, Cuchulainn went to one of his saddlebags. Curious, she saw the firelight catch on whatever he held in his hand. But he didn't return to her right away. Instead he bowed his head and she noted the tension in his shoulders. Then he drew a deep breath, and took his place beside her.

"I have something for you. I meant to give it to you last night, but…" He moved his shoulders. "Last night…"

"Last night didn't end as it should have," she said. "Tonight will be different."

"Tonight you should have this." He held up the silver necklace and let the turquoise stone dangle.

"It's Brenna's stone," she gasped, cupping the blue-green rock in her hand.

"It's your stone now. She gave it to you. I think she would want you to wear it." He placed it over her head so that the stone hung between her breasts. "I've not felt her presence since the day she was killed, but I want to believe that she would approve of us."

Brighid closed her eyes, trying to sift through the rush of her mixed emotions. "She came to me, Cu."

"What!"

"In my dream, like you did when your soul was shattered. We met at MacCallan Castle. She told me that she'd given me the turquoise stone and she also said she wouldn't be haunting MacCallan Castle." Brighid opened her eyes and looked through tears at her husband. "She said it wouldn't be good for any of us if she did."

"What else did she say?" His face had gone very still, and he was keeping his voice carefully controlled, but Brighid could hear the pain in his words.

"She said she was happy, and that she had fulfilled her destiny." Brighid managed a weak, half smile. "Her scars were gone, Cu."

He bowed his head and she could see the tears that fell, glistening, onto the blue and green of his kilt.

"She didn't talk with me for very long. She just made me give her my oath, and then she was gone."

"Your oath?" He raised his head and wiped at his cheeks with the back of his hand.

"She made me swear that I would keep an open mind to the impossible," Brighid's voice had dropped almost to a whisper.

A single tear made its way down Cuchulainn's face. "So she knew about us."

The Huntress nodded. "And she approved. She said that she was leaving you to me, freely and without any hesitation." Brighid's laugh sounded choked. "It was the night we were at Guardian Castle. I thought she was talking about your soul retrieval. It was only yesterday that I realized she knew I loved you, even before I knew it myself."

"And when did you know it?"

"The first time I kissed you." Gently she brushed the tear from his cheek. "I'm not her, Cu. I'm not as good as she was, not as kind, not as compassionate. But I'm loyal and I'm faithful. And I do love you."

"Brenna's gone," he said through a throat thickened with emotion. "I didn't handfast with you because I wanted you to be like her."

"Why did you, Cu?"

He took her hand and kissed it. "Because you hold a piece of my soul, my beautiful Huntress. And to be whole, I need to be near you."

He kissed her with the salt of tears mixed with the intoxicating taste of man. She drank him in and wondered if she would ever be able to get enough of him.

"I dreamed of you last night," he said as his mouth moved to the hollow of her neck.

"I dreamed of you, too," she said, busying her hands with untying the lacings of his shirt.

"I came to you in the fog," he said.

She paused, fingers still at the lacings of his shirt. "And you were naked."

He lifted his lips from her skin and met her eyes. "A woman's voice told you to speak what was in your heart."

"And I told you that I wanted you. All of you." Her hand touched his face. "It was more than a dream."

"Yes."

"The woman's voice. I think it was the Goddess," she said.

He smiled. "I think you're right."

"I want to see you again. Like you were last night."

"Naked?"

She nodded. "I'm no silly young virgin. I won't pretend that I haven't had my share of centaur lovers, but I've never seen a naked man before. Not this close. Not like this. I mean, except for last night in my…our dream." She drew in a deep breath. "I want to see you."

"Harrumph," he grunted.

She raised one brow at him. "Are you being shy, or do you not want to be naked with me?"

"Neither," he said. "I'm just…" He hesitated, and then ran his hand through his hair and gave her a little chagrined smile. "This is new to me, too. I've had lovers before, you know that, plenty of them. But none of them have been centaurs. I'm not sure—"

He broke off when she pressed her fingers against his lips. "How about we both stop thinking so much."

The smile that lit his face transformed him from hesitant lover to rakish young warrior. "Makes sense. Love has little to do with thinking anyway."

Still smiling, Cuchulainn stood and with a quick, practiced movement he unwrapped the kilt from around his waist and pulled it away so that he stood before her, naked.

Brighid swallowed. Her eyes moved down from his face to

the broad width of his chest, which was handsome and familiar—normal. He could easily have been a centaur male. In his
torso he carried a centaur's power and grace. But he wasn't a
centaur, she told herself, he wasn't and he would never be. Get
used to it. Accept him for what he is, as he clearly accepted
her. She held her breath and let her eyes drop.

His legs were long and muscular. She'd seen quite a bit of
them before, of course. He wore a kilt often and that left them
bare from his knees down. But she'd never before seen his
thighs or the muscular ridges that covered his buttocks and
dipped fluidly in at his waist. And she'd never seen his naked
manhood.

"I wish you'd say something," Cu said.

She let her breath out in a puff. "It's not as bad as I thought
it would be."

"Well that's certainly flattering," he said.

She reached out and caught his wrist. "I'm really not very
good at this," she sighed. "What I'm trying to say is that you
aren't as scary as I thought you would be. Naked, I mean."

"Scary? You're scared of me?"

"A little. I just wasn't completely sure what to expect. Last
night it was all sensation and heat. Nothing was very clear."
Her eyes dropped back to below his waist. "Tonight everything
is very clear."

"And that makes you afraid of me," he said, shifting her
grip so he could lace his fingers with hers.

"Now that you're here, in the flesh, in front of me, I don't
think fear is the right word for what I'm feeling." Hesitantly,
she touched his thigh and let her fingers play over the thickness of his muscle as she watched his body stir and react.

"What is the right word for what you're feeling?" His voice
sounded strained.

She glided her hand up so that it smoothed over his tight,
flat stomach. "Fascination…" she breathed. "Your body fasci-
nates me. It has for a long time, much longer than I was willing to admit to myself." When she took his hard length in her

hands he gasped and her eyes flew to his. "If you want me to stop you'll have to tell me."

"I don't want you to stop," he rasped.

She didn't want to stop. That her touch, just the smallest flick of her tongue or stroke of her hand, could effect him so profoundly made her feel powerful and passionate. It was something that went beyond centaur or woman. Exploring Cuchulainn's body made her revel in her own femininity. She stroked his amazing, fascinating length of hardness sheathed in skin the texture of silk. When she brought him to climax with her hands, and later with her mouth, she found a different kind of passion than she'd experienced with centaur lovers. She knew the joy of her lover's pleasure, and she reveled in how his satisfaction touched the very core of her being.

That night they slept dreamlessly, hands linked together, bodies pressed so close that in the darkness it was hard to tell where man and woman ended and centaur began.

When the bay stumbled for the third time Cuchulainn pulled him up. Brighid had to watch her own stride. Her overtaxed muscles felt alarmingly loose, and she was afraid she had little more control over herself than the poor horses had over their equine limbs. She concentrated on gradually changing her gait and stopping more slowly so that she wouldn't embarrass herself by collapsing in a heap. Drawing in careful, controlled breaths she circled back to where Cu stood next to the trembling horse.

"He can't go any farther. He's game—he'll try, but it'll kill him. I'm going to leave him here. He'll rest and then eventually find his way to McNamara Castle. Or maybe one of the small farmhouses will take him in," Cu said.

Brighid wiped sweat from her face. "The buckskin is in better shape, and we should find a place to camp soon."

"It's true, he isn't at the point of collapse yet, but I think it would be wise if we slowed some."

"Agreed," she said, careful to keep the relief from her voice. She didn't want Cuchulainn to know just how close she was to collapsing herself.

Brighid looked around them as Cu unsaddled the exhausted horse. They'd pushed hard since dawn, choosing to avoid McNamara Castle and the luxuries it could afford them. Instead they'd saved time by cutting across fertile farmland and angling into the well-kept forest on the south side of the Calman River, which had led them—finally—into the Blue Tors. Now as night fell Brighid was surrounded by reminders of why the tors were named so. The gentle rolling hills were covered with ancient trees whose thick leaves appeared a smoky blue-green in the waning light. *Like Cu's eyes,* she thought. *Let's hope that's a good omen.*

Damn, she was tired! She felt shaky and light-headed, and she suddenly understood all too well how Niam had run herself to her death. Brighid, too, was nearing the end of her strength. Maybe they should just make camp at the next clearing and look for a place to quest for Epona's Chalice tomorrow—after they'd slept.

The turquoise stone that hung between her breasts had grown uncomfortably warm and the hawk had to repeat its call three times before its cry registered in Brighid's exhausted mind. When she finally looked up she saw the bird circling in a tight spiral overhead, a distinctive gold and silver slash against the mellowing sky. The moment her eyes found the hawk, it broke from its circle and moved lazily to the south, keeping low over the trees.

Come…

Brighid's skin prickled as the silent call washed through her mind.

"Cuchulainn, we need to go," she said.

"What is it?" he asked, slapping the bay's rump before he pulled himself wearily aboard his reliable buckskin gelding.

"I think I know how to find our campsite."

Squinting, he followed her gaze skyward. "That's not your mother's raven, is it?"

"No," she said softly. "It's my hawk."

She followed the bird with Cuchulainn staying close behind her. She could hear his muffled "harrumph" and didn't need to see his face to know he was frowning up at the sky. She should probably remind him that he'd better start getting used to the presence of the spirit realm in their lives. But she was too damned tired—plus, more often than not she tended to agree with his mistrust.

The hawk called again, bringing Brighid's wandering attention back into focus. She forced herself to kick into a lumbering trot and heard the gelding blow wearily through his nose as he struggled to keep up with her. She just needed to concentrate on placing one hoof before the other and following the golden bird as it led them deeper into the Blue Tors, taking them on a winding path that cut across the tree-filled, rolling hills. The bird flew on and on, totally unmindful that it was leading them on a route that was ignoring the few trade roads and that it would soon be too dark for them to see anything—even a golden bird.

Brighid clambered up yet another of the gently rounded hills and then had to struggle to maintain her footing as she slid down the surprisingly steep far side of it. When she hit the bottom of the decline, she stood still, breathing heavily, thankful that exhaustion hadn't caused her to misstep. In her condition it would be a simple thing for her to snap one of her equine legs—a simple thing with disastrous consequences.

"Are you all right?" Cuchulainn's gelding stumbled to a halt beside her, and the warrior was off the horse and running his hands down her legs in an instant.

"I'm not hurt," she assured him, and then passed a shaky hand over her face and tried to laugh. "I'd say today was becoming dreamlike, but lately my dreams have been much better than this."

The hawk shrieked at her again and she frowned at the sky—then was surprised to see that the bird had perched on the top branch of a tree not far from them.

Soon, Huntress...we shall meet again.

With another cry it lifted, beating the warm evening air with its massive wings. Then it seemed to evaporate into the sky.

"Did that bird just disappear?" Cuchulainn said.

But Brighid wasn't looking at the bird, her gaze had shifted to where it had led them. They were standing at the edge of a small clearing that appeared to be encircled, horseshoelike, on all sides except one, by a ring of hills. She walked forward on legs that trembled to the far edge of the clearing, the side that wasn't closed in by the green of foliage-covered hills, and even in the vague, shadowy light of evening she could see that the world dropped away from her and the land spilled out and down until it emptied into...

"The Centaur Plains," Cuchulainn said, walking up to stand beside her.

"I hadn't realized we were this close," she said, straining her eyes to see through the encroaching darkness to the waving grassland that had been her home. "So the hawk was leading us there."

"Actually I think it was probably leading us here."

He pointed over her left shoulder. She followed his finger to see that what she had originally discounted as just another tor, was actually the large open mouth of a cave. A stream ran from the interior and waterfalled over the edge of the clearing. Her stomach tightened.

"It's an entry to the Underworld," she said. "Just like your father said."

"Not tonight it isn't." Cuchulainn walked back to the gelding and began pulling the saddle and packs from the horse's sweaty back while he spoke. "Tonight it's just shelter and a ready campsite. Neither of us is in any shape to travel anywhere else—be it in the physical world or the Realm of Spir-

its." He glanced over his shoulder at her when she didn't respond, noting the stubborn set of her shoulders. "Do you
want to chance facing your mother's spirit tonight?"

She blanched. "No."

"Neither do I. So tonight we sleep. Tomorrow we worry
about the Otherworld."

She nodded, relieved beyond words that he was there to as-
sert logic and sanity into a journey that was neither logical
nor sane. She knew her time was short—that Bregon might
have already managed to drink of Epona's Chalice—but the
fog of exhaustion that was smothering her body and mind told
her that questing for the Chalice that night would be futile,
perhaps even dangerous.

"I'll get the firewood," she said.

Before she could stagger to the tree line Cuchulainn
stepped in front of her. He took her hand and raised it to his
lips.

"You're reminding me of Niam tonight," he said, studying
her with concern.

"Niam?" She shook her head in confusion. "I don't—"

"Your eyes are hollow. Your skin is flushed and you're walking like you could fall over at any moment."

"Niam pushed herself for at least two more days. She probably didn't stop to sleep or eat at all. And she wasn't a Huntress. She wasn't accustomed to exerting herself physically.
I'm—"

"You're exhausted," he cut her off again. "Take the gelding
over to the stream. Let him drink. Let yourself drink. I'll get
the firewood."

She began to protest, but his next words stopped her.

"Please let me do this for you."

The night before he'd given himself to her, freely and with
such complete intimacy that it had amazed her that the man
who had trembled under her touch was the same warrior who
had bloodied a sword beside her. Could she not learn to allow
him the same access to her? He wasn't asking to make love to

her, but he was loving her all the same. Wasn't her allowing him the intimacy of caring for her just another kind of surrender?

She bent and kissed him, letting her lips linger on his.

"I'll take the gelding to the stream," she said.

He smiled and touched her face. Then he walked off into the darkening forest. Brighid led the exhausted horse to the stream and let him drink his fill before she rubbed him down and then hobbled him and watched him settle down to some tired grazing. Then she stood beneath the crystal waterfall and let it wash the sweat and dirt from her body as she gazed into the black distance that concealed the land of her youth. It was appropriate that her first sight of the Plains was shrouded in darkness.

"What misery are you leading them into, Bregon?" she whispered. "Why can't you just let her die?"

Cuchulainn came back to find Brighid standing near the edge of the clearing, staring into the darkness. He felt a little prickle of unease. It wasn't the first foreboding he'd experienced that day. Ever since they'd entered the Blue Tors he'd been uneasy. At first he believed it was a symptom of exhaustion. His Huntress had not been exaggerating when she'd bragged about her stamina. She'd set a pace that would have been impossible for a single horse and rider to match. Not for the first time he breathed a prayer of thanks for his father's suggestion that he trade off mounts.

But now he decided the unease had little to do with their grueling journey. Before Brenna had been killed Cuchulainn would have pushed aside any hint of intuition or Feeling that could not be explained by something as mundane as exhaustion. Brenna's tragic death had taught him that it was unwise as well as dangerous to ignore Feelings of any type. He had learned a painful lesson—and he had learned it well. Unlike the day Brenna had been killed he would be vigilant and wise in protecting Brighid. He would not have another love snatched from him. He couldn't survive it. If something happened to Brighid his soul would fragment into so many pieces it would be impossible to put back together again.

Which was why he kept his sword nearby and his senses alert as he built a fire at the mouth of the cave, unloaded their packs, and simmered the food he hoped would revive Brighid. When she didn't move from her place near the clearing's edge his unease increased. When he spoke his voice was unintentionally gruff.

"I thought you didn't like heights."

She didn't respond at first but then her equine coat quivered. The stone centaur she had seemed to be drew a deep breath, became living flesh again. She turned to him. Her eyes were dark and shadowed with weariness and worry, but she smiled and managed a teasing tone.

"Why is it everyone knows that I don't like heights?"

He shrugged and waggled his brows at her. "I thought it was a well-known centaur thing." He held a wineskin up and jiggled it so she could hear its heavy sloshing. "I have wine."

With a sigh she walked slowly into the cave and took the skin from him. Drinking, she looked around. Its opening was spacious. The top didn't end till well above her head, but the inside didn't live up to the entrance's promise of space. The smooth, sand-colored walls looked like they had been formed by a giant's spoon hollowing out a taste of the gentle tor, but they narrowed to a tunnel in the rear corner that was barely big enough for the clear stream of water. Cuchulainn's fire licked the walls with flame, changing the brown to gold and orange. As she stared the colors ran together and blurred, so that it seemed for a moment that the walls around them had been turned to flame. She heard a whoosh, followed by a crackling roar that could not have come from the tame campfire. She felt heat blazing against her skin and she closed her eyes on its fury.

"Brighid!" Cuchulainn was at her side, touching her face and smoothing back her still damp hair. "What is it?"

The centaur shook her head, blinking her eyes clear. "I'm— I'm just tired. I need to sleep."

He led her back to the fire where he had arranged their blankets in a makeshift pallet. When she reclined, letting her legs collapse and fold under her, he handed her a hot slab of meat surrounded by thick slices of bread and cheese.

"Eat first. Then you can sleep."

She nodded and automatically chewed the food, even though she felt strangely detached from the heat it spread throughout her body. She and Cuchulainn didn't speak, but their eyes met often—his filled with worry—hers dark with exhaustion.

"Tomorrow," she said when she'd finished eating. He glanced up from adding more wood to the fire, his look a question. "Tomorrow we must begin the quest for Epona's Chalice."

"Then it will be tomorrow. Tonight I want you to clear all thoughts of the Otherworld from your mind. Sleep, Brighid." He knelt beside her and kissed her gently.

"I may not awaken till well past dawn," she said, breathing in his scent and touch.

"It doesn't matter when you wake. I will be here," he murmured.

Brighid closed her eyes and surrendered her mind and body to the intoxication of sleep.

CHAPTER
FORTY-THREE

If someone had asked Brighid if she'd wanted to dream that night, she would have answered with a resounding "no!" She just wanted to sleep—to give her body time to reenergize so that when she asked more of it later the deep wells of her power would be refilled and available to her once more.

No, she had no interest in dreams that night.

So when she felt herself being pulled from her body, she was more annoyed than alarmed or afraid. Irritated, she opened her eyes to find herself gazing down at her sleeping form. Cuchulainn was still awake and sat vigilantly beside her, staring somberly into the campfire. He looked tired. The lines in his face, that had softened after she'd retrieved his soul, were back. Automatically she reached out to him, but instead of touching him, she was lifted up and up, through the roof of the cave and into the night sky.

The Huntress gasped and swallowed down a terrible rush of dizziness. Oh, Goddess! What was happening to her?

Be at peace, my child. Do not fear.

Epona's voice! Brighid's heart hammered painfully in a chest that was clearly more spirit than body. She looked wildly around, but saw nothing more than the fully risen moon that was perfectly round and butter-colored in the clear night sky. As she hung there, trying to control her mixed feelings of awe and panic, she felt her spirit body begin to move. Slowly, at first, she floated north. Below her the Blue Tors were dark and silent. Then her speed increased and it seemed only an instant had passed. She was across the wide Calman River. McNamara Castle sped by her and the vineyards blurred beneath her. She wanted to slow, to control the terrible speed of her journey, but her spirit was in the Goddess's hands—and Epona was quite obviously in a hurry.

The moon glistened off the black liquid expanse of the B'an Sea. Brighid focused her eyes on its vastness that stayed the same, no matter how quickly her spirit sped over it. It helped to quell the dizziness she couldn't quite shake off, and it was only when her spirit slowed noticeably that she allowed her gaze to move from the water to the land. The Huntress sucked in a breath in surprise.

Below her MacCallan Castle was alight with life. Torches blazed from the battlements and the inside walls. Though it was late, the sentries were attentively pacing the newly reconstructed walkway. The sight of her adopted home was bittersweet. She loved seeing it again, but it also saddened her. It reminded her too well of how much she and Cuchulainn would rather be there than sleeping in a lonely cave at the edge of the Centaur Plains.

Fate has decreed otherwise, child.

The Goddess's voice soothed her mind like a gentle caress and she felt her melancholy ease. Then the Huntress shook her head, ashamed of herself. Who was she to question fate and the Goddess's will? Brenna had met her fate willingly.

Niam had embraced hers honorably. Could Brighid do any less?

You may question, child, just as you may choose. I believe that you will choose wisely when the time comes.

Brighid bowed her head, humbled by the trust in the Goddess's words.

Now observe so that you will have the knowledge you need when the time comes...

Her body dropped down at a speed that had her eyes blurring until she was jerked to a sudden halt. Blinking to clear her vision, she realized she was hovering near the ceiling of the Great Hall. Below her, sitting at their usual places at the Chieftain's table were Elphame and Lochlan. The only other person in the room was the head cook, Wynne. She was standing in front of the table. Between them, on the tabletop, was a mound of freshly picked herbs. Elphame was absently feeling the broad green leaf of one of the plants that Brighid thought she recognized as basil.

When Ciara hurried into the Great Hall, everyone's attention shifted from the herbs to her.

Her smile was open and curious as she approached the table and curtsied gracefully. "You sent for me?"

"Yes," Elphame said. "I know it's late, but Wynne only just told me about this. And I wanted to speak to you at once."

"This?" Ciara asked.

"The herbs the children have been tending," Elphame said, pointing at the fragrant pile.

Ciara's forehead wrinkled as her brows drew together. "Have the children done something wrong? They're usually so good with plants I didn't think they would cause any problem in the kitchen's gardens. But if they've harmed something I will see that—"

"They dinna harm the wee plants, Shaman," Wynne blurted, interrupting Ciara's apology. "They made them grow."

Obviously confused, Ciara looked from the pile of herbs to the cook, and then back at the herbs. "I don't understand."

Only Brighid noticed that Etain had entered the room and was listening to the exchange with interest.

"Well, I donna understand either, but I do know what I see with me own eyes and touch with me own hands. In the space of the three days the bairns have been tending them, they have grown more than they would have in three weeks. The bairns made the herbs grow," she said firmly.

"But weren't they already growing? All the children did was water and weed them."

"I think the children did much more than that." Etain's voice came from the doorway.

"Mama." Elphame sent the High Priestess a relieved look and motioned for her to join them. "I was just going to send for you."

Etain smiled at her daughter, but kept most of her attention trained on Ciara.

"Touch the plants, Shaman. See if they can tell you what it is Wynne already knows."

Hesitantly Ciara placed her slender hand atop the pile of herbs. She closed her eyes and took several deep cleansing breaths. Then her mouth formed a surprised little "O" and she gasped. When she opened her eyes Brighid could see they were filled with unshed tears.

"Tell my daughters what it is you have discovered, Ciara," Etain said.

"The children did make the plants grow! Oh, Goddess!" Overcome with emotion the winged woman bowed her head and pressed her hand against her mouth.

"Mama, what is it? What has happened?" Elphame asked.

"Epona has given the New Fomorians a great gift," Etain said.

"They were born from death and destruction, and they have lived with madness and loss," Ciara said through tears of joy. "And now our great Goddess has granted us the ability to nurture life."

"It's not just now," Etain told the Shaman. "They've always

had the gift—*you've* always had the gift. How do you think you were able to bring forth life and hold to love and hope and not give in to utter despair in the desolation of the Wastelands?"

"It is, indeed, a great gift," Elphame said, taking her husband's hand and looking into his beloved face. "And we have been richly blessed to have you here with us."

"You are our home, my heart. There is nowhere else we would choose to be," Lochlan said, gently touching her cheek.

"Think of what this will mean, Elphame!" Ciara gushed. "We can be useful and bring forth food, not just for MacCallan Castle, but for trade and..."

Brighid lost the rest of Ciara's words as her spirit drifted up through the ceiling of the Great Hall and into the night sky. This time when the earth blurred as her spirit sped back to the south, Brighid's thoughts were too preoccupied by what she had just witnessed for her head to spin and become dizzy.

Epona had given the New Fomorians the ability to nurture life from the earth. Little wonder Liam had shown such an aptitude for understanding the spirits of animals—he had been gifted with an affinity for the earth and for growing things. The leap to understanding the spirits of animals wasn't a long one.

Brighid was glad for them. They were a people who had overcome great evil and exhibited great good. It was just that they had been given the ability to nurture, renew, and grow.

Remember when you awake, child.

The Huntress's spirit settled back into her body and she heard Etain's words echo from her memory. *Tell my daughters what it is you have discovered...* The priestess had said daughters, not daughter.

She must have known that Brighid was there. *Not surprising,* the Huntress thought sleepily. *Etain seemed to have eyes and ears everywhere.*

The Huntress slept, dreamlessly, for the rest of the night.

* * *

The enticing scent of roasting venison penetrated through the blanket of sleep, and Brighid finally opened her eyes, blinking against the bright light of midday. Cuchulainn tended a bubbling haunch of meat that he had spitted over the fire. His eyes lifted when she stirred. He watched her stretch and she saw relief soften his face.

"Good morning," she said. "That smells wonderful."

"Good afternoon," he replied and used one of his throwing daggers to slice a piece of meat from the haunch and then skewer it. Smiling, he walked over to her, kissed her, and handed her the morsel. "Welcome back."

She nibbled at the hot meat and quirked an eyebrow at him. "Are you trying to take over my job?"

"Hardly. If I were MacCallan's Huntress the Clan would probably starve. It took me most of the morning and four arrows to bring down this one young, rather stupid deer."

She smiled. "His lack of intelligence has definitely not adversely affected his taste."

"Probably because he was too stupid to do much running," he grumbled.

She laughed out loud. "See, you're a better Huntress than you thought."

"No, I'm not, but I did dig up some early potatoes and wild onions." He prodded what she would have otherwise taken for rocks within the edges of the campfire with the toe of his boot. "You need to eat as much as you can today. Even I know that a journey into the spirit realm can appear to take only a few hours but turns into days."

"So you're not just trying to make me fat and unattractive to other men?" she said, wanting to tease the worried shadows from his eyes.

"I'm trying to keep you alive."

"Cu, has something happened?"

"No…yes… I'm not sure," he said, running his hand restlessly through his hair. "I've been uneasy since we entered the tors. And this place—" he gestured at the cave "—has my teeth set on edge."

"But you haven't had a specific Feeling?"

"No. And I've tried. I've listened with that other sense." He sighed. "Nothing. I don't know if it's because of my ineptitude or if it's because there's nothing specific there."

"Perhaps the Feeling was sent to remind you to stay vigilant."

He started to snap at her that of course he would be vigilant—then he remembered that he hadn't always been so. He had been prewarned of Brenna's death and he had done nothing to prevent it.

"Perhaps…" he said. "The spirit realm is a mystery to me." He glanced up at her and forced himself to smile. "But I do know enough about it to be certain that you are well fed before we visit there." He carved off another hunk of meat and brought it to her.

"Visit—that sounds so much nicer than journey or quest," she said. "I should tell you that I visited MacCallan Castle last night in my dreams."

His eyes shot to hers. "Brenna?"

She shook her head and pushed down the jealousy that his quick look and tense tone made her feel.

"No, it wasn't anything like the times you or Brenna came into my dreams. Last night my spirit was awake and aware. I watched myself lift out of my body and travel to MacCallan. And I heard Epona's voice."

"The Magic Sleep," Cuchulainn said thoughtfully. "My mother has described it many times. It is the way Epona often communicates with her and allows her to see important events as they take place." Then his contemplative look became alarmed. "Was everyone at the castle well?"

"Very," she assured him. "But I do think I witnessed an important event. Apparently there's more to the New Fomorians than their goodness and tenacity. Epona has gifted them with the ability to nurture growing things—and according to

Wynne's report—this ability allows them to hasten the growth of plants."

"That should make Wynne happy."

"It pleased everyone, including your mother." Brighid paused. "But I don't understand why that was important for me to witness."

"Maybe Epona wants us to know that all is well with the Clan so we won't head into the Otherworld with worry to distract us."

"Maybe…" she said. "Did your mother ever say anything about being seen when she was on one of her Magic Sleep journeys?"

"Not that I remember. Did they see you last night?"

"No one acted like it, except your mother said something that made me wonder."

He grinned and carefully pulled a hot potato from the coals. "You know it's impossible to keep anything from my mother."

"Anything important," Brighid added.

"Trust me, often it feels like she knows *everything*."

They chatted about home and the Clan and the fallout of the New Fomorian's unexpected gift while they ate the nourishing meal of venison, potatoes and wild onions, and Brighid felt her strength returning. Afterward she stood under the gentle fall of cold cave water and gazed at the beauty of the Centaur Plains. The land called to her soul. She could find belonging and comfort at MacCallan Castle, but she knew it would never have the ability to move her like the open land of her birth did. It was late spring and in some places the grass would already have grown past her withers. The brilliant blues, pinks and reds of spring wildflowers would have given way to the long, lace-topped white flower known as snowpeak and the tall, brown-eyed daisies that could be found in un-expected fields alive with the summertime sound of buzzing bees. She held her hand up to shield her eyes from the glare of the midday sun and thought she could just make out dark dots on the horizon that could be bison. Then the Huntress frowned as what else she was seeing registered in her sharp eyes.

"Drought," Cuchulainn said. He was standing above her at the edge of the clearing and he, too, was gazing out at the rolling grasslands.

"It's been a dry spring at MacCallan, but I had no idea it was affecting the plains so drastically." Her sharp eyes narrowed as she discarded the romantic haze her vision had been peering through and looked with new eyes on the grasslands. "It should be green, so rich and alive that from this distance it should look like the landscape has been painted the color of emeralds." She shook her head, feeling her gut clench with foreboding. "But it's the brown of fall."

"I haven't seen it this dry for years, maybe for as long as I can remember," Cu said.

"What began the Fomorian War?"

Cuchulainn's brow tunneled. "Their attack on MacCallan Castle, of course."

She shook her head, tasting the bitterness of foreboding in the back of her throat. "Before that. Decades before that. Why were they in Partholon?"

His turquoise eyes widened in understanding. "They were driven from their lands by a great drought."

"It's a bad omen, Cu. I Feel it, deep within my soul. I think it's time we followed this hunt to its conclusion."

"Agreed."

"Good. Then let me tell you what my mother taught me of the Quest for Epona's Chalice."

CHAPTER
FORTY-FOUR

"If you keep looking so damned gloomy you're going to make me nervous," Brighid told Cuchulainn.

"Sorry. I've spent so much of my life avoiding the Otherworld that it's hard for me to step willingly into it."

"So then don't think of it as stepping into the Otherworld. We're following a trail, remember? We've hunted together before, Cu. This will be no different."

"You mean except for the spirits and the fact that we won't be in our bodies."

She frowned at him.

"All right!" He raised his hands in surrender. "We're going on a hunt."

"Good. Let's review what we know one more time." She held up her hand to tick off her fingers. "First, we've readied the labyrinth."

Cu's eyes went to the spiraling circle of stones they had

placed in the center of the cave. The stones unwound smoothly around and around until they led to the small tunnel and the stream of water.

"I still don't like that," Cu said, staring claustrophobically at the constricting hole in the back of the cave.

"I don't particularly like it, either, but it fits with everything your father and my mother have said about the beginning of the spirit journey. Midhir directed us here because the tors have always been linked to the Underworld. My mother told me many times that using a labyrinth was one easy way to begin a spirit journey, as well as to return at the end of one."

"We're just following a trail," Cu repeated.

"That's all we're doing," Brighid agreed. "But I want you to remember that the labyrinth is the path back to this realm."

"I'll remember," he said, his jaw tightening. "But I will not return without you, and you should remember that."

She met his eyes. "We return together or not at all."

He scowled, but the mischievous glint was back in his turquoise eyes. "I prefer the together part of that."

"Stop worrying," she said.

"Next."

"Next—" she held up a second finger "—you join me in my dreams."

The warrior sighed. "You say that like it happens every day."

"Cuchulainn, in less than half a cycle of the moon you have entered my dreams four times."

He grinned. "I don't think you can count that last one."

She gave him a stern look. "Actually it counts for even more. We shared the same dream and neither of us had shattered souls, which means our spirits met somewhere in the Otherworld. All we need do is just to repeat what we've already done." He raised his eyebrows and coaxed a small smile from her. "Minus the sex," she added.

"So I join you in your dreams."

"That's the easiest way of putting it."

"Just now your tone, the way you looked at me, reminded me of my father," Cu said.

She curled one side of her smile. "Is that supposed to make me feel better about this journey or are you telling me our marriage is in trouble?"

He grinned at her. "You're not concentrating."

"Third—" she lifted another finger "—when our spirits are together we follow the labyrinth, beginning in the center, around and around to the tunnel entrance."

"Then we slide down into the Underworld." All trace of humor had left his voice.

"Yes, but only because that is where a Shaman Journey typically begins. We won't stay there. Your father said Epona's Chalice will not be found in the Underworld, and my mother often implied the same. I believe Epona's Chalice is in the highest realm of the spirits—the Upperworld—the realm where the Goddess is most often found." She took his hand. "Remember, Cu, there are three levels of the spirit realm— the Underworld, the Middleworld and the Upperworld. We cannot afford to get lost in the first two. Always follow the path upward and don't let anything persuade you to turn aside from our purpose."

"I'll remember. I'm ready."

"Cuchulainn, there were several things my mother made very clear to me about this journey. The first is deceptively simple because it is what even the smallest children learn as they begin to practice rituals and test their aptitude for the spirit realm."

"Leave the problems of life in the physical realm. Do not carry them with you into the Otherworld," Cu said. "I know that as well as you."

"You know it—I'm just reminding you to abide by it," Brighid said sternly. "For both of us."

"For both of us," he repeated, kissing her hand. "I'll bank the fire and make sure the gelding is seen to."

Brighid nodded and gave him a smile that was meant to

cover up the fear and doubt that lurked just beneath her confident facade. As he set their camp to order she paced the length of the cave, going over and over the small, disjointed details of a High Shaman's spirit journey her mother had sprinkled throughout her childhood. One thing her mother had said kept circling around and around in Brighid's head. *Before you drink of the Chalice you must face your greatest ally and your most powerful enemy—and the two are one in the same.*

She hadn't known what her mother had been referring to then, and she certainly hadn't received any illuminating information that would clear up the riddle now. She'd just have to take the leap and trust herself, her Goddess, and the man at her side.

"All is ready," Cuchulainn said, striding back into the cave. "It's only early evening, hopefully we'll be back before morning."

"Don't count on it. Time passes differently in the Otherworld."

"Then let's get it over with."

Cuchulainn held out his hand to her and she joined him on the pallet they had made up carefully in the center of the labyrinth of stones. Beside them they had placed a full wineskin and a loaf of wrapped bread and cheese. The first thing they must do when they returned would be to eat and drink so that their bodies would reground in the physical realm.

"We're missing something," Brighid said. She looked around the cave till she found what she needed sheathed in Cuchulainn's scabbard. Carefully she pulled the gleaming blade free and rejoined her husband in the center of the labyrinth. He cocked an eyebrow at her.

"I'd feel better if you held this," she said. "I know you can't physically take it with us, but all things are ensouled. Perhaps the spirit of your blade will deign to accompany us."

"It would relieve my mind greatly if it did," he said, closing his hand around the familiar hilt.

They lay on the pallet, fitting their bodies together. Brighid sighed, glad that the physical awkwardness that had once been between them was gone. She pressed her head against his broad chest. Before she closed her eyes she touched the turquoise stone that hung between her breasts.

"Just breathe, Cu. Relax your body and will your soul to follow the beat of your heart to me," she whispered.

"I'll be there. I won't let you be alone," he said.

She kissed him before she closed her eyes and began the deep cleansing breaths that would take her into a trancelike state. It was an easy exercise for her. She used it often to follow the spirit trails of animals. So she fell into a meditative state quickly. Only this time instead of focusing her concentration on her chosen prey, the Huntress blocked out everything except the beat of Cuchulainn's heart.

The Shaman drums are the easiest way to find an opening to the Otherworld. All of life beats with them. Listen and you will find an opening to the spirit of the earth.

Her mother had said those words to a very young Brighid when she had complained that Mairearad had taken too long choosing a simple drum. Brighid remembered that she had been eager to leave the crowds and heat of the open air market, and for once her mother had not snapped at her for her complaint. Instead she had explained to her daughter why choosing the correct drum was important for a High Shaman.

Then Brighid had discounted her mother's words, and had only been grateful she had somehow avoided a reprimand. Now she used the memory to begin her own High Shaman quest. They didn't have a drum, and even if they had she knew that Cuchulainn would not have been willing to remain in this realm to beat it while she entered the Otherworld alone. She'd pondered her mother's words, trying to find a compromise. Mairearad had said that all life beats with the sound of drums…life…the heartbeat of life…and it had come to her with sudden clarity. Her husband's heart would be the life beat she would follow into the Otherworld.

So she pressed her head against his chest and let the strong beat of his heart guide her.

Thump-thump…thump-thump…thump-thump…thump-thump…

It was more magical than a drum, more primitive and real, and she would gladly follow it even to the ends of the earth.

When her spirit lifted from her body it was a much different sensation than she had experienced during her dreams or even the Magic Sleep. Her spirit was surrounded by the warmth of Cuchulainn's heartbeat and for a moment she stood beside their bodies, listening with her soul.

"You were right. It wasn't as hard as I thought it would be," Cuchulainn said. He was standing next to her and his body was illuminated by a gentle golden glow. In his hand he clutched a shimmering white sword.

"It came with you," Brighid said.

"I think my hold on it was so tight that it had little choice," the warrior said. Then he lifted his other hand and touched her face. She felt the caress like a warm breeze against her spirit. "You're incredibly beautiful like this, all silver and shining."

"You're golden," she said, touching his shoulder gently.

He looked down at his spirit form and grunted. Then lifted his eyes to hers. "Let's go."

"We follow the labyrinth. Always to the right in the journey there, and to the left when we return," she said, turning in the proper direction and beginning the circular spiral.

As they followed the path of stones Brighid noticed that the walls of the cave changed, darkening into a cavern so vast that by the time they reached what used to be little more than a small gap in the back of the cave they were instead standing before a rough rock door over which was written *awen*.

"Inspiration," Brighid whispered. "It's what it means in the ancient language of Shamans."

"Your mother told you that?"

Brighid felt her soul shiver with excitement. "No. No one told me. I just understood it."

"Then this is the way we go," Cu said. He opened the door and raised his sword protectively. But before he could step ahead of her she touched his arm.

"I have to lead here, Cu."

His nod was little more than a jerk of his head, but he stepped aside and let her precede him through the doorway. She gasped, and then disappeared.

"Brighid!" he cried, holding his sword before him and preparing to plunge into the darkness after her.

Then her laughter bubbled up from below. "It's nothing bad, just relax and let yourself go with it."

He'd go with it because she was down there, but he certainly wouldn't relax. Gritting his teeth and holding tightly to his sword he stepped through the doorway and his body fell. It spiraled gently round and round to the right, reminding him of the few times it had snowed enough at his mother's temple for the ground to be covered in slick whiteness and how he and El and the twins had fashioned childish sleds and sped down and around any surface that was at all hill-like.

His feet hit the ground and he took a moment to reorient himself. This time he and Brighid were standing directly in front of a round portal. Brighid touched his arm again.

"Be careful. This is the entrance to the Underworld. It is not our destination."

Without waiting for his reply she stepped into the portal and emerged into a sea of fog. The gray mist licked her spirit body and she shivered. She heard Cuchulainn's surprised grunt and she quickly stepped back to him and laced her fingers through his.

"By the hand of the Goddess! This was where we met in our last dream," Cuchulainn hissed.

"Brighid…" The disembodied voice came from the mist and it tingled along the centaur's spine. "Brighid…" the voice repeated.

"We're not to stay here." Cuchulainn's voice reflected his tension.

"Wait, Cu. I know that voice."

The mist in front of them parted and Niam appeared.

"Niam!" Brighid cried, automatically moving forward to greet her, but her sister stepped back at the same time Cuchulainn's grip tightened on her hand.

"Sister, in this journey you are not to enter the Underworld." Then she smiled and her beautiful face lit, making Brighid's heart catch. "I am only here to pose one question to you. Your answer will decide whether you move on or whether you return to the physical realm." But instead of asking the question, she turned her attention to the warrior at her sister's side. "And what will you do if my sister does not drink of the High Shaman's Chalice? Will you call your handfast a mistake and return to the comfort of your castle and those who love you there?"

"In life you didn't know me, so I will not take offense at your question. I do not believe you mean to insult me, and because of that I will answer you. Whether Brighid does or does not drink of Epona's Chalice our marriage will not end. Where she goes, I will go. I will stand beside her if fire should try to burn us, if the seas should try to drown us, and if the earth should shake in tumult. And I will cherish her name as my own unto death and, if Epona wills it, beyond."

"Because you swore an oath that was much like your answer?" Niam's spirit asked, unmoved by the warrior's passionate reply.

"Because when I swore an oath I gave her my heart. To me they are one in the same."

Niam finally smiled, looking very much like her older sister. "Though you are only a man, you may be worthy of her." Then her gaze left the warrior and refocused on her sister. "Why do you wish to become a High Shaman, Brighid?"

Taken aback by her sister's question she could only blink and stare at the lovely centaur who had been so fragile in life and who now, in death, appeared so strong and confident.

"Answer now, Brighid Dhianna!" Niam's mouth formed

the words, but the voice was strange and powerful. It worked on Brighid like a goad.

"I wish to become a High Shaman because I am weary with trying to escape the responsibilities I was born to. Too many tragedies, from the death of a young girl long ago, to your recent death, happened because I refused to face my fate."

"What is your fate?"

"To heal the blight my mother's reign has spread."

"And what of your personal desires?"

Brighid raised her chin. "I belong to Cuchulainn and he to me—with or without me attaining the ability to shapeshift."

Niam smiled and her voice returned to her own. "When I said personal desires I wasn't referring to your new husband, sister. As a High Shaman you will wield great power. What of that?"

This time Brighid thought before she answered. She had always liked the sensation of Feeling the spirits of animals. She had relied on it and used it for good. And she remembered the rush of excitement breathing in Cu's spirit had brought her. It had been a heady Feeling. Not just kissing him for the first time, but having the power to guide his spirit back to his body. She could protest to Ciara, Cuchulainn, and even to Etain, but she knew that deep within her soul she delighted in the power that simmered in her blood.

Slowly she met Niam's eyes. "What I think is that I will have to be very careful to wield great power wisely—to listen to the Goddess and my conscience more than my emotions and desires."

Her sister's smile was radiant. "Then may Epona bless you with her Chalice." Niam made a wide, sweeping motion with her arm and to the right of the Huntress and the warrior the mist roiled and bubbled before parting to expose a flight of gray stone stairs which led straight up and disappeared into more grayness.

Brighid turned to say goodbye to her sister, but the mist had already closed, obscuring the centaur's form. The Huntress drew back her shoulders and said to Cuchulainn, "Let's climb."

CHAPTER
FORTY-FIVE

The stairs were wide enough to allow Cuchulainn to ascend them by her side. As they entered the mist again, he held his sword at the ready. Perhaps it shouldn't have comforted her, but it did.

Finally the stone stairs ended and a warm wind swept against their faces, dissipating the fog to reveal that they were standing on a platform overlooking a shining river of light. Brighid's and Cu's eyes were drawn compulsively to the glistening waters. As they stared the lapping liquid swirled and scenes from each of their past lives took ghostly form within the crystal depths.

Cuchulainn as a boy hefting his first real sword…Brighid running with wild abandon across a sea of flank-high grasses…Cuchulainn holding the wounded Elphame tightly in his arms as Brighid carried both of them back to the safety of MacCallan Castle…Brighid bending over talon-shaped tracks and reading the story of Brenna's death…

"Stop!" Brighid cried, taking Cu's shoulders and pulling him around to face her. "Don't look into the river!"

"What is it?" His voice was hoarse and he was clearly shaken to his core. "Why are we seeing the past?"

"It is the Middleworld." At his blank look she wanted to curse and berate him for not paying better attention to his childhood lessons of the Otherworld. *Later he must learn more.* But now was not the time to berate him, instead she hastily explained. "The Middleworld is the place of time and space journeying. The river will show you your past—my past—our world's past, and even other worlds and places foreign to us. It would be easy to become lost here—many have. But we cannot let it capture our souls, Cu. We must go on."

"It can show me Brenna, her death, or even the last time we were together in life."

"It can," Brighid said, pushing aside the pain his words caused her. "If you truly desire it you can stay here in the waters of the past. I will not hate you for it. I will even release you from your oath to me." Then she drew a deep breath and let none of the heartache or longing she was feeling tinge her words. Her voice was that of a Huntress strong in her convictions and confident in herself. "But know this, Cuchulainn. I want you to make this decision and I want you to make it now. Choose Brenna and your past, or me and our future. I loved her, too, but I will not share my husband with a ghost."

He jerked as if she had struck him and then blinked and looked around them like he was only then understanding fully where they were. When his eyes touched the river's beckoning surface, he looked hastily away.

"I choose you and our future. I chose that when we handfasted and I have no desire to be free of that oath now or ever. No matter how beguiling this Realm of Spirits makes the past," he said.

"Then let's go on," she said, not wanting to give voice to the relief his words brought her.

"Where?"

The Huntress jerked her chin to their right. "Through there."

Cuchulainn turned and saw an open door that led into the black interior of what was obviously a burial mound, the outside of which was covered with grass and flowers. Great flat white stone slabs lined the doorway. Cuchulainn moved aside and motioned for Brighid to precede him, carefully keeping his eyes on the Huntress and not the silver river that twinkled alluringly at the edge of his vision.

As Brighid entered the dark mound the sound of a raven's angry screech echoed behind them, and with intuition that Felt preternaturally enhanced by the power of the spirit realm, she knew that her mother had somehow orchestrated Cuchulainn's Middleworld temptation.

Which meant it must be important that the warrior accompany her—if he was insignificant, he would not be a target for Mairearad.

"Are you well? Why have we stopped?" Cuchulainn's voice came from the darkness behind her.

"All is well, Cu." Even though he couldn't see her through the blackness, she nodded to a faint pinprick of light ahead of them. "We follow that light."

They moved quickly, and soon found themselves on the threshold of another door, which was lit by moonlight. Together, they stepped through the door and into the Upperworld.

In front of them stretched a thick forest. Even in the silver moonlight they could see that the trees and grass and flowers were painted in colors that were unusually bright. Three paths led from the doorway where they stood, each disappearing into the green depths of the forest.

"Which one do we take?" Cu asked.

Brighid cleared her mind and tried to Feel the way, and then sighed in frustration when she was guided to none of the paths in particular. Actually, as she studied each of them more carefully, she realized that she had been mistaken. It wasn't that none of the paths called to her. The truth was that they all beckoned her. The music that flowed from each of them was alluring and magical, and she wanted nothing so much as to shake off the net of responsibility in which this quest was trying to snare her. She could stay here and follow these paths for an eternity. She could run down them, just as she had raced over the Centaur Plains of her youth. She would be free and happy and filled full with music, and then…

"Brighid!"

The centaur blinked and shook her head, trying to rid her mind of the seductive call of the music.

"Brighid! You cannot leave me!"

Her eyes cleared at the same moment the music stopped. Cuchulainn was staring wide-eyed at her. He had thrust the point of his sword into the ground between them and with both hands he gripped hers as she tried to pull away from him and dash down any of the three paths.

"I'm—I'm here. I'm back," she said, her voice growing stronger as she continued to speak. "It was the music. Did you hear the music calling me?"

"I heard nothing except the call of a raven." His voice was raw. "Nothing else, Brighid. You made no sound. At first you didn't move—didn't breathe—didn't respond to me. Your eyes were empty. Then you started to move forward as if you were one of the walking dead. Even when I grabbed you to keep you from leaving you acted like I wasn't here at all—or maybe it was that you weren't here any longer."

"I'm back." She touched his cheek gently, shivering from the knowledge that her mother had tried to bewitch her, too. "You called me back."

"I'll always call you back from wherever you've gone." Reluctantly he let his hands fall from hers. Cu pulled the sword from the ground and ran a hand through his hair. "But I would appreciate it if you didn't go away again."

She smiled at him before turning her attention back to the three paths. This time when alluring music whispered to her, she resisted it, refusing to give in to its seduction. And as she resisted it the music changed until it was no more than the echo of an angry bird's cry. Then she felt the stone that dangled from the chain between her breasts warm. Instinctively, she closed her hand around the turquoise and odd, hollow-sounding words drifted through her mind as the spirit of the stone spoke to her.

Remember how I was given you.

"The hawk," Brighid murmured. Then she smiled and spoke the words with confidence. "I call for my spirit guide, the golden hawk!"

The bird's cry echoed from the moonlit sky as it shot from above, circled Brighid once, and then perched regally in the lowest limb of one of the ancient oaks at the edge of the dense forest.

Brighid bowed her head to the bird and elbowed a staring Cuchulainn so that he did the same.

"Thank you for answering my call," Brighid said.

The golden hawk cocked her head to study the Huntress.

Do you wish to continue your quest? The question rang clearly in Brighid's mind. From the corner of her eye she saw Cuchulainn jerk in surprise, and she understood that he could hear the bird, too.

"I do," she said.

Then tell me, Huntress, which of the three paths would you choose?

"None of them." Brighid didn't hesitate, but gave the answer that felt most true to her soul. If her mother's creature had tried to compel her down the paths, she would refuse to go, even though the logistics of entering the forest through any other way appeared impossible. It seemed that even in the short time they'd been standing before the ancient forest its trees had thickened and what had at first appeared as a soft carpet of grass had morphed into a barrier of brambles and briars. Clearly the only way into the forest was one of the three paths—all of which she had just rejected.

You have chosen wisely. Follow me, Huntress, and become who you are destined to be.

The hawk lifted from the tree, flying impossibly low between two great oaks and directly into the foreboding forest.

"Maybe I should lead this time," Cuchulainn said.

She nodded, relieved that he hadn't argued with her or questioned why they were following the hawk into a mess rather than entering the forest through the clearly marked paths.

The warrior raised his sword and slashed at the dangerous-looking thorns. Brighid heard him grunt in surprise. She peered over his shoulder to see that as the white light of his sword touched the prickly barrier, the plants disappeared in little puffs of green smoke. Cu glanced back at her, grinned, and then strode into the forest after the bird. Eagerly Brighid followed him, noting that, once again, the hawk was taking them purposefully away from any preestablished trail—just as she had when she'd guided them through the Blue Tors.

The forest gave way before Cuchulainn with increasing ease. Soon he no longer needed to use his sword, and they followed the hawk easily. What had at first appeared to be impenetrable had changed completely. It was still lush with ancient trees, but the forest bed was clear and flat and carpeted with a loam of fragrant leaves. Traveling through it was a marvel, not a hardship.

Then Cuchulainn abruptly stopped walking. "By the Goddess…" he breathed. "Look at that."

Brighid's eyes followed the warrior's gaze and she gasped. Well to the left of where they stood the forest floor opened suddenly like the maw of a great, dark beast. Each of the three paths that had beckoned her with her mother's seductive music emptied into that gaping hole. She knew she wouldn't even have seen it. The music would have blinded her and she would have fallen into the pit. The Goddess only knew where it emptied, but it certainly didn't lead to Epona's Chalice. Had Brighid chosen one of the three easy paths her quest would have ended there.

Sometimes choosing what seems impossible is the only way to find your path to the future.

The hawk's voice sounded in her mind again as its wings ruffled the air over their heads, leading them farther away from the pit. They followed the bird.

They hadn't walked much longer when the forest gave way to a grassy clearing, bright with the silver light of the moon. In the center there was a stone basin, which was covered with carvings of ancient knots and runes, all entwining to form the graceful shape of the Goddess with her arms raised over her head, so that it appeared that Epona's hands were touching the water as it bubbled up from the spring. On the edge of the basin sat a gleaming golden Chalice with Epona's triple knot of mares decorating it. The hawk circled the clearing three times before perching on the single oak that shaded the bubbling well.

"It's Epona's Chalice," Brighid said in a voice hushed and reverent.

"Go, my love. Take what is rightfully yours."

"Only if you come with me," she told him.

He kissed her gently. "Where you go, so there will I be, too."

Together they walked to the basin, but as they drew near it Cuchulainn instinctively slowed his steps and let her draw ahead of him. He would watch over and protect her, but he could not share in what she was about to experience.

Slowly Brighid went to the basin. But instead of instantly filling the Chalice and drinking of it, she focused her attention on the water. It bubbled up from the center of the basin, sparkling like liquid light. Brighid dipped her hand into the water. It felt alive. When she lifted her hand the water that dripped from it looked like beads of moonlight falling from her fingers. Then she stared down into the basin and its surface quivered, as if a gust of stormy wind had just blown over it. Brighid's eyes widened. Within the water she saw her brother's reflection take form. He, too, was standing before the basin. As she watched he peered down into the depths of the water, just as she had been doing. But he did not touch the water, and his face did not register the awe that had filled Brighid upon entering Epona's grove.

"Enemy—ally…I have no time for this!" Bregon's voice echoed eerily from the reflected past. *"What is most important is that I have been well trained and that I will use my power for my herd."* Without another word his hands closed possessively around the Chalice of Epona. He plunged it into the water and then lifted it to his lips and drank greedily. When he was finished drinking he tossed the Chalice into the basin, threw his head back and shouted victoriously.

Though her gut felt tight and sick, Brighid kept watching as her brother turned away from the basin and disappeared into the forest. Then her breath caught in her throat. When she looked back at the basin the faint outline of her brother's spirit still stood there. In the middle of the grove another silhouette of a centaur formed, then near the tree line the glistening outline of another and another appeared. *Goddess! They're all Bregon!* In each of the apparitions his body was almost completely transparent and she could only vaguely make out his form by focusing on the faint glimmer of silver that outlined his body. All of her brother's spirits were silently staring at the most substantial of all of them, the centaur who stood beside the basin. His head was bowed and while the others looked on he retrieved the discarded Chalice and set it reverently back in its place. He looked up from the reflection and directly into his sister's eyes. His ghostly face was awash in tears.

Then he and the others disappeared.

Brighid knew what she had just witnessed had been her brother drinking of Epona's Chalice. He was a High Shaman now—she was sure of it. As sure as she was that what else she had seen in the basin's reflection of the past had been the shattering of Bregon's soul. A sudden rush of sadness overshadowed the worry she felt for her herd. Bregon had left so much of his soul behind! Cu had only experienced a single loss of spirit, and it had caused him to be a sad shell of himself, so bereft and hopeless that he thought of ending his life. She couldn't imagine what must be happening to her brother. How could he survive so fragmented?

Brighid sighed and let her fingers trail through the living water again. It was all so wrong. How could the poison of one woman be allowed to live on after her death to destroy the next generation?

"You're late, sister."

With a gasp, Brighid spun around. Her brother stood before her. Not the sad, broken fragments of himself she had just been lamenting. The centaur who faced her radiated power—a power she had not yet tasted.

CHAPTER
FORTY-SIX

Brighid drew around her the mantle of cool aloofness she had worn for most of her life. Her smile was polite and disinterested.

"Hello, Bregon."

His eyes narrowed to slits. "Drop your pretenses and leave, sister. There is no reason for you to drink of Epona's Chalice. You chose another path for your life. Our mother was satisfied with your choice. I am satisfied with your choice. Go back to the forests of the people you love so well. Our herd does not need you."

"Our mother was a sad, twisted centaur whose lust for power caused her to never be satisfied with anything, Bregon. The day you accept that is the day you will be free of her ghost."

"So you know she's dead."

"Yes, I know. Niam told me."

Bregon's lips twisted in a sneer at the mention of their sister.

"She died bringing me the news," Brighid continued.

The haughty expression slid from Bregon's face. "Niam? She's dead?"

"Our sister ran herself to her death. Ending the hatred that our mother bred meant more to her than her own life."

Bregon wiped his hands over his face and when he looked up at her Brighid got her first true glimpse of the iron-souled stranger her brother had become.

"Niam was always foolish and weak. She lived that way. She died that way."

"It is not foolish or weak to give your life for another," Brighid said.

"It is if your oh-so-valiant effort is for naught," he sneered.

"Look around you, Bregon. It is because of Niam that I am here." Her voice intensified as she hurled the words at him. "It is because of Niam that I will drink of Epona's Chalice. And it is because of Niam that I will return to the Centaur Plains and take the position my birthright assures me—High Shaman of the Dhianna Herd."

"No, sister. I don't think you will." As Bregon spoke his eyes turned sly, and he moved forward toward Epona's Chalice.

With the grace of a Master Warrior, Cuchulainn stepped smoothly between Brighid's brother and the Chalice.

"I would think again, Bregon," Cuchulainn said, his voice deceptively nonchalant.

Bregon pulled up in surprise. Then his expression changed to amusement. "A man?"

"See there, Brighid, just when I was beginning to doubt your brother's intelligence he manages to dazzle me with his sharp powers of observation," Cuchulainn said amiably.

A roll of laughter escaped from Brighid before she could stop it, and its sound seemed to ignite Bregon.

"How dare you speak to me in such a way you impudent little man!"

Cuchulainn raised his brows as if Bregon had just amused instead of insulted him. "It is true that I am just a man, but this—" he brandished the gleaming white sword between them "—tends to make up for my lack of hooves."

"You're in the Otherworld now, you fool. Swords are a weapon of the physical realm. Here you need power gifted from the spirits. Power such as this." Bregon swept his hands through the air around him, as if he was catching invisible insects. Then he muttered a few unintelligible words and threw the invisible nothing at Cuchulainn. Instinctively, the warrior raised his sword and a ball of light crackled and burst against the white blade.

"But that's not possible!" Bregon sputtered. "It shouldn't have protected you. It's a sword," Bregon said.

Cuchulainn pulled back his lips in a snarl. "It is the spirit of a sword. Now who is being foolish, Bregon? For what reason would a sword become tangible in the Realm of Spirits?" When the centaur just stared at him without speaking, Cuchulainn answered his own question. "My sword has power here because it is aiding me to fulfill an oath that is binding in all realms."

"An oath? What—"

"Bregon, meet Cuchulainn MacCallan, son of Midhir and Etain. He is my lifemate," Brighid said.

Bregon's face went slack with shock. "You handfasted with this man?"

"She did," Cuchulainn said. Then he began striding toward Bregon. "And even in the Otherworld my sword will protect her life because I have sworn that it is more dear to me than my own." He stopped when the tip of his sword pressed against the centaur's chest. "Now you should leave before I do something that would suggest that I am not honoring her name even as I do my own."

Bregon backed slowly away from Cuchulainn, who followed him, careful to keep his sword held ready. Just before the centaur reached the forest edge he looked back to where his sister stood beside the basin.

"I will not give up what I have fought to win," he said.

"I hear you, Bregon. Now you hear me. I will bring an end to the hatred and dissension our mother sowed during her unhappy life. I give you my oath on that. You can choose to be for me or against me. But if you go against me I will cull you from the herd as I would any other traitor."

"I have already made my choice. When you enter the Centaur Plains you had better come with more than this little man." Bregon spat at her, and then he disappeared into the forest.

Cuchulainn stayed near the forest's edge, keeping his keen eyes trained on the shapes and shadows that flitted within.

"Brighid, it would make me breathe much easier if you drank from the Chalice now and we returned to the cave."

"Just a moment more," she called to him. "I have to be sure that…" Her words trailed off as her fingers touched the side of the Chalice. She had to be sure of what? She didn't know—she only knew that she was not her brother and she would not take the cup and callously use it and cast it aside.

It is your turn now, beloved child.

Brighid looked up from the Chalice. A woman, clothed in a gown of rich white samite, was walking across the glade toward her. She seemed to move in a pool of silver moonbeams. As she approached Brighid the woman shifted shape, changing from a beautiful blond-haired maiden, to a middle-aged matron whose body was strong and useful, to an ancient crone with hair the color of snow. But her form did not stop there—one instant she was a woman, the next she was an elegant silver mare, then a powerful centaur who carried the bow of a Huntress clutched in her right hand, and then she grew wings and took the shape of a New Fomorian girl child.

Breathless with awe, Brighid averted her eyes and bowed deeply to the Goddess.

"Hail Epona!" she said. "Goddess of things wild and free. I have come to your grove because—"

"Child," the Goddess said in a voice that was surprisingly gentle. "I know why you have come."

Brighid's eyes lifted. Epona had taken the form of a woman in the prime of her life. She was still clothed in the gown of white samite, and it slicked over her generous curves showing the voluptuous beauty that was the Divine Feminine.

"Of course you know why I've come. I'm—I'm sorry, I didn't mean to…" This time Brighid interrupted herself. She closed her eyes and tried to control the trembling within her. When she opened them she said, "Epona, I ask your permission to drink of your Chalice and to assume the responsibilities of High Shaman for the Dhianna Herd."

Epona studied her carefully. "You watched your brother in the basin reflection."

It wasn't a question, but Brighid nodded. "Yes, Goddess."

"Did you notice that he did not ask my blessing? He took and drank and then he departed."

"I am not my brother, Goddess."

Epona's full lips tilted up. "You have the look of your mother, but you do not have her heart. You have chosen a different way."

"I hope so, Epona."

The Goddess's gaze shifted to the far side of the grove and the smile that had been teasing her lips widened. "Ah, Cuchulainn! You may approach me."

Cu had dropped to his knees the moment Epona had materialized in the grove, and now he stood and approached the Great Goddess with his heart hammering painfully in his chest.

"Hail Epona!" he said and bowed low to her.

"I am pleased to see you here in my sacred grove, Cuchulainn. As the son of my Beloved Incarnate I have been disappointed that you refused the gifts I granted you out of love for your mother."

"Forgive me, Goddess. It has taken me a long time to grow up."

Epona nodded thoughtfully. "A wise and truthful answer." The Goddess gestured at the gleaming sword he still clutched in his hand. "Would you have spilled Bregon's blood here in my grove?"

Cuchulainn answered without hesitation. "To protect Brighid, yes, I would have."

"Even if it earned you my displeasure?"

"I can only hope that you would want me to honor the vow I made to Brighid, witnessed by you and my mother, and that because of that vow you would be merciful and forgive me for defiling your sacred grove." Cuchulainn bowed again humbly to the Great Goddess.

Epona was silent, studying the warrior. When she spoke her voice was thoughtful. "I believe I granted you the wrong gifts. A warrior would consider visions and preordained Feelings as something he should struggle against. Little wonder they have been an uneasy fit within your spirit. I take my gifts back, Cuchulainn." As she spoke Epona made a beckoning gesture with her hand and Cuchulainn gasped and staggered. "In return I grant you the gift of second sight." The Goddess dipped her hand into the basin and then sprinkled three glowing drops of water on the warrior. "From here on you have the ability to see in a sacred manner the shapes of all things in the spirit. You will know the true soul that fills the shell of the body. You will see through the darkness of life."

Cuchulainn fell to his knees, overcome with the rush of power that rained into his body.

"Use your gift wisely, Cuchulainn MacCallan, son of my Beloved Chosen One. Never let your sword end the life of someone whose spirit is redeemable."

"I will try to be wise, Great Goddess," Cuchulainn said in a choked voice.

The Goddess smiled and touched his head. Then she turned to the Huntress.

"Why did you hesitate to drink of my Chalice after your brother left my grove?"

"In my youth my mother told me several things about her quest to drink of your Chalice. Much of what she said I have forgotten—and she quit speaking to me of the Otherworld when she realized that I wouldn't follow her path."

"But there is something she said to you that you have never forgotten," the Goddess said.

"Yes. My mother told me that before I drank of the Chalice I must face my greatest ally and my most powerful enemy."

"And the two are one in the same," the Goddess finished for her.

"Yes. All that I've faced in your grove has been my brother—and I don't believe he is my greatest ally, though he could be my worst enemy."

"He is neither," Epona said. Then she gestured at the basin. "Look within the waters, Brighid Dhianna, and you will find what it is you seek."

Resolutely, Brighid turned back to the basin and peered down into the water. The living liquid swirled and then became still and glassy, perfectly reflecting her face. She looked deeper, bending over the basin, and her body jerked. She was staring at her own reflection, yet within it she could clearly see her mother's face. And she suddenly understood. Her greatest ally and most powerful enemy was herself. If she accepted the power of a High Shaman, she would also be drinking in that which had corrupted her mother—and that capacity for corruption lurked within her. It had been born there, with her spiritual gifts.

"You can let the knowledge paralyze you," the Goddess said. "Or you can accept that she is a part of you and know you must guard against her weaknesses, which are also yours, as well as embrace her strengths."

Brighid turned from the basin and met Epona's eyes. "Why do you allow those who can be corrupted to drink of your Chalice?"

The Goddess smiled kindly at her. "I granted my children free will. It is the greatest gift of all, but with the freedom comes pain and evil, as well as love and courage. Great good is not possible without great evil. One cannot exist without the other. And, child—" she touched Brighid's face in a motherly caress that had the centaur's eyes filling with tears "—just because there is a chance of corruption it does not mean that chance will grow to fruition. Remember always that I believe in the good within you, Brighid."

"Thank you," the centaur whispered to the Goddess. Then Brighid closed her hand around the thick stem of the Chalice, dipped it into the basin, and while the Great Goddess and Cuchulainn watched, she drank of the living waters.

Power flooded Brighid's body, and within its swirling chaos she felt her mind unravel and unfold. She was at once a part of the earth and the heavens and the moon, sun and stars. She saw that everything was, indeed, ensouled and that they were all interrelated. The concepts of real and unreal stretched and bent within her and she understood with a new sense that the spirit realm and the physical world were nothing more than points on a flexible branch that could be bent, curved and re-woven so that the end points of reality and unreality could meet and become one in the same.

It's how I will shapeshift to mate with Cuchulainn. I will simply bend reality… The thought emerged from her tumultuous mind, and it grounded her. She blinked her vision clear and she was once more standing in the Goddess's grove beside the sacred basin, holding Epona's Chalice.

"Brighid?" Cuchulainn was there beside her, looking worried and, she thought, rather pale.

"All is well." She smiled reassurance to him. Then she bowed deeply before the Goddess. "Thank you for your great gift, Epona."

The Goddess cupped Brighid's chin in her hand and raised the centaur's face. "I believe that you will use it wisely, child." Then she smiled at both of them. "Now you must return. You were right to act with haste. Time is short and you have much to do." Epona clapped her hands together and the ground gave way beneath Brighid and Cuchulainn's feet. They floated down in a gentle spiral unwinding to the left. From behind them Epona's powerful voice cradled their spirits and held them awash in warmth and love.

Know that my blessing goes with you, my children…

CHAPTER
FORTY-SEVEN

Coming back into their bodies was definitely not the gentle experience departing them had been. Brighid found herself gasping and coughing and struggling not to retch.

"Here, drink this. It helps."

Cuchulainn was holding the wineskin against her lips. She obeyed him, drinking deeply. As the warmth of the wine spread throughout her body she felt her trembling cease and the nausea recede.

"Your turn," she gasped, handing him back the wineskin so that he could drink his fill.

"My father," he said, then paused as he drank. "He was always pale after a spirit journey, and when I was a boy that used to frighten me. Then he explained that it was really not so bad as long as he ate and drank quickly after his spirit returned."

While he was talking Brighid unwrapped the loaf of bread

and cheese, broke off a hunk of both and handed them to Cuchulainn. He smiled his thanks.

"Next time I see Father I'll have to tell him that 'really not so bad' does not come close to describing being tossed back into your body."

"I'm grateful that because of him you thought to leave all of this ready for us." She bit into the bread and then frowned. Brighid sniffed the cheese. She looked at Cuchulainn and saw that he was doing the same.

"It's old," he said.

"The bread is stale and the cheese is half covered with mold."

Then their eyes met and widened with understanding.

"I left the venison hunk hanging in a tree."

He chugged another drink of wine, then stood unsteadily. Brighid surged up, hating the way her legs quivered and her powerful equine muscles twitched. Cuchulainn handed her the wineskin.

"Drink some more of this. I'll check on the venison." He stumbled from the cave.

She was too weak to argue with him. Instead she knocked the mold off the cheese and ate several bites quickly, as well as forcing herself to chew a hunk of the stale bread. When her legs felt like they would carry her, she followed Cu out of the cave. It was a clear, warm night. Brighid thought back. When they began the spirit journey it was early evening, and it felt as if they had been gone from their bodies only minutes. But the facts were that the bread was stale and the cheese…

Brighid had been staring out at the night and suddenly what she was seeing registered in her mind.

"The meat is totally rancid, and the damned gelding broke his hobbles and is gone. First thing in the morning I'll have to—" He broke off, noting the shocked expression on Brighid's face. "What is it?"

"The moon. It's in its fourth quarter."

Both of them gazed at the crescent-shaped sliver of light that hung in the inky sky.

"But it was full just last night. Wasn't it?" he said.

She nodded. "It was full the night before we entered the Otherworld. I remember it because it illuminated everything so clearly."

"During your Magic Sleep journey to MacCallan," he said.

"Ten days, Cu. It is at least ten days from the full moon to the phase of the last quarter."

Cuchulainn ran his hand through his hair. "No wonder we feel so awful."

"Cu, it might have been days since Bregon left the grove. We have no way of knowing how long we were in the presence of the Goddess."

He took her hand. "It's true. We have no way of knowing right now—and there is nothing we can do about Bregon or the other centaurs of your herd tonight." When she started to speak he shook his head. "No," he said firmly. "It would be foolish of us to do anything tonight except eat and sleep and replenish our bodies and spirits. In the morning I'll track the gelding and we can decide what to do from there."

"I already know what we must do," Brighid said. "Bregon's words were blustering and bragging. I won't need an army to take my rightful place as High Shaman of Dhianna. Once the herd knows I drank from Epona's Chalice they will accept me."

"What of the centaurs who are loyal to Bregon?"

"There will be a few, but much less than you believe." Finally she smiled. "You see, my warrior husband, no centaur female would ever refuse allegiance to the first-born daughter of their High Shaman."

He returned her smile. "So those who side against you will be choosing very long, lonely lives."

"Exactly," she said.

He linked his arm through hers and they made their way slowly back to the cave, leaning a little on each other and occasionally stumbling.

"That does make me feel more hopeful about this. Perhaps the transition to your leadership won't be as traumatic an event as we anticipated."

"Perhaps," she said thoughtfully. "But there is still my brother to deal with. He's made it clear that he will not easily give up the position he has usurped."

"Then we will simply have to show him that he has no choice." Cuchulainn's voice was flint.

"Cu, when the basin showed me Bregon drinking of the Chalice I saw something else. When he left the grove ghostly wisps of his spirit stayed behind in the Otherworld. His soul has been shattered, Cu, terribly." She touched her husband's face. "Promise me that you will remember that he is not whole when you confront him."

"I promise," he said, and kissed her hand. "But you need to understand that no matter what pity I might feel for him, I will not allow him to harm you."

"I can't believe that he would really hurt me, Cu. I still remember the sweet child he used to be who wanted nothing so much as his mother's love and approval."

"He's not a child anymore. But don't worry, my beautiful Huntress, I will always remember that he is your brother." He kissed her hand again and then began feeling around the dark mouth of the cave for the fire starting implements he'd left ready at hand. "I think if we boil some of the dried meat left in our packs it would make a decent broth to soak that stale bread."

"I'll knock the mold off the rest of the cheese," Brighid said.

"Thank Epona for my mother's love of wine, at least we have plenty of that."

They built a quick fire and pieced together a decent meal, talking quietly about their experiences in the Otherworld, most especially about the awe they both felt when in the presence of the Great Goddess. Brighid watched Cuchulainn speak, thinking again how blessed she was to have such a valiant and loyal mate. Then, with a little start, she realized that she now had the power to shapeshift and join fully with him. It was that thought that had her lips curving into a smile even as she lost the battle with her exhausted body and she, and then Cuchulainn, fell into a deep, healing sleep.

When Brighid opened her eyes the cave was just beginning to be illuminated in the dreamy light that was the harbinger of newborn dawn. She stretched, careful not to wake the warrior who slept so peacefully beside her, and then stood, testing her body to see if it was still as weak and unreliable as it had been the previous night. *No,* she thought happily, *I feel wonderful!*

She left the cave and made her way quickly to the waterfall. Taking off her vest she stood naked under the cold spray. Lifting her face to the crystal current she opened her mouth and drank of the water. By the Goddess, she felt so incredibly alive! Her skin tingled under the water's caress, but it was more than that—Brighid felt an awareness in the world around her that she had never before experienced. It was as if until that morning the trees and rocks and the very earth herself had been slumbering—and now everything had awakened with her.

Laughing softly, she stepped from under the waterfall and gazed out at the Centaur Plains. There wasn't light enough yet to see definitions in the waving grass and gently rolling land. It was still shrouded in darkness, but the sky had begun to blush in anticipation of the sun and her eyes drank in the hazy morning view.

"Home…" She breathed the word aloud and the spirit within her body leaped at the admission. "I'm going home."

Brighid ignored the vest she had left on the rock beside the waterfall. She felt powerful and beautiful and filled with the passion of purpose. When she reentered the cave Cu stirred, rolled over, and then slowly opened his eyes. Seeing her silhouetted against the predawn sky he smiled and raised himself up on his elbow.

"Standing there all naked and wet you look like you could

be one of the fairy folk who slipped away from the Other-world," he said, his voice still rough with sleep.

"That doesn't surprise me," Brighid said, throwing her arms over her head as if she could embrace the day. "This morning I feel so different—like I'm not completely of this world."

Cuchulainn sat all the way up. "You are different, my beautiful Huntress, you are a High Shaman."

Brighid met his eyes, looking carefully to see if there was any reticence or withdrawal from her lurking there. Then she smiled, because she saw only Cuchulainn and the love he felt for her reflected in his gaze.

"Do you think people will stop calling me Huntress now?"

"Would that make you sad?" he asked.

"Yes…yes it would. At the core of my being I will always be a Huntress."

"Then—" he swept his arm in a courtly flourish "—to me you will always be my beautiful Huntress."

"I hope so, Cu. I really hope so," she said. When he started to get up she shook her head. "No. Don't come to me yet. I want you to stay there."

He tilted his head and studied her. "What are you concocting?"

"I'm—I'm not sure. Just give me a moment."

"I'm not going anywhere, Huntress," he said, leaning back on his elbow and taking a pull from their wineskin.

Brighid bowed her head and closed her eyes. Then she reached out with the new senses that had blossomed into life in the grove of the Goddess. Her mind swirled…

Everything was, indeed, ensouled…interrelated… The spirit realm and the physical world were nothing more than points on a flexible branch that could be bent, curved, and rewoven so that the end points of reality and unreality could meet and become the same. Centaur…man…woman…hawk…tree…grassland…they were all spirit-filled and touched by the Goddess. It was a simple thing, really, this shifting of shape and molding of matter…

Brighid raised her head and smiled beatifically at her husband. "I'll need you to be very quiet. I know I can do this, but I must have your word that you will not fragment my attention."

Cuchulainn's expression became tense and serious. "Brighid, you just returned last night. I think you should wait before you attempt—"

Her look stilled his words.

"Do you believe in me?" she asked.

"Yes."

"Do you desire me?"

"Of course," he said. Then he nodded. "I understand, my love. You have my oath that I will not fragment your attention."

She gave him a quick smile of gratitude before turning her attention inward. *Help me, Epona, guide me, aid me. I've barely tasted my new powers—I feel them, but I have no training...I don't know...* She drew a deep breath. *I cannot do this without Your loving touch.*

Suddenly words flooded her mind. The centaur bowed her head and gave words to the magic that was surging through her soul.

I am the wind that blows across the sea;
I am the wave of the deep;
I am the roar of the ocean;
I am the stag of the forest;
I am a hawk on the cliff;
I am a ray of sunlight
and the greenest of plants.

As the tempo and volume of Brighid's voice increased, she began to lift her arms, holding her palms out, fingers spread wide. She did not shout, but the power within the words was so great that it raised the hair on the back of Cuchulainn's neck. Then a shimmering covered her body. She glowed. The brilliance that danced along her skin seemed to be moving, but it wasn't the light that was moving. It was the Huntress's skin, rippling and liquefying. Brighid closed her eyes and lifted her arms and head together in time with her words.

> I am the wild boar
> and the salmon in the river;
> I am a lake on the Plain;
> I am the word of knowledge
> and the point of a spear;
> I am the lure beyond the ends of the earth
> and I can shift my shape like a Goddess!

As she shouted the last line her body exploded in a shower of light and her wordless shriek of agony echoed off the walls of the cave.

Despite his oath, Brighid's scream had Cuchulainn on his feet and rushing to her. But he stumbled to a stop when he saw the woman. She was kneeling in the exact place Brighid had been standing. Her head was bowed and damp hair covered her face. One of her hands rested on the ground and the other was still raised above her. She was breathing hard and her naked body was glistening with a slick film of sweat. With a moan, she raised her head and shook back her hair.

"I wish someone had warned me about how much that hurts." Brighid's voice sounded raspy.

"By the Goddess! Brighid!" Cuchulainn made a movement toward her, and then checked himself as if he was afraid to come too close to her.

She peered up at him through a curtain of silver hair. "If you tell me you're afraid to touch me I can promise you that I'm going to be very upset."

"Of course I'm not afraid to touch you. I just…" He breathed a curse and closed the space between them. He bent and carefully gripped her arms, helping her to stand. "I just didn't want to hurt you," he finally said.

"You're not going to hurt me." She glanced down at her body and her eyes widened. "I had no idea how strange this would be."

He put his arm around her waist. "Maybe you should come over to the pallet and sit down."

She nodded and stumbled a couple of steps forward. Then stopped and looked down at her legs again. "I'm so small!"

She thought his bark of laughter sounded a little hysterical. "You're not small—look at you—you're almost as tall as I am."

"Wait, let go of me and let me…I mean I need to…" She sighed at his perplexed expression. "Cuchulainn, I want to stand on my own *two feet* for a moment and get used to this new me."

"Oh! Of course," he said, carefully disentangling one arm from around her waist and the other from under her elbow.

He stepped away from her. She straightened and then looked down at herself again. Her torso was unchanged, but from her waist down she was another being entirely. Her powerful equine body had been exchanged for two long, lean legs. She glanced behind her and had to blink hard to keep from feeling dizzy and disoriented.

"Goddess! There's nothing back there," she blurted.

This time the warrior's laugh sounded more normal. "Of course there is! You have very shapely buttocks."

She met his eyes. "My shape is attractive to you?"

"Very," he said. "Not that I don't think you're beautiful as a Huntress, too," he added hastily.

"I already know you find me attractive as a centaur. This body is new to me. Naturally, I would wonder if…"

"You don't need to wonder, Brighid. You are an exquisite woman. In this light you look like a satin-skinned Goddess who somehow fell from the morning sky." He reached out and let a strand of her silver hair fall through his fingers. "And I am the luckiest of men to have discovered you."

She saw the desire in his eyes and the knowledge of it

started a hot quiver low in her belly. She smiled and let her gaze move back to her body. Carefully she stretched one of her legs forward. Pointing her toes she swung the leg forward from her hip. "Legs…toes…it's all so ordinary and yet extraordinary."

"I think it's completely extraordinary." His voice raw with emotion. "You did it, Brighid! You mastered that which only a High Shaman can command—the power to shapeshift."

"We did it," she said. "If you hadn't been with me I would never have reached Epona's grove. And now I need you to help me with something else."

"Anything, my beautiful Huntress."

"Show me how to become one in the flesh with you."

Wordlessly Cuchulainn took her hand and led her to their pallet, which they had not moved from the middle of the labyrinth. As she walked across the cave her steps became more sure, and though she missed the power of her natural form, she was able to appreciate the capacity for grace in her woman's body. She lay beside her husband and, filled with curiosity and wonder, she let her hands caress her naked body, learning how it responded to touch and finding the small secret spots that were especially sensitive.

"My skin is so soft. It amazes me," Brighid said. "I had no idea it would be like this." She smiled up at Cuchulainn who had propped himself on his elbow beside her and was watching as she explored herself.

"You make me breathless," he said huskily.

"Don't lose your breath," she murmured, taking his hand and guiding it to her thigh. "If you can't breathe, how will you tell me about the pleasures of this new body?"

He moaned her name and whispered against her lips, "I'll show you."

But he didn't just show her. As he touched her with his hands and mouth he spoke to her, asking what caress she most preferred and where and how his touch pleased her. His hands, roughened by years of swordplay, felt sensuous against the smoothness of her skin and Brighid found that she could not get enough of the feel of that roughness cupping the softness of her buttocks. When his mouth moved to her core and tasted fully of her, she did not look away, but watched him as he finally learned what she had known before him—the joy of a lover's pleasure.

When she was slick and ready for him, he entered her gently, allowing her time to stretch and receive him. And then they linked hands as they began the ageless give and take of lovemaking. She arched to meet him, reveling in the knowledge that their bodies had finally been able to experience what their souls had already known—the joining of two. When he cried her name and spilled his seed into her she held him close and crested the wave of sensation with him.

"Changing back is much easier," Brighid said, twitching her tail and stomping her hooves as if she was worried that something might not have completely transformed back to equine shape.

"It's amazing," Cu said. "All these years and I have never once seen my father shapeshift." He gave her a lopsided, boyish grin. "Although there were a couple of times when I burst into my mother's chamber and he was there in man form." He chuckled. "It never failed to surprise me. The last time I was about ten or eleven, and I couldn't really see him very well. I remember thinking that some stranger had gone mad and was ravishing her, so I brandished my not particularly dangerous wooden practice sword and yelled for him to unhand the Goddess Incarnate."

"What did he do?" Brighid asked, smiling.

"He looked up at me and said, 'Later, boy, right now your

mother and I are rather busy.'" Cuchulainn shook his head. "But that wasn't the worst of it. My yelling brought my mother's palace guards running—they don't take the ravishing of the Chosen of Epona lightly. There followed an embarrassing several moments that my father didn't find amusing. At all. When the 'later' came he sat me down and had a very long, very detailed talk with me about husbands and wives and lovemaking in general. He also explained to me in detail why he had to shapeshift, and why when he did it was a very private moment between my mother and him."

Brighid tried unsuccessfully to smother her laughter. "That sounds like a very awkward conversation."

"It wasn't a conversation. He talked—I listened. Then he asked me if I had any questions."

"Did you?"

Cuchulainn snorted. "Are you kidding? I was completely embarrassed, besides that all I could think of was why in the name of the Goddess anyone would want to do the things he was describing—and even if he did—why my mother would tolerate them."

Brighid's laughter turned into unexpectedly girlish giggles. "Stop, you're hurting me."

He smiled at her, wrapped one arm around her waist and kissed her soundly.

"I do remember in particular one of the things my father explained to me about shapeshifting during that awkward lecture."

She raised a silver brow.

"He said a High Shaman can only maintain another shape for a limited amount of time."

Brighid nodded. "It is common knowledge that a High Shaman must return to her natural form in no longer than the span of one night."

"Is it also common knowledge that once a High Shaman has returned to her natural form that it takes at least the span of another day for her body to reenergize?"

"No." Brighid looked surprised. "That part is not well-known." She let out a long, frustrated sigh. "There's so much I don't know, Cu. I feel the change within me, and I sense the world around me in a different way. But I know so little about how to wield this new power."

"Go easy on yourself. Most High Shamans have prepared for years, and are still being mentored by another High Shaman."

"That's the problem. I don't have a mentor."

"One step at a time, my beautiful Huntress, one step at a time. First you reclaim your birthright. Then you find a mentor. It just so happens that your husband does have connections with at least one High Shaman, and I can promise you that he would be more than willing to mentor his daughter-in-law." Cuchulainn grinned at her.

She draped her arm around his broad shoulders and nuzzled his ear. "Who knew a man would be such a good thing to have around?"

He chuckled and kissed her. "Don't tell the other centaur Huntresses—they'll all want one of their own."

She bit his neck and he gave a little yelp. They both laughed.

Then Cuchulainn sobered and touched the side of her cheek. "I was serious about what my father said, Brighid. A High Shaman's body is depleted after shapeshifting, so you take care today. Don't push yourself and don't expect too much from your body."

"I'm just hunting deer. I could do that even as a woman— I think," she added with a quick smile.

"Hunt your deer carefully. By the time you gut it and bring it back here I should have found that damned gelding."

"I can help you find that damned gelding of yours," Brighid said.

"I'm sure you could track him in half the time, my beautiful, talented Huntress, but we need the fresh meat, so I'll have to muddle through without your expertise."

"I don't have to come with you, Cu. I just have to—" She rolled her eyes when his amused expression turned guarded and strained. "Cuchulainn," she said sternly, "you're married to a High Shaman. You're going to have to get used to my evoking aid from the Otherworld." She shrugged her shoulders and smiled a little sheepishly. "I have to get used to it myself."

He sighed and raised her hand to his lips. "You're right. And, yes, my beautiful Huntress, I would welcome your help."

"Just give me a moment and don't—"

"I know," he said laughingly, "don't distract you."

She gave him an exasperated look before closing her eyes and grounding herself with three deep, even breaths. Then she thought about Cuchulainn's gelding—the sturdy, well-trained mount her husband depended upon…and quickly, much more quickly than she was used to, that extra innate sense that had always helped her track animals rushed from her body in a wave of sweeping power. Almost instantly she was drawn to a place not far from their cave where a lone dark blue spirit light burned steadily. The gelding. By the Goddess, that was easy! Then another, smaller, spirit light very near the gelding caught her attention, and she focused on it, wondering at its energetic golden aura, and suddenly she understood what she was seeing and wanted to laugh aloud. She almost broke the trance immediately so she could tell Cuchulainn, but the pull of other spirit lights called to her.

With a sense of wonder, she thought of the deer she planned to hunt, and little dashes of fawn-colored illumination flickered all across the tors and out into the Centaur Plains. Well, she thought happily, she certainly wouldn't have any problem finding that venison.

Then something quivered at the very edge of her spirit vision. It was coming from the north. An emerald glow so bright that its light was blinding, and it made her spirit give a little startled jump, breaking the meditation trance she had so easily fallen into. Her eyes fluttered open and she felt an unaccustomed weariness drag against her body and soul. Cuchulainn was watching her closely, worry shadowing his eyes. Instinctively, her first thought was to reassure him, and she pressed the mystery of the green light from her mind. *Later, after I've eaten and I'm not so tired I'll figure out what it is…it's probably only the green glow of the northern forests…*

Mentally she shook herself and gently touched her husband's face. "Cu, I've been using my affinity with animal spirits to track game for years. It's nothing to worry about. I'm a little tired, but I'm fine."

"I know…. It's just." He shook himself and smiled at her. "You're right. I'm being foolish. Did you find my errant horse?"

"Yes, and he's not far from here. Head northwest and you'll find a deer track. Follow it to a clearing and a pond. That's where he is. At most he's an hour's easy walk from here." Then she grinned at him and added, "And your gelding is not all you'll find of yours in the clearing."

He raised his brows at her. "You aren't going to tell me what else is there?"

"How about I give you a clue. She's furry and very, very annoying."

"Fand?" he said immediately.

"None other."

Cuchulainn burst into laughter.

Brighid gave an exaggerated sigh.

Still grinning, Cuchulainn lifted the bridle over his shoulder. "I'll go capture my beasts and meet you back here."

"I'll bring the dinner."

"I'll bring the wine and the company."

Brighid's laughter followed him as he strode toward the northwest, climbing the gentle slope of the rolling tor. When he stood at the top of the little hill he turned back and watched his wife gather her bow and strap her quiver of arrows over her shoulder.

"I love you, Brighid," he called and then shook his head at his own romantic silliness. She was too near the waterfall to hear him, and he could see even from that distance that the concentrated look of a Huntress was back on her face. Right now the only thing she would pay any attention to would be the scent or track of a deer.

"That's my beautiful Huntress," he murmured to himself. She was powerful and sensuous and intelligent. With her beside him he believed there was nothing the two of them couldn't accomplish. Tonight they'd eat and restore the energy the past days had sapped from them. Tomorrow they'd enter the Centaur Plains. He'd make sure she got to the Dhianna Herd and took her rightful position as their High Shaman. Then they could sort through the misunderstandings and hatred her mother's leadership had bred. Man and centaur could live happily together. His parents were proof of that—he and Brighid were proof of that. And the New Fomorians weren't a threat to anyone in Partholon. There was no need for the centaur herds to war against them. They were not the demons that had decimated the warriors of Partholon—both centaur and human—so long ago. Together he and Brighid would just have to make her herd see reason.

Cuchulainn let his gaze scan the Centaur Plains. Even browned with drought the land was still beautiful. It was open and free. The few times he'd traveled to the plains with his father he had been intrigued by the vastness of it. Perhaps it was a result of his father's centaur blood, but the thought of spending the rest of his life on the grasslands gave him a feeling of satisfaction. He had no doubt that he could find contentment and a home there with Brighid beside him.

Whistling happily, and thinking how good it would be to see his wolf cub, he hitched the bridle over his shoulder and headed into the northwest.

Brighid stood at the edge of the Centaur Plains and drew in a deep, joyous breath. It had been worth it. Yes, there were deer much closer to their cave than the plains, but Cuchulainn would be gone at least a couple of hours. She'd have plenty of time to track, kill and gut a deer, and get back to their cave before Cu had even returned, or at least that's how she'd rationalized her decision to ignore the weariness in her body and slide down the last of the gentle tors to hunt the venison of the plains.

Weary or not, it felt good to have her hooves in the rich soil of her homeland! She'd chosen a different life and she'd left her home believing she would never return—and she had made that work within her mind. But now she could admit that her spirit had never been easy with her choice. Inside of her there had been a yearning to return, and a restless stirring that she now realized had been the dormant High Shaman.

No more, she promised herself. *From here on I will use the gifts granted me by Epona and I will take the position I was born to.*

She decided quickly not to take herself back into a meditation trance to locate a herd of deer. This was her homeland. If she couldn't hunt venison here she didn't deserve to be called Huntress. Her sharp eyes scanned the land in front of her. At the edge of her vision she could see the familiar green dotting and a dip in the horizon that signified an area of crosstimbers. There were always small creeks or streams that meandered through the plains, and they were surrounded by a sandy grove and hardy trees. Even in times of drought, water from underground springs fed the crosstimbers area. Where there was water deer usually congregated. And there's where she would hunt.

She forced her body into a smooth canter and smiled as the wind and grass swept past her.

By the time she'd reached the crosstimbers line she was almost ready to admit that her decision to hunt the plains had been a hasty one—if not an outright mistake. Sweat soaked her body, and she was having trouble concentrating. She'd crossed several different centaur tracks, though she hadn't met anyone. She could see the dark spots of bison not far to the east, but she hadn't found any deer tracks at all, which was decidedly strange. Unless a centaur village was near, there should be plenty of deer all around a crosstimbers area—and she knew of no centaur village so close to the borders of Partholon. The luster of hunting on her homeland was definitely wearing thin. If she didn't find sign or spoor of deer soon, she would have to use her spirit powers to locate one. Just the thought of it made her groan in exhaustion.

The grasslands began to give way to the blackjack and post oaks that predominated the crosstimbers, and she let herself slow to a listless walk.

She just wanted to find the deer and get it back to their camp. With gratitude she thought about Cuchulainn waiting there. He could do the cooking.

Later, she couldn't decide if it had been her weariness or their stealth, but she heard and saw nothing before the rope snaked around her neck. Her hands were instantly up trying to pull the noose free, then she felt another rope catch her hind leg. She was jerked roughly off her feet, hitting the ground so hard that the air rushed from her. Her head cracked against a rock and blackness engulfed her.

CHAPTER
FORTY-NINE

Consciousness came back in a painful rush. Hard hands were holding her on her feet. She felt battered and bruised and her head ached with a hot, piercing pain that beat in time with her pounding heart.

"Stand up by yourself!" a rough voice said. "Dragging you here was hard enough. I'll be damned if we're going to hold you upright, too."

Dragged? I've been dragged?

Hands tied behind her back she struggled suddenly and violently. Half blind with pain she tried to strike out with her powerful equine hind legs—and her throat closed. The harder she struggled the tighter the rope that cut off her breath.

"Be still or choke yourself to death!" the voice boomed.

Trembling, Brighid forced herself still and the rope around her neck loosened enough for her to suck in a breath and cough spasmodically.

"Don't fight it and you'll be fine. Fight and you won't breathe."

Trembling, Brighid blinked her vision clear and time seemed to slow. She felt as if she was moving under deep water as she tried to comprehend the contradictions in what she saw. She was standing in the middle of a centaur tent—that much was easy for her to understand. It was one of the large, five-sided tents made of beautifully dyed and elaborately decorated bison skins that her mother used to insist be erected and readied for her with every luxury in place well before she arrived at wherever she was visiting. The opening was directly across from Brighid and through the half-pulled-back flap she could see that it was dark. How long had she been unconscious? Her mind struggled to clear. Everything was wrong and she was unable to understand what had happened to her.

The tent was familiar, but the interior wasn't richly appointed with the thick pallets and low-standing tables centaurs preferred. The only decoration was several free-standing iron candelabrums that cast shadowy light around the tent. The rest of the tent was empty—except for the four male centaurs who surrounded her. She tried to pull her hands free again, but they were securely tied behind her back. She could feel ropes on her neck and body. In a haze of disbelief, she saw that she was standing, with her torso cross-tied, between the two center poles of the tent. Her front legs were hobbled. Two ropes were tied around her neck. Each of them was attached to a noose around each of her rear legs—she could feel them chafing painfully just above her hooves. The hobble and the cross-tie made certain she could not move. The neck-leg restraint rendered her hind legs impotent. She was very effectively trapped. Brighid raised her eyes to the centaur who stood closest to her and his sneer of superiority had time and noise and sensation flooding back to a normal tempo.

"Fully awake now, my beauty?" he sneered. "Good. No sense in damaging your pretty neck—that is any more than it has already been damaged." He chuckled and the other three centaur males laughed, too.

Thunder rolled in the distance and lightning flashed in the opening of the tent, helping her to identify the other centaurs. They were Bregon's pack. She'd thought of them as that since the day they'd killed the young girl. They went everywhere with her brother, following him in everything he did. *Like the pathetic sheep they are,* she thought.

"Gorman." Brighid pitched her voice to perfectly mimic her mother's most angry tone. "Release me at once, you coward!"

Lightning flashed again, and from the edge of her vision she saw one of the other centaurs, Hagan, flinch at the familiar sound of her voice. The other two males were brothers, Bowyn and Mannis, and their eyes went large and round as she spoke. But she kept her attention focused on Gorman, Bregon's best friend, and partner in all he did.

"You sound like her. You even look like her. But you are not her." Gorman spat into the grass in front of her. "You were never as strong as Mairearad. You never will be."

"Define strength, Gorman," she shot back, forcing the exhaustion from her voice and mind. "Is it the ability to manipulate and use others? Or would your definition of strength be dependent upon ropes? No, wait. I seem to remember that you enjoy terrifying small girls. Pity you had to sneak up on me and tie me up. Was there no wagon available to conveniently roll over me?"

"Strength," he said darkly, stepping forward so that he sprayed spittle in her face as he spoke, "is defined by the victor!"

"Where is my brother?" she said, refusing to react to his blustering.

"You brother is making certain that Partholon knows that once again Fomorians have been loosed upon their world."

"Have you gone mad?" she said. "There are no more Fomorians."

"Really? Then what do you call those winged creatures you and Midhir's son guided into Partholon?"

"I call them the same thing Midhir and Epona's Chosen call them—New Fomorians. You know Elphame lifted the curse from them. They are no longer a demonic race." As she spoke she tested the bindings around her wrists, vying for a way to get her hands free. "This is ludicrous. I demand to see my brother."

"Patience, my beauty. Bregon has been very busy and wasn't able to greet you properly upon your arrival." Gorman laughed and the three watching centaurs chuckled nervously along with him. "He asked us to keep you…occupied…until he could join us."

Brighid felt her face go cold. "Bregon could not know what you have done to me."

Gorman shrugged. "He commanded that you be kept from reaching the herd until it is too late. He left the means up to us. This—" he gestured to the cross-tie poles and the ropes that would strangle her if she attempted to fight "—was my idea."

"It's already too late. I have tasted of Epona's Chalice. I am the Dhianna High Shaman."

"Yes, we're aware of that. Bregon told us. Fortunately none of us thought to tell our mates. Such a shame that the females of the herd won't find out until it's too late."

"You are mad," she told Gorman, and then carefully turned her head so that the next time the tent glowed with lightning she met the eyes of the dark bay centaur who had remained farthest in the shadows. "Get my brother, Hagan. No matter what has happened between us he will not look kindly on this treatment of his sister." Then she narrowed her eyes and filled her voice with all the power she could siphon from her exhausted spirit. "And even if Bregon would be willing to allow it, he knows, as do I, the anger that would fill Epona at such treatment of her High Shaman!"

Hagan flinched and opened his mouth to speak, but Gorman cut him off.

"And what did your precious Epona do when your own mother was spitted through the gut and lay dying in agony?" Gorman's face was florid with the passion of his emotions. "Nothing! Your Goddess let Mairearad suffer and die. Apparently Epona no longer cares about what happens to her centaur High Shamans."

Brighid turned her gaze slowly and deliberately back to his. "You blaspheme and have turned from the Great Goddess. I give you my oath that you will pay for it."

Thunder growled through the night and lightning spiked as if Epona had heard and acknowledged her Shaman's oath. Heedless, Gorman sneered.

"We shall see who pays for what, Brighid Dhianna. After all, it is you who helped to bring the demons back into Partholon. Perhaps the people you chose over your own herd will not open their arms to you with such enthusiasm when they realize what you have done."

"The New Fomorians are not demons, you fool! They are a kind people who nurture life, not death. And that is what all of Partholon will know."

Gorman's eyes turned sly. "You seem to be forgetting one very special *Fomorian*." He enunciated the word carefully.

Brighid narrowed her eyes at him. "Fallon is jailed at Guardian Castle awaiting the birth of her child and her execution. She will pay for her madness, even though what she did was only a result of the depth of her love for her people. She is an aberration. The rest of the New Fomorians are not like her."

"So what you're saying is that they wouldn't help her escape and then join her in small but deadly strikes against Partholon?"

"Of course not."

"But what if they did? What if a winged creature who came from the southwest—the exact area of MacCallan Castle—

managed to break into Guardian Castle and free the insane Fomorian, leaving blood and death in their wake? What would the Guardian Warriors do?"

"This is a ridiculous guessing game. It could not happen. The New Fomorians want nothing more than to live peacefully in Partholon. They wouldn't do anything to jeopardize that."

Gorman's laughter filled the tent, almost drowning out the next roll of thunder. Bowyn and Mannis smiled, and their teeth flashed white in the flickering lightning.

"She knows as little as Bregon said she would about it," Mannis said.

Brighid's eyes snapped to his. "You have a tongue? I thought you and your brother were only mouthpieces for Bregon. If he's not present feeding you your words I didn't think either of you—" she let her disgusted gaze include Bowyn "—could actually speak for yourself."

"You always thought you were so much better than us," Bowyn said angrily.

"Not better, just more humane," Brighid said.

"Don't you want to know what the 'it' is?" Gorman interrupted, calling her attention back to him.

"I don't care about anything you have to say, Gorman."

"Really? Perhaps you will. 'It' is shapeshifting. Bregon told us the people of Partholon know as little about shapeshifting as his own newly made High Shaman sister. And that he would use their ignorance to his benefit."

"What are you…" With a shudder of horror she knew. The "Fomorian" who helped Fallon to escape would be Bregon. "Oh, Goddess! No!"

"Oh, Goddess! Yes!" Gorman mocked. "But don't think it was Bregon who thought of the plan."

"Mairearad." She breathed her mother's name, remembering the raven's obscene shriek for vengeance.

"Of course it was Mairearad. Even dying she was brilliant. She orchestrated the revenge for her own death. She told Bregon to enter Guardian Castle at night and alone, and find the Fomorian. Then he was to kill everyone who had seen him enter in his true form, shapeshift into a Fomorian, and allow the creature to escape—only then would he let any of the warriors who saw him live."

"Because they wouldn't see him. They would see a Fomorian," she said, shaking her head back and forth in horror, remembering the kindness the Guardian Warriors had shown the children. But that wouldn't matter, not if they believed Partholon was being attacked by the race they had been commissioned to defend her against.

"Yes." Gorman chuckled. "And they'll follow a Fomorian's trail that will lead back to MacCallan Castle. What do you think Clan MacCallan will do when the Guardian Warriors surround their castle?"

"They won't give up the children," she whispered, more to herself than to Gorman. "They'll fight to protect them."

"We're counting on that," Gorman snarled.

"Why? Those people have done nothing to you. Why would you want to destroy Clan MacCallan?"

"For the same reason you should. They killed your mother."

"That's crazy. Clan MacCallan could not possibly have harmed my mother."

"She died in a pit dug by humans." Gorman moved quickly to a dark corner of the large tent and picked up a wad of material from the floor. He returned to stand in front of Brighid and shoved the bloody cloth into her face. "This is what the humans were wearing. Do you recognize it?"

It was the MacCallan plaid. Brighid's stomach pitched as she remembered Elphame telling her of the clan members who had chosen to break their oaths and leave the castle, making themselves unacceptable to any other clan. They must have made their way to the vast Centaur Plains, probably thinking to begin anew, maybe even found their own clan.

Instead they'd founded a war.

"These people were not a part of Clan MacCallan. Several clan members broke oath and left—these had to be those people. Where are they? I'll recognize them if I see them."

"You wouldn't recognize them now, not even with your excellent Huntress vision," Bowyn said sarcastically.

"You killed them!" she said.

"We did. It was the beginning of your mother's vengeance."

"This has to be stopped before the world is awash in blood," Brighid said.

"Let it be awash!" Gorman shouted. "While you were chatting with your uncaring Goddess, Bregon was going about your mother's business. He's already been to Guardian Castle, and should return to the plains any day with news of his bloody success. The wheels are spinning past the point of no return, and it is impossible for you to stop them."

Brighid's eyes went cold. "Don't ever tell me what's impossible, you pathetic sycophant. What would you know of the impossible? All you've done your whole life is follow a centaur who is little more than a petulant colt and lust after a female who knew more of hatred and manipulation than love. I pity you, Gorman."

"You *pity* me!" he screamed, blowing spittle in her face. "We'll see very shortly who's to be *pitied*."

Thunder roared ominously and lightning flared outside, brightening the tent with a surreal, fitful light. Breathing hard Gorman sidled closer to her and fisted his hand in her hair, jerking her head back painfully.

"Bregon had more to report from the Otherworld than the news that you'd finally managed to taste of the Chalice." With a single, violent movement, he ripped the vest from her chest, exposing her breasts. "He also said something we found very shocking. He told us that you had mated with a man. Could that really be truth?" With his other hand he lifted her breast so that he could easily bend his head over it. When his tongue flicked out to lick her nipple, she surged so violently away from him that her world began to blacken as the rope cut off her air supply.

Then two other sets of hands pressed against the other side of her body as Bowyn and Mannis held her upright so that the rope loosened and her breath returned in panting gasps. In a gray haze it seemed that the eyes of the three centaurs burned with an unnatural light. Their faces were flushed and their breathing had deepened. Where their hot hands touched her she could feel their lust burning into her.

"Answer him," Bowyn said, his voice gruff and breathy. "Did you mate with a man?"

"I did," she ground between her teeth, fighting off panic. "Cuchulainn MacCallan is my husband and lifemate, and when I lead the Dhianna Herd I will do so with him at my side."

"That will never happen!" Gorman shrieked.

"Perhaps she has been too long without a centaur lover, and she has forgotten true passion," Bowyn rasped between ever-thickening breaths. His hand closed over her other breast and as he squeezed and prodded the nipple he bit into her shoulder so hard that his teeth drew blood.

Gorman's low chuckle sounded near her ear as his tongue flicked up and down her neck. "Perhaps you are right, Bowyn."

She could feel Mannis moving behind her, his hands and teeth taking painful turns at kneading and then biting her haunches. Frantically her eyes searched the tent for Hagan, but the centaur had disappeared into the storm-filled night.

"If you do this thing I swear by the Goddess Epona that I will not rest until each of you are dead," Brighid hissed. She struggled against the blackness that kept narrowing her vision by concentrating on the warmth that had begun to spread from the turquoise stone that hung between her naked breasts.

"And how will you fulfill that oath?" Gorman whispered, his hot breath coming fast and heavy against her skin as he nipped and licked the mound of her breast. "Will your puny man mate track us down and scare us to our deaths with his overwhelming strength?"

"He won't have to. He's going to kill you tonight where you stand," Cuchulainn said from the opening of the tent.

CHAPTER
FIFTY

The deadly sound of Cuchulainn's sword being drawn free of its sheath was echoed by a wolf's low, menacing growl. When the warrior moved Fand struck. Bowyn was the first to go down, screaming as the wolf lunged under Brighid's body to get to his rear legs. With one powerful tear of Fand's teeth, Bowyn was hamstringed and floundering in his own blood on the grassy ground.

Cuchulainn didn't move like a man. He moved like a malevolent spirit—silent, all-knowing, deadly. With speed that caused his sword to become a silver-white blur he whirled and lunged past the fallen Bowyn, slicing his throat in a neat, scarlet arch. The centaur's last breath escaped his open mouth in a gurgling gasp.

The warrior closed on Mannis without making a sound. The centaur was scrambling back from Brighid's haunches, his body still engorged with his obscene lust, when Cuchulainn struck. He skewered him in the chest, pulled his sword free and whirled past him, dragging the blade along his equine belly and disemboweling him.

"I won't be so easy to kill," Gorman said, hefting the long sword he'd retrieved while the man had been kept busy with Gorman's comrades.

Cuchulainn's only response was to move relentlessly toward the centaur. He didn't speak and he didn't break his stride. With speed that had been honed like the edge of a blade, he made the centaur look old and clumsy in comparison. Cuchulainn ducked smoothly under Gorman's sword, but instead of going for a killing blow, he sliced at the centaur's front hock.

Gorman hissed in pain and stumbled back—and right into the wolf's path. Fand wasn't as silent a warrior, but she was just as deadly. Thunder blanketed Gorman's scream and, in turn, lightning illuminated the torn flesh that dangled from his rear hamstring. He collapsed and Cuchulainn closed on him.

"No!" Brighid yelled.

Cuchulainn's body jerked to a halt. The face he turned to his wife was one she had only seen once before, when they had fought side by side against Fallon and the misguided Fomorians who tried to protect her. But his blood-spattered warrior's mask did not frighten or repulse her. She knew her own visage was a reflection of the same cold intensity.

"Cut me free," she said.

"Fand! Watch him," Cuchulainn ordered. The wolf slunk over to stand near the centaur's bleeding hindquarters, fangs bared.

Cuchulainn sheathed his sword and pulled free the dagger from his belt. With swift, sure movements he cut the ropes from his wife's body.

Without asking, Brighid pulled his sword free, and then, bare-chested and holding the bloody blade before her she approached Gorman.

He looked up at her, eyes glazed with pain and fear.

"Don't kill me! I'll do anything!" he pleaded.

"Don't speak to me," she ground between her teeth. Without looking at the warrior who was standing beside her she said. "Cuchulainn, Epona gave you the gift of seeing the soul. What do you see within this centaur's soul?"

She heard his sharp intake of breath and knew that this was the first moment he had used the gift newly given to him by the Goddess.

"I see rot and darkness."

With no hesitation, Brighid plunged her husband's sword into the centaur's heart. In almost the same motion, she jerked it free and handed it back to Cuchulainn.

"I have to get out of here," she said.

Cuchulainn nodded tightly. Before he followed her through the open tent flap he stopped to pick up her torn vest, and the Huntress's bow and quiver of arrows that had been thrown into one of the tent's corners.

"Fand! Come," he said.

The warrior and wolf walked out into the night to find that Brighid had stumbled several steps from the tent. She had dropped to her knees and was being violently sick. Fand lay close by, whining worriedly. Cuchulainn stroked her back, held her hair, and murmured wordless sounds of comfort, all of which were drowned out by a deafening crack of thunder, followed by a blinding blaze of lightning. Brighid's head jerked up.

"There's no rain," she said, wiping her mouth with the back of her hand.

"No, love," he said gently. "There is no rain."

The Huntress drew in several deep breaths. "I can smell no rain in the air, either. It's a dry storm. By the Goddess, I've always hated the damned things! Dangerous—they bring deadly lightning and the chance of…" With a look of horror, she stood. Orienting herself quickly, she turned so that the wind was blowing directly into her face while she looked southward out across the length of the Centaur Plains. "Oh, Goddess, no!" she cried.

Cuchulainn followed her wide-eyed gaze. The horizon was on fire. As they stood staring with horrified awe, a shaft of lightning snaked to the ground, igniting another, closer, section of the grasslands.

"We have to get off the plains. Now," she said, slipping on her vest and strapping the bow and quiver in their proper place over her back. "A grassfire is deceptive. In no time it can engulf you."

"The gelding isn't far from here."

"Wait," Brighid said before Cuchulainn sprinted off. "Help me cut two pieces out of the tent."

He didn't question her, but went to the tent and began to slice through the thick hide.

"Big enough to cover us," she said, grasping the torn edge and pulling it so that it would tear more quickly.

"Cover us?" His cutting faltered.

"If we can't outrun the fire we have to find a gully, or better, crosstimbers with a stream. We get in the streambed and cover ourselves with the hides. If we're lucky the fire will pass over us."

"If we're not lucky?" he said.

"We suffocate or burn to death."

He grunted and began cutting the sections from the side of the tent with renewed energy. When the two pieces of the tent fell free, neither Brighid nor Cuchulainn spared a glance at the silent, bloody remains within.

The gelding was hobbled not far from the tent. Cuchulainn flipped open his saddle pack and tossed a skin of water to Brighid. She drank greedily while he rolled up and then tied one of the pieces of the tent to Brighid's equine back, and the other behind his saddle. When he was finished he turned to the Huntress. She was standing with her head down, petting Fand and murmuring endearments to the whimpering wolf cub.

Cuchulainn didn't let himself dwell on what he had found in the tent and what had almost happened to his wife. He couldn't. If he did, he would be lost. His stomach was tight and hot, and he still felt the preternatural clearness that always came over him during battle. He'd need a warrior's strength to get them through what lay ahead. But he couldn't stop himself from going to her and lifting her face. Holding it between his hands he felt the shudder that passed through her body when she met his eyes.

"You came in time," she whispered. "Thank you."

He couldn't speak. He could only kiss her with an intensity that edged on violence. She met his passion with her own, wrapping her arms around him and drinking him in.

Lightning streaked across the sky, breaking their kiss.

"We have to ride hard. The wind is with the fire," Brighid said.

"Back to the tors?"

"No. There's not enough water there to stop the fire, and we couldn't climb fast enough to get away from it."

"East, then. The tributaries of the Calman River finger into the plains between the tors and Woulff Castle. My father and I fished there often in my youth."

Brighid nodded. "Let's hope the drought hasn't dried them up."

"If it has then we'll just have to make it to the river itself," Cuchulainn said, swinging aboard the gelding.

He might be able to make it. The gelding is fresh and well-rested. I won't.

"Brighid," Cuchulainn turned in the saddle and their eyes met in the next flash of lightning. "I will never leave you. We either live or die—together."

She knew he was speaking the truth. This man would never leave her, not even to save himself. *Then Goddess help me not to get us both killed.*

"You lead. I'll be right behind you," she said.

The warrior dug his heels into the gelding's sides and

they raced into the northeast with the wolf cub streaking behind them.

Their flight from the Centaur Plains seemed to be a descent into an Underworld that had been abandoned by the Goddess. The thunder and the lightning served to illuminate vignettes of a nightmarish reality. Animals of the plain rushed past them—deer, fox and other small mammals like rabbits leaped hysterically into their path before bounding away. And with the animals came the smoke. At first it was just a brief, bitter taste on the southern breeze, but as the night lengthened the air became thicker until Cuchulainn pulled up his gelding, and tore his shirt into long swatches of linen that he soaked with water from one of the skins.

"When it gets really bad tie it around your nose and mouth. It might help."

Gasping for air Brighid nodded, and they both drank thirstily from the skin. "I wish it was wine," she said between coughing fits.

Cuchulainn smiled at her. "It will be soon. My mother's temple isn't far from the Calman tributaries."

"I don't suppose I need to ask whether she'll know to be there to greet us." Brighid tried to keep her tone light, but she was still struggling to get her breathing under control, and the intermittent flashes of lightning clearly showed how hard her equine body was trembling.

"Mother will probably have dancing girls and a parade all prepared for us," he said, attempting to match her tone, but he guided his gelding close to her. His face was drawn and his eyes worried as he studied the Huntress. "Let's rest here. We have some time."

"We have no time," Brighid said. Fand came panting up to them and Brighid bent, pouring water in her hand for the wolf to lap. "There's a brave, good girl," she told the wolf. Then she glanced up at Cuchulainn. "You lead. I'll follow."

Cu nodded tightly and pointed the gelding's head to the north again, and kicked him into a steady lope. Suddenly lightning forked the night with brightness, clearly illuminating the shape of a lone centaur moving almost parallel to them. In the white light his coat shone gold and sliver, an exact copy of his sister's.

"Give me your bow," Cuchulainn said.

"No. If it's to be done, I'll do it." At a gallop she notched the bow and waited for the next strike of lightning. When it came she sighted and let fly an arrow, which embedded itself in Bregon's flank, causing him to stumble and fall hard to the ground.

At a flat run, Cuchulainn's gelding beat Brighid to her brother, and the warrior leaped from the horse's back, drawing his sword and pressing it against the centaur's heaving chest so hard that it broke the skin. The next lightning flash illuminated the scarlet drops that trailed down his colorless chest as if he was a half-finished painting.

"This is just so that you don't doubt that my sword works in this realm," Cuchulainn snarled.

"Don't kill him, Cu," Brighid said quietly, putting a trembling hand on her husband's arm. "At least not yet."

But her brother was ignoring the warrior. Instead he was staring at the rope burns and teeth marks that had left red, angry wounds on his sister's body.

"What happened to you?"

Cuchulainn's growl matched the wolf's low angry rumble. "The centaurs you left behind did as you ordered them. They captured her. They bound her with ropes so that if she moved she would choke herself. Then they began to rape her." With each sentence he pressed the sword more firmly into Bregon's chest and fresh blood welled under the razor-like blade. "I made certain they didn't complete your orders."

"No," he said faintly, eyes widening in shock. "They were just supposed to hold you until I returned."

"Until it was too late to stop the war!" Brighid cried. "How could you do it, Bregon? How could you cause such bloodshed and hatred? Wasn't our mother's hatred enough to fill you full for a lifetime?"

A shudder passed through his body. "I just wanted to make her happy."

"That was an impossible task for anyone, Bregon," she said. Then the pitying look in her eyes hardened. "Have you done it? Have you freed Fallon?"

Bregon closed his eyes and nodded.

"Open your eyes and look at the man who is going to kill you!" Cuchulainn ordered.

Again, Brighid's hand lightly touched her husband's arm, and with obvious effort he stopped himself before plunging the blade the rest of the way into Bregon's chest.

"Where did Fallon go?" Brighid asked.

"Into the mountains. That's all I know," Bregon shuddered again. "She was horrific." His expression of shock was receding and an arrogance that reminded her of her mother was creeping into his tone. "How can you defend those creatures? They are evil. Even pregnant she ripped and tore the guards with her hands and teeth to get free. Taking their form, even temporarily, was a ghastly experience."

"They're not like Fallon! The New Fomorians are gentle and kind. Epona has even gifted them with the ability to nurture life." Brighid shook her head in disgust, feeling thoroughly sick and so weary it seemed every word was a struggle for her to form. "You've always been like this, Bregon, unable to see beyond your immediate needs and desires."

"I don't believe those winged creatures should be allowed to live," he said.

"It's not your choice! And what of the Guardian Warriors? How many of them did you kill? And how many more did Fallon kill?"

"And what of the Clan MacCallan?" Cuchulainn said between clenched teeth.

"They killed my mother!" Bregon cried.

"You young fool, the men who were on the Centaur Plains had broken with the clan," Cuchulainn told him. "Why else would they have been there trying to forge a new life?"

"And no one killed our mother, Bregon. It was an accident—an accident which would have been avoided if she had given the little group of people permission to settle in one small part of our land."

"They had no right to be there! They cannot trespass upon the herd's land!"

"No!" Brighid made a violent cutting motion with her hand, and the sudden, violent motion made her feel light-headed. "The plague of hatred our mother spread ends now. You will come with us to Epona's Temple. There you will tell Etain what you have done and let her decide your punishment."

"I won't go!" His breath started to come in hard, shallow pants and his eyes darted around, as if searching for aid in the smoky darkness that surrounded them.

"If I have to hamstring you and drag you behind my horse I will," Cuchulainn said.

Brighid's skin began to tingle just before the sound reached them. Then the roar built. It was thunderlike, but more living—more intense. The earth beneath them began to vibrate.

"Bison," Brighid said, staring at her brother incredulously. "You have an affinity with animals, too."

Her brother returned her gaze steadily. "We do have some things in common, sister."

"What's happening?" Cuchulainn said.

"He's stampeded the bison. Get mounted," she said quickly, carefully keeping the panic from her voice. "We'll deal with him later."

Cuchulainn didn't move, but kept his blade pressed against the centaur's bleeding chest.

"Cuchulainn! If we don't move and move fast we will be killed."

"We'll lose him."

"We may, but he cannot hide from Epona."

With a frustrated snarl, Cuchulainn stepped back. The instant the sword was no longer against his chest, Bregon surged up. He turned to his sister.

"Forgive me," he cried, stumbling toward her.

Automatically her arms went out to catch him, but instead of embracing her, his hand snaked out, grabbing the rolled up bison skin from her back. Before Cuchulainn could react, he spun away, and melted like a blond spirit into the smoke.

Cuchulainn swung aboard his gelding, who was restlessly skittering to the side, ears cocked at the rumbling darkness, and made to go after him.

"Let him go," Brighid said heavily. "He's not worth your life." With a mighty effort, Brighid scooped Fand up and tossed her over the saddle in front of Cu. "Keep her with you or she'll be trampled!" She had to shout over the growing noise. "Keep a firm hold on the gelding. He'll want to panic, but you'll be safe as long as you're mounted on him."

An enormous dark shape thundered past them.

Brighid met her husband's turquoise eyes and smiled. She was near the end. The shapeshifting, and then her abduction and fleeing from the grassfire had depleted even her deep reserves of Huntress strength. She would not be able to keep up with the stampeding bison, but she would not have his last living memory of her be of tears and regrets. "I love you, Cuchulainn," she said, and saw his face soften in response.

"And I you, my beautiful Huntress."

Another beast rushed past them and Brighid drew a deep breath before slapping the gelding on the rear and shouting, "Now ride!"

CHAPTER
FIFTY-ONE

Gelding and centaur leaped forward together and then they were consumed in the mass of stampeding creatures. Their scent hit Cuchulainn—musk mixed with smoke and panic. He could hear nothing except the pounding of their hooves. Frantically he tried to guide his gelding so that they remained beside Brighid, but it was impossible. The ocean of bison separated them until all he could see was her silver-blond hair as it streamed behind her. And then he was pulling too far ahead of her and he lost her completely.

Fear exploded within him. He couldn't lose her! Slowly he managed to angle his gelding so that they were very gradually cutting through the running creatures. The horse was more agile than the lumbering bison and they finally made it to the edge of the herd. He slowed the horse to a steady trot and scanned the dark beasts for any sign of Brighid's silver coat.

The herd thinned and as stragglers staggered past him a

new sound reached his ears. It was a distinctive crackle and popping that was followed by an ominous *whoosh* of air. He turned his head as a sudden updraft cleared the smoke and the gelding squealed and fought to lunge away as the wall of flames materialized. From within the orange fire, Cuchulainn could see a young bison calf and its mother being consumed.

He spun the gelding around and began crisscrossing the flattened grass path left by the herd.

"Brighid!" he yelled, eyes searching for a spot of silver in the empty plain.

He would have passed her if Fand hadn't begun to whine and wriggle frantically to be free. Brighid had fallen to her knees and was bent forward at the waist, resting her hands against the ground and gasping for air.

He raced to her and dropped from the gelding to her side. She raised her head and looked up at him, her eyes large and glassy.

"No," she whispered. "You were supposed to be safe."

"I told you I wouldn't leave you," he said. Turning quickly to the gelding he grabbed the water and held the skin to her lips. She gulped and then turned away to cough.

The whoosh and crackle of the fire had her head snapping around. "Get out of here!" she yelled at him.

"Only if you come with me," he said.

"There's no point." She gestured to her right foreleg, which was bent at the wrong angle along the ground. "It's broken. Quickly, Cuchulainn. Leave me!"

"I will not! Where you go I go—if you die I die! I will not lose you, Brighid. I could not survive it."

"Please don't do this," she said brokenly.

Then his eyes widened. "Shapeshift!"

"Cu, I—"

"You can! You must. Shapeshift and the gelding can carry us out of here. If you don't, we die here."

Live, child...

The gentle, familiar voice of Epona drifted through her

mind, calming and soothing her. Brighid bowed her head and began whispering the words as she steeled herself for the pain of the Change.

Her skin had barely stopped glowing from the transformation when Cuchulainn lifted her to the gelding's back. The fire was so close that the heat seared their skin and sparks rained around them.

"It's going to catch us," Brighid panted against his ear.

Cuchulainn leaned forward and dug his heels into the gelding, who lengthened his stride, but they couldn't pull away from the flaming monster that pursued them. Brighid closed her eyes and clutched the turquoise stone that dangled from around her neck.

I need you again, my winged friend.

The hawk's cry sounded above the spitting flames and her mighty wings beat against the smoke that surrounded them as she circled over them once and then dove like a plummeting star to their right.

Come...

Cuchulainn reined the gelding to the right, and followed the soaring bird to the riverbed.

The water was shallow—only reaching just above the gelding's hocks. And they weren't alone. They had joined an odd assortment of deer and coyotes, all of whom were cringing into the water and staring with hypnotic fascination at the approaching wall of flames. When Fand leaped the bank and splashed to them, not even the timid deer spared him a glance.

"Get the skin off the gelding!" Brighid yelled over the thunder of the flames. "Let him go. He can outrun it without us."

She gritted her teeth against the pain in her broken leg as he helped her from the horse's back. She balanced on one leg in the muddy water while he tugged off the saddle, packs, and bison pelt, and shooed the gelding away. Then Cuchulainn lowered her with him as he sank into the water and called Fand to them. Wrapped in each other's arms with the wolf pressed closely, Cuchulainn covered them with the bison pelt and their world went black.

They lost all sense of time, and knew only the heat and the terrible, deafening sound of the feeding fire. The water around them hissed and steamed. Brighid held tight to Cuchulainn and tried to control the instinctive panic that made her want to fling off the oppressive bison skin. Her pulse beat painfully in her broken leg and her body felt horribly weak, and amidst the heat she began to shiver and she knew that shock was setting in. *That could kill me as surely as the fire.* The thought was detached from her, and she knew she should force herself to care—to struggle to stay conscious and aware…but it was so much easier to sleep…and it was so very cold…

Then she heard the singing. Her lips tilted up as she recognized the voices of the winged children and remembered that it was the song they sang the day they began their journey from the Wastelands.

Greetings to you, sun of Epona
as you travel the skies on high,
with your strong steps on the
wing of the heights
you are the happy mother of the stars.

"Do you hear them," she whispered to Cuchulainn.

"I do," he said, his voice hushed. "I hear them even though they can't be here."

"They aren't—" Brighid's voice was choked with tears "—but their love is. Gorman was wrong, Epona still cares about what happens to her High Shamans." As she listened to their disembodied song of praise she felt the strength of love fill her body and expand around her as she tapped into and focused it, blanketing them in a mother's protective touch.

You sink down in the perilous ocean
without harm and without hurt.

You rise up on the quiet wave
like a young chieftain in flower,
And we will love you all the days
of our lives!

"It's over," Brighid said quietly when the singing stopped. "The fire has burned itself out. I can Feel it—its anger is gone."

Slowly Cuchulainn raised the thick pelt from them and gazed into the alien dawn of a much-changed land. He stood and lifted Brighid, with Fand following closely, and carried her from the riverbed that had dried to little more than a puddle and was littered with the scorched bodies of animals. He climbed the eastern bank to stand on the rise amidst the blackened corpses of trees. The series of tributaries that fingered into the Centaur Plains from the main river had finally broken the line of the fire, and the green that still covered the ridge behind the last of the waterways looked bizarrely out of place in a world of black and gray. Before he could turn to face the south and what was left of the Centaur Plains, Brighid spoke.

"Let me stand," she said. "I want to Change back."

He lowered her feet to the ground. When she had her balance, he took a half step away from her, and then shaded his eyes as the brilliant light of the Change engulfed her body. Back in her natural form, she stood awkwardly on three legs, but she met his eyes resolutely.

"I'm ready to see it now," she said.

Together, the two of them turned to face the south. Brighid could hardly comprehend what she was seeing. The sun was rising over the eastern edge of the horizon, casting cheery pink and gold into the sky over a sea of ruin. The plains were gone. In their place were still-smoldering ashes that clumped in grotesque charred formations. Trees were indistinguishable from bodies. Nothing moved except small trails of rising smoke.

"Oh, Goddess." Brighid pressed her hand against her mouth to keep from sobbing aloud. *Could anything survive it?*

"Yes, child." Etain's voice came high and sweet from behind them.

They turned to face the Goddess Incarnate and Brighid gasped. Etain sat on the silver mare at the edge of the blackened line. Midhir stood to her left. To her right were Elphame, Lochlan and Ciara. And stretching behind them were all of the winged children.

"Now tell me, my daughter, how could anything survive such devastation?" Etain asked Brighid.

The Huntress's eyes went from the Goddess Incarnate, to Elphame, and then to Ciara and the unusually silent children and, finally, her gaze lifted to her husband's turquoise eyes. With a rush of clarity, Brighid finally understood—and it was at that moment that the Huntress fully became the High Shaman.

"With hope and love anything can be survived," she said, and her words rang with Goddess-enhanced power so that they carried not just to all the children, but spread like ripples in a still pool across the Centaur Plains.

Etain smiled her approval.

Suddenly there was shouting from behind the children and dark-clothed warriors appeared with their bows and swords drawn. Brighid felt Cuchulainn tense at her side, and she opened her mouth to call a warning, but Etain raised one silk-clad arm and the sun glistened off the palm of her hand as if she had called its rays to her.

"Hold, Guardian Warriors!" she commanded without glancing behind her at the approaching army. "I did not allow you to follow them here for misplaced retribution. You are here to witness rebirth. Stand silently and observe." Then her voice changed, and softened and she finally did glance behind her, but not at the warriors. The High Priestess smiled at the children. "Come," she said.

The group descended from the green ridge and crossed the fire line without hesitation. When they reached Brighid and Cuchulainn, they halted. Brighid wanted to greet her friends, Elphame, Ciara and the small winged figure of Liam, but the preternatural tingling was back all over her skin and it seemed that her blood hummed with a sudden surge of wordless desire—something that was just beyond the reach of her mind and spirit—but something she wanted…had to have.

"Lead them, Brighid, High Shaman of the Dhianna Herd. It is your love and their hope that will heal the soul of the land," Etain said.

"Let me lean on you?" Brighid asked Cuchulainn.

"Always, my beautiful Huntress," he said.

With her arm around his broad shoulders she limped down the embankment, crossed the scorched river, and with the rustle of the moving wings that followed her, Brighid, Cuchulainn and the New Fomorians stepped onto the destroyed plain.

Brighid turned to face the children and their Shaman. "Will you help me make it grow again?" she asked them.

"Yes, Brighid!"

"Of course, Huntress!"

"Yes!"

"Yes!"

She smiled as their joyous voices sang over the deathly stillness of the burned land. "Then join me." She held out her hand and Liam ran to take it. Ciara stepped up next and took Liam's hand. Then Kyna skipped up to clutch Cuchulainn's hand and grinned toothily up at him. And one-by-one, the New Fomorians linked hands and spread out in a semicircle, facing the destruction of the southlands.

"I—I'm not sure…" Brighid said quietly.

Ciara caught her eye and smiled that joyous smile of hers that was so full of love and kindness. "Yes, you are, Brighid. Just let your heart speak."

And then Brighid opened her mouth and her heart poured forth.

Gracious Goddess Epona!
Guardian of those wild and free,

we seek Your blessings upon this place.
It was a place of hatred and strife,
but it has been purified with fire,
now let it be rebuilt as a
place of happiness and love!
A place of refuge and peace,
A place of enchantment!
Wild and free as the Goddess who created it…

Brighid paused as Ciara, and then the children following her, began to hum a wordless, lilting melody that reminded her of the wind as it swept through the long grasses of deep summer. At the same time an emerald glow began to emanate from all of the New Fomorians. Cuchulainn's hand tightened on hers as Epona's voice, filled with love and happiness swept over them like a magical wind from the depth of their hearts.

"I consecrate you, Brighid Dhianna, as Guardian of the Centaur Plains. You are tied to it through blood and love and hope— and now by my sacred trust!"

Overcome with emotion, Brighid bowed her head in acknowledgment, recollecting herself before she could complete her prayer. When she spoke again her voice was thick with the love and happiness that surged through her.

O Gracious Goddess!
Divine protectress of those wild and free,
Be always present
in this place of beauty!
Hail Epona!
So may it be!

As she spoke the last words of her prayer the emerald glow that had been hovering over the children suddenly exploded, and like a jewel-colored whirlwind that had the power to blow away the past, it swept across the plain, removing the ugly black ash and smoke to suddenly expose the beautiful new growth that was already pushing through the rich soil underneath.

With tears streaming unheeded down her face, Brighid watched her homeland be reborn. And then, before she could comprehend the enormity of what the Goddess-blessed children had done, there was a stirring in the newborn land as centaurs suddenly appeared. They were led by a silver-blond male whose hair had been singed from his body and whose skin was blistered and burned.

Brighid stood very still in the center of the line of linked hands while he and the other centaurs made their way slowly to her. As they drew closer she recognized many of them, especially the females, as Dhianna Herd members, but the focus of her attention remained on her brother.

Bregon stopped just a few paces before her. Slowly, deliberately, he executed the low bow of respect paid only to centaur High Shamans.

"Forgive me, Brighid." When he raised his face to her, his soot-covered cheeks were awash with tears. And then he dropped to his knees. Keeping his eyes on his sister, he began speaking in a deep, earnest voice.

"Through the deep peace of the flowing air I bind myself to you.

"Through the deep peace of the crackling homefire I bind myself to you.

"Through the deep peace of the quiet earth I bind myself to you.

"Through the four elements I am bound to you, Brighid Dhianna, High Shaman and Guardian of the Centaur Plains, and through the spirit of our herd I seal this bond. Thus has it been spoken, thus will it be done."

Shocked, Brighid could only stare at her brother and the other members of the Dhianna Herd who had all knelt as her brother had spoken the ancient words of binding.

"You must accept them or not," Cuchulainn said quietly. "It is your decision."

"Rise, Dhianna centaurs. Your High Shaman accepts you."

With a glad shout, the centaurs rose—all except her brother—who bowed his head again and wept openly.

There was a stirring in the line to Brighid's right, and Ciara dropped the hands of the children on either side of her. With that grace that was so singular to her, the winged Shaman approached Bregon. He raised his face and stared into her eyes. Brighid saw the jolt that went through his body, and she began to limp forward, but Cuchulainn's hand on hers restrained her.

"Wait," he whispered.

Slowly Ciara wiped the tears from Bregon's cheeks and then she offered him her hand. The centaur took it, and lurched up so that he was standing again. Keeping his hand in hers, the winged Shaman turned to face the children.

"This is Brighid's brother," she told them. "Let us make him welcome."

Instantly the little winged dam broke free and small bodies clustered around the singed centaur, jumping about and asking their usual assortment of unending questions.

"Look at him, Cuchulainn, and tell me what you see within his soul," Brighid said.

The warrior watched his wife's brother, and then his eyes shifted to hers.

"I see redemption, my beautiful Huntress."

Far to the north, deep in the Trier Mountains, a heavily pregnant Fallon leaned on her mate's arm as they entered the dark slash under the rocky outcropping through which they had spotted the single trail of smoke.

Inside a small fire burned in the center of the cave. At the sight of the newcomers the wings of the huddled creatures stirred and lifted dangerously. Fangs and claws glinted, even in the weak light of the waning fire.

She'd known it! She'd known that they hadn't all perished! It hadn't been possible that beings who were so strong, so filled with the will to live, had all died. No…they'd been here, waiting for her…just as she'd dreamed…just as she'd hoped.

"Who are you?" one of them snarled.

Fallon shook off Keir's arm and drew herself up to her full

height, showing off the living bulge that mounded her abdomen.

"I am your salvation!"

* * * * *

*Go back to Partholon's past
with P.C. Cast's next two novels!
DIVINE BY MISTAKE, available September 2006
and
DIVINE BY CHOICE, available December 2006.*

Award-winning author P.C. Cast is a dynamic, entertaining orator and an extraordinary teacher. Currently she lives in Oklahoma, where she resides with her daughter and her spoiled cat. She is hard at work on her next novel, but she always loves to hear from her fans. Please visit her at www.pccast.net.

LUNA™

LUNA™

A sweeping fantasy set in an ancient Greco-Roman civilization. A goddess has been born—the daughter of Epona's beloved Incarnate Priestess and the centaur High Shaman. Elphame is unique. Her story of self-discovery is an epic adventure that will lead to her destiny and an unexpected love.

Visit your local bookseller.

THE **TEARS** OF **LUNA** ST

A shimmering crown grows
and dims and is always
reborn. Luna has the power
and gift to brighten dark
nights and lend mystery to
the shadows. She will
sometimes show up on the
brightest of days, but her
most powerful moments are
when she fills the heaven
with
mo
cares
tal
lo
p
st
cri
ling
on
fin
b
enc
th
f

This year LUNA Books and
Duirwaigh Gallery are proud
to present the work of five
magical artists.

This month, the art featured
on our inside back cover
has been created by:

Thomas Canty

If you would like to order a

A